"May I ask why you decid

"After careful thought, I decided your offer was simply too good to refuse, Lady Pomeroy. I shall gain a wife, a substantial fortune, and eventually the heir I require."

"And I shall gain control of my own purse strings," Clarissa reminded him, regaining some of her formal wit.

Simon's eyes gleamed with brief amusement. "Without interference or inquiry."

"I will have your pledge, sir," Clarissa urged him.

His gaze hardened at the unintentional insult. "You have my word," he said firmly. "As long as we are husband and wife, there will be no interference or inquiry into the spending of your personal funds."

Clarissa breathed a sigh of relief. She knew the earl would keep his word. It was the reason she'd gone to him in the first place.

"Before I have the banns posted," Simon continued, "perhaps it would be best for us to discuss my conditions."

Clarissa gave him a puzzled look. "*Your* conditions, my lord?"

"Like you, there are certain things I want from our marriage."

"An heir," Clarissa said, trying not to blush at the thought of how that heir would be produced.

"That goes without saying," Simon replied. "I'm talking about my *personal* expectations."

Clarissa sat very still. The tone of the earl's voice told her more than she wanted to know. With the memory of his kiss still lingering on her mouth, she forced herself to meet his gaze. "I'll do my best to make you a good wife."

"Will you?" Simon asked in a low voice. "There is more to being a wife, Lady Pomeroy, than seeing that my dinner is served in a prompt fashion. A wife has other duties, as well. Will you perform those as willingly?"

THE LADY'S PROPOSAL

Patricia Waddell

ZEBRA BOOKS
Kensington Publishing Corp.
http://www.zebrabooks.com

ZEBRA BOOKS are published by

Kensington Publishing Corp.
850 Third Avenue
New York, NY 10022

First Printing: May, 2001
10 9 8 7 6 5 4 3 2 1

Printed in the United States of America

One

Sheridan Manor
Coventry, England 1886

Marriage.

The word made her shiver. It made her stomach knot and her head ache. It made her feverish with excitement and cold with apprehension. Marriage was the ultimate sacrifice, to Clarissa Pomeroy's way of thinking. A woman was born, educated in the proper manner of dress and speech, taught to move gracefully when she walked into a room, tutored for hours in the arcane rules of etiquette and introduction. Then, without any explanation or regard, she was paraded through the ballrooms of London in the hopes of gaining a proposal of marriage.

It was insulting.

It was maddening.

It was the way of things.

Clarissa gazed out the window of the carriage. It was an unusually bright spring day, suitable for a ride in the country but not at all appropriate to the task at hand. She decided the day would be more reflective of her mood if the sky were a dingy gray and rain was making muddy puddles along the dirt road that led from London to the country estate. She gave the issue of the day thoughtful deliberation as the driver kept the horses moving at a smart pace through the wrought-iron gates and along the cobblestone drive that curved in front of the prestigious country estate.

When the carriage came to a halt, the footman hurried down from his perch and opened the door. Clarissa gathered her courage and the leather pouch containing the ridiculous conditions of her grandfather's will before she accepted the servant's outstretched hand and stepped from the carriage. Once outside, she looked at the grand country home, built during the reign of James II. It's three-story gray granite walls were draped with ivy, cut away from the tall lead-paned windows by a skillful gardener. Around the flat roof there was a stone railing decorated with gaudy marble gargoyles and fanciful winged beasts. The front entrance boasted large double doors carved from wood that had been stained dark by time and weather. Like the man who lived inside, Sheridan Manor was the epitome of everything proper and English.

Simon Aloysius Sinclair, the earl of Sheridan.

The name gave Clarissa pause, as did the scheme she was being forced to undertake. If her beloved but irritating grandfather hadn't died, she wouldn't be worried about whether or not the earl found her attractive.

But Clarissa *was* worried.

Since her grandfather's untimely death, she had done little but pace the floors of Hartford Hall, wearing out her feet in hopes of finding a more suitable solution to her dilemma.

The elaborately carved doors of the house opened in harmonious unison with the carriage door being shut behind her. Clarissa gathered up the skirts of her black mourning dress and ascended the wide, flat stone steps that led to the entryway. A shallow-faced butler with a blue-veined nose and thin white eyebrows stood like a statue, holding the door open as she swept inside.

"My lady," he said, executing a perfect bow.

"Is Lord Sheridan in residence?" Clarissa asked, anxious to have the ordeal over and done with before she lost the last of her courage and returned to her carriage with specific orders that the driver not stop until she was reinstated at Hartford Hall.

"He is waiting for you in the library. This way, my lady."

Clarissa followed the dark-suited butler across the tiled vestibule floor. It reminded her of a chessboard, done in large squares of black and ivory marble. Being reminded of the game of kings and warriors forced her to perform a quick rethinking of her strategy. Although the earl wasn't a stranger, she knew little about Simon Sinclair on a personal plane. He had shared some investments with her grandfather, and their business relationship had prompted several invitations to the earl to dine at Hartford Hall. She had never engaged in more than polite dinner conversation with the him, and none of the words they had shared had given any hint of her personal feelings for the man.

Each time that Clarissa had encountered Simon Sinclair, he had been extremely polite, the perfect example of an English gentleman. Following that description, he had been careful to avoid any subject at the dinner table that could jolt or jar the sensibilities of a lady.

The first time that Clarissa had met the earl, she couldn't help but reflect on the words of an article by Newman, from *The Idea of a University*, defining the desired qualities of a gentlemen. *"He observes the maxim of the ancient sage, that we should ever conduct ourselves towards our enemy as if he were one day to be our friend."*

Keeping that thought in mind, Clarissa took a

calming breath as the butler pushed open the pocket doors of the library and announced her arrival to the earl of Sheridan. She stepped into the room. It was done in dark walnut furnishings, with deep tones of hunter green in the carpet and drapes. The lingering scent of cigar smoke and beeswax tickled her nose. Two of the room's towering walls were confined to bookshelves. Row after row of leather-bound volumes were stacked shelf upon shelf from floor to ceiling. The southern wall was consumed by tall, stately windows that lent the day's sunlight to anyone relaxing in the leather chairs while they read.

Clarissa's eyes were quickly drawn to the earl of Sheridan, standing behind an elegantly carved desk. The earl was a tall man with dark brown hair and even darker eyes. As always, Simon's intensely masculine presence affected her. His gaze held a penetrating quality that had often made her think he could see past her clothing and into her soul. It was a disturbing thought as she walked across the thick Oriental carpet to face him.

"My lord," she said, managing a polite but indifferent enunciation of the words.

"Lady Pomeroy," Sinclair replied before glancing over her shoulder at the servant who was awaiting his orders like a soldier. "Bring us some tea, Higgins."

The doors closed behind the obedient butler with a soft rumbling sound of wood moving over polished tile. Hiding her nervousness as well as a trained actress on a London stage, Clarissa walked toward the seat indicated by a graceful sweep of Lord Sheridan's hand. For the next few moments, the only sound in the library was the gentle rustle of the three starched petticoats under her dress as Clarissa seated herself in one of the two leather chairs facing the desk.

Simon returned to the stiff wood-trimmed chair behind the desk. The piece of furniture reminded Clarissa of a throne. Covered in rich black leather with an ornate design around the top and arms, it suited the earl's handsome features. Like the room, Simon Sinclair carried an innate air of quality about him. His jacket was a dark fawn color that complemented the walnut shade of his hair and eyes. His shirt, faultlessly white, was made of the finest linen. Although she couldn't see his boots, Clarissa was certain that they would reflect his features as clearly as the large gilt mirror she'd passed in the vestibule.

"My condolences over the loss of Lord Hartford," Simon added, gracefully hinting that regardless of the circumstances, it wasn't normal for a young lady in mourning to be calling upon a gentleman.

Clarissa nodded in lieu of words. It had been almost a full year since her grandfather's death. During that time, she had refrained from parties and social gatherings. But she couldn't wait until her black dresses were finally relegated to the attic before calling upon the earl. Time was of the essence.

"Thank you," she said, realizing that the earl was making as much of an impression on her senses now as he had in the past.

There was something strangely compelling about the man. It went beyond his handsome features and the impeccable cut of his clothing. The earl had a reputation for being extremely intelligent, very dignified, and unquestionably pompous when it came to matters of society. He was also said to be quick to temper if anyone mistook him for a fool. None of those qualities were of any particular interest to Clarissa. The reason she had decided upon Simon Sinclair was simple. He could be trusted. His honesty and honor were without dispute. His name was totally untarnished by word or deed.

He was, for lack of a better term, perfect.

At least he was perfect for Clarissa's purpose.

The requirements of her grandfather's will were ridiculously restrictive. She needed a man she could trust if she wanted to carry on the charitable work she'd begun at Haven House.

The small amount of conversation stopped altogether as a maid tapped lightly on the door, then entered carrying a silver serving tray. The earl dismissed her with another wave of his hand once the tray had been placed on a small oval stand situated between the leather chairs.

When the earl stood up and came around the corner of the desk, Clarissa felt a rush of heat through her body. She tried to understand the complex tangle of emotions that were forming a knot in the pit of her stomach. There was physical attraction mixed with a strange yearning that she hadn't yet given a name. Added to that was the overshadowing effect the man seemed to have on her normally mild disposition. Being alone in the room with Simon was a bit unnerving. So much so that she avoided his gaze while he poured the tea. She accepted the cup he offered, then immediately averted her attention to the oil painting behind the desk.

Simon used the opportunity to study his guest. He had known Lady Pomeroy for the last several years, and his eyes had always been drawn by her luxurious auburn hair and the deep violet blue of her almond-shaped eyes. Framed by perfectly arched brows, her eyes had an iridescent quality that contradicted her calm, ladylike mannerisms. Simon had always thought her a bit of a paradox. More so since becoming close friends with her late grandfather and hearing from the old gentleman himself that Lady Clarissa was given to a willful nature if left unsupervised.

The death of the earl of Hartford had prevented the young woman from being seen at the endless parties and soirees that filled London's seasonal schedule. Simon had heard that she had retired to her grandfather's estate near Norwich to mourn the passing of her grandfather. He'd also smiled when the rumor that Lady Pomeroy hadn't worn a corset to her grandfather's funeral had been repeated in one of his clubs. He'd attended the services held in St. Paul's Church. He hadn't been able to comment on the gossip one way or the other. Clarissa had been draped in a black cloak that had covered her from head to heel. He noticed that her hair wasn't covered today and wondered if she found the fashionable bonnets of the day as uncomfortable as corsets.

Looking at her now, Simon decided that black suited her. Few women could wear the midnight color as fashionably as Clarissa. It accented her flawless complexion and the rich coloring of her hair and eyes. It also reminded him that she was unchaperoned.

Needless to say, he'd been surprised by her note of the previous week requesting a visit. He'd responded in the affirmative, frankly curious about why she had insisted upon a meeting with him. Not as patient as many thought him to be, Simon sipped his tea quietly while he looked at the young lady sitting in front of him.

"May I be so bold as to ask what matter of urgency has brought you to Sheridan Manor?" he finally inquired, sitting his cup down on the dark blotter pad that was used to keep ink from staining the top of the two-hundred-year-old desk.

"The urgency is my grandfather's," Clarissa replied, reaching for the leather pouch and withdrawing the papers she'd brought with her. "This is his last will and testament."

She stood up and placed it on the desk in front of Simon, then returned to her seat.

He studied the document for a moment without touching it. "I'm not sure I understand."

"It's a lovely day," Clarissa told him. "I can wait in the garden while you read it. Once you have, I'm sure you will understand my reasons for seeking an appointment with you."

Simon's curiosity was piqued. He had thought of several plausible reasons why Clarissa might seek his advice. Richard Pomeroy had been an avid businessman, with investments that ranged from one end of the expanding British Empire to the other. He had thought that the earl's granddaughter might be in need of advice on how to maintain those investments, or perhaps she had found them overwhelming and sought his recommendation about whom to consult if she wanted to expand or terminate a portion of the funds. Neither reason required the presentation of the earl's last will and testament.

"I would not want to impose on such a private matter as your inheritance," Simon responded, still not touching the long legal document lying in front of him. "Are you sure?"

"I'm sure," Clarissa said, coming to her feet. "Knowing your ability in matters of business, my lord, I'm confident that you will grasp its meaning quickly enough."

"As you wish," Simon said, standing. "The east garden should be pleasant this time of day. I'll escort you."

Clarissa followed him out of the library and across the hall into a large, spacious, and expensively decorated parlor. French doors with twin panels of glass and white Irish lace drapes were opened, allowing the brisk breeze to freshen the room. The doors didn't belong in a house that was several centuries old, and Clarissa recalled hearing Simon discuss with her grandfather the renovations he had undertaken at Sheridan Manor. He had spent a small fortune making the seventeenth-century estate more comfortable and convenient for living.

As he walked beside her, Clarissa realized that she had more than one reason for choosing the earl of Sheridan. Simon was very tall, well over six feet, which suited the unusual and unladylike height she had inherited from her Scottish mother. Although he had never partnered her on a dance floor, Clarissa was certain they would make a suitable couple should they ever find an opportunity to waltz.

"Do you require a shawl?" Simon asked as they stepped outside the parlor and onto the small veranda that was furnished with marble benches and well-manicured marigolds growing in large Grecian pots on either side of the doorway.

"No, thank you," she told him. "I find the breeze quite pleasing."

Leaving her to enjoy the solitude of the garden, Simon returned to the library. His boots clicked musically on the parquet floor of the parlor as he tried to sort out the confusing circumstances of Lady Clarissa's visit. One of the few facts he had gleaned from his discussions with the late earl had been the lady's reluctance to accept any of the numerous marriage proposals that had come her way. Simon assumed her to be twenty years of age, if not a year or two older. Most young ladies were married by that time.

He walked into the library and picked up the earl's will. Settling into the chair closest to the window, Simon began to read. A few moments later, he arched a dark brow. By the time he finished reading the document, he was frowning.

He had always considered the earl of Hartford a meticulous man, but the terms of Richard Pomeroy's will went beyond precision. They were absolutely rigid.

Clarissa was the earl's only heir. As such, she was due to inherit a sizable fortune, one that came close to surpassing Simon's. But that inheritance was based upon her complete and total submission to the terms of the will. Any deviation and she would find herself as penniless as a dockside trollop. The terms didn't surprise Simon as much as the timetable attached to them. Clarissa was to marry within fourteen months of her grandfather's death, and not a day later. That would allow her the year's mourning period required by polite society and give her two months to find a suitable husband once she returned to London. Her husband was also required to meet a stringent set of rules. The lady's father had held the title of Earl of Farlow, passed on to him by a distant maternal uncle, and Lord Pomeroy's will required Clarissa's future husband to hold an equivalent rank. The man was to be of good moral character and willing to have his accounts audited by the earl's solicitors to guarantee that Clarissa was not being married for her fortune alone.

The Hartford fortune, consisting of several country estates, a London town house, two railroads, a tea plantation in Ceylon, three large farms in Africa, and one Yorkshire coal mine, was to be under the complete control of Clarissa's future husband, with the exception of a *reasonable allowance to the lady* that was to be determined by her benevolent spouse.

Simon put down the will and poured himself a drink.

So much for financial advice, he thought. Apparently, Lady Clarissa had sought him out because she found herself in dire need of a matchmaker. The idea irritated Simon more than he liked to admit. He had no inclination to marry, being perfectly content with his life as a gentleman and an active member of the House of Lords. Still, there was the problem of an heir—one he would be forced to solve in the future. Having just celebrated his thirty-second birthday, he felt no immediate need to rush into taking a wife. There was plenty of time to make a selection from the endless parade of well-behaved, well-bred ladies of society.

Further analysis brought Clarence Albright's name to mind. The Viscount Thornton was Simon's best friend and was currently contemplating marriage because his age was advancing to the time when he could no longer put off the inevitable sacrifice of taking a wife in order to produce an heir. Clarence was considered handsome by the ladies, a gentleman by his peers, and a decent man by all. He would have no trouble passing the financial scrutiny of the late earl's solicitors, nor would he be unkind to the woman he eventually wed. His rank didn't qualify him, of course, which made his candidacy irrelevant. It was the thought of another man holding Clarissa in his arms, the mental image of another man taking down her luxurious russet hair and kissing her, that made Simon stare out the window in disgust.

Of course, there was the slight possibility that the lady hadn't come to him seeking direction. Could she possibly have asked him to read the will in hopes that he would find the terms agreeable? That he would find her agreeable?

Simon returned the will to the leather case Clarissa had left behind and walked out of the library and toward the garden, where he had left her. He saw her sitting on a stone bench, the seat supported by two granite angels with their wings spread wide. The sunlight danced brightly over the dark cinnamon coloring of her hair as she came to her feet in a graceful movement that forced Simon to admit that although she was tall and slender of form she was very nicely put together. He walked up to her, casting a quick glance at the hawthorn bushes to her right and the invincible English ivy behind her, creeping up and over the garden's brick wall.

Clarissa felt her heart start to pound as Simon approached her. Once again she was struck by his impressive presence. Tall and lean and aristocratically handsome, she began to suspect that there was more behind the gentlemanly veneer he wore as easily as his well-tailored jacket. His dark gaze held a mystery, she decided, as if he were amused by people's efforts to see beyond what he wanted them to see. He was intriguing, Clarissa decided, and perhaps a little dangerous.

She couldn't deny the female curiosity that was responsible for her reaction every time she encountered Simon. By rights, she ought to find him totally unappealing. They had nothing in common. Although she was careful to keep her unorthodox viewpoints well hidden, Clarissa couldn't think of a single political issue upon which she and the earl would agree. He was so conservative as to be considered immovable when it came to matters of progressive thinking, such as women's rights, a subject that was of extreme importance to Clarissa.

"Would you like to return to the library, or shall we remain in the garden?" Simon asked, stopping a few feet in front of her.

"I prefer the garden, my lord."

"Very well," he said, then handed her the leather pouch that contained her grandfather's will. "I find the terms somewhat stringent but not totally surprising. Your grandfather was a man given to detail.

I'm certain that whatever conditions he placed on your inheritance were put there with the best of intentions."

"He feared I would never marry," Clarissa said, stripping away the polite adjectives and getting to the truth of the matter. "This is his way of forcing me to take a husband."

Simon couldn't argue with the obvious. "It seems that you find the prospect upsetting."

Clarissa released a frustrated sigh. "I find the idea of being controlled from the grave upsetting, my lord. Although I adored my grandfather, we did not always see eye to eye on things."

Simon gave her a light smile. If his memory was correct, Richard Pomeroy had once admitted that he was tired of pushing eligible bachelors under Clarissa's very choosy nose.

"Marriage is a respected institution, Lady Pomeroy."

"So is Parliament, my lord, but I do not see a requirement in my grandfather's will for me to apply for a seat in government."

Simon had to smile. The idea was preposterous. The concept of women debating on the floor of the prestigious government house sent cold chills up and down Simon's spine. He had been right about the spark in Clarissa's violet eyes. The lady had spirit. Studying the tilt of her chin, Simon decided that Clarissa also possessed a touch of Scottish stubbornness, inherited from her mother's side of the family, and a dash of too much boldness for a woman of her age.

His male instincts told him it would be very interesting to tame her unruly traits, but not as interesting as discovering if she was as passionate in body as she was in spirit. The intriguing thought sent a rush of heat through Simon. His body tightened with sexual tension, and he suddenly had an overwhelming urge to kiss her. The primitive response took him by surprise. It wasn't like him to be affected so easily by erotic thoughts or the mere sight of a woman. Regaining his control as quickly as he'd lost it, Simon's expression hardened.

Clarissa watched him as he reacted to her remark. If her plan was to work, there could be no lies between herself and the man she hoped to marry. She knew Simon could not abide a lie. It pricked at everything he stood for. He was reputed to be honest to the marrow of his bones. If he thought that she was set on deceiving him, there would be no way he would consider taking her as his wife.

No. She wouldn't lie to him. Not about her true nature. As for the rest, it wasn't a lie. It was merely a necessary lack of information. Unless she could maintain the secrecy of her work at Haven House, it had no chance of surviving. And her work had to go on. It was too important to be cast aside because society, and men in particular, were too narrow-minded to accept its substance.

"Do you have a gentleman in mind?" Simon asked matter-of-factly.

Clarissa met his penetrating gaze and felt something deep inside her melt. She couldn't let this man's effect on her change her original course of action. It would ruin everything if she became more enthralled by him than she already was.

"I have given the subject a great deal of thought," Clarissa replied, folding her hands in front of her. "It would seem an easy choice if one considered rank alone. There are several men who meet my grandfather's requirements in that area."

"But you are thinking of more than a man's nobility."

Clarissa ignored the slight lacing of sarcasm in Simon's comment. "I have several requirements of my own," she told him. "The man I marry will have to meet both my conditions and those listed in my grandfather's will."

"And what would those conditions be?"

Clarissa cleared her throat. "The first and most important one would be the deciding factor. I plan on selecting a man who has no heir at this time. In doing so, he will receive the full inheritance when we marry, minus the monthly allowance I am to be given."

Simon began to see the way of things. He gave Clarissa a knowing smile. "You wish to have your allowance set at a specific amount."

"Whomever I marry must pledge me no less than one-fourth of my grandfather's estate. It is a *reasonable* amount considering the vast sum of the Hartford coffers, wouldn't you agree?"

"Is my agreement necessary?" Simon urged softly. Lady Clarissa wanted him to be her husband. Strangely, the idea didn't offend him in the least. She was certainly beautiful enough to make the task of producing the heir he required more pleasure than duty. She was young and healthy, with just enough spirit to make the liaison interesting. She was also in need of a firm hand. Any woman who thought she could dictate to her husband needed a good lesson in who established the rules and who obeyed them. "Am I to understand that you wish me to consider the position?"

"I do not like games, my lord, unless they are confined to a gaming parlor," Clarissa said, deciding it was time Simon learned a few things about her. "Why else would I reveal the terms of my grandfather's will?"

"I'm flattered, my lady."

Clarissa found his gaze disconcerting as he studied her with dark, unmoving eyes that told her little of his thoughts. She had expected the man to show some reaction. After all, she was asking him to marry her. The act deserved more than an unblinking stare.

"Is my proposal something you would take under consideration?" Clarissa dared to ask. She'd never accomplish her goal if she let Simon's unnerving proximity distract her.

"Perhaps," he replied honestly. "But before I decide, let us discuss the rest of your *conditions.*"

Clarissa's fingers clinched in the folds of her black cashmere dress. She had come to Sheridan Manor prepared to discuss marriage as calmly and as rationally as any other business proposal. It was, after all, that and nothing more. There were no feelings of affection between herself and Simon Sinclair. The truth be known, they were almost strangers. The few times he'd been at Hartford Hall for dinner certainly didn't constitute a relationship. They were social acquaintances, nothing more.

Still, she knew enough about the earl to realize that he wasn't a man to be led about on a leash. "Shall we walk?" she prompted, taking a step toward the large fountain at the end of the garden.

Simon followed her along the cobblestone path that weaved through the freshly trimmed elm trees and rosebushes. Keeping his hands folded behind his back, he glanced at her from the corner of his eye. The urge to kiss her hadn't passed. In fact, it was stronger than ever as she moved alongside him, matching his pace with long legs that gave her walk a ballerina quality.

"My conditions are minuscule compared to those of my grandfather," Clarissa began. "I have no real desire to marry at all, but unless I wish to keep my virtue in a penniless state, I also have little choice in the matter."

"I see," Simon said quietly. "You feel as though you are being forced to take a husband."

Clarissa stopped and looked up at him. "I am being forced," she said adamantly. "I'm honest enough to admit that living in poverty holds no appeal for me. What purpose would it serve except to put another homeless woman on the streets of London?"

"What purpose indeed," Simon replied. "Please go on."

Licking her lips, Clarissa chose her words carefully. What passed between herself and the earl now would set the pace for whatever future they might share.

"Like my grandfather, I would like a man of good character. A man who does not find me repulsive, a man who would conduct himself in a gentlemanly fashion once we are married."

Insects hummed in the garden shrubbery as Simon studied her in an ominous silence that made Clarissa wish he'd hurry up and say what he was thinking. The man had an uncanny knack of making her extremely nervous. And he was looking at her as though she'd just disrobed for his inspection. It was making her angry, and she didn't want to lose her temper.

"I assure you, my lady, I find nothing repulsive about you. In fact, I find you just the opposite. But then, I'm sure you realize your appeal."

Clarissa wasn't sure how to respond. She wasn't given to vanities, so she had no idea how men viewed her. Nor had it been important—until now. Being told that Simon found her attractive eased some of her fears. It also made her insides go soft and her pulse quicken until she was certain that Simon could see it beating like the wings of a wild bird.

"I'm more concerned about your thoughts on marriage in general," Clarissa responded. "I do not wish to bind myself to a man who thinks to exile me to the country while he enjoys the vices of London." She looked him right in the eye. "Being unmarried, you have the freedom to do as you wish. You are discreet, but it's no secret that you keep a mistress. Should you plan on doing so after we marry, I will tell you right now that I will not tolerate such brazen disregard of our marriage vows."

Simon laughed.

The soft rumbling sound surprised Clarissa.

"You call me brazen." He chuckled. "How brazen is a young woman, still in mourning for her only relative, when she invites herself to a gentleman's home and proposes marriage as easily as she would summon tea from a maid?"

Clarissa eyed him thoughtfully. "You think me too bold."

Simon's smile all but disappeared. "I think you are a young lady who finds herself between a proverbial rock and a difficult solution to her problem," he countered smoothly. "Although I do understand your concerns, I have to admit I find your way of addressing them rather unusual."

"What way would you recommend, my lord? Should I beseech my grandfather's solicitors to find me an amiable husband? Or perhaps I should conduct interviews. I have hired several maids and a gardener. They have all proven themselves satisfactory employees. Does that mean I am a good judge of character? If so, I should have no problem at all in weeding out the unsavory fortune-hunting gentlemen who would come knocking at my door if the terms of my grandfather's will were made public."

"Your temper is showing, my lady."

"Ah, yes, my temper," Clarissa said pointedly. "A fault you should know about beforehand. I am not considered of a very cordial nature when I am upset, or so my grandfather frequently told me. I'm also very strong-minded about other things. One of them is my fierce determination not to become a puppet at the end of some man's strings."

"Which is no doubt the reason that you expect your future husband to give you such a generous allowance," Simon remarked, not bothering to hide his amusement.

When Clarissa was angry, her eyes darkened to a rich sapphire blue. Simon found himself momentarily trapped by their cavernous depths as he imagined their wedding night.

She frowned at him. "I suppose you have already decided that a match between us would not be what you seek in a marriage."

"And what do you think I seek from marriage should I pursue it?"

Was Simon saying he wasn't interested in marriage, or was he teasing her? It was hard to tell when his expression didn't change.

"I think when it comes to marriage, my lord, that your wants aren't that different from any other man. You want a wife who obeys you with the enthusiasm of a genie summoned from a brightly colored bottle."

Her analysis earned Clarissa a fierce scowl.

"You have a quick tongue, Lady Pomeroy."

"But an accurate one," she retorted. "Am I wrong, my lord? Have I misjudged you?"

Simon smiled. "I fear not. You are absolutely correct in thinking that I will expect my wife to keep her vows, including the one of obedience. But unlike you, I see a reason for my expectations. Like it or not, my lady, we live in a world where women are not equipped to protect themselves."

Clarissa almost laughed. She knew all too well how dangerous the world could be for women. She had ample proof at Haven House. Still, she had to curb her tongue and hope that she could make Simon more than interested in marrying her. As much as it dented her pride to do so, Clarissa softened her approach.

"Forgive me, my lord. I do understand the necessity of being able to depend upon one's husband to take care of the more strenuous problems of life, but that does not make it easy for a woman to relinquish her every thought to a stranger."

"I do not consider us strangers," Simon replied seductively.

The change in his tone made the skin on the back of Clarissa's neck tingle. He was looking at her differently, too. The unreadable quality of his eyes had softened until she thought she saw something burning in their dark depths, something soft and reassuring. Her heart leaped in her chest. Could it be possible? Could the earl actually feel the same strange attraction that she felt?

For a brief moment, Simon wanted to pull Clarissa into his arms and give her the comfort she needed, even if she didn't want to admit the vulnerability of being left alone in the world. Alone and at the mercy of the terms of her grandfather's will. He pushed the temptation aside. There would be plenty of time for that later. He continued watching her eyes. They told him more than she realized. "As I said, I do not find my expectations unnatural. I do not require whomever I marry to forfeit her very soul to me, Lady Pomeroy. I only expect what any husband would expect. That my wife honor and respect me in the same fashion that I vow to honor and respect her."

Clarissa walked closer to the fountain. The wind gathered up the artfully directed water and carried a light mist toward her. The mist dampened her face as she tried to think of the best way to detail her most important request. She could feel Simon watching her. It was an intangible sense of awareness that made her skin tingle and her pulse race.

"We avoid the real subject at hand, my lord," she said, finally turning to face him. "Do you find my proposal one you would consider?"

Simon nodded.

"Good," Clarissa said, finding the word inadequate but sufficient for the moment. "Then we should discuss my allowance."

"Ahhh, yes, the very *reasonable* allowance." Simon arched a dark brow. "Perhaps you should be more specific as to why you would desire one-fourth of your grandfather's estate. I assure you, if we marry, I will not have you begging for enough coins to buy a new hat."

"I'm not that inclined to fashion, my lord," Clarissa told him. "The allowance is more than money to me. It's the principle behind it that gives it importance."

"The principle?"

"I realize that the sum seems rather large, and you must be curious as to why I would demand it, but I assure you the funds will not be spent on hats and slippers. In the last few years I have become increasingly interested in various charities. I want the allowance to make sure that my expenditures in those areas are not limited by my husband's disagreement on the worthiness of such issues."

Simon's gaze became skeptical. "A gentleman applauds charity, Lady Pomeroy. He does not limit it if his wife feels inclined to be of a generous nature. Your explanation leaves something amiss in my mind."

Bracing herself for the closest thing to a lie she hoped to ever have to speak to the earl, Clarissa glanced down at the ground, then back up, meeting his gaze. "I'm sure you have already reached the conclusion that I'm not given to the old-fashioned manner of putting coins in a poor box and walking away. Our society is not as progressive as it should be when it comes to seeing that orphans are fed and that people shivering in the winter wind are provided a warm cloak to ease their distress."

"Are you saying that you prefer taking a more active role in dispensing the funds you donate?"

"Yes," Clarissa replied earnestly. "I have founded several accounts for the poor, although I prefer to keep my part in such works unknown. There is little charity in the act of giving if the giver uses the platform as a way to bring attention to themselves."

"A noble concept," Simon mused aloud. "Go on."

"Needless to say, my grandfather thought my endeavors overly zealous. He did not restrict my allowance, but he did lecture me about it. I wish to end those lectures, my lord. In exchange for full control of three-quarters of my grandfather's estate, I merely ask that my future husband give me full rein over the remaining portion. To do with as I see fit. Without interference or inquiry."

"And again, I must ask, why me?"

Clarissa gave her response careful consideration. It would serve no purpose if the earl knew that she was attracted to him. Marriage would force her into his bed. Time and his male virility would make her the mother of his children. The laws of the land would make her his chattel, a possession to be treasured or tolerated, depending upon his personal preference.

"You are known to be a man of your word, my lord. An honorable man. A man who would not withdraw a promise once it has been given. I find that aspect of your personality the most appealing. It is the reason that I came to Sheridan Manor today."

"I see," Simon replied thoughtfully. "Knowing that you have only the word of your husband to keep him from denying you the privacy you desire once the marriage is legally recorded and consummated, you seek out a man with a reputation for being true to his word."

"Exactly, my lord."

"Again, I'm flattered," Simon told her. "Extremely so. I pray that there are other such men in our country, but I find myself grateful that you decided upon me."

"Then you will marry me?"

"I will think about it," Simon replied with a fleeting smile.

Clarissa frowned.

"Don't be impatient, my lady," he said, stepping closer. "Marriage is a big step for any man, regardless of the awards waiting for him at the altar. I am not given to impulsive behavior or rashness when it comes to such decisions." He smiled encouragingly. "I will call on you at Hartford Hall by week's end."

Reaching down, Simon took hold of Clarissa's ungloved hand and lifted it to his mouth "Until then."

"Until then," she replied, feeling as awkward as a child. She'd had men kiss her hand before. But none of them had ever turned the acceptable gesture into an intimate caress. The soft pressure of Simon's mouth on her bare skin made her feel almost weightless. Clarissa looked down to make sure her feet were still firmly planted on the ground.

When Simon straightened to his full height and smiled at her, Clarissa looked away for a pensive moment, hoping she could hide what she was feeling. The socially acceptable kiss had been her first physical contact with the earl, and she was afraid that her eyes might give away the secret her heart had been keeping for the last two years. She was in love with Simon Sinclair, and she had no illusions about his returning the affection. If the earl married her, it would be because he found the arrangement both profitable and convenient. Nothing more.

Simon glanced toward the house, unconsciously wondering if he dared to pull Clarissa into his arms and kiss her the way he really wanted to—until she was trembling and clinging to his shoulders as tightly as the ivy hugging the garden wall. His common sense overruled the impulsive thought, and he stepped back.

"I will see you to your carriage," he said.

Clarissa didn't trust herself to speak. Gathering up the skirts of her black dress, she turned toward the house, grateful that her back was to the earl as she inhaled deeply and willed her traitorous body to calm itself. If she was going to marry Simon, she had better get used to being kissed by him. Of course, telling herself that and actually doing it were two entirely different things, and for the first time in weeks Clarissa began to wonder if she hadn't lost her mind along with her heart.

Two

Clarissa tossed the leather pouch on the mahogany table in the foyer at Hartford Hall and gave the butler a frustrated glance. "Please have tea served in the parlor, Huxley."

The butler motioned to the maid lingering in the shadows of the hallway to hurry and put a pot on to boil. "Was your trip a success, milady?"

"I suppose you could say that," Clarissa told him.

In the flesh, Huxley fell somewhat short of the customary image of an English butler. He was short and stout, with wide amber eyes, reddish brown hair, and a crooked smile. His black jacket was buttoned snugly over his plump middle, placing a strain on the buttons when he sat down, and he wore a mustache, something rarely seen on the face of a servant. His hands looked more like those of a butcher than a butler, and his voice had the voluminous quality of a street vendor. But in spite of his unusual features, he carried an extraordinary briskness about him that kept most guests from questioning his rank in the household.

He was also Clarissa's best friend.

She knew her camaraderie with the butler would shock her peers if it was ever discovered. It wasn't proper to interact with, or react to, servants. They were considered invisible people, unseen until a lady or gentleman wanted a cup of tea poured or a cloak fetched.

Following his mistress into the tastefully decorated parlor, Huxley added some wood to the fire, which was needed to take the chill from the night air. He drew the drapes, turning up the gas lamps on either side of the room to ease the shadows that had overtaken the parlor with the setting of the May sun.

"From your earlier comment, am I to assume that your meeting with Lord Sheridan went according to plan?" Huxley asked once the fire was crackling to his satisfaction.

"I'm not sure." Clarissa sighed, tossing her shawl over the back of a brocaded settee and slumping onto its cushiony surface. "The earl is to call at the end of the week and give me his answer. He thinks marriage important enough to ponder for a day to two," Clarissa clarified.

"An understandable point of view," Huxley said.

"I thought I understood him," Clarissa mumbled to herself, then looked at the servant who had become her secret cohort. "I'm not so sure now."

"It has been over a year since Lord Sheridan attended dinner," Huxley reminded her. "Perhaps your perception of his response is clouded by the stress you've been feeling of late."

"Stress!" Clarissa snorted the word. "I've been going out of my mind with worry, and you know it. I can't let Haven House become a deserted estate in upper Yorkshire again. My ladies are depending on me."

The butler knew that the ladies weren't ladies at all, but unwed mothers. Women of the lower classes who had found themselves with child and without a husband.

Social standards being what they were, it was unthinkable for a lady of quality to even know about such unfortunate things. Helping such women was something no one in her right mind would consider for more than a moment. Buying an estate in Yorkshire and sheltering them, giving them medical care and emotional support, was so outrageous as to be unthinkable.

Yet that was just what Clarissa was doing.

Huxley was one of the few people who knew about Clarissa's unorthodox charity. He considered himself honored by her trust, and he did everything within his power to maintain it.

The unique relationship he and Lady Pomeroy shared had begun some fifteen years ago, when she'd arrived on her grandfather's doorstep. Orphaned by the unfortunate accident that had claimed her parents' lives, the little girl with ginger curls and bright blue eyes had immediately claimed the butler as her playmate. No matter where Huxley went, Clarissa had trotted behind him, asking countless questions and insisting that talking to him was much more interesting than playing with dull porcelain-faced dolls in the nursery.

"Do you think he will agree to your conditions?" the butler asked, being privy to the details that Clarissa wanted satisfied before she took a husband.

"I'm not sure," she sighed. "He seemed reluctant, but then I expect any man would be. I'm not being very proper about things."

Huxley smiled. The term *proper* didn't suit his mistress at all. Clarissa was open-minded and generous and far too caring to be considered a proper lady of the times. Unlike her peers, she cared little for wealth and position. Instead, she saw herself as a vessel to use those things for the good of others. It was a sweeping concept, one that would leave her at the mercy of gossips and shunned by society if they ever found out how deep the currents of her heart actually ran.

It was for that reason, and the heartfelt affection he held for her, that Huxley assisted Clarissa in matters concerning Haven House. His role was simple. He carried messages when asked, made sure she was given the privacy she needed to conduct her business, and otherwise assisted in anything that made her life more comfortable. In his very biased view, Lady Pomeroy was a living, breathing angel of mercy.

"What if he declines my proposal?" Clarissa voiced her biggest fear. "I can't think of another man who comes close to the earl in integrity. All will be lost if he doesn't marry me."

"He hasn't declined your offer as yet," Huxley said, reassuring her. "And I don't think he will."

"Why not?" Clarissa prompted.

The butler's reply was postponed as the maid carried in a tray of tea and sweet cakes. Once the parlor door was shut again, Clarissa looked at her dearest friend in the whole world, needing his assurance now more than ever.

"The earl thinks more of you than you realize," Huxley said, speaking candidly because he'd never been any other way with the lady. "I have often suspected that his eagerness in accepting your grandfather's invitations was due to your presence."

Clarissa laughed. "You're imagining things."

"Am I?" the servant said, pouring her a cup of tea. "I think not. Lord Sheridan is known to be a man with a discerning eye, and you are a lovely lady."

Clarissa wasn't sure she liked the direction the conversation was taking. Although she trusted Huxley more than any man, she couldn't bring herself to discuss the strange, exotic feelings that came her way whenever she thought of Simon Sinclair. It was more than physical attraction, she was sure of that.

The thought of actually living with Simon Sinclair created an anxiety in Clarissa that bordered on panic. How could she live under the same roof, eat at the same table, and sleep in the same bed with the man without revealing her feelings for him? How could she share the intimacies of marriage without exposing her most private thoughts? How could she hide the love that seemed to radiate from every pore of her body, or at least that was how it felt whenever she allowed herself to think about Simon Sinclair. Clarissa wasn't as naive as most women her age. Her anxiety didn't stem from a virgin's fear of the unknown. The tight tingling in her chest, the breathlessness she felt whenever Simon was near, came from a natural female curiosity about what it would feel like to have his body lying next to her, to be able to hear the soft cadence of his breathing, to have her senses of taste and sight and sound totally absorbed by the man.

Clarissa almost laughed at herself for indulging the foolish notion of being completely captivated in such a way. The ladies at Haven House should be more than enough to squelch any foolish notion she might have about romance. The women weren't, as society would so callously label them, whores. They were normal women; shop clerks and maids, women who had let their hearts carry them beyond the boundaries of common sense and reasonable thought. Women who had fallen in love and, by doing so, had given their bodies to the men who they had foolishly believed loved them in return.

Clarissa didn't judge them or belittle them for having loved. Instead, she did her best to help them through a difficult time. Her reasons were her own. She'd always remember seeing a serving maid being cast out into the street, the man who had employed her yelling and calling her the most vile of names, the poor girl left crying and bruised in the gutter while people of quality drove by in their sleek carriages and turned their noses up, dismissing the girl's treatment as justified.

For weeks after that she had thought about the young maid. What had happened to her? Had she died in one of the cold, rat-infested houses that lined London's east side? And why hadn't anyone cared enough to help her?

The last question had plagued Clarissa the most.

She had seen enough of polite society to know that charity was considered something one gave—money dropped into an alms box, coins tossed at a problem without getting one's hand dirty by actually touching the person who needed help.

The concept chilled her heart, just as the memory of the young girl had chilled her mind. She'd done the unthinkable even then. At the age of fourteen she'd gone to Huxley and begged him to seek out the girl, to discover her name and whereabouts. The butler had been reluctant to help her at first, citing all the reasons it wasn't proper for her to get involved in such an unsavory thing at such an early age. In the end, she'd won him over. A week later, he'd told her that the girl was living in the back of a millinery shop. Clarissa had raced upstairs and emptied the sock where she kept her money. It wasn't much, but it would help to keep the girl fed and perhaps buy a blanket for the child when it arrived.

Her first act of charity hadn't been enough. The shopkeeper, the girl's aunt, had not had a very successful year, and there was little money for food or coal for the small stove that heated the shop. The young serving maid had taken ill and died.

When Huxley told her the unpleasant news,

Clarissa had cried for hours. She'd done the unthinkable again when she'd talked the butler into taking her to the pauper's grave that had become the girl's final resting place. There she'd met the girl's aunt. A plump lady with a tear-streaked face who had thanked her for trying to help.

That graveside encounter had formed the second strongest friendship in Clarissa's life. Meriwether Quigley and Clarissa shared similar points of view about the plight of young ladies whose only sin had been to love. Together they had grieved and talked, and they had stumbled upon the idea of a place where such women could go, away from scalding words and cold stares. A place where they could live in peace and relative comfort until their babies were born.

When Clarissa reached her eighteenth birthday and inherited the money from her mother's estate, she had put the funds to good use. She'd purchased a deserted, run-down estate in upper Yorkshire and started Haven House.

No one knew about her shocking charity except Huxley, Miss Quigley, Dr. Hayward, the gentle country doctor who attended the mothers, and of course, Mrs. Flannigan, the stout Irish widow who ran Haven House. The circle of friends was small and a well kept secret.

"If only society weren't so close-minded," Clarissa said as she sipped her tea. How she hated the restrictions and unwritten regulations adopted by generations of snobbish men who thought themselves superior because some long forgotten relative had done some equally long-forgotten king a favor. "I have always thought it disgraceful to have to keep Haven House a secret. How hard our hearts are to be ashamed of giving an unborn child the opportunity God wishes each of us to have."

"I share your philosophy," Huxley told her. "But

there is little you can do about others. What you are doing is much more than most. Be content with that, if you can."

"Without a husband, I shall have to be content to do nothing," she said wearily. "I pray that Lord Sheridan will accept my offer. I admit feeling more than a small reluctance at taking another man as my husband."

If Huxley thought her comment strange, he didn't indicate it. Instead, he refilled her teacup and insisted that she go straight up to bed after emptying it. She had had a long day, and it was time she rested.

Lying awake in the huge four-poster bed, Clarissa tried to think of the good one-fourth of her grandfather's estate would accomplish, but her thoughts kept wandering back to the garden at Sheridan Manor and how it had felt to have Simon's lips brush over her hand.

A strange sort of recognition had taken place inside her at the touch of Simon's lips. It was the first time he had made any physical contact with her, and the moment registered in her mind like a long-hoped-for dream that had suddenly become a reality.

Clarissa had left one of the windows of her bedchamber open, enjoying the cool, brisk air that blew in from the southern regions of the North Sea. Norwich was set a short distance inland from the stormy ocean, and it was not uncommon to feel the effects of a storm as it swept down from the cold currents of the North Sea toward the narrow English Channel that separated the island country from the Continent. Thinking about Simon sent a shiver through her, but it wasn't from the cold night air.

Until today, Clarissa hadn't allowed herself to think beyond her motives for taking a husband. She had received the terms of her grandfather's will with mixed emotions. A great deal of it had been anger, but she'd soon resolved herself to the fact that unless she did as the will decreed, she would be as much in need of assistance as the ladies she was trying to help.

Not the same assistance, but she would still be without means to support herself. It was a difficult, eye-opening situation, and she'd accepted it the same way she accepted most things that couldn't be changed. She tried to find a way around it.

The earl of Sheridan had come to mind almost immediately. She knew Simon would be the best man to see that her grandfather's fortune wasn't squandered away. His business abilities were highly respected, and it was rumored that he frequently advised the queen herself. Knowing that she needn't be concerned about finding herself as penniless married as she would be if she remained single, Clarissa had turned her thoughts to more important things.

Unfortunately, she'd overlooked the possibility that her initial reaction to the earl would send her wits flying out the nearest window.

If her bones turned to jelly at the slightest touch of his hand, what would happen to her when he actually kissed her?

If he kissed her?

One thought quickly took Clarissa to another until she blushed in the dim moonlight that was drifting through her open window. How could she imagine such things?

Yet she was imagining them. Simon looking down at her with soft dark eyes, his head lowering until their mouths were scant inches apart, and finally, blessedly, a kiss that left her clinging to him.

Clarissa's eyes popped open with the realization that she was very close to losing more than her wits where the earl of Sheridan was concerned. She knew in her heart that she was more than mildly attracted to the man. She'd known it from the very first time he had come to Hartford Hall, arriving in a sleek brown-and-gold coach, with the Sheridan coat of arms embossed on the doors.

He'd stepped down from the carriage and right into her dreams. Tall, dark, and such a perfect gentleman, the earl of Sheridan was the stuff of midnight fantasies and fairy tales.

The thought of marrying had not occurred to her then. That dream had never materialized, partly because Clarissa did not view marriage in the same naive light as other young women. She saw it as a confining, restricted state of affairs that frequently left the woman regretting her actions.

Not that she didn't believe in love.

She did.

But love was elusive, as fleeting as a spring butterfly and harder to capture. On the other hand, the unhappy results of taking a husband because it was a woman's fate to marry was a harsh reality. She'd seen more than one charming young lady swept off her feet by a gentlemanly smile, only to appear in town the next season, looking sad and forlorn after the glitter of her wedding vows had tarnished in the cold light of discovering that her husband thought her little more than a witless possession meant to warm his bed and bear his children.

Clarissa wanted more than cold reality.

She wanted the warming comfort of her husband's arms. She wanted his smile and the tender glances she knew existed with real love. She wanted more than the security of a man's title and name; she wanted something of the man himself.

But her grandfather's death and the rigid terms of his will had banished those daydreams. She was obliged to marry in order to maintain an inheritance that should have been hers without question or concern. Clarissa wasn't angry with her grandfather. He had been of the old school; men who saw all women as helpless and in need of a husband to see to their affairs. She had loved him in spite of his antiquated ideas, and he would continue to hold a place in her heart.

Unfortunately, Simon was of the same school of thought, although he was much younger. It was the opposite side of the coin from the trusting man she needed. But she had to take the good with bad, or in this case, the old-fashioned with the necessary.

It wasn't the thought of having a man in her life that disturbed Clarissa. It was the thought of having Simon Sinclair in her bed that had her palms sweating and her heart pounding so rapidly, she doubted she would be able to fall asleep.

What would it be like to lie beside Simon throughout the night? To hear him breathing, to feel the warmth of his body? To know him in the intimate way that husbands and wives knew each other? Afraid that she might not like the answers, Clarissa ordered her eyes to close and took long, deep breaths until the tightness in her body relaxed and she finally drifted off to sleep.

Simon offered his friend a brandy. "I thought you were going to be spending the week in Dorchester?"

"So did I," Clarence Albright said, sitting down in the chair opposite Simon's desk. "But my plans were unexpectedly altered. Lord Barton sent around a messenger saying he had to return to London on a matter of urgent business. I have a week to while away before purchasing one of his thoroughbreds."

"So you decided to while away the time at Sheridan Manor," Simon said, pouring himself a drink.

"Something like that." Albright chuckled. "I have no desire to return to London and another of my mother's parties." His shoulders slumped, and he rolled his eyes toward the vaulted ceiling of the earl's study. "It's damned tiring seeking out a wife, I tell you. After a week they all start looking alike. Polite smiles, coy glances, girlish giggling. God, how I hate girlish giggles. It's enough to send a man to his club for a few hours of peace and tranquility."

Simon laughed. "If you weren't in your dotage, you wouldn't be looking for a wife."

"I'm not that old," Albright grumbled. "If I were, I wouldn't have to worry about producing the next viscount of Thornton."

"It's the price we pay for being titled gentlemen," Simon said sympathetically.

"Well, it's a bloody high price, I tell you. Just wait, my dear friend. Your turn is coming."

"Perhaps I won't have the same difficulty."

The quietly spoken reply made Albright sit up and take notice. "Who is she?"

Simon gave him a thin smile. "Lady Clarissa Pomeroy."

"Hartford's granddaughter!" The viscount was impressed. "I thought she was rusticating in Norwich."

"She is, or should I say, she will be for another few days."

"Damn it all, Sinclair, you've been courting the girl and keeping to yourself about it. I thought we were friends."

Simon saw no need to explain the details of his relationship with Clarissa, brief as it might be. It would serve no purpose to disclose the terms of their marriage to anyone, including the viscount. If society reached the same conclusion as Albright, that the earl of Sheridan had intended to seek Clarissa's hand and her grandfather's death had postponed the engagement, then all the better.

It wasn't until that very moment that Simon realized he had no reservations about taking Clarissa as a wife. Whatever reluctance he had demonstrated yesterday in the garden had been for her benefit. The lady's boldness needed to be curtailed. Letting her worry over the outcome of her brazen proposal might be just the thing to make her pause and take thought before she did something as daring in the future.

"Will you stand with me?" Simon asked as his friend sipped the imported French wine.

"Need you ask?" Albright retorted, then quickly added, "I'll expect the same of you when the times comes for me to make the sacrificial walk down the aisle."

Simon laughed. "It's strange, but I'm discovering that I'm not as hesitant as I thought I would be."

"I'd feel the same way if I were marrying a beauty like Lady Pomeroy."

Simon frowned. "She is beautiful, isn't she?"

It was Albright's turn to laugh. "As if you hadn't noticed."

Simon had noticed, which meant that other men would notice to. Funny, but he hadn't thought of anyone seeing the subtle charm of Clarissa's appearance in quite the same way that he had seen it. Not that she wasn't pleasant to look at. She was. It was just that she wasn't inclined to seek out a man's eye when she attended a ball or the theater. In fact, he had gotten the impression since she'd come of age that she avoided men whenever possible. It was another one of the things that had made her so intriguing to him, a woman who didn't flirt and wave her fan like a peacock in heat. Clarissa was quiet and self-contained in public. He'd seen another side of her personality in the garden. The loss of her temper had amused him, and at the same time it had made his body hum with the delightful sensation of passion.

Simon was aware of his reputation as a reasonable, pragmatic man who enjoyed politics and a good game of cards. He also enjoyed women, albeit discreetly. It had been a long time since he had felt an uncontrollable bout of lust, one that took him by surprise and left him feeling frustrated. His last recollection of wanting a woman and not being able to satisfy his desire was so long ago it barely registered in his memory. He was pleasing to a lady's eye, titled, and extremely wealthy. Those attributes guaranteed him a bed partner anytime he wanted one.

"If you're about to take on the yoke of matrimony," Albright said, interrupting Simon's private thoughts, "I suppose you won't be needing the services of a mistress."

Simon gave him a knowing smile. "I've always suspected that you were attracted to the lovely Nanette."

The lady under discussion was Simon's current mistress. He had thought about returning to London and spending a night or two at the town house he rented for the petite French countess who made her way by keeping certain gentlemen of the town happily occupied in her bed. But instead of satisfying the desire Clarissa had kindled, Simon had retired to his study and worked on the speech he was scheduled to deliver to Parliament when it reconvened at week's end.

"Who wouldn't be interested in the lovely widow," Albright mused aloud, smiling over the rim of his brandy glass. "Perhaps I should deliver the news of your recent engagement. If the lady needs a comforting shoulder to shed her tears, I wouldn't mind volunteering."

"Be my guest," Simon replied, coming to his feet. "And please inform the lady that I will see the rent paid until the end of the year in lieu of a personal visit to announce my regrets at having to take leave of her entertaining company."

"I'm sure she'll be appreciative of the message," Albright said, grinning.

"And the messenger," Simon replied dryly.

"Without a doubt." His friend laughed, raising his glass in a mock salute. "By the way, when are the nuptials to take place?"

"At the end of June," Simon replied, looking out the window and wondering what his future wife was doing at that precise moment in time. "I'll have my secretary send around the details. It will be a small wedding. Although Clarissa is officially out of mourning, I'm sure she will prefer a private ceremony."

"I'll keep my calendar clear," the viscount told him. "Until then, pray for me."

Simon looked over his shoulder. "And for what shall I pray?"

"For patience," Albright groaned. "I've vowed to select a wife before Boxer Day. That means another six months of tolerating my mother's good intentions and the countless young ladies she has found for my ultimate selection."

Simon smiled. "Keep your chin up, old friend. Remember, it's the duty of a gentleman to take a wife and provide the nursery with at least two sons."

The viscount mumbled something about keeping more than his chin up as he set his brandy glass on the table and left Simon to finish the draft of his speech to Parliament.

Simon returned to the window. Since he'd apparently decided to marry the lovely Lady Pomeroy, it was time he devoted some thought to more than his future wife's enticing violet eyes and pleasing female form.

There was, of course, the not-so-small matter of the Hartford inheritance. Simon was wealthy in his own right, but adding the bulk of the late earl's estate would make him one of the richest men in the British Empire. Nothing to turn up one's nose at, to say the least. The son Clarissa would eventually give him would inherit both titles, ensuring him a respected rank throughout the empire. Then there was the relief of not having to suffer his friend's current plight by being forced to search for a wife. That alone was enough to make Simon sigh with relief.

It was the lady herself that was giving him some doubt.

He was fast discovering that Lady Clarissa Pomeroy was a paradox. She was known for being polite but somewhat reserved when it came to social functions. The few facts he had gleaned from her grandfather pointed toward a willful nature. The two impressions contradicted one another. So which lady would be his wife? Or would he be forced to watch a constant transformation from polished lady to temperamental female, depending upon her mood?

Simon suspected there was more to Clarissa than she wanted people to see. He also imagined that there was more to her demand for privacy in the handling of her personal accounts. Her explanation had been flimsy at best.

If he accepted her proposal, and he had done so by announcing their engagement to the viscount, then he would have already given his word that he would not interfere or inquire into the spending of her share of the inheritance. Simon didn't begrudge her the funds she wanted to spend on orphans or the poor. It was an admirable pursuit for a lady of her means. What he did question was her inclination to think that by doing the proposing she was somehow setting the pattern for their future relationship.

He'd be a fool to let her think that he could be led about by the nose. Since he wasn't a fool, he had to find a way to make the lady realize that promising her privacy in the disbursing of her funds didn't make him a eunuch. When Clarissa said her vows, Simon wanted to make sure she understood what they meant.

The earl's dark eyes took on a mischievous glow as he thought of the perfect way to turn the bold Lady Pomeroy into a submissive and obedient wife.

Three

"Lord Sheridan has arrived, m'lady."

Clarissa almost jumped out of her skin. She'd been so engrossed in the daily news of a London newspaper that she hadn't heard Huxley enter the parlor on the second floor of Hartford Hall where she was enjoying a leisurely cup of afternoon tea.

Coming to her feet, she sucked in a large breath of air and smoothed the wrinkles from the black dress she was wearing. "Show him into the library," she told the butler. "I'll be down momentarily."

Simon was here!

Surely he planned on accepting her proposal, if not, it would have been easier to have sent a note penned with gentlemanly courtesy. But then again, perhaps not. He had told her he would come personally to deliver his answer. And he was a man of his word. That was the reason Clarissa had chosen him.

With a head filled with apprehension and a stomach filled with fluttering butterflies, Clarissa descended the staircase to the long, narrow foyer that separated the formal front parlor from the library and downstairs dining rooms. Hartford Hall was relatively small compared to her grandfather's other estates, but she had always enjoyed its quaint comfort and the personal privacy it gave her. The kind of personal privacy she would forfeit if she became the earl's wife.

Huxley was waiting for her at the bottom of the stairs. "I offered the earl a brandy."

"Does he seem anxious to see me?" Clarissa asked, then waved the answer aside before Huxley could give it. "Never mind. It's difficult to read his moods."

Deciding she'd endured all the waiting her nerves could handle, Clarissa swept into the library in a rustle of black satin and lace. Her dark reddish-brown hair was swept up in a stylish coiffure. The only jewelry she wore was a pale cameo brooch that her grandfather had given her on her eighteenth birthday. The elegant simplicity of her dress and jewelry, combined with the rich color of her hair and the iridescent sparkle of her eyes caught Simon's attention immediately.

He stepped away from the window where he'd been standing. "Lady Pomeroy."

"My lord."

Clarissa's breath caught in her throat at the sight of him. Outlined by the late-afternoon sun that was flooding into the library, Simon was a fine figure of a man. Her gaze lingered on the powerful lines of his body and the muscular grace of his movements. His dark hair absorbed rather than reflected the sunlight, and his eyes seemed to reach out and touch her. His expression softened as she stepped farther into the room.

"You look surprised to see me," he said.

"Not at all, my lord," she said, hiding her nervousness behind a warm smile. "I hope your journey from Coventry was an enjoyable one. The weather has been unseasonably pleasant."

"I didn't come here to discuss the weather," Simon said, setting his brandy glass down on the edge of the mahogany desktop.

The movement made Clarissa notice his hands. He was wearing a gold signet ring. He had large hands with long, lean fingers and neatly trimmed nails. The thought of those hands caressing her body was enough to make Clarissa's mind go momentarily blank. An invisible shiver traveled from her stomach to her toes, and she realized that she was on the verge of letting Simon see how much his physical presence influenced her.

"Of course," Clarissa said, squeezing in a short, silent prayer before she settled down on the edge of the velvet settee. "I assume that you've reached your decision."

"I've decided to accept your proposal."

His curt statement caused an explosion of mixed feelings inside Clarissa. Relief first, then an odd warming sensation that made the butterflies in her stomach settle down and the tension in her spine relax. She was going to be Simon's wife! Deep inside her, Clarissa knew her secret dream was coming true. But the knowledge was spoiled by an even deeper sense of regret that Simon didn't return her feelings.

"Have you nothing to say?" Simon urged her, wondering if she was having second thoughts.

Clarissa stared at him for a long moment. What did a woman say to the man who had just agreed to marry her? For the first time in her life, Clarissa was speechless. She searched for the appropriate phrase. Her mind couldn't find a single word that suited the auspicious occasion. When Simon sat down beside her and reached for her hand, Clarissa had to force herself not to jerk back as if she'd been burned.

"You have very nice hands," Simon remarked,

splaying her fingers across his open palm. "Do you play the piano?"

"Not very well," Clarissa admitted. He'd taken off his gloves. The abrasive glide of his fingertips over the back of her hand had the same effect as the kiss he'd given her in the garden.

Goose bumps sprouted on her skin underneath the sleeve of her dress and moved upward until the hair on the back of her neck was bristling like an instinctive alarm. When he turned her hand over so it was lying palm up, cupped gently within the valley of his own palm, Clarissa couldn't take her eyes away from the sight of his fingertips gently tracing the lines of her inner hand. Her sensitive flesh reacted to the feathery touch, and she smiled.

She looked up to find Simon smiling back at her. She'd never seen him smile before, not a full-fledged smile, but one that made him look several years younger and much less menacing. Seconds turned into an immeasurable span of time as Simon continued his gentle exploration of her hands. When he lifted one to his mouth and placed a chaste kiss into the center of her open palm, Clarissa felt the contact all the way to the soles of her black leather slippers.

"Have you nothing to say to the man who is going to be your husband?" Simon teased lightly.

This was a side of the earl Clarissa had never seen. A side she'd only imagined existing in her dreams. Simon was still holding her hand, and his voice had softened to the texture of velvet. Smooth and seductively supple.

"Thank you." She whispered the words.

She was looking at him with such undisguised gratitude that Simon was hard-pressed not to laugh. Something about her reply puzzled him. There was a sincerity to it that made him wonder if Clarissa had truly entertained the idea of being cast out like an unwanted shoe. Surely she knew that any number of men would flock to her side to keep that from happening. Was her shyness an act or just another part of her complicated personality?

"You're quite welcome," he replied in a husky voice.

Another silence ensued, one that was filled with the erratic pounding of Clarissa's heart and the return of butterflies to her stomach. Her mind did somersaults as it jumped from feverish images of their wedding day to their wedding night. Feeling the heat of her thoughts go from her mind to her face, Clarissa tried to withdraw her hand. Simon tightened his hold on her.

"You have to accustom yourself to my touch," Simon told her. Watching her with an almost predatory intensity, his thumb began rubbing the base of her wrist where her pulse was beating rapidly. "Tell me, Lady Pomeroy, have you ever been kissed?"

Before she could answer, Simon's mouth was pressing lightly against hers. Clarissa's heart contracted, and for a brief second she thought it was going to stop beating altogether. She started to pull away, but one of Simon's hands curved around the nape of her neck, keeping her in place.

If she had managed an answer to the earl's question, it would have been no. No, she'd never been kissed. And she'd never imagined how it would feel to have a man's mouth pressed so intimately against her own. Even with her mouth closed, she could taste him. The intoxicating flavor of the brandy he'd been sipping when she entered the room was as much a part of the kiss as the warm, moist pressure of his lips. A rising sense of being cast under some strange spell filled Clarissa's body as Simon ended the chaste kiss and moved back.

His smile was half male arrogance, half smug satisfaction, as he looked at her.

"A kiss is the customary way of sealing an engagement," he said calmly.

As if drawn by an invisible force she couldn't control, Clarissa's gaze moved downward from Simon's mysterious dark eyes, over the tanned planes of his face, to the line of his mouth. Unconsciously, she licked her lips. She tasted Simon and the brandy again.

His eyes never left her face as he brought his hand up and traced the outline of her mouth. It was the most sensual touch Clarissa had ever experienced. Suddenly afraid that he'd somehow reach inside her and steal her very soul, she stood up and turned away, keeping her back to the earl while she frantically searched for the composure that made most people think she was untouchable.

Satisfied that his future bride was as pure in body as she was in reputation, Simon left the settee and walked back to where he'd left his brandy glass. He sipped at the contents, using the time to contain the unruly desire that had rushed over him during the chaste kiss. He had admitted an acute attraction to Clarissa several years ago, but it wasn't until now that Simon realized how much he had always wanted her. He wanted to strip the black satin away from her pale skin and taste the different textures of her body. He wanted to run his tongue over the hard peaks of her breasts and kiss the soft flesh of her belly. He wanted to feel her female heat surrounding his male flesh until there was nothing but the promise of ecstasy and she was moaning his name. It was a good thing they would be married soon. Simon knew he would not be content until he possessed Clarissa completely.

Giving her an extra few moments to regain her composure, he waited until he heard the sound of her satin dress brushing over the starched lace of her petticoats before he turned around once again.

"I believe you have met Viscount Thornton before, have you not?"

"We were introduced at one of Lord Sommerfield's parties," she replied, thinking the question odd under the circumstances.

"He called on me at Sheridan House," Simon said matter-of-factly. "We have been friends since Oxford. I asked him to stand as my witness. I assume you want a small, private ceremony. Is the last Saturday in June agreeable?"

"Yes," Clarissa said, surprised that he could kiss her one moment and then discuss the plans for their wedding so casually. Her body was still reverberating with emotion. It was a heady sensation, one she'd never felt before, and she wondered if she'd suffer the same fate every time he touched her. If so, she was going to have a harder time keeping her feelings hidden than she'd first suspected. One kiss and she felt as weak as a newborn kitten.

Of course, the kiss hadn't been Simon's first. She was still reeling from the effects, and he looked as calm as an English elm on a windless day. It was irritating to think that the kiss had been nothing more than a way to finalize a business contract. She needed to keep that in mind. Simon was marrying her because . . .

"May I ask why you decided to accept my proposal?"

"After careful thought, I decided your offer was simply too good to refuse, Lady Pomeroy. I shall gain a wife, a substantial fortune, and eventually the heir I require."

"And I shall gain control of my own purse strings," Clarissa reminded him, regaining some of her formal wit.

Simon's eyes gleamed with brief amusement. "Without interference or inquiry."

"I will have your pledge, sir," Clarissa urged him.

His gaze hardened at the unintentional insult. "You have my word," he said firmly. "As long as we are husband and wife, there will be no interference or inquiry into the spending of your personal funds."

Clarissa breathed a sigh of relief. She knew the earl would keep his word. It was the reason she'd gone to him in the first place. Realizing that she had dented his pride by asking him to actually speak the promise she required, she searched for a way to make amends. If she was going to be the earl's wife, she needed to learn to get along with him.

She resumed her seat on the settee, trying to think of something to say to erase the tension in the room. Nothing came to mind.

"Before I have the banns posted," Simon began, "perhaps it would be best for us to discuss my conditions."

Clarissa gave him a puzzled look. "*Your* conditions, my lord?"

"Like you, there are certain things I want from our marriage."

"An heir," Clarissa said, trying not to blush at the thought of how that heir would be produced.

"That goes without saying," Simon replied. "I'm talking about my *personal* expectations."

Clarissa sat very still. The tone of the earl's voice told her more than she wanted to know. With the memory of his kiss still lingering on her mouth, she forced herself to meet his gaze. "I'll do my best to make you a good wife."

"Will you?" Simon asked in a low voice. "There is more to being a wife, Lady Pomeroy, than seeing that my dinner is served in a prompt fashion. A wife has other duties, as well. Will you perform those as willingly?"

Clarissa knew he was talking about their marriage

bed. One would think that with all the experience she'd gained from running Haven House, she wouldn't be embarrassed by the subject of husbands and wives and marriage beds, but she was. Holding another woman's hand while she cried about a lost lover wasn't the same as looking a man in the eye and announcing that she'd willingly become his bed partner.

"I'm prepared to do my duty," Clarissa said, giving him the answer she thought he wanted to hear.

Simon was obliged to admit that the answer would have pleased him had his future bride been anyone but who she was. Although he expected Clarissa to come to him willingly and do her duty, he also wanted her to come to him with desire. He'd felt the sensual shiver caused by the suggestive kiss he'd placed in the palm of her hand. There was no doubt the lady was capable of desire. It was up to him to teach her that it wasn't something shameful, to be hidden behind closed doors in a darkened room.

"Ahhh, yes, your duty," Simon said dryly. "The word sounds rather boring when used in the context of one's marriage bed."

Unsure where the conversation was leading, Clarissa thought it best not to comment at all.

"Come here." Simon said in a soft but commanding voice.

When she hesitated, Simon smiled. "Come now, a lady bold enough to travel all the way to Coventry to propose marriage shouldn't be shy about standing by the man who's agreed to become her husband."

She looked at his outstretched hand. Instinctively, Clarissa knew that if she accepted it, she was going to find herself back in Simon's arms. Her first thought was to ignore the softly spoken request, but she couldn't. It had felt so good when he'd kissed her before, and even though she was upset with him for acting so casually about it, she did want to feel that way again. She prided herself on being a sensible person. Of course, the problem with being sensible was having your head argue with your heart, knowing all the while which one was going to win.

Slowly, she came to her feet and walked to where Simon was standing beside the desk. Accepting his hand, Clarissa looked up at him. She could tell by the intense look in his eyes that this kiss was going to be different.

And it was.

Wordlessly, Simon pulled her close. His left hand found its way to her waist while the other traced the contours of her mouth. His eyes never leaving hers, Simon teased her mouth with the tips of his fingers. "I like your mouth," he said. "And the feel of you in my arms."

Uncertainty surged through Clarissa as a riot of exotic sensations traveled through her body like the warm feeling one got after sipping a cup of hot tea. Keeping his eyes open, Simon lowered his head and pressed his lips ever so gently over hers. Clarissa wanted to close her eyes and savor the strange and wonderful pleasure that was overtaking her, but Simon's dark gaze held hers captive while his tongue traced the seam of her closed lips. The warmth that had invaded her body began to turn into sensual shivers that marched up and down her spine like tiny soldiers. Unable to keep her eyes open any longer, her lashes lowered, and she leaned into the kiss.

Taking his time, Simon molded his lips to hers, teasing each curve of her mouth with deliberate patience, until he felt her mouth soften and her lips part. When they did, he slipped his tongue inside.

Clarissa stiffened at the unexpected trespass, but she didn't pull away. The intimate exploration of the kiss started her head to swimming and her knees to wobbling. Every nerve in her body hummed, and her hands instinctively found their way up and around Simon's neck until she was clinging to him. Before she realized what he was about, Simon had lifted her off her feet and onto the desk.

"My lord?" She managed the shaky protest.

"Hush," Simon urged softly. "We're to be married. There's nothing wrong in allowing me to kiss you."

His hands, around her waist now, tightened and held her in place while he brought one leg forward and slipped it between her knees, gently forcing them apart. Clarissa gasped as she realized what he was doing, but the sound was muffled by his mouth. The kiss became more demanding as he pulled her forward until he was cradled between her thighs. Her dress and petticoats didn't keep her from feeling the heat of his body, wedged so intimately against her.

Simon could feel her breasts pressing against his chest. He resented the clothing that kept him from feeling all of her. With one hand on her hip, he moved the other around to her back, rubbing it lazily up and down her spine, applying just the right amount of pressure to slowly ease her more closely against his body. He kissed her until he had to stop or die from lack of air, then he moved his mouth to her neck and the graceful curve of her throat just above the buttoned collar of her black dress. When she arched her neck to give him better access, he took it, nibbling at her ear, then moving back to her mouth for another breathtaking kiss that left them both shaking.

All sensibility failed Clarissa as desire took over.

Returning his kiss, she rode the sensual wave of feeling that had her floating while being held tightly in Simon's arms. Never had she imagined that a man's touch could be so debilitating. She couldn't seem to focus on anything in particular, yet she was acutely aware of everything around her: the warmth of Simon's hands as his thumb pressed against the pulse point in her throat, the soft rustle of her petticoats as he moved against her, the scent of his cologne, the flavor of French brandy. It was intoxicating, this feeling of being absorbed by another person, of relinquishing one's will until all you could do was experience a precise moment of life.

Feeling her response, Simon continued his sensual game of teasing Clarissa senseless. When she moaned softly and pushed against him, letting him feel the hard nubs of her breasts, he knew he'd pushed himself close to the breaking point. If he didn't stop now, it wouldn't end until he made love to her completely. Reminding himself that the kiss was supposed to be a lesson in establishing who set the rules and who obeyed them, Simon gradually lessened his hold on her and pulled away.

He smiled at the results he'd obtained. Clarissa's face was flushed with newly discovered passion, and her eyes were glowing like polished gems.

Still lost in the storm of sensations he'd aroused, Clarissa blinked her eyes and fought her way back to reality. She was sitting on the desk, and Simon was looking at her as if he'd just won the stakes at Epsom Downs.

"That's what I want from our marriage," he said simply.

"I don't understand," Clarissa mumbled, still overwhelmed by her first real sampling of desire. My goodness! No wonder women found themselves overcome by passion. It was a remarkable experience.

"Don't you?" Simon replied, smiling smugly. "Then perhaps I should clarify myself."

"Please do," Clarissa snapped, realizing how easily she'd fallen into his arms. She needed to get the situation under control, and quickly. If Simon discovered that she had feelings for him, she'd be at his mercy.

"It's very simple, dear lady. You extracted a promise from me, so it's only natural to expect one in return."

"You're getting the bulk of my grandfather's estate. Isn't that enough?"

Her temper was starting to show. Simon wasn't sure if he liked Clarissa's eyes best when they were sparkling with anger or glowing with passion, but he had the distinct feeling he was going to have ample opportunity to decide.

"Money has nothing to do with honor," he told her. "And let's not forget what you're getting, Lady Pomeroy. Or do you think you can exact the same agreement from another man? If so, I'm willing to forget our engagement."

Damn the man! Just when she thought everything was going to be all right, Simon had to remind her how insufferable men could be. And there wasn't a thing she could do about it. She needed a husband she could trust, and time was running out.

"What kind of promise?" She gave him a skeptical look.

Picking up the brandy glass he'd set aside before lifting Clarissa onto the desk, Simon took a sip before replying. "In return for promising not to interfere or inquire into the spending of your rather generous personal allowance, I want your promise that you will perform your wifely duty whenever and wherever I am inclined to enjoy it. In other words, my lady, whenever, wherever, and however I wish."

"And you call me bold!"

"More bold than a woman should be," Simon countered smoothly. "But still intelligent enough to realize that very few gentlemen, if any, would agree to the absurd conditions you have placed on marriage. Many would agree, only to withdraw their word once they are within their legal right. If I am to be bound by my honor, then so shall you."

Clarissa couldn't remember the last time she'd been so furious. She was getting ready to slap the conceited smile off Simon's face when she realized she'd be right back where she started from if she didn't agree to his outrageous terms. Worse yet, her ladies would be out in the cold with her.

"I suppose you want me to refuse," she said, trying to sound just as smug as her future husband. "That being the case, you'd feel justified in poking your handsome nose into my business whenever or wherever you're so inclined."

Simon smiled at her wit. "The decision is yours."

Clarissa's temper wanted to deny him the satisfaction of defeating her, but her sensible side returned, bringing with it the image of eight ladies and their unborn babes. There was a taut silence as reality came crashing down around her. She'd picked this particular path, not Simon. She'd proposed, offering the bulk of her grandfather's estate as her dowry. She'd asked the man to marry her, committing her body and her loyalty. If Simon was being an insufferable ass about things, she had no one to blame but herself.

"Very well, my lord. *After* we are married, I will perform my wifely duties whenever and wherever you are inclined to enjoy them."

"Excellent," Simon announced. "Parliament is scheduled to reconvene at the first of the week. If you require any assistance in planning the ceremony, contact my secretary."

"I can manage," Clarissa said, fisting her hands behind her back to keep from boxing the man's ears. "Is the chapel here at Hartford Hall agreeable?"

"It's agreeable." Simon replied. "I have a box at the opera. Arrange to be in London two weeks from today and we shall show ourselves to society."

"Is that really necessary?"

"Your mourning is over, Lady Pomeroy. Once our engagement is announced in the papers, people will expect us to be seen together. Besides," he added, "I find myself anxious to enjoy your company again."

Clarissa glared at him. If the earl thought she was going to fall at his feet the next time they met, he was going to be greatly disappointed. As much as she'd enjoyed the kisses they'd just shared, she'd also learned a very valuable lesson. She couldn't trust her own emotions, which meant she had to keep them on a tight leash or she'd quickly find her feelings exposed and her heart broken. "My promise doesn't have any validity until after we're married, my lord."

"I can be a patient man when it suits me," he said.

"And an arrogant one," she retorted.

Simon laughed.

She was on the verge of telling the earl a thing or two when Simon gave her a quick, hard kiss, then walked out of the room, leaving Clarissa to wonder if she'd solved one problem only to find another at her doorstep.

Four

The day after Simon's brief but eventful visit to Hartford Hall, Clarissa found herself staring at a sheet of writing paper and wondering how in the world she was going to concentrate on anything long enough to get the three dozen things listed on the paper accomplished within the next few weeks. There were wedding invitations to issue and menus to prepare. She'd need a wedding gown, of course, not to mention the endless, sundry items that went along with a bride's trousseau. Simon's announcement that they'd be married in less than six weeks' time hadn't included any hint of whether or not they'd be taking a honeymoon trip. Would she need warm clothing or gowns more suited to cooler evenings and foggy mornings?

Then there was the question of who would walk her down the aisle.

Her heart wanted to ask Huxley, but it wasn't reacting normally. Neither was any other part of her body since Simon had kissed her senseless in the library. Of course, no proper lady asked a butler to escort her to the altar. The only other man she could think of was Dr. Hayward, and she didn't dare ask him without provoking questions that she had no intention of answering. Besides,

Bonnie Lullumber's baby was due in six weeks, and Clarissa didn't want to run the risk of having the cordial country physician in the chapel at Hartford Hall when he needed to be in Upper Yorkshire delivering a child.

There were no relatives to ask, no distant male cousin or wayward uncle to do the honor. There was Mr. Knightley, her grandfather's solicitor, but the man was well past his prime and suffered from severe gout that kept him confined to a chair most of the time. The aging officer of the court was nice enough, Clarissa supposed, but she didn't relish the idea of walking down the center of the chapel draped on the arm of a man who barely stood five feet tall.

Scratching out one of the three dozen items, she decided she'd go it alone. After all, the few guests who would be invited to the private ceremony were well aware of her shortage of relatives and would certainly understand her decision to make the honored trek to the altar sans the customary escort.

With one decision made, another followed. She'd not only walk down the aisle alone, she wouldn't waste her time in dressmaker shops being poked with needles and muddling over which color cloth best suited gowns that she didn't need. If she lived to the ripe old age of one hundred and one, she'd never wear all the dresses she already owned.

Clarissa was in the act of scratching the second item off her list when Huxley tapped on the parlor door.

"Excuse me, your ladyship," the butler said. "The post has arrived."

"Is there a letter from Mrs. Flannigan?" Clarissa asked, putting the list aside and coming to her feet.

"Yes," Huxley replied, coming into the room and shutting the door behind him. He placed several letters on the table next to the serving tray that had provided Clarissa's morning tea, then handed her the correspondence from the Yorkshire housekeeper.

Anxious to read whatever news the stout Irish woman had written, Clarissa opened the letter with eager hands and began pacing the room as her eyes scanned the neatly penned words. "Miss Lullumber is doing well," she said, giving Huxley the gist of the first paragraph. "The west-wing nursery has been freshly painted and is awaiting the new babe."

"That's good to hear," Huxley replied, refilling Clarissa's teacup and pouring himself one as well. "I wager it's going to be a boy."

"As long as it's healthy," Clarissa said. "Oh," she added, smiling.

Huxley gave her a pensive look over the rim of his teapot. "Good news?"

"The very best," Clarissa told him, sitting down again so she could reread the wonderful tidings Mrs. Flannigan had written. "Apparently one of the men employed to redecorate the nursery is smitten with our Miss Calberry. He's actually proposed!"

"That is good news."

"Mrs. Flannigan writes that Martha was reluctant to accept his attention at first, but after several weeks of cordial but persistent determination, the young man has convinced her that he'll do right by her and the baby. She's promised to give his proposal serious consideration, adding that she wants me to meet him before she renders her final decision."

Miss Calberry's decision didn't come as any surprise to the Hartford butler. The eight ladies currently residing at Haven House all thought of Lady Pomeroy as their benefactor.

Clarissa's smile faded as she put down the letter and looked at her faithful servant. "There isn't enough time to travel to Haven House and appraise the young man properly. Simon expects me in London in two weeks. But I hate to think of giving Martha too many days to deliberate the proposal. She's barely beginning to show her pregnancy. The wedding would be less cumbersome if she doesn't keep the young man waiting too long."

"There's always the train," Huxley pointed out.

Clarissa chewed on her bottom lip. Traveling by train would make the trip much quicker. With the rise of the working classes, trains were becoming a more economical way to travel. Some lines had even increased their fares to discourage workers from filling up the cars, leaving more room for the refined lords and ladies who had taken to using the trains. The English rail system had advanced by leaps and bounds in the last several years. One could reach the farthest corner of the British Isles within days. Clarissa preferred traveling by private carriage lest someone recognize her and inquire about her destination, but time was of the essence in this particular situation. Very few women in Miss Calberry's situation were given the option of marriage. It would make the child legitimate, and if the young man proved to be sincere in his intentions, it offered the shy young woman a chance at happiness.

"There's so much to be done here." Clarissa sighed, torn between her newly acquired obligations to the earl of Sheridan and the eight women who depended upon her for their welfare.

Huxley followed her gaze to the list she'd discarded when he entered the room. Picking it up, he quickly scanned the neatly listed tasks. "I'll send Mrs. Garris ahead to London," he said. "She's a capable housekeeper. She can open the town house and have everything ready upon your arrival. You can pen Mrs. Quigley a note, telling her the news of your upcoming nuptials and requesting a visit as soon as your London schedule permits."

"What about the wedding?" Clarissa asked, knowing she'd worked herself into a tizzy for nothing. Huxley had the organizational skills of an army field officer.

"There's little to do but shine the silver and have the maids give the upstairs a good cleaning before the guests arrive," he said, undaunted by the prestigious event. "Once you're settled in London, being fitted for your wedding dress and enjoying the opera with his lordship, Mrs. Garris can return to Hartford Hall and begin the final preparations. Don't fret, my lady, all will be well."

"I would like to see the nursery," Clarissa said, daring to think that she could sneak away to Yorkshire without anyone missing her. "Mrs. Flannigan's letters are informative, but I prefer seeing things for myself."

Parliament would keep Simon busy enough, and there had been nothing in his parting words to make Clarissa suspect that he'd return to Hartford Hall prior to the wedding. If she left immediately, she could call upon her ladies, inspect the young gentleman who'd supposedly fallen in love with Miss Calberry, discuss her plans for additional renovations with Mrs. Flannigan, get an update from Dr. Hayward, and still meet Simon for an evening of opera.

"Purchase the necessary tickets," Clarissa told her butler. "A private car, of course."

"Of course," Huxley said, gathering the teacups and placing them on the serving tray.

The color had crept back into Clarissa's cheeks by the time the butler exited the parlor. She began pacing the room, mentally rattling off all the things she wanted to get done in the short time she'd be at Haven House. There were two more babies due before summer's end, and she wanted to make sure the workmen had the west wing ready in case her excursion to London supplied her with any more candidates for the home. Mrs. Quigley always seemed to have another lady in the wings, waiting to be discreetly interviewed by Clarissa before being offered shelter at the isolated Yorkshire estate.

Haven House wasn't for everyone. Clarissa insisted that her ladies understand the rules that went along with the opportunity to bear their children in a safe and comfortable environment. First and foremost was the necessity for discretion. If anyone in proper society got wind of what she was doing, all would be lost.

Mrs. Quigley made sure the ladies understood that Haven House provided food, clothing, and shelter, along with the services of Dr. Hayward. Once their babies were delivered, they could remain at the estate, earning their way with honest, respectable work, or they could give their infants up for adoption and return to their former lives. The decision was theirs. So far, none of the ladies had forsaken their children, which meant that Haven House had three single mothers, two male toddlers, and a chubby-cheeked four-month-old little girl named Meredith. Clarissa suspected that little Meredith belonged to a lord of the realm, but it was only a suspicion.

Another rule of Haven House was that none of its ladies were forced or obligated to reveal the identity of their child's father unless they wished to do so. Clarissa saw no point in knowing the names of the men who had sired the children she had come to think of as nieces and nephews. The women she took in deserved the chance to redeem their lives. There was no judgment passed upon them. Mrs. Flannigan wasn't one to ridicule or criticize unless a particular lady forgot her manners or became lazy in her studies or the simple tasks assigned to her to keep her hands busy and her mind occupied with things other than self-pity or guilt.

Hearing the foyer clock chime ten, Clarissa gathered up her list and went upstairs. She took the unopened mail with her, since the train trip would offer ample time to respond to the letters. Lillian, her maid, was tidying up the bedroom as Clarissa entered.

"I'll be leaving for London in the morning," she announced, keeping to her rule of never sharing her Yorkshire travels with anyone but Huxley. "We'll need to start packing."

"Yes, milady," Lillian said hurriedly. "Huxley told us about your engagement. The house is abuzz with the news." Smiling from plump ear to plump ear, the maid bobbed a curtsy. "Congratulations. Lord Sheridan is a fine gentleman."

"Thank you, Lillian," Clarissa replied, folding Mrs. Flannigan's letter and placing it into the pocket of her black skirt.

She assumed that the rest of the servants shared Lillian's apparent joy over the wedding announcement. She'd been reared by the staff of Hartford Hall as much as she'd been raised by her grandfather. She knew each one by name, as well as the names of each member of their families. Her grandfather hadn't been a miser when it came to wages, and the staff was loyal and attentive, especially Lillian. The fleshy maid with friendly brown eyes and curly blond hair had the protective instincts of a mother lion when it came to her mistress.

"It will be nice to see you dressed in something besides black, milady," Lillian said, scampering about the room like a girl half her age. "I loved the late earl, but it's time you got on with your life." She glanced over her shoulder as she opened the wardrobe doors. "Lord Sheridan is a handsome man."

Clarissa's first inquiries about what happened between a man and a woman in the privacy of their bedchamber had been answered by the robust maid, and she knew Lillian was hinting that it wouldn't be long before all her questions were answered by Lord Sheridan.

Clarissa kept her expression bland and her private thoughts to herself. She'd tossed and turned most of the night, her dreams clouded by Simon's face and her body restless with an unnamed tension that still had her head aching. Walking to the windows that overlooked the back gardens, Clarissa turned her reaction to Simon over and over in her mind. There was no disputing that she'd enjoyed his kisses. She had silently yearned for years to know what it would feel like to have him kiss her. Now she knew.

The experience had been both thrilling and frightening. His mouth had felt like molten fire, burning her senses until she'd been unable to do nothing more than cling to his shoulders like a damp cloak. When he'd walked out of the library, she'd been sorely tempted to rush after him. The temptation had been hard to resist, and Clarissa was honest enough to admit, at least to herself, that she was looking forward to knowing Simon on a more personal level. Which only added another problem to her growing list. Could she separate her emotions from the physical reaction Simon had expertly drawn from her? Could she willingly submit her body without surrendering her heart?

"I'll have your traveling suit brushed and aired," Lillian said, laying the green suede garment on the bed. "Do you want the gray cloak or the brown one."

"It doesn't matter," Clarissa replied, only half hearing what the maid was saying.

She couldn't get Simon out of her head. Every time she closed her eyes, she could feel the pressure of his mouth, as though he were still kissing her. What would it be like to lie naked beside him, to have him holding her against his own naked body? Would he be rough or gentle? His kisses had been both, coaxing and demanding things she hadn't imagined she could give a man. She knew the mechanics of taking a husband, but there was nothing to help her comprehend what it might feel like to actually have a man invade her body. She turned away from the window, managing to maintain a tenuous control over her emotions.

"Most of my gowns are still in London," Clarissa said, pushing thoughts of her wedding night aside for the time being. She had six weeks to worry about it. "Pack what's practical, but nothing more."

Simon climbed the steps to his club as the clock in the nearby park chimed six. It had been a mild day, with little rain to speak of and a clear sky that promised bright stars and a good view of the quarter moon. He'd dismissed the carriage driver so that the man could enjoy a pint of ale at one of the local taverns while Simon met his mother's only brother, Sir Richard Haston. Richard was also Simon's only relative. The Sinclairs and Hastons weren't known for having large broods of children, something Simon had never given much thought to until now. Clarissa was certainly healthy enough to give him more than the required heir, and he found himself smiling at the thought of filling Sheridan Manor to overflowing with rambunctious sons and violet-eyed little girls set on mischief.

Forcing a rigid expression to his face, Simon

handed his hat to the club's footman and walked into the grand salon. A quick glance located his uncle. Simon approached the table, signaling for the steward to bring him his customary glass of wine. The announcement of his upcoming wedding would be in the London papers the following morning, and he owed his uncle a personal invitation to the wedding.

Sitting down, Simon noted that his uncle, whom he hadn't seen for several months, had lost some weight, making his already slim features appear almost gaunt. As always, a pair of wire-rimmed spectacles were perched on his uncle's narrow nose. His head was half-crowned with a circle of silvery gray hair. Feeling both respect and affection for the old codger, Simon accepted the man's outstretched hand. His uncle was a congenial fellow, with an uncanny ability to understand human nature. Richard Haston had been knighted for his military endeavors in India, and after his return to England, he'd found himself doing the queen's bidding when she refused to budge from her self-imposed seclusion in Balmoral after the prince consort's death in 1861.

After Albert's death, the queen had been obsessed with her grief, practically exiling herself for ten years. Although her mourning attitude had lightened in the last fifteen years, it was still an important part of her personality. She tolerated politics in general and had an active dislike for anyone who criticized the conservative regimes of Europe. Her position didn't surprise Simon, since most of the Continent was ruled by her relatives.

"It's good to see you, lad," Richard said. "The morning papers praised your eloquence in Parliament this morning. You always did have a way with words."

"Let's hope some of them reached the right ears," Simon replied, sinking into the plush leather chair across from his uncle. The club was one of the most conservative in London, and it wasn't unusual to see some of society's most outstanding members sipping brandy and smoking cigars in the salon at this time of day. "Gladstone's position on Irish home rule has most of my colleagues gritting their teeth."

"He's going to split the Liberal Party in two if he keeps up," Richard retorted.

The conversation was interrupted as the steward appeared with a bottle of wine and two crystal glasses. He poured each man a drink before nodding his head respectfully and exiting the area.

"Gladstone will get what he wants eventually," Simon replied after taking a sip of the rare vintage. "Not as quickly as he would like, of course."

"He always was an impatient bugger."

Simon laughed. He shared his uncle's conservative views, along with the brown eyes that were prominent on his mother's side of the family. "Speaking of impatience," he said, then paused to light a cheroot. "You can forgo your routine lecture on the responsibility of finding myself a wife and getting on with the business of procuring an heir for the Sinclair title."

Richard's eyes went wide and, at the same time, a crooked smile lit up his aging face. "Who is the lucky lady?"

"I'm not sure luck has anything to do with it," Simon replied. "The morning papers will announce the engagement and forthcoming marriage of Lady Clarissa Pomeroy, granddaughter of the late earl of Hartford, to yours truly."

"Hartford's granddaughter!"

Simon smiled as the fragrant smoke of his cheroot drifted toward the vaulted ceiling of the club's grand salon. The expression on his uncle's face attested to his surprise and ultimate approval of the next Lady Sheridan.

"When did all this come about?" his uncle asked once the initial shock had passed. "The last I heard, Lady Pomeroy was keeping to herself. Some minuscule estate in Norwich, I believe."

"She was raised at Hartford Hall," Simon replied, knowing his uncle would have every last sordid detail of the unexpected engagement before he gave up his inquisition. "The wedding will take place in the chapel at Hartford Hall. Although we haven't discussed the details, prepare yourself to escort the bride to the altar. With Clarissa just out of mourning, a small ceremony is more appropriate than a grandiose wedding. Don't you agree?"

"I'd be honored to stand in for her grandfather. I always thought Hartford a decent man. And I couldn't care less where the vows are spoken as long as they see you happily wed," Richard said. Lifting one silver brow in an inquisitive manner, he added. "You will be *happily* married, won't you?"

Simon gave the question a moment's thought before replying. "Yes," he admitted less reluctantly than he would have thought possible a few days ago. "I see no reason why Clarissa and I shouldn't be blissfully happy together."

"Excellent. I promised your mother, God rest her generous soul, that I'd see you wed with children on your lap before I departed this good earth," his uncle said with conviction. A mischievous smile crossed his face. "Hartford's granddaughter! I'll be damned. If memory serves me, she's a pretty thing."

Simon couldn't contain his smile. "I find nothing displeasing about Clarissa's appearance."

"The girl's a bit on the stubborn side, if I recall Hartford's appraisal," his uncle goaded in a good-natured way. "Not the sort of woman I thought you'd be attracted to. Always thought you preferred the meek and mild sort. I remember you telling me that the only thing you required from a wife was obedience and a healthy womb."

"There's nothing meek about my future bride," Simon said, remembering the way Clarissa had proposed marriage and how she'd responded to his kisses.

"Just as well," Haston said. "A boring woman makes for a boring marriage bed and an even more boring life. The Sinclairs have always appreciated spirit. That's why your father married my sister. Elizabeth was never boring."

"Clarissa has more than enough spirit to keep boredom at bay," Simon said, laughing.

The conversation turned back to politics and the queen's Golden Jubilee, to be celebrated the following year. Plans were already being made to spruce up London for the prestigious parade Her Majesty's carriage would make through the streets. Several of the government buildings were to receive fresh paint once the summer months forced the peerage to leave their elegant city homes and take up residence in the country until the heat abated.

Simon was savoring the last of his wine before excusing himself for a dinner engagement with the earl and countess of Derby when his uncle broached the subject of Clarissa's inheritance.

"Taking Lady Pomeroy to wife is going to increase the Sheridan holdings twofold."

Simon nodded. Since his uncle helped him oversee a portion of the Sheridan estates, it wasn't an intrusion for Richard to comment on the vast wealth that would come under Simon's control on his wedding day. "Hartford had a way with business," he said. "I'm meeting with his solicitors in the morning."

"It's going to be a long meeting," his uncle remarked. "Amos Knightley might look like a wrinkled old prune, but his mind is as sharp as a new ax blade. Looked after Hartford's accounts for more years than I can remember. I'd keep him on if I were you."

"I plan to," Simon told him. "What do you know about Hartford's steward?"

"Prebble?"

"That's his name," Simon replied, remembering the list of employees who had been given a generous bonus in the earl's will.

"Honest as they come, or so I've always heard. Ran Hartford's lands like they belonged to the queen herself."

"Let's hope he hasn't changed," Simon remarked, realizing that taking on Clarissa and her inheritance was going to demand a great deal of his time. "I don't relish the thought of replacing half of the staff. A bad steward can suck an estate dry in a year's time."

"I'd be glad to keep an eye on things while you're showing your bride the Continent," his uncle offered.

It was customary for newly married couples of the peerage to take a tour of Europe after their nuptials. Some were even venturing across the Atlantic to New York City. A disgusting thought as far as Sir Richard Haston was concerned. America was much too barbaric to have any appeal. The rebellious country needed a few more centuries to gain respectability.

"No need," Simon told him. "Parliament consumes more and more of my time. Its summer adjournment can't come too early for me this year. Lady Pomeroy and I will marry the last Saturday in June. A few quiet weeks in the country should be enough to seal our bargain."

"Not too quiet, I hope. A man is entitled to enjoy

his bride," Haston teased. "And marriage is no bargain, lad. I don't know how most men find the patience to deal with wives. Being forced to procreate never aroused my interest."

"Nor mine," Simon admitted. "But Lady Pomeroy is an exception. In fact, I find myself looking forward to my wedding night."

"Then I wish you stamina and a fruitful honeymoon," his uncle said, raising his glass. "When do I get to meet the lady?"

"Thornton's mother is using Clarissa's arrival in London as an excuse to give a party. Your invitation will be arriving by post."

"I assume she's also going to use your upcoming marriage as an excuse to remind her son that he's yet to find a wife for himself."

"Thornton has promised to marry before Boxer Day." Simon repeated what the viscount had told him when he'd shown up at Sheridan Manor.

"I can't imagine the womanizing bounder married to anyone," Richard said. "Rumor has it that Dalton is ushering his niece off to Scotland to visit a maiden aunt just to keep Thornton from getting too close to the chit."

Simon searched his mind for an image of Lord Dalton's niece. All he could find was a vague recollection of a petite young girl with shy brown eyes who preferred looking at her shoes instead of at a man's face. Definitely not Thornton's type, he thought, and said as much.

"That's why I don't put much stock in the gossip. Thornton likes his women wild and reckless."

"Thornton likes his women any way he can get them." Simon laughed. He didn't bother telling his uncle that he'd relinquished his mistress into the handsome viscount's care. Richard would hear of it soon enough.

Coming to his feet, Sir Haston congratulated Simon once again, telling him that he looked forward to Lady Thornton's party with enthusiasm.

Wishing he hadn't accepted an invitation to dinner, Simon left the club shortly after his uncle. The carriage ride across town to Lord Derby's residence offered Simon some time to himself. He relaxed while the driver maneuvered the busy London streets, dogging gin-soaked whores and plodding hackneys. As the carriage turned onto Wembley Street, Simon's thoughts once again drifted to his future bride. He had enjoyed kissing Clarissa in the library at Hartford Hall, and although he'd admitted to his uncle that he had no argument against taking the lovely lady as his wife, Simon was beginning to wonder what it was about her that had his mind so unsettled since his return to London. Although he was almost certain she'd never been kissed before, he surely had no excuse for being so befuddled by the exchange. Yet he couldn't deny the primitive need that had been lingering in his loins since he'd walked out of the library.

The last few days had found him waking up to a body dampened by sensual sweat and a mind fogged by dreams of a violet-eyed temptress. His imagination had taken to running wild during the night, leaving him with an insatiable hunger that he knew no woman but Clarissa could satisfy. His unruly need perplexed him almost as much as the lady's demands for financial privacy.

Perhaps Mr. Knightley would be able to shed some light on Clarissa's unusual conditions. As the carriage came to a stop in front of a red brick town house, its windows ablaze with gaslights, Simon remembered his pledge. *No inquiries and no interference.*

Being a man of his word, Simon didn't intend to actually question Mr. Knightley about Clarissa's personal accounts. Of course, if the man offered information, Simon wasn't going to turn a deaf ear. His male instincts told him that his lovely bride-to-be had something up her proverbial sleeve. And that something was more than a strong sense of charity.

Climbing out of the carriage, Simon once again told the driver to be at ease. Dinner parties, especially those hosted by the earl and countess of Derby, were known to go on for hours. The night was bright and crisp, and there was no reason why the driver should be confined to the carriage while his employer enjoyed roasted lamb and French champagne.

Taking a deep breath of the evening air to fortify his lack of interest in social chatter, Simon strolled up the steps. A butler, dressed in the customary black suit and stiff white shirt, opened the door.

Several hours later, Simon departed the town house on Wembley Street, well fed but exhausted. One last carriage ride delivered him to his home not far from Regent Park, where he was greeted by his own butler, who was intuitive enough to take Simon's cloak, then leave him with a brandy and the warming light of the library fire.

Ignoring the brandy, Simon slumped into a chair and stared at the fire blazing in the hearth. As tired as his body was, he knew sleep wouldn't come easily. His body was tight with apprehension, and he didn't have the slightest idea why. The debates in Parliament over Irish home rule were heated but not unlike similar debates in the past. He was used to the verbal jostling that went on between the conservative and more liberal elements of government. Granted, the House of Lords was taking up a lot of his time, but he had never been a man who liked to idle the days away with nothing more than his stables or his estates to keep him busy.

It was Clarissa Pomeroy and her violet eyes that had Simon so preoccupied. Being reminded by

Richard Haston that he had indeed once stated that his requirements for a wife were limited to obedience and a healthy womb was forcing Simon to reevaluate his reasons for marrying Lady Pomeroy. She certainly didn't fit the first requirement. In fact, Simon had little doubt that Clarissa would gladly exclude the vow of obedience altogether if the clergyman performing the ceremony would allow the omission. Reflecting upon the possibilities of what marriage to the brazen young woman might be like brought a smile to Simon's face.

He'd seen the fiery indignation in her eyes when he'd told her of his own conditions, and he'd felt it when he'd pulled her into his arms. She hadn't wanted to surrender to his kiss, but she had. Knowing that Clarissa had the potential for passion was more than enough to keep Simon from concentrating too hard on her lesser qualities. Given time and the temperance that sharing his bed would teach her, Simon was confident that their marriage would prove to be favorable to both of them.

Their children would certainly benefit from the union. Whatever the number of offspring, with him as their sire and Clarissa as their dame, the next generation of Sinclairs wouldn't lack courage or spirit.

Five

Eleven days after Simon had kissed her and two days before the opera, Clarissa walked up the front steps of her grandfather's London town house. She was so tired, she could barely put one foot in front of the other. Not wanting to encounter anyone who might question why she'd arrived on a train from Manchester rather than the one that ran regularly from Norwich to London, Clarissa had insisted that Huxley schedule their arrival at Paddington Station at an inconspicuous time. Which meant it was only an hour before dawn. Unable to sleep on the train, Clarissa had sat up most of the night, listening to the incessant hum of steel wheels rolling over steel rails. She'd gone from smiling over Martha Calberry's good fortune at finding herself such an amiable young man to frowning over her own set of circumstances.

"You can sleep the day away," Huxley said as he opened the front door of the Park Lane house. Thick fog blanketed the lush greens of Hyde Park, on the western boundary of the plush residential neighborhood that was only a short distance from Buckingham Palace.

Clarissa gave him a weary smile as she stepped into the foyer and shrugged out of her rain-dampened cloak. The hem of her royal blue skirt was streaked with the murky residue of water and coal dust from the puddles that had formed on the station platform. In spite of her appearance, Mrs. Garris greeted Clarissa with a warm smile, telling Huxley to get her settled in the parlor while she fetched her ladyship a nice cup of herbal tea.

"Then right to bed with you," Huxley declared, bending down to pick up the cloak Clarissa had shed and dropped to the floor like a butterfly's cocoon. "If Lord Sheridan sees you looking so tired, he's likely to summon a physician."

"You think he'd be that concerned?" Clarissa asked, unsure how Simon felt about her and their upcoming marriage.

"Lord Sheridan isn't a man to disregard the health of his intended bride," Huxley replied. "He has a reputation for taking care of business."

Business!

But then, that was what her upcoming marriage to the handsome lord was all about. Business, pure and simple. In exchange for the freedom to handle her own money, Simon would get a wife. Their relationship was contractual, not romantic.

Still, the thought of seeing Simon again was enough to resurrect some of Clarissa's energy. Her steps were more lively as she walked into the small parlor, where a fire was still smoldering on the hearth. The opera was tomorrow night. Would Simon kiss her again?

"I'll see that all is ready upstairs," the butler said once the maid had brought in a tray with steaming tea and moist sweet cakes. He stoked up the fire, then closed the parlor door, leaving Clarissa alone for the first time in days.

The last week and a half had been a whirlwind of activity. She'd spent endless hours on the train, leaving Norwich for Carlisle, then Carlisle for London. More than eight hours had been spent in a rented carriage drawn by a set of thick-chested Breton horses that had been hired to take her from the railroad depot in Carlisle to the secluded Yorkshire estate that she'd named Haven House. In between the train and carriage rides, she'd met and approved of Myles Garfield, arranged for the remaining four bedrooms in the west wing to be painted, and helped Mrs. Flannigan select cloth for draperies and bedspreads. She'd transferred the last of her mother's inherited funds into her Carlisle account so the Irish housekeeper could purchase a new stove for the kitchen and roses to replenish the manor gardens, leaving Clarissa nothing but the living allowance that was part of her grandfather's will. She had spent time with the ladies discussing names for the babies to be delivered that summer and listening to their plans for the future.

Dr. Hayward had called, assuring her that each and every resident was healthy and for her to return to London and stop "fretting" over them long enough to enjoy her own wedding and honeymoon.

The news of her upcoming marriage to Simon Sinclair had been greeted with mixed emotions. Some of the ladies feared that her husband would eventually find out about the Yorkshire estate and order its doors locked and barred. Others hugged and kissed her and wished her nothing but happiness. Mrs. Flannigan had smiled, and Dr. Hayward had teased her about soon needing his services. He'd assured her that he'd be honored to deliver the next earl of Sheridan. No one but Huxley and Mrs. Quigley knew that she was being forced to take a husband in order to maintain financial security.

Clarissa sipped the tea, relishing its spicy aroma and warmth. She remembered that Simon had tasted like brandy and—her weary mind couldn't find the right words. It still amazed her that a kiss could encompass so many things. Sensations and smells. Tastes and texture. Like the tea, Simon's mouth had warmed her from the inside out. The memory of it was still strong enough to heat her blood and make her head swirl. And soon she'd be seeing him again, looking into his vibrant brown eyes and wondering if he could ever come to care for her.

Truly care.

The way young Myles Garfield cared for Martha Calberry. The Yorkshire-born lad was only a year or two older than the expectant mother he'd promised to love, honor, and cherish. It had taken less than ten minutes for Clarissa to give her blessing to the unexpected union. Myles had stood straight and tall in front of her, his plaid cap held firmly in his right hand as he'd declared that he meant to marry Miss Martha Calberry, whether her benefactor approved or not.

"She's going to need someone to look after her and the babe," he'd said. "I'm a hard worker and an honest man. It doesn't matter that the babe isn't mine. The man I call my father isn't my real dad. Mine was killed in the mines before I was born. But he raised me just the same. And I don't give a tinker's damn, pardon the language, m'lady, that Martha thought herself in love with another man before she came here. It's me she loves now, and that's all that matters. She's a bit shy about it, but she does love me. And I her. I'll do right by them both. God be my witness."

It had been the love and devotion in the young man's eyes that had convinced Clarissa, not his words. She'd searched his face, looking for doubt or selfish motives, but all she'd been able to see in Myles Garfield's eyes was honesty. Honesty and a sincere love for the young woman who had sat quietly on the sofa while he bluntly stated his very honorable intentions.

If only she could see the same honesty shining in Simon's eyes. Would he ever look at her with love, or was she destined to be only an object of sexual attraction? A curiosity that would soon outgrow its novelty. A wife who had come along at the right time with just the right amount of money to entice him to the sacrificial altar?

Why had Simon agreed to marry her?

Clarissa had spent the weeks before her outrageous proposal convincing herself that like other men of his rank and responsibility, the earl of Sheridan needed an heir, and thus an acceptable wife. And the granddaughter of the earl of Hartford was nothing if not acceptable.

Feeling a headache coming on, Clarissa set her teacup aside and stared into the crackling flames of the fire. Dawn was creeping over the city, sending light into the fog-filled shadows and awakening the noisy street peddlers who would soon be selling their wares in the business district. She could already hear the clacking of the cab wheels stopping at regular intervals along the cobblestone street outside so that the young boys who rode in the back of the canvas-covered wagons could make deliveries to the kitchens in the prestigious Mayfair neighborhood.

She went upstairs, stripped out of her stained traveling suit, put on a white nightgown, and crawled under the covers. Clarissa was asleep within seconds, all worries about her wedding night and the dashing earl of Sheridan replaced by fatigue.

Having received a note announcing Lady Pomeroy's arrival, Simon stepped down from his carriage and walked toward the ten-foot wrought-iron gates that separated the expensive red brick residence from the street. He lifted the latch, closing the gate once he was inside, and proceeded up the steps toward an ornately carved door of English oak that was as sturdy and dependable as the aristocracy it represented.

"Good day, your lordship," Huxley said.

Simon handed over his black beaver hat and calfskin gloves before asking if his fiancée was in residence.

"Lady Pomeroy is in the library," Huxley replied, placing the earl's hat and gloves on a narrow teakwood table, garnished with a tall Chinese vase filled with fresh flowers. "This way."

Simon followed the stout butler across the tiled floor toward the library. Having visited the late earl of Hartford on several occasions, the interior of the house didn't come as a surprise to Clarissa's future husband. The majority of the first-floor furnishings were of rich, warm walnut. The chairs in the library and parlor were large and comfortable, upholstered in soft leather. The draperies were green and gold, with braided fringe that whispered across the floors when they were opened or closed, depending upon the time of day. The house silently shouted of good taste and an elegant grace that Simon suspected was more to Clarissa's credit than her grandfather's.

He'd never been upstairs, but the earl of Sheridan also suspected that the remainder of the London residence was as stylishly decorated as the dining room and salon. The size of the house was only slightly larger than his own home in Belgrave Square, and for a moment he pondered the thought of moving into the Park Lane residence once he and Clarissa were married. As the doors to the library were opened by the stout butler, Simon decided it would be foolish to give his lovely bride the advantage of living in a house where she felt perfectly at ease. Once Lady Pomeroy became Lady Sheridan, she was going to have to acclimate herself to being his wife. That included living anywhere her husband wanted her to live.

When Huxley announced the earl, Clarissa's heart tightened for a moment as she looked up. As always, her first glimpse of Simon made her stomach quiver with strange sensations. Dressed in an autumn brown jacket and matching trousers, Simon walked into the room with the manly grace of his breeding. His white cravat and shirt were of fine linen, and they accentuated the healthy tan of his skin. His brown eyes focused on her immediately, and Clarissa prayed that she'd had enough sleep to erase the fatigue of the last ten days from her features.

"Bring us some refreshments," Clarissa said to Huxley as the butler exited the room, leaving the door open.

"My lady, I trust you are well," Simon said, in a clear strong voice that offered no hint of his reaction at seeing her again.

"Yes, thank you," she told him, telling herself it was only a small white lie. She hadn't been herself since the day she'd proposed marriage to the earl of Sheridan, but there was little to be done about it now. One of the items she'd read in the papers that had been accumulating in the library since Mrs. Garris had opened the house was the news of their upcoming nuptials.

Unknown to Clarissa, Simon was having more than a little difficulty adjusting to the sight of his future wife. The mourning black was gone. In its place was a gray broadcloth skirt that fit snugly about her narrow waist, flaring softly over her womanly hips as she came to her feet. She was wearing a pale blue silk blouse with a high collar and pearl buttons. Her thick auburn hair was woven into a nest of sleek curls at the nape of her neck, and Simon wanted to unleash it from its restrictive pins and feel it slide through his hands.

"I was just reading about your speech," Clarissa said, indicating the scattered newspapers on the floor next to the divan, where she'd been sitting. "The prime minister is not happy at having his plans for Irish home rule so eloquently defeated."

Simon noted several letters and a splattering of party invitations on the neighboring ottoman. His bride had been busy catching up on the London news. He'd given the speech more than a week ago.

"Gladstone is rarely defeated," Simon said with a crooked smile that was out of place with the accounts she'd read in the papers. "He has the tenacity of a Scottish terrier."

"As well he should have," she countered. "It's never easy to change things when the majority of people are content to leave them be. Complacency doesn't get the job done."

"Do I detect a hint of liberalism in your words?" Simon asked, not totally surprised by Clarissa's sympathies.

A good many women applauded the liberal party's approach to social change. But most of them kept their opinions to themselves. It wasn't considered fashionable for a lady of breeding to be interested in politics. The Married Women's Property Act, passed four years before, enabled women to buy, own and sell property, and to keep their own earnings. The act didn't apply to his free-thinking fiancée. Clarissa wasn't a married woman yet, and she hadn't earned the Hartford fortune. She'd inherited it. And only a portion of it, if her grandfather's will was to be satisfied.

"I rarely hint at things, my lord," Clarissa replied, wondering how Simon would react if he ever discovered that she financially supported the majority of legislature he so eloquently spoke out against. "I prefer candor to coyness."

"It isn't necessary to remind me of your frankness," he said, approaching her with a predatory gaze.

His dark eyes roamed over her in a bold, sensual sweep that started at the toes of her black leather shoes and ended when he stopped to stare at her mouth. There was a possessive, almost challenging, quality to his gaze, and Clarissa feared he would kiss her again, making her forget her resolve to keep him at arm's length until they were legally married.

She stepped behind the desk that had been her grandfather's personal domain, using the sturdy piece of furniture like a shield to defend her wavering emotions. If Simon kissed her, it would only inflate his arrogance and weaken her determination to keep her heart safe. "I received a note from Lady Thornton. It appears that a party is being held in our honor this evening."

"That's one of the reasons I came to see you," Simon replied, amused by her blatant attempt to keep him at a distance. He decided to indulge Clarissa's female stubbornness for the moment. But he didn't intend to take his leave without reinforcing the terms of their relationship. He wanted to kiss her again. "Lord Thornton has agreed to be my best man. It's to be expected that his mother would want to be the first to acknowledge our engagement. I'll call for you at eight."

Huxley brought in a tray of tea and fresh baked bread squares covered in rich strawberry jam, one of Clarissa's favorite treats. She adored strawberries and frequently had them for breakfast, sliced, with a sprinkling of sugar.

Excusing the butler once the tea had been poured, Clarissa motioned for Simon to take a seat.

He declined the invitation and walked to the windows overlooking the small but meticulously kept courtyard at the back of the London house. A wall kept the small garden and green lawn separated from the neighboring residences. It was a brisk spring day, making the roses along the walkway stand tall to absorb the sunlight.

Clarissa sipped her tea and tried to think of something to say. She wasn't usually tongue-tied, but for the life of her she couldn't think of a single, cordial topic to end the silence that seemed to permeate the library.

Suddenly, Simon turned and looked at her. The china teacup stopped midway to her mouth as Clarissa felt the eerie beckoning of his gaze. It was as though she were a ship lost at sea and Simon was the saving grace of a welcoming lighthouse. For a brief moment, all she could do was look at him, feeling as if he'd somehow managed to burrow his way beneath her skin and take up residence dangerously close to her heart.

"My uncle, Sir Richard Haston, will be attending the party tonight," Simon told her. "Our last meeting didn't offer the time for me to inquire into your preferences as to how the ceremony will be conducted. If you desire the customary amenities, my uncle would be honored to escort you down the aisle."

Clarissa was surprised. Both by the gesture and Simon's eloquent reminder of their last meeting. They hadn't had the time to discuss the wedding details because he'd delivered the arrogant conditions of their marriage, then kissed the blithering wits out of her.

"I'm the one who would be honored," Clarissa replied, feeling a rush of heat as Simon approached the desk once again. "My grandfather always held Sir Haston in the highest esteem."

"Then we'll tell him tonight," he said, his voice low and seductive.

When he came around the desk and reached for her hand, Clarissa could no more refuse him than she could sprout wings and fly. She found herself following him to the door, being led across the Persian carpet like a puppy on a leash. She was calling herself a coward for not insisting that he unhand her when the click of the library door being closed and locked brought her head up. For a long moment she couldn't free herself from the captivating intensity of his eyes. A feeling began to settle in the depths of her being so strongly that it threatened to steal her next breath. She longed to know what Simon was thinking at that exact moment, but like always, his features gave no hint of his emotions. She stared into the walnut depths of his eyes and prayed that her own eyes weren't flooded with the same sensations that were already overtaking her body. If so, she knew Simon could see her anticipation as surely as she could feel it boiling up inside her.

"I've missed you," Simon said, engulfing her waist in his large hands and pulling her toward him. "A gentleman expects to be greeted more cordially by the woman he's soon to wed."

"A gentleman doesn't take advantage of a lady," Clarissa told him, placing her hands against the soft wool of his jacket and straightening her arms to keep the earl from holding her any closer. "After all, my lord, we are barely more than strangers."

More intimidated than she liked to admit, Clarissa did her best to ignore his soft chuckle. The man was entirely too smug for her liking. If he thought he could sweep her off her feet with more of his debilitating kisses, he was in for a surprise.

"We are engaged to be married," he reminded

her in a confident tone. "That makes us much more than strangers."

Although he wasn't pulling her any closer, he hadn't released her either. Clarissa decided it was time to take control of the situation before she found herself surrendering to any more of the earl's tempting charms. "Truth be known, I'm not sure what our engagement makes us, my lord. Granted, we have met on several occasions, and you were considered a trusted friend by my grandfather, but that hardly makes us—"

"Lovers," Simon teased, enjoying the way Clarissa's eyes darkened to a dazzling blue whenever she was upset about something. He knew he was encouraging a display of her temper, but he couldn't resist teasing her. It was a delight to watch her eyes sparkle with female indignation and feel her body so close he could detect the light tingling that said she was just a little afraid of him.

"We are not lovers," she said, giving him a firm shove to set herself free.

Simon's grip on her didn't lessen. He merely smiled and pulled her against his chest, letting her feel the heat of his body beneath the smooth silk of his tailored shirt. "Not yet, but we will be."

Clarissa bristled as his hands moved from her waist to her back, trapping her in a sensual grasp that was far from proper. She could feel the steely strength of his thighs as he stepped closer, leaving little between them but the heat of their bodies and the clothing that kept them from feeling the texture of each other's skin.

"We will be husband and wife," she informed him briskly. "A man and woman can hardly be lovers without loving one another. We don't share that particular affection. On the other hand, having observed the state of most aristocratic marriages, I'm reluctant to call us more than business partners."

It was a half-truth, to be sure, but Clarissa needed to remind herself that Simon's attention wasn't motivated by the same thing that had her heart melting inside her chest.

Another soft chuckle sounded before Simon tipped her chin up with the knuckle of his index finger, forcing Clarissa to look directly into his eyes. Standing so close, she realized that his brown eyes were tinged with gold flecks and framed by thick dark lashes. There was a sprinkling of gray at his temples and the slightest shadow of a beard on the lower half of his chiseled face. His hand moved slowly up her back, not stopping until he was cradling her head to hold her in place while his mouth lowered to kiss her.

His lips brushed tentatively against hers, teasing and tasting and making her want the kiss so much, she almost forgot that she was supposed to be scolding him, not deflating like a hot-air balloon at his slightest touch.

Simon forced himself to go slow, to control the unruly need to carry his soon-to-be wife to the green velvet divan and make love to her while the sunlight streamed through the lead-paned windows of the library. He could feel the rise and fall of her breasts under the blue silk blouse. The hand holding her about the waist tightened just enough for him to confirm the rumor that Lady Clarissa Pomeroy rarely wore a corset. At that moment, Simon wanted to strip her naked and gaze at the softness of her body, to claim each and every womanly curve, to feel the pleasure of having her twist and moan beneath him as he taught her what being lovers really meant.

Clarissa made an incoherent sound in the back of her throat as Simon gradually turned the chaste kiss into one that demanded her full attention. Her hands took on a will of their own as they circled his neck, and her body eased against his, closing the gap between them like drifting sand filling the crevices of a rocky beach. His mouth pressed harder, his tongue intruding and retreating like an ocean tide. Clarissa gasped as he tasted her, taking his time, making her head spin and her knees threaten to give way beneath her.

The intimacy of the kiss shocked her. She could feel her heart beating more rapidly with each passing second. When his arm moved to her waist, then lower, cupping her hips and lifting her against him, Clarissa decided kissing was the most wonderful thing in the world.

Holding her against him, Simon allowed himself the pleasure of fantasizing how nice it was going to be to do the same thing when Clarissa was wearing nothing but her sparkling blue eyes and luxurious auburn hair.

Feeling his self-control waning, Simon forced himself to break the kiss. He looked down at Clarissa's flushed face and swollen mouth and smiled.

"Husbands and wives can be lovers," he said, his voice husky and thick with the passion that was evident if anyone but glanced at him. "And that's what we're going to be. Lovers and partners."

Clarissa shook her head to clear it of the sexual cobwebs the earl's kiss had created. She searched his eyes for the slightest glimmer of love, but all she could see was the dark fire of passion heating them to a warm, liquid brown. Hating her inability to deny him the kiss he'd so arrogantly forced upon her, Clarissa disengaged herself from his arms and stepped back.

"I distinctively remember telling you that I don't intend to meet the brazen requirements of our marriage until *after* it has taken place," she said, raising a trembling hand to her hair to straighten the pins. "Please remember that you're a gentleman. I would hate to take myself back to Hartford Hall before enjoying the opera."

Simon was still smiling when he called her bluff. "And I distinctively remember how much I enjoyed kissing you that day in the library. You enjoyed it, too, or you wouldn't have kissed me back just now."

"I did no such thing!" Clarissa was horrified that he could insult her without blinking an eye. "Perhaps you should leave now, my lord. I will welcome your escort to the opera, but I have suddenly found myself indisposed to your arrogance."

Simon laughed, then walked to the desk where he'd left his teacup. He took a slow drink, keeping his back to Clarissa as she realized he wasn't going to be tossed out into the street like an unwanted suitor.

For a long moment, she considered unlocking the door and calling for Huxley. The stout butler would see Simon out if she insisted, but Clarissa didn't reach for the brass doorknob. She had been the one to ask Simon to marry her, not the other way around. And she'd been the one to agree to the outrageous conditions he'd set. Could she blame him for thinking that she enjoyed his advances?

She had enjoyed the kiss, but she wasn't about to admit it. Not now, when Simon looked very much like a man who'd just been proclaimed king of the world. That was what was really upsetting Clarissa. In a few short weeks she would become the earl's wife, and in doing so, she'd be expected to treat him like a king. Centering her life around his wants and needs, taking his name and submitting to his desires, until she feared that her own identity would be absorbed and one day she'd awaken to question who and what she'd become.

That was her biggest fear.

Losing not only her heart but her soul.

And Simon Sinclair was the kind of man who could steal a woman's soul. He wouldn't do it maliciously. He'd simply seduce her senses until she didn't know up from down, leaving her totally dependent upon him for the love she so desperately needed. The kind of love most men refused to admit existed. Men, especially conservative-thinking men like the earl of Sheridan, preferred passion to the romantic notions of love that sustained a woman's dreams.

Deciding that if he gave Clarissa too much time to recover from the intoxicating effects of their kiss she might flee to the safety of her bedroom, Simon turned back to her. She was still standing in front of the door, her mouth still moist from his kisses and her eyes focused on nothing in particular, as if she were looking inward, trying to sort out some perplexing problem.

"I met with Mr. Knightley yesterday morning," Simon said matter-of-factly.

Clarissa blinked, bringing herself back from the fanciful world in which she'd imagined that Simon might actually love her. "I received a note from him as well," she said, forcing herself to walk to the desk and retrieve her teacup as though she hadn't been clinging to Simon's broad shoulders a very short time ago. "He told me that your meeting went well."

Simon almost smiled again, but he didn't. If Amos Knightley's definition of well meant four and a half-hours of legal details, finished off with a firm lecture about the responsibilities of assuming the late earl of Hartford's place in the world, then the meeting had gone well indeed. Under other circumstances, the earl of Sheridan would have been insulted by the discussion, but Amos Knightley was close to eighty years old, and any man, titled or not, less than sixty was considered little more than a lad by the aging gentleman. Simon had also noted a genuine concern for Clarissa's welfare in the old man's words, another reason why he'd suffered the sermon. Apparently Clarissa often visited the gout-stricken solicitor for no other reason than to see if he was doing well and to bring him a homemade tonic that Knightley insisted made him feel much better. Simon suspected it was Clarissa's attention that momentarily expelled the pain of growing old, just as it had erased an afternoon appointment from his mind.

He glanced at his pocket watch. He had less than an hour's time before meeting his own solicitors and arranging for the transfer of properties and monies that would come on the day Lady Pomeroy became his wife, as well as the generous monthly allowance that would allow her to contribute to every charity known to mankind.

"I must take my leave," he told Clarissa. "I have an appointment that forces me to cut our reunion short."

Since Mr. Knightley's note had stated that Simon had agreed to the terms of her allowance without a moment's hesitation, Clarissa didn't goad him by asking if he'd been impressed by the actual listing of her grandfather's estate. Nor did she voice her regret that he would soon be leaving. Let the man think that she didn't care in the least if he waltzed into the library, kissed her, sipped some tea, then waltzed back out again.

Simon picked up her hand and raised it to his mouth, giving her a wicked smile before he placed a kiss in the center of her palm.

"I'll call for you at eight," he said, releasing her hand and reminding her of the party, where they'd be formally viewed as an engaged couple.

"Eight," Clarissa said, her voice barely audible.

Six

Clarissa stared at her reflection in the mirror. She hadn't worn a party gown in over a year. She'd decided upon a pale yellow satin gown. It buttoned up the back, and the tiny pearls sewn into the lace bodice glittered like milky raindrops when she moved. Unsure about her first appearance in society in over twelve months and not wanting to disturb the fragile tolerance that existed between her and the earl of Sheridan, Clarissa had allowed Lillian to lace her into a corset. As much as she hated the dreaded undergarment, she was wearing it. Simon was the epitome of English propriety when he mixed with his peers, and she wasn't ready to risk his displeasure. They weren't married yet, and her allowance could vanish as quickly as smoke up a chimney if she didn't keep her temper on a leash and her wits about her.

"The earl will be speechless," Lillian declared, handing Clarissa a pair of pearl droplet earrings. "I've never seen you look lovelier."

Clarissa put on the earrings, then added a priceless strand of pearls around her neck. The smell of light perfume filled the bedchamber as the maid helped her finish her toiletry for the Thornton party. Clarissa walked over to a small dressing table and picked up the a pair of white gloves.

Drawing them over her hands and up her arms until they reached her elbows, she wondered who else would be attending the party. She knew Viscount Thornton, or at least she'd made his acquaintance at the balls she'd attended prior to her grandfather's illness and death. He was a dashing figure of a man with a reputation for charming the ladies. He was also Simon's best friend, which meant Clarissa would be seeing a lot of him from now on.

She supposed the viscount's friendship could come in handy. No one knew Simon better than Clarence Albright. If anyone could give her an insight into the earl's personal life, past and present, it would be the rakish viscount.

Clarissa gave her reflection one last, quick glance before stepping out into the hall. The second and third floors of the town house opened onto a balcony that formed a semicircle above the white tiled foyer. The light of the gas-fueled brass chandelier, suspended from the vaulted ceiling by chains that could hold the Devil himself in bondage, offered more than enough light for Clarissa to see that her fiancé looked as handsome in evening clothes as he did in everything else.

Simon looked up as she began descending the spiral staircase, catching her eyes and holding them as she took one graceful step after another, coming closer and closer to the moment when he would take her hand and lift it to his mouth again. The gloves would keep her from feeling the warm, moist pressure of his lips on her bare skin, and Clarissa wasn't sure if she liked or disliked the idea. This was their first formal outing together. Once they entered the grand salon of the Thornton's home, everyone in London would consider her Simon's personal property. She would be draped on his arm like a fashionable peacock for society to see and admire. People would flock around them, bestowing congratulations and wishing them years of happiness. But only she and Simon would know the truth.

A question flashed through her mind as Clarissa reached the landing between the first and second floors. What if Simon had told Viscount Thornton of her unusual proposal and his own outlandish terms of marriage? And what if the viscount told someone else? All of London would know in a matter of hours.

Clarissa hesitated at the bottom of the stairs, her hand resting lightly on the mahogany banister as Simon smiled and walked toward her. Her fears were squelched as he looked at her, and she knew that this man wasn't one to boast or brag. Dressed in black evening clothes and a white silk shirt with jet studs, he looked so handsome, Clarissa could barely contain her feelings. No, Simon hadn't told Clarence Albright, or anyone else, about their unusual engagement. Whatever was between them would remain between them, whether a secret contract or the passion that Clarissa could no longer deny.

"You look lovely," Simon said, reaching out to gently lift her hand away from the banister and lead her toward the center of the foyer, where Huxley was waiting with a white ermine wrap to ward off the chill of the evening air.

Simon took the fur and draped it over Clarissa's shoulders, leaning down and whispering into her ear. "I'm tempted to forgo the party and drag you off to the library again."

Clarissa kept her eyes forward and her reaction contained as she thought of Simon's smoldering kisses and where they would lead if she didn't keep her defenses up and the earl at a safe distance. Outside, the night air was cool with the promise of rain, and the fog hung over the city like a white blanket. His hand firmly holding her elbow, Simon bid Huxley good night and steered Clarissa down the steps and into the private coach, pulled by a matched pair of dark bay horses with glossy black manes and neatly cropped tails that kept them from getting tangled in the harness.

Once the carriage door had been shut by the footman, Simon relaxed against the dark blue cushions and tapped on the roof. The wordless command made the driver's whip crack harmlessly over the rumps of the sleek-muscled horses, and the carriage rolled away from the curb. Gaslights glowed in the murky gray fog, doing little to illuminate the night. The light posts outlined the streets, and their amber glow offered the numerous coaches and private carriages a boundary of trespass. The viscount's London house wasn't all that far from Park Lane, and Clarissa knew she would only have a few minutes alone with Simon before they reached their destination.

As if he had come to the same conclusion, Simon looked at her, his smile still in place. "I don't think I've ever seen a more beautiful woman," he said, meaning every word of it.

The last year had added a certain female maturity to Clarissa's features, and she knew that the yellow gown complemented her coloring. But she wasn't concerned about her appearance. She was worried about the look in Simon's dark eyes. He was about to kiss her again, and she couldn't let him. She'd never survive the evening if she didn't keep her resolve in place this time. There was too much at stake. Namely—her heart.

When he moved from his seat opposite her to fill the empty space at her right, Clarissa turned her attention to the window and the expensive houses that lined the streets of Mayfair. When Simon chuckled softly and reached around to gently grasp her chin and turn her head, Clarissa resisted him.

"What's this?" Simon asked. "Don't tell me you're still angry because I kissed you this morning."

"I'm not angry," Clarissa told him, maintaining her dignity even though her body was already tingling in anticipation of what it would feel like to dance with Simon. "I'm merely looking out the window."

"The fog is thicker than gravy," Simon pointed out. "You can't see anything."

Clarissa sighed. So much for being polite. "Very well, I'm doing my best to reiterate my original declaration," she admitted. "I am not at your beck and call until after the wedding, Lord Sheridan, and I ask you to remember it."

Simon's soft laughter filled the coach, making Clarissa want to slap the man more than ever. He was intentionally goading her temper, and if he wasn't careful, the earl would soon discover how formidable it could be. Counting the draped windows that allowed tiny slivers of gold light to escape the parlors that fronted the street, Clarissa bit her tongue and reminded herself that she had a lifetime in which to argue with the man sitting beside her. And that's exactly what they'd do, argue like fishmongers on the East End docks, she was sure of it.

Clarissa wasn't the carriage's only determined passenger. Knowing the game his lovely bride-to-be was trying to play, Simon smiled and turned her face back to his. "You can count lampposts or quote Shakespeare until you've recited every sonnet he ever wrote, but it isn't going to make me disappear."

Clarissa stared at him. How in the devil did the man know she was counting things in her head, trying to ignore him? She didn't like his uncanny ability to read her thoughts. She was about to open her mouth and chastise him for the arrogant remark when his fingertips moved from her chin to the pearls looped around her neck. Ever so gently, he traced the path of the lustrous beads, his finger moving slowly from one bead to the next as he outlined the oval trail of the expensive necklace.

Clarissa sucked in her breath. Never had a man touched her so intimately without touching her at all. The foggy night took on an eerie silence, the sound of her breathing the only sound her ears could hear. Simon's eyes followed the path of his fingertip, and the intensity of his gaze made the strangeness of his actions even more erotic. Clarissa's brain told her hands to move, to close the ermine wrap and end the sensual game Simon was playing, but her muscles didn't respond to the command. Instead, she sat helplessly at his side while his fingertip retraced its original path.

She looked into his eyes and felt lost, as if she'd been sucked into some deep, dark abyss. There was no time, no place, nothing but the gentle glide of Simon's fingers and the erratic beating of her heart. She managed to fight the temptation to lay her hand over his and press it more firmly to her breast. His touch inflamed her, making her desire more, making her want things she had only imagined in the shrouded privacy of her dreams. Underneath the heavy satin of her Paris gown, Clarissa felt her breasts swell and her nipples harden. When he reached her collarbone, Simon lifted his fingertip and placed it over her parted lips.

Clarissa closed her eyes in an effort to contain her emotions.

"As much as I believe in keeping a lady chaste

until marriage, I disagree with the theory of keeping them totally ignorant," he said softly. "Passion isn't shameful, Clarissa. It's as natural as breathing to most people. Don't ever be ashamed of how you respond to my touch. Passion suits you."

Embarrassed that he knew how her body was reacting, Clarissa pushed his hand away and stiffened her shoulders until she looked more like a soldier on sentry duty than an engaged woman on her way to a ball. "I'm not ashamed of anything," she told him emphatically. "You're the one who should be ashamed."

"Of what? Our mutual attraction to one another? And it is mutual, my dear. Your sweet mouth can deny it all you like, but I can feel your body trembling the same way it was trembling this morning in the library."

Clarissa's temper flared with the passion Simon's touch had ignited. "How can a man who's such a prude in Parliament be such a womanizer in private? You're despicable!"

"Politics has nothing to do with passion," Simon told her. "I have no intention of debating reform issues on our honeymoon. And I will not abide a wife who cringes under the coverlet like a sacrificial lamb. I want a woman in my bed, not a martyr."

"You made your intentions very clear when you forced me to accept your outrageous conditions," Clarissa snapped, so angry her hands were shaking.

"Forced!" He laughed. "There was no force involved, Lady Pomeroy, and you know it. One good turn, deserves another, shall we say? You proposed marriage, adding the stipulation that you are to have free rein over a *very* generous allowance, then accuse me of being outrageous. I think not, my lady."

"Then why did you accept the proposal?"

"Because I want you," Simon admitted candidly.

"And I intend to have you. Fighting and screaming or purring like a contented kitten. It's your choice, my lady."

"You're being rude."

"Honest," he corrected her. "I'm a gentleman, not a monk," Simon replied, undaunted by her outrage. "And you're no nun, Lady Pomeroy. You're a hot-blooded, free-thinking female who's in dire need of a firm hand."

"You sound like my grandfather. He was constantly telling me that I was too outspoken."

"You are that," Simon agreed. "But you're also going to be my wife. Engaged couples kiss. It's the way of things. It's also a very pleasant pastime," he added, reminding her once again that she hadn't resisted him up to now. "Not as pleasant as what's awaiting us in our marriage bed but pleasant enough to make the time between now and then very tolerable."

"Most engaged couples feel an affection and a mutual respect for one another," Clarissa remarked. The man could at least pretend to feel *something* for her.

"I respect you," Simon said honestly. "But I also desire you."

"I prefer respect to lust," she told him, preferring love above them both but knowing that was an impossibility, at least for now. "But I fear our definition of the word differs. If you respected me, you wouldn't—"

"If I didn't respect you, Lady Pomeroy, your bodice would be down around your waist, and you'd be moaning in delight instead of debating definitions."

Impatient with her attitude and knowing the viscount's home was only a few blocks away, Simon grabbed her by the shoulders and turned her around. Clarissa's protest turned into a jumbled mass of mumbled words as Simon covered her mouth. The kiss was hard and demanding, forcing her head back against the carriage cushion and making her body tighten in instant recognition of what he'd primed it for earlier.

She kissed him back. Her resistance was gone, evaporating under the heat of his mouth.

The kiss was over much too soon, and Clarissa stared up at Simon's face as he drew the white fur snugly around her shoulders before returning to the seat across from her. It was too dark to see his face, but she knew he was smiling that damn smug smile again.

"You are impossible," she snapped.

"I'm also the man you're going to marry in a month's time," he stated just as firmly. "You're the one who wanted this marriage," he reminded her. "And I'm the one who intends to do a hell of a lot more than kiss you after the vows are spoken. Unless you'd prefer to terminate our agreement and find another trustworthy gentleman to keep your personal account stocked with money."

Clarissa was fuming as the carriage came to a stop in front of the viscount's London residence. The windows were aglow with light, and the three-story houses looked to be filled to overflowing if the number of carriages lining the street was any indication of the guests who were already enjoying the festivities. Simon waited for the footman to open the door before he stepped free of the carriage and offered Clarissa his hand. She accepted it, vowing once again to keep her temper leashed and a smile plastered on her face for the duration of the evening.

She had to stop reflecting upon Simon's kisses and start thinking about the ladies residing at Haven House. Her work had to go on. It was too important, too necessary.

The grand salon of Viscount Thornton's London house was filled with elegantly dressed lords and ladies who turned like one person as the butler announced the arrival of Lord Sheridan and Lady Pomeroy. Clarissa felt the roomful of eyes watching her as Simon escorted her down the three marble steps that led into a small ballroom. They were greeted with nods and smiles as their host approached them. Clarence Albright was boasting his customary smile. Dressed in black evening attire, his pale blonde hair was rakishly tousled over his forehead, and his blue-gray eyes danced with merriment as he bowed to Clarissa and proclaimed that his best friend was blessed with the most beautiful woman in the room.

The compliment didn't sway Clarissa's opinion of the viscount. Clarence Albright was known for his flattering way with women as well as the ability to entrap their hearts. Like Simon, he carried himself with a confident grace that drew a woman's admiration and made her wonder what thoughts were going on behind his unreadable eyes.

"You are a lucky devil," the viscount declared as Simon gave him a censoring scowl that said he'd been a bit too enthusiastic in his greeting. "And you, my dear lady," the viscount added, turning his attention back to Clarissa, "must promise me a waltz later this evening."

Albright's mother came rushing across the room, her massive bosom bouncing up and down as she made her way through the throng of people who had gladly accepted the invitations that would offer them a glimpse of Lord Sheridan and his unexpected fiancée.

Clarissa knew she was the talk of the town. There had been nothing to make anyone suspect that she would marry Simon. Pleased that she'd once again managed to outwit society, she greeted Lady Thornton with a bright smile.

"You're even more lovely than I remember," Lady Thornton told her. "When Clarence told me of your engagement to Simon, I was pleasantly surprised. It's time this gentleman married, and I couldn't be more pleased at his choice of brides." She smiled at Simon, then took his arm. "You've taken my son's last excuse away," she told the earl. "He's kept me at bay by vowing that he couldn't possibly marry before you did."

"I've got until Boxer Day," the viscount reminded his mother. Then, offering Clarissa a smile, he added, "Until then I'm free to enjoy my bachelorhood."

Clarissa wasn't sure exactly what Simon, Lady Thornton, and her notorious son were smiling about, but she was content to let them share their amusement.

"Lord Patterson is here," the viscount told Simon.

Clarissa heard Simon groan under his breath. Lord Patterson was a supporter of Gladstone's bill for home rule in Ireland. Although the party was being given in honor of her and Simon's engagement, it wasn't exempt from the politics that followed society from ballroom to ballroom. The current form of English government thrived in the cluster of elegantly dressed gentleman and bejeweled ladies that attended parties and soirees. With summer gaining on them and Parliament about to adjourn, Lord Patterson wasn't about to miss an opportunity to try to convince Simon to be more tolerant of Gladstone's agenda.

"Excuse us," Simon said to their hosts.

Lady Thornton waved at one of the guests and took her leave as her son gave the earl a meaningful smile before sauntering off to claim the hand of a very pretty young lady and leading her onto the dance floor.

With spotless manners and an aristocratic air that parted the crush of guests like Moses' staff separating the Red Sea, Simon led Clarissa across the polished floor toward a small group of elderly gentlemen. She recognized the tall and thin Sir Haston immediately. There was a hint of youthfulness about his eyes that lightened Clarissa's mood. Supporting his frail weight on a cane with a silver head crafted into the shape of a lion's head, Sir Haston gave the impression of a man who had learned a lot from the life he had enjoyed so far.

"Lady Pomeroy"—Sir Haston acknowledged her with a bow and a smile—"I must say, I couldn't be more pleased. I considered your grandfather a valued friend, and I know he would have looked upon your marriage to Simon with as much pleasure as I do."

"Thank you," she said, suddenly realizing that, like her, the earl of Sheridan had almost no family. Sir Haston was not a young man, and once he was gone, Simon would be alone.

No. Not alone. He'd have a wife. And she'd have a husband. It was some comfort to know that neither family would end too soon. She wanted children, and if Simon's current passion for her was any example of what the future held, Clarissa was certain that she'd give the earl more than one child.

"Simon has told me of your generous offer, Sir Haston," Clarissa said. "I'd be honored to have you escort me to the altar."

"Then by all means let me escort you to the punch bowl," the elderly man replied, gently pushing Simon aside. "While we enjoy our refreshment, I'll tell you about the time Simon fell out of a boat trying to bring in a trout. He was only six at the time, of course. Not much bigger than the fish that had latched onto his line."

Clarissa laughed at the image of a little boy struggling to land a reluctant trout while the boat rocked like a cradle, eventually dumping him into the stream. She accepted Sir Haston's invitation, smiling over her shoulder as Lord Patterson came swooping across the room like a hawk honing in on a rabbit. A few moments later, she was sipping champagne punch and listening to Simon's uncle recite stories of his nephew's childhood mischief, while Lord Patterson cornered her fiancé and began what could turn out to be an endless conversation about the pros and cons of letting the Irish have some say in their own country.

London parties being what they were, several hours passed before Simon found his way back to Clarissa's side. He'd barely heard a word Lord Patterson had said, for he'd been busy watching his fiancée move about the room like a yellow butterfly in a garden of brightly colored satin gowns and glittering jewels. She was tall and elegant, and he felt a sense of pride at being able to claim her as his intended wife. Simon found himself approving of Clarissa's more modest taste in clothing. The pearl earrings and necklace were the only jewelry she wore, and they glowed with the heat of her skin. Her dress was of French design, very expensive but tastefully cut, and it called attention to the perfection of her figure. Simon had noticed the hungry gazes that had passed her way as the gentlemen attending the party found one excuse after another to offer their congratulations. She'd declined several invitations to dance, and that pleased him more than anything. He didn't like the thought of another man holding Clarissa in his arms.

Seeing Thornton heading her way, Simon mumbled an excuse to the chatty Lord Patterson and strolled across the room, regaining his position at Clarissa's side before his friend could claim her for a dance. The melodious strains of a waltz filled the room as Simon offered his arm, then silently whisked her onto the dance floor.

"This waltz was promised to Thornton," Clarissa told him as they joined the other dancers.

"Nothing about you is promised to anyone but me," Simon said rather arrogantly, smiling the entire time.

Clarissa frowned at the man who was holding her so effortlessly as the musicians played on and the room began to turn into a rainbow of swirling colors as they turned and danced. The strong hand holding hers felt warm. Simon's other hand was around her waist, holding her just the right distance away from his broad chest. Reminding herself that everyone was watching them, Clarissa turned her frown into a smile and let the music replace the doubts in her head.

Simon was right. She was promised to him, bound by the honor of their agreement and the feelings that had captured her heart, if not his.

The music reached a sweet crescendo as Simon pulled her closer than propriety allowed. The rainbow of colors swirled faster as the dancers let the music rule their movements. Their jewels glinted, and Clarissa felt as if she were dancing on a cloud surrounded by a thousand tiny stars, twinkling and laughing. The warmth of Simon's touch seeped through her glove and the satin of her gown, heating her skin, as the music warmed her blood. But there was more than the music and the gaiety of a party; Clarissa could feel it in her heart. It was alive and strong and vibrant, like the colors of a summer day.

She met Simon's gaze, and for a brief moment Clarissa let herself believe that the emotion in his eyes was love instead of desire. Her fingers tightened on the sleeve of his upper arm, and Simon's head lowered as if he were going to kiss her right there in front of everyone.

She couldn't have stopped him if he had, but the opportunity vanished as the music came to a whirling, high-pitched end. The party guests looked on as Simon held her a moment longer, his hand flexing softly around her waist, the same way it had that morning in the library.

Clarissa felt her mouth go dry, and she wet her lips with the tip of her tongue. Simon stiffened, then released her. Without a word of invitation or intention, he began leading her toward the patio doors that opened onto the gardens. Out of the corner of her eye, Clarissa saw the viscount smiling.

The evening air hit them with a blast of coolness, ending the stifling heat of the ballroom and the warmth of the passion that ignited each time they touched one another. Clarissa stepped to the stone railing and placed her trembling hands palms down on its steady surface. The marble felt cool and reassuring as she looked up at the clouds shrouding the moon. A few stars twinkled here and there against the black velvet mantel of the night sky.

Simon stood next to her, his very presence a reminder of what had almost happened in the ballroom. It would have been scandalous for him to have kissed her, but a small part of Clarissa found herself wishing that he had. What was happening to her? Why did Simon's touch send every rational thought racing from her mind? How in the world was she going to survive being married to the man without eventually losing her heart completely?

Beside her, Simon was having his own doubts. Dancing with Clarissa had unleashed a recklessness in him that he hadn't known existed until tonight. He wanted her. Yes. But wanting a woman and almost kissing her in front of half of London were two entirely different things. Perhaps it was because she'd defied him so valiantly in the carriage. And perhaps it was because he felt more for her than he wanted to admit.

The questions hung between them like the waning moon suspended between the stars. The silent tension sizzled as the chatter of the party guests drifted though the doors and into the night. The band was playing another waltz, and Simon was tempted to drag Clarissa into the dark shadows of the garden and dance with her again, where no one could see them.

He took a deep breath to steady his raging emotions, then looked at Clarissa. Her eyes were closed, her head lifted toward the midnight sky. So beautiful, Simon thought to himself, and so very mysterious. Yes. That's what appealed to him the most, he was sure. Clarissa was a mystery. A puzzle that needed to be solved. He'd always enjoyed a challenge, and he had to admit that this particular woman offered him just that.

Clarissa opened her eyes to find Simon staring down at her. She could feel his gaze, so aware of it that her pulse quickened and her hands gripped the marble railing to keep from reaching for him. She was too inexperienced to understand the strange, intangible yearnings that filled her mind and body, but her heart understood them. Love wasn't an action; it was a reaction. And she knew that the heart she was struggling to keep safe was more exposed at that moment than it would ever be again.

Her eyes pleaded with him for just one word of encouragement, but he said nothing. He only continued to stare at her, his eyes as dark as the shadows in the garden, his expression as unreadable as the fog that was seeping over the brick wall.

"Would you care to dance again?" Simon heard himself asking.

Clarissa shook her head. She didn't trust herself. Not yet. It was too much too soon, and she needed time to get over the effect Simon had had on her in the carriage and again on the dance floor. "I'd rather talk."

"About what?"

"Anything," she told him. "Tell me about your family."

"My family's history is common knowledge. There are no pirates or unsavory characters in my lineage, if that's what you're worried about."

"What a shame." Clarissa laughed. "I was looking forward to finding a ghost or two at Sheridan Manor."

Simon smiled, and she felt her heart swell until she thought it might burst. He was so very handsome, and she loved him so very much.

"There is my great aunt Abigail," he said teasingly. "Although I've never seen her ghost, it's said her reputation haunted the family in other ways."

"How so?" Clarissa found herself curious about anything that touched this man's life. His family, his friends, his favorite wine. She wanted to know everything about him, and she knew so very little.

"She was quite lovely and very precocious," Simon explained. "It's rumored that she was Silly Billy's mistress for a short time."

Clarissa laughed. William IV had reigned for a short time before Queen Victoria had taken the throne. He'd been a naval man, not expecting to inherit the title because he was the third son. His tactlessness and lack of style had earned him the name Silly Billy. Although he had married much later in life, his only children had been illegitimate, ten of them by the actress Mrs. Dorothy Jordan. To think that a member of the esteemed Sinclair family had actually been involved with one of the less savory kings to grace the throne of England was enough to make most people raise a brow in astonishment.

"Of course, it's only a rumor," Simon added, knowing full well that it was truth, not fiction. His great aunt had lived to a ripe old age, and he could still remember the stories she'd told him about being whisked off to one of the royal hunting lodges for a long weekend with her lover.

"Your great aunt Abigail sounds interesting," Clarissa remarked, thinking she shared some of the lady's sense of adventure. It was certainly risky to be doing what she was doing. If Simon ever discovered her favorite charity, he'd probably lock her away in some unused wing of Sheridan Manor, never again to see the light of day.

"I can tell by your expression that I shall have to keep a close eye on you," Simon responded with a hint of humor in his voice. "The Sinclairs aren't given to scandal. What would people think if I took a wife who actually enjoyed being outrageous."

Clarissa knew he was referring to the remark she'd made in the carriage, calling his conditions outrageous. Of course they were. No gentleman demanded that his wife submit in such a manner, but then, she was beginning to suspect that Simon's gentlemanly graces were limited to his public life, not his personal one.

"The Pomeroys aren't given to scandal, either, my lord. Although we are, shall I say, less stringent in our attitudes than the Sinclairs."

"How so?" he asked, mimicking her previous question.

Clarissa hesitated for a moment. Simon might think he knew her, but he didn't. They were complete opposites in most things. Still, she didn't want to offer him a false picture of the woman he was soon to marry. "The Reform Bill, for instance," she said. "If what I read in the papers is to be believed, the next session of Parliament will debate the issue rather feverishly."

"It has its merits," Simon acknowledged. The proposed legislation would offer the vote to more than two million men, forcing a redistribution of the ruling houses of Parliament but giving the country a more thorough representation."

"Do you support it?"

"I don't oppose it," he replied, noting her skeptical reaction. "Things are changing rather quickly nowadays, and government must change with them."

Clarissa laughed again. "Can I believe my ears? Is the most conservative lord in Parliament actually telling me that he envisions a day when the staunchest of British institutions may actually think of the future instead of the past. What if progress goes so far as to make the peerage antiquated and unnecessary? Surely you can't support the progressive thinkers of our time to that extreme."

"You have a sharp tongue, my lady," he replied. "And I'm not so conservative that I cannot see or appreciate the advances of science and society. My concern isn't with change but with our reaction to it. Discretion and patience are the key to good government, not embracing every folly that comes down the pike."

"Ahhh, yes," she said pensively. "Like the folly of women's rights."

"Women don't need to vote. What they need is the good sense to let their husbands take care of them, as God intended." He shook his head, clearly disgusted with the concept of a bunch of female minds muddying the pristine waters of English politics.

"What about our beloved queen?" Clarissa asked. "She's a woman. Yet she sits on the throne of England, ruling by divine right, if the authority of her rank is to be believed."

"That's something else altogether," Simon chided her for even comparing Victoria to the free-thinking females that were predicting equality of the sexes by the next century.

"How so?" Clarissa prompted, knowing she was venturing into dangerous territory but not caring. Simon may never come to love her, but she wanted his respect. In fact, she intended to demand it.

Simon gave her a fierce frown. "I'm not surprised that you embrace the recent campaign for women, but I am surprised that you admit it. Most ladies don't."

Ladies meaning the privileged peerage, of course.

"I'm not a coward," Clarissa said, tilting her chin up. "And I don't blame most *ladies* for not marching up and down the street, banners waving. Why should they? It won't accomplish anything but a scorching lecture from their fathers or husbands. Whenever I tried to engage my grandfather in a meaningful conversation about women's rights, he refused to listen and changed the subject before it had barely begun."

Simon could understand why. Clarissa was very well educated, highly intelligent, and quick of wit. He had no doubt that she would be an admirable campaigner if she ever took to the pulpit. Something he was going to make sure never happened. The last thing he needed was a wife who gathered women around her in the public square, climbed onto a wooden box, and began spouting speeches about females being deprived of their natural rights. The very thought was enough to make him need a brandy.

Another thought flashed through Simon's mind. He gave Clarissa a hard look. "You don't by chance consider women's rights a charitable endeavor, do you?"

Taking a moment to straighten her gloves and hide her smile, she finally returned his gaze. "No, my lord. I'm more concerned with the safety and physical welfare of the less fortunate in our country than I am with recruiting a mob of London ladies and storming Parliament."

"Excellent," Simon said, finally trusting himself to touch her again. He took her by the arm and began leading her back into the ballroom. "I have not forgotten my pledge to refrain from inquires or inquisitions into your charitable finances, but that doesn't mean I'll tolerate my wife involving herself in public scandal."

That takes care of that, Clarissa thought. Simon would never understand her endeavors at Haven House or the reason why they were so important to her. His main concern was, and would continue to be, the reputation of his family name and his conservative politics. Proper ladies didn't do improper things. Passion aside, Clarissa knew from his remarks that she'd have to be very careful not to raise any suspicions. Simon wasn't a man who was easily fooled, and no matter how much he *wanted* her, he wouldn't refrain from closing her accounts and exiling her to the country if he thought she'd overstepped her boundaries.

Seven

Clarissa woke up the morning after the Thornton party with a pounding headache. Putting on her robe and walking to the window, she wasn't sure if her distress was caused by the champagne punch she'd drunk the night before or the lack of a goodnight kiss from her betrothed.

After reentering the ballroom, Simon had assumed an air of propriety. They'd danced several more times, but the magic feeling they'd shared during their first waltz had evaporated. He'd kept her on his arm—a telling sign, to be sure—as they'd walked into the dining hall for a lavish meal of poached salmon and thinly sliced beef served with spicy stewed tomatoes, but his conduct had been nothing less than exemplary the rest of the night.

Viscount Thornton had even commented on it during their one dance, telling Clarissa that Simon had a tendency to become somewhat brooding at times, especially when something was on his mind. She'd tactfully inquired into what that might be, only to have the viscount laugh and tell Clarissa that she only had to look into a mirror to find her answer.

His remark had given her some hope, which had

been dashed as soon as they took to the carriage to return to Park Lane. Instead of kissing her or teasing her, Simon had sat silently across from her, saying little. When he'd escorted her up the steps of the Mayfair house, Clarissa had found herself hoping for one more of his ravishing kisses.

But he hadn't kissed her.

Instead, he'd apologized for being unable to ride with her the next morning, stating several pressing appointments as his excuse, then reminding her of the opera and saying that he'd reserved a table for them to dine afterward.

She'd gone to bed wondering if she hadn't overdone herself by discussing the unsavory idea of women's rights. The earl had reacted very adamantly to her remarks, and Clarissa hoped she hadn't given him food for thought. Although he'd teasingly challenged her to find another trustworthy gentleman to meet her conditions, they both knew that was very unlikely. The idea of Simon's withdrawing his promise and perhaps even ending their engagement had kept her awake almost until dawn. She'd finally consoled herself by admitting that he was a man of his word and, as such, would never withdraw their wedding announcement. Still, she had to be more careful. There was too much at risk for her to let her personal feelings get in the way.

It was enough to give anyone a headache.

One minute, Simon was seducing her senseless; the next, he was acting as if their time together were nothing more than an inconvenience. A necessary preamble to their upcoming marriage.

Deciding her headache would only increase with the strain of trying to decipher Simon's actions and reactions, Clarissa went about her morning toiletry, determined to make the most of the day. She had penned Mrs. Quigley a note that she would be stopping by the millinery shop at the earliest opportunity, and since there would be no morning ride in Hyde Park, Clarissa planned on visiting with her friend and secret cohort that very day.

Dressed in an emerald green suit with black piping and large, shiny jet buttons, she descended the staircase to find Huxley pouring tea. Clarissa preferred taking her morning refreshment in the library, where she could read the paper, rather than lingering in bed. Since she was residing in the house alone, she saw no reason for the staff to muddle up the dining room or second floor parlor with her meals. She preferred her privacy over everything else.

"Huxley, please arrange for the carriage to be ready within the hour," Clarissa said, sitting down to a cup of hot tea and muffins generously smeared with strawberry jam. "I shall call upon Mrs. Quigley after I've done some other shopping."

"As you wish," the butler replied, knowing his mistress was anxious to see the plump lady who ran the hat shop just off Bond Street.

While Clarissa read the morning paper and planned an afternoon fitting for her wedding gown, Simon was pacing the floor of his study, trying to understand why he'd been caught in his own trap. Fortunately, he'd come to his senses in time. The thought of what had been going through his mind when the first waltz ended was enough to make his body start throbbing all over again. He'd almost kissed Clarissa right then and there! It was unbelievable to think that he, a man of experience and good breeding, could let desire overrule his common sense so easily. It was more than unbelievable. It was absurd. And Simon was determined not to let it happen again—until he was married, of course. Then he'd indulge himself in Clarissa's lovely charms until he was too exhausted to get out of bed.

When he'd decided to accept Clarissa's unusual proposal of marriage, he'd also resolved to temper her willfulness with a taste of passion, thus teaching her that he wasn't a man to jump at the pull of a string. He still thought his strategy worthwhile, but at the same time, he was discovering that he wanted more than her willing performance in bed.

He wanted to understand the defiant gleam that flashed in her violet-blue eyes and discover the secret she had tucked up her female sleeve. And Simon was sure there was a secret. In fact, he'd almost bet Sheridan Manor on it, and the house had been in his family for generations.

His morning sabbatical was interrupted as Higgins announced that Viscount Thornton had arrived. Simon frowned. The last person he wanted to see at that particular moment was Clarence Albright. If anyone had noticed his blunder at the party, it had been the keen-witted viscount.

"I say, Sinclair," Thornton chimed, coming into the study with a rush of early-morning enthusiasm rarely found in a man who had been up most of the night socializing with his peers. "I never would have thought it of you."

"Thought what?" Simon asked, dismissing Higgins with a wave of his hand. If the viscount wanted a cup of tea, he could bloody well pour it himself.

Albright's laughter echoed off the walnut-paneled walls. "Actually falling in love with the lady. What else?"

Simon's expression took a downward plunge. He would admit, only to himself, of course, that Clarissa did stir an unusual response in him, a nameless emotion he couldn't identify because he'd never felt it before. But it certainly wasn't love. Lust—most definitely. But not love. Love was for romantic schoolgirls and gullible young fools. He was neither. Whatever he felt for Clarissa was yet to be determined. That was as far as he'd go in admitting that he felt anything beyond a very strong physical desire for her.

"That's lunacy," Simon snorted. "Complete and utter lunacy."

"Is it?" his friend inquired, pouring himself a cup of tea and adding a dash of brandy instead of the usual cream. "I don't think so. Saw you myself. My God, man, you would have ravished her right there for all of London to see. Incredible, that."

"What's incredible is your tendency toward the absurd," Simon told him in a sharp voice. "I'm marrying Lady Pomeroy for the same reason any man of my age and rank marries."

The viscount drank his tea while he studied Simon over the rim of the cup. "I don't think so," he finally said.

"I hope it doesn't shock your fragile sensibilities to know I don't particularly give a damn what you think," Simon said back to him. "As for Lady Pomeroy, she isn't a topic I wish to discuss at the moment."

The viscount laughed. "Very well. Let's talk about the opera. I'll be escorting the very prim and very proper Miss Avondale. My mother's idea, of course. Afterwards, I thought to drop by Nanette's for a few hours. Can I deliver a message for you?"

Simon smiled. He hadn't given his old mistress a second thought since coming to London. It was another sign that he'd become much too enthralled by Clarissa to think about another woman. Maybe he should see Nanette again, personally voice his regrets over neglecting her, and avail himself of her sympathetic charms. "No," he told Thornton, changing his mind almost immediately. "I have nothing of interest to say to the lovely widow."

"Just as well," the viscount told him. "She's furious at you for dropping her like a muddy shoe. Of course, she said it in French. Much more dramatic that way."

Simon didn't have to be told about Nanette's dramatic nature. He'd witnessed it a time or two and suspected that she used it as a sort of foreplay. It was stimulating to tame a shrew, after all. As the viscount rambled on about the superb hunter he'd purchased from Lord Barton, Simon thought about taming another shrew. The more he thought about Clarissa's naturally defiant nature, the harder he got, until he didn't dare stand up from behind his desk without exposing his condition to the visiting viscount.

Damn the woman! She was in too many of his thoughts, taking up too much of his time. He had the last weeks of Parliament to contend with and his own businesses, plus those he would begin to oversee once he married. His only consolation was the certainty that a two week honeymoon would take the edge off his lust and he'd be able to function normally again.

The bell over the shop door jingled merrily as Clarissa opened it and walked inside. Mrs. Quigley came prancing out from behind the counter, her pewter gray eyes sparkling. She was a short, round-bellied woman, and Clarissa loved her liked a second mother.

"It's so good to see you again," Meriwether Quigley exclaimed, giving Clarissa an affectionate hug. The counters and display cases were filled with fashionable ladies' headwear and evening bags and gloves, but for the moment the shop was void of customers.

Clarissa had chosen the noon hour to come calling, knowing that the young girl Mrs. Quigley employed as a clerk would be taking her lunch.

"I couldn't believe my eyes when I read your letter," Mrs. Quigley went on. "Lord Sheridan, of all people. Are you sure you know what you're doing?"

"No," Clarissa admitted with a sad smile. "But he has agreed to my conditions, and I trust him to keep his word."

"I'm sure he will. He has a certain reputation in that direction, or so I've heard."

There was little Mrs. Quigley didn't hear. She was one of the most popular merchants on Bond Street, although her shop was actually around the corner from the bustling business district. Nevertheless, her hats were fashionable and just expensive enough to make them chic, which meant that every lady in London visited the shop, giving Mrs. Quigley an earful of gossip any time she chose to listen.

"Come," Mrs. Quigley said, taking Clarissa by the arm and leading her toward the stairs. The older lady lived in a cozy apartment on the second floor. "We both have things to tell one another."

"What about the shop?"

"I will hear the bell if anyone comes in. We can have tea and talk about the charming earl of Sheridan."

Clarissa started up the stairs. Meriwether Quigley was one of the few people who didn't care about titles and social status. She was unique in that way, and it was the primary reason why Clarissa loved her so much. With Mrs. Quigley, Clarissa could be herself.

Once they were seated in the parlor of the apartment, the older woman turned to Clarissa. "Now, you must tell me all about the earl. I saw him once from a distance, but I dare say he was handsome enough to hold my eye for quite a while."

"I'm not sure I've got much to tell," Clarissa said somewhat sadly. "Simon is handsome, of course, and very well known for his speeches in Parliament. As for other things, I'm still getting to know him."

"You're to be married at the end of June," Mrs. Quigley reminded her, then smiled. "You're in London now, which means you'll be keeping company with the gentleman. I've always said the best way to get to know a man is to listen to him. They love to talk about themselves, you know. Or at least my dear departed Henry did. He never seemed to tire of talking. God rest his soul."

Clarissa had never met the former Mr. Quigley. The man had died some years ago, leaving Meriwether just enough money to open the shop. But Clarissa had heard more than one affectionate story since becoming the shopkeeper's friend. If only she could have memories like Mrs. Quigley's; fond, loving memories to keep her smiling in her old age. But Simon wasn't Henry Quigley, and she wasn't Meriwether.

Knowing she only had a short amount of time to visit before her appointment with the seamstress, Clarissa decided to forgo any conversation about her upcoming nuptials and get down to the business that had become the focal point of her friendship with the shopkeeper.

"Have you heard of anyone who might be needing the hospitality of Haven House?" Clarissa asked her.

"Perhaps," Mrs. Quigley replied thoughtfully. "A lady's maid came into the shop a few days ago. She discreetly pulled me aside and asked if I might be the one who had a friend in Yorkshire."

"When I told her that I had several friends in Yorkshire, she said she was looking for a particular kind of friend. One who might be gracious enough to offer someone a few months of much-needed privacy in the country."

Clarissa set her tea cup aside and moved to the edge of the settee. "And . . ."

"She's to call again tomorrow morning. If I find the maid's *friend* truly in need, I shall pen you the customary note."

The customary note was a short message informing Lady Pomeroy that the blue hat she had requested was ready and could be picked up at a specific time. The code was simple and to the point. Clarissa would respond with her own note, telling Mrs. Quigley that she'd be by the shop to take delivery of the hat. In actuality, Clarissa would come by the shop and meet with the young lady in question. The meetings were handled very discreetly. A dressing screen would be placed in the center of the apartment parlor, with the young lady on one side and Clarissa on the other, similar to a church confessional. If the young lady decided to handle her situation in another way, she was wished the best of luck and told to leave the shop by the back stairs, never having seen the face of her would-be benefactor. If an understanding was reached, arrangements were made for the young woman to be taken to Haven House, under the watchful eye of Huxley, the butler. A new arrival at the Yorkshire estate wasn't told Clarissa's true identity until Huxley, Mrs. Quigley, Mrs. Flannigan, and the current ladies in residence were in unanimous agreement that she could be trusted.

The survival of Haven House demanded the discretion of everyone involved.

Over a second cup of tea, Clarissa shared the news of Martha Calberry's marriage to Myles Garfield. The older woman was elated to find out that the shy Miss Calberry had found a sturdy young man to be her husband. "You are a messenger of so much good news," Mrs. Quigley told Clarissa. "I'm sure it's only a matter of time until the doubts about your own marriage will vanish. I know you harbor deep feelings for Lord Sheridan. Give him some time. Men are such stubborn creatures when it comes to surrendering their hearts. But the right man is worth all the aggravation in the end."

I sincerely hope so, Clarissa thought, then added aloud. "I'm sure the earl and I will get along very well."

Mrs. Quigley shared the latest gossip with Clarissa, remarking that most of it had been centered around the announcement of Lord Sheridan's engagement. "Most are saying that your grandfather's untimely death prevented the engagement from being announced last year. It's the match of the season, others are saying, and I most wholeheartedly agree," the shopkeeper added. "This morning I overheard Lady Berryman telling Miss Sophy Randolf, of the Dorchester Randolfs, that she'd seen you dancing with her lordship at Viscount Thornton's party and it was undoubtedly a love match."

Clarissa managed not to blush as the memory of her first waltz with Simon came rushing back into her mind. Lady Berryman was a voracious gossip. By now, most of London would think that Simon was smitten with her—and she with him. Well, at least Lady Berryman had gotten half of it right. Clarissa was smitten. Simon had managed to steal her heart as expertly as a pickpocket swiping a gold watch.

Hearing the shop clock chime the hour, Clarissa thanked Mrs. Quigley for the tea and gathered up her hat and gloves. "I shall look forward to hearing from you," Clarissa said. "In the meantime, I have a task for our friend Mr. Nebs."

Lionel Nebs was a charming man in his mid-forties with an enthusiastic smile and an uncanny knowledge of things that went well beyond Mrs. Quigley's or Clarissa's expertise. He knew London as well as any coachman for hire and possessed the ability to procure almost anything that was for sale. Mrs. Quigley had made his acquaintance some years ago and had frequently employed him to perform discreet investigations into the personal history of the ladies she interviewed.

"What would you like Lionel to do?"

"I'd like him to make a few inquiries for me," Clarissa began. "With my marriage to Lord Sheridan announced and his promise of a generous allowance, it's time to think beyond Haven House. Although some of the ladies will stay on to help with future residents, there are others who will want to begin their lives anew. I want Mr. Nebs to look into some acquisitions for me. He can use the pretense that he is inquiring into potential investments for his cousin."

"And I'm to be his cousin," Mrs. Quigley said, smiling as she began to see the direction of Clarissa's thoughts. "How marvelous. You're right, of course. I daresay most of the ladies we've taken under our wing are more than capable of providing for themselves, given the opportunity."

"I couldn't agree more." Clarissa smiled in return. "The possibility of another millinery shop comes to mind. And perhaps a seaside resort or two. Holiday excursions are becoming more and more popular of late. I see no reason why a respectable *widow* with a young child couldn't oversee such a resort. I would supply the initial investment, and once the inn was operating at a profit, the debt could be satisfied in small monthly installments, which would allow us to invest in more businesses."

"You are brilliant!" Mrs. Quigley said, clapping her hands together. "What about a music hall?

They're becoming quite the thing, you know. And very profitable."

"One business at a time," Clarissa said, grimacing inwardly at the thought of Simon's reaction to a music hall. "For now, I'd like to concentrate on finding some coastal property that might meet our requirements. Have Mr. Nebs begin his inquiries in Portsmouth."

"I'll have him look into the matter right away," Meriwether said, coming to her feet. "It's all so exciting."

"Yes, isn't it," Clarissa agreed. She brushed aside the uneasiness she felt about the future. She couldn't let herself become rooted in the fear that one day Simon would discover what she was doing with her money. She needed to concentrate on the reason she'd asked him to marry her in the first place. Haven House and the future of the women who lived there and the children who would be born there. They needed her. Simon only wanted her.

As she took her leave of the shop, Clarissa asked Mrs. Quigley to design the veil for her wedding.

"Pearls and ivory lace," Meriwether said without hesitation. "Your coloring begs for ivory, not white. The softer shade will complement your hair."

"Thank you," Clarissa said, leaning down to place a kiss on the woman's cheek. "Ivory it shall be."

The rest of the afternoon was spent convincing the flamboyant Madame Boise to use ivory satin instead of the virginal white preferred by other brides. Once the robust Frenchwoman relented, Clarissa stood for a fitting. Several hours later, Clarissa took her leave with Madame Boise's promise that the gown would be as unique as the bride wearing it.

She returned home to take a short nap before beginning her preparations for another evening in Simon's company. Soaking in a bath of scented, steaming water, Clarissa watched the late afternoon sunlight fade to the ghostly shades of twilight. Although she had a good head for business, she lacked the experience of dealing with men in general. For the most part, she'd spent the years since her sixteen birthday ignoring the opposite sex. The only man she'd spent more than a smidgen's worth of time thinking about had been Simon. Her daydreams had been romantically mild compared to what she'd experienced as his fiancée.

As she left her bath, Clarissa tried not to think about what she would experience as Simon's legal wife. He'd made his intentions perfectly clear the day he'd accepted her proposal. He wanted a willing wife who would submit to his passionate endeavors whenever the mood struck him.

Clarissa hadn't had much time to give the conditions a thorough thinking over, but then, what was there to think about? Simon expected their marriage bed to be kept warm in exchange for his indifference about her personal accounts. She would eventually give him an heir, and he would eventually lose his enthusiasm for her company. Their life together would become boring and mundane unless she could reach Simon's carefully shielded heart.

As she dressed for the opera, Clarissa realized she had a lot more than Haven House and the expansion of her charitable pursuits to challenge her if she wanted to win Simon's heart. And she did want to win it. The thought of spending the remainder of her life without love was enough to make Clarissa angry. *No,* she silently declared as Lillian came into the room with a royal blue gown draped over arm. *No. I won't become complacent in my attitudes. One way or the other, I'm going to make Simon fall in love with me.*

Eight

As Simon placed a white flower in the lapel of his gray pin-striped jacket, he took a moment to praise himself for his control over the last few weeks. It had nearly been his undoing on several occasions, but he'd managed to maintain his dignity and his manners where his fiancée was concerned. It hadn't been easy. Especially after allowing himself a taste of her charms. But he'd been determined to keep their relationship in perspective. His friend's remarks the day after the party had been more than enough to caution Simon that his brief engagement to the lovely Lady Pomeroy could easily lead him astray.

He wasn't a prudish man, but he did believe that a man ruled his own home and in doing so ruled those who lived under its roof. Since acknowledging his desire for Clarissa, he'd almost forgotten that simple truth. Her ability to make him forget everything but the throbbing need of his loins was reason enough to reaffirm his role as the superior male. Archaic as it might be, Simon intended to keep control of his marriage—and his wife.

Now, as the guests were strolling into the small private chapel of Hartford Hall, Simon was convinced that he'd done the right thing by keeping his time with Clarissa limited to chaperoned social engagements and rides in Hyde Park. She'd remained in London for almost a month before returning to the Norwich estate to supervise the final details of the wedding that was to take place in a few minutes.

Across the gray and white tiled vestibule of the family chapel, Clarissa was pacing in another anteroom, wondering if she'd survive the day. She'd never experienced such a case of nerves, and it was disconcerting to think that she was finally going to walk down the aisle and stand beside Simon while they repeated vows that would bind them for life.

The last few weeks had been a jumble of emotional battles. The month she'd spent in London had tried her patience almost as much as it had tested her resolve to make Simon fall in love with her. Although she'd seen him several times a week, he had taken on a new identity, one she wasn't sure she liked. His manners had been impeccable, his speech eloquent and well-versed, and his touch almost nonexistent. Their trips to the opera and several parties had been devoid of any kisses except for a gentlemanly bow over her hand and the light brush of his mouth over her glove as he'd bid her good night. The few times they'd danced, she had hoped to rediscover the magic of their first waltz, but it had eluded her, along with Simon's teasing remarks and seductive glances.

All in all, she felt as if the man who had ravished her mouth so thoroughly in the library had somehow been transformed into someone else altogether. The only thing that forced her to admit that the original earl of Sheridan hadn't been abducted and replaced by a look-alike was his unbending attitude about women in general. They'd argued quite adamantly during one of their morning rides, so much so that Clarissa had expected him to cancel their dinner engagement for that evening. Having heard that women in America often rode astride rather than sidesaddle, she'd voiced an interest in doing the same. From Simon's reaction, one would have thought that she'd expressed a desire to gallivant about London in her petticoats. The only thing that had kept the argument from becoming an out-and-out shouting match was the timely appearance of Clarence Albright. The viscount, having caught just enough of the conversation to know that it would turn into an all day affair unless he intervened, politely reminded Simon of an appointment, ending their ride and beginning what Clarissa was sure to be one of many unsettled issues between them.

A soft knock on the door brought Clarissa's pacing to an end.

"It's time, my lady," Sir Haston's voice sounded through the closed door, along with the soft musical strains of a traditional hymn being played by the vicar's wife.

Clarissa took a deep breath and straightened the cap of her veil. Gathering up the bouquet of white carnations and vibrant violets that Lillian had placed carefully on the room's small table, she walked to the door and opened it.

Sir Haston, dressed in a well-tailored black suit, was waiting on the other side. "You're too lovely for words," he said, offering her his arm. "Shall we have a go at it?"

Clarissa smiled as she took his arm. "My knees feel like jelly."

"Then hold on tight," Sir Haston said teasingly. "It's not far and Simon is waiting. He won't let you fall."

I've already fallen, Clarissa admitted silently. *I've fallen in love with the man I'm going to marry in a few moments and I haven't the foggiest idea how he feels about me in return. If the last few weeks are any indication, our marriage is going to be more than I originally bargained for.*

As two blue and gold uniformed footmen opened the doors of the chapel, Clarissa pushed her worries aside and concentrated on getting to the altar without stumbling. The little chapel, with its vaulted ceiling and Italian frescoes, stood at the north end of Hartford Hall. The family plot, where her grandfather was buried, was to the chapel's right, and a small, well-manicured garden with fruit trees and wild roses was to the left. The sun was shining, promising a beautiful June day for the celebration that was to follow the ceremony. After a luncheon and champagne toast, the bride and groom would leave for Sheridan Manor and their country honeymoon.

Clarissa took one more deep breath, then stepped forward, beginning the journey that would take her from the status of a single lady to that of a married woman. Every eye in the chapel turned to gaze at her as the vicar's wife began playing the wedding march. The guests, seated in the narrow walnut pews that lined both sides of the quaint chapel, smiled as the bride came into view. The light of six dozen candles, arranged in brass sconces along the walls, reflected off the pearl-like quality of the ivory satin of her wedding gown. Favoring the style that was common to French fashions at the turn of the century, the gown fit snugly over Clarissa's breasts before cascading to the floor in elegant folds that lengthened in the back, forming a wide satin train decorated with pearls and handmade lace. Her bodice was covered with hundreds of tiny pearls that formed a deep vee between her breasts. The pattern was repeated on the ivory lace that formed the gown's sheer sleeves and again on the long satin train, gliding along behind her.

Mrs. Quigley had outdone herself with the veil. It was the sheerest of lace, sewn into a small, round cap that hugged the crown of Clarissa's head. White satin rosettes and pearls adorned the small hat before allowing the lace to fall gracefully down Clarissa's back. Although her face was covered in traditional bridal fashion, the ivory lace was sheer enough for everyone in the chapel to see the lovely features behind it. With her auburn hair artfully arranged and her violet eyes gleaming to match the flowers she carried in her bouquet, the guests started mumbling among themselves that the earl of Sheridan was indeed a very lucky man.

As predicted by Mrs. Quigley, the groom couldn't take his eyes off Clarissa as she walked toward him. Simon couldn't remember when he'd ever seen her looking more lovely, and he swelled with pride at the thought of finally being able to claim her as his wife. He had thought long and hard about the ring he would soon place on her left hand and had decided upon a gold band embellished with sapphires and diamonds. He'd also purchased a matching necklace and looked forward to seeing his new wife dressed in nothing but expensive jewelry.

"I say, Sinclair. She's enough to take a man's breath away," Thornton whispered as Clarissa approached the altar, where the vicar was waiting to perform the ceremony.

Simon gave his friend a censuring look, then turned his attention back to the bride. He didn't like the thought of anyone coveting Clarissa, even though he knew Thornton's friendship would keep the viscount's thoughts from becoming more than platonic in nature. He trusted few men, but he did trust Clarence Albright. In spite of the viscount's insatiable appetite for women, he was an honorable man and had proved himself to be a trustworthy friend.

The short distance from the chapel's double entry doors to the altar seemed to take on the proportions of a Greek odyssey as Clarissa found her gaze drawn to Simon. The stained-glass window behind the altar, depicting a scene from the book of St. James, was ablaze with sunlight, and the bold colors formed a saintly rainbow around the man waiting for her. Gripping Sir Haston's arm a bit more firmly, Clarissa stared at the handsome picture Simon made, dressed in a perfectly tailored gray suit and white silk shirt. The viscount wore similar attire, but the other man didn't have Simon's masculine appeal. The earl's dark eyes seemed to probe beneath the ivory lace of her wedding veil, demanding that Clarissa bear her very soul to him.

Her blood began to warm as Sir Haston came to a stop. The music ended, and the guests once again took their seats. Clarissa had noted Mr. Knightley among them and was pleased that the aging solicitor's gout hadn't kept him from attending the ceremony. There were approximately fifty people in the quaint family chapel. Most of them were mutual friends of Simon's and her deceased grandfather, and Clarissa realized that the man she was about to marry was one of the most respected men in the British realm. She quenched the disappointment she'd felt at not being able to invite Mrs. Quigley to the wedding, but the shopkeeper's presence would have raised entirely too many questions.

Simon stepped forward to take her hand, and Clarissa found herself being led forward. The music had stopped, and the vicar was patiently waiting to begin the honored task of uniting Lady Clarissa Pomeroy and his lordship, the earl of Sheridan, in holy matrimony.

As they turned to face the vicar, Clarissa felt the fiery touch of Simon's hand as surely as she felt the hundred butterflies fluttering in the pit of her stomach. Sensing her uneasiness, Simon squeezed her fingers slightly, causing her to look at him. His face lacked emotion, but his eyes were like fire, burning through her nervousness and rekindling the passion that he had intentionally put to rest over the last few weeks.

He held her hand throughout the entire ceremony, repeating his vows in a calm, clear voice as Clarissa's mind raced with the consequences of their actions. As Simon slipped the beautifully jeweled wedding band on her finger, Clarissa got a glimpse of the viscount, standing to the groom's right. Thornton was smiling like a proud father, and Clarissa wondered if all of Simon's friends approved of his choice as keenly as Clarence Albright.

That thought was quickly pushed out of reach as the vicar pronounced them man and wife and Simon reached out to raise her veil. His eyes lingered on her face for a breathless moment before he lowered his head and kissed her. It was a chaste kiss, suited to the public occasion, but Clarissa couldn't help but feel the promise in Simon's mouth as it pressed lightly against her lips. The look in his eyes as he turned her to face the wedding guests held the same promise. He was done with keeping his distance.

The chapel bells rang out in joyful announcement of the morning's event as Simon led her from the small church. Outside the brown stone chapel, the steps were lined with well-wishers from the estate staff and the nearby village. Rose petals were tossed into the air as the groom escorted his new bride down the stone steps and along the cobblestone path that led to the main house.

The reception was held in the formal dining room. Huxley had had the chairs removed and the long, cherry-wood table transferred to the east side of the rectangular suite, where sunlight poured through the windows, displaying an endless array of food for the wedding guests. Silver trays, laden with sliced beef and fresh vegetables, sat beside more silver trays bearing a tasteful variety of sliced fruit and small sweet cakes sprinkled with sugar and cinnamon. A small trio of musicians played while the guests mingled about the dining room, filling their plates with food before joining the newly married couple in the east garden. Simon had thoughtfully sent several of his footmen ahead to Hartford Hall, offering their services to Huxley. The butler had the additional servants scampering about the house, offering the guests drinks from skillfully balanced serving trays.

Clarissa had decided just that morning, after awakening to a perfect spring day, that the reception would go beyond the boundaries of the country house. She'd requested that the east garden be decorated with white streamers and urns of fresh-cut flowers. The chairs and tables, normally reserved for croquet matches, had been brought out of storage and washed clean so that the guests could sit without soiling their clothes. The rosebushes were heavy with small pink-and-red blooms, and the breeze softly rustled the leaves of the elm trees that created an informal wall around the garden.

Clarissa had dismissed herself momentarily so that Lillian could pin up the train of her ivory wedding dress, which had drawn a string of compliments from the ladies who swept through the receiving line before filtering into the dining room. Her veil was secured away from her face by pearl-tipped pins as she composed herself. Simon hadn't spoken a word to her since saying his vows in the chapel, but Clarissa had felt his presence like the rumbling thunder of an approaching storm. The few short glances she directed at him had been met with a fiery gaze that held promises of the night still to come.

"Your lordship will be getting anxious," Lillian reminded her as Clarissa stole another moment of privacy. Her last for a very long time, she was afraid. The thoughts of two weeks with Simon as her constant companion was enough to make her stomach start churning again.

"I'm ready," she told the maid as a light knock sounded on the closed bedroom door.

Lillian opened it and dipped into a respectful curtsy as Simon stepped into the room. Clarissa reacted with a fluttering heartbeat that was quickly brought under control as he crooked his arm and silently beckoned her to take her rightful place at his side. Together they walked down the staircase, through the dining room, and out into the garden. The guests were gathered in small clusters here and there on the lawn, nodding and approving of the newly married couple, as Huxley stepped forward and voiced his personal congratulations before offering Simon a glass of French champagne.

They mixed and mingled as the occasion required, and Clarissa found herself smiling in spite of the apprehension building with each glance from Simon's dark eyes. Music flowed into the garden, reminding her of the waltz they'd shared, and she couldn't prevent the excitement that joined her apprehension. The two emotions twisted and turned like dancers until she was quickly wishing that the festivities would end and the inevitable wedding night was over and done with.

It was midafternoon before they made their final goodbyes. Clarissa had changed into a peacock blue suit. As Simon helped her inside the waiting coach, the guests offered them a rousing cheer of congratulations. The door closed behind her husband, and the coach surged forward.

Clarissa did her best to relax as Simon stretched out his legs in the limited confines of the expensive carriage. He was a big man, albeit a graceful one, and Clarissa found herself growing more and more curious about what kind of life they would share. If the emotions rushing through her veins like a summer storm were any indication, it wouldn't be a boring one.

While his bride's mind was wandering from one question to another, Simon loosened his cravat and tried to make himself comfortable. They wouldn't arrive at Sheridan Manor for several hours, and as much as he wanted to pull his new wife onto his lap and ravish her, he wasn't about to consummate their marriage in a cramped carriage. The image of it brought a wicked smile to his face as he regarded his *wife*. It was undeniably arousing to know that Clarissa actually belonged to him now. There was no reason why he couldn't indulge in a few kisses to ease the tension that had been mounting between them since she'd walked down the aisle of the country chapel.

Huxley had supplied them with a basket of fresh fruit and thick wedges of baked bread, along with a bottle of French wine. Simon helped himself to a shiny red apple. The sharp crunch of his teeth biting into apple drew his wife's elusive violet eyes. When he leaned forward, offering her a bite of the once-forbidden fruit, her cheeks took on the blushing hue of a new bride for the first time since he'd kissed her at the altar.

"You didn't eat very much at the reception," he said, motioning toward the basket.

"I wasn't hungry," Clarissa told him, wishing she didn't sound so breathless. She'd been in carriages with Simon before. Why was she acting so shy now? *You weren't his wife then,* she reminded herself.

"Come sit by me," he said, making room on the green cushioned seat.

The words had been softly spoken, but Clarissa didn't mistake the tone of authority he'd used in pronouncing them. Simon was her husband now, and he fully expected her to obey the request.

Gathering up the full skirt of her traveling suit, Clarissa made the transfer from one side of the carriage to the other with the assistance of her husband's helping hand. She was straightening the folds of her skirt when Simon's hands reached out once again, bringing the activity to an abrupt end.

"Look at me," he said, his voice low and seductive, the way it had been that night in the carriage when he had escorted her to Lady Thornton's party. The night he'd so brazenly traced the path of her pearl necklace.

Clarissa hadn't worn the pearls since that night. They were carefully packed away in the jewel case that would follow her to Sheridan Manor, along with Huxley, Lillian, and a hodge-podge of trunks and hat boxes.

Acutely aware of his bare hands resting on top of her gloved one, Clarissa turned her head until she met Simon's gaze. Slowly, he pulled her hands away from her skirt and began to peel the gloves away. He tossed them aside, then studied the ring on her left hand with male satisfaction. When he turned her left hand palm up and placed a kiss on her bare skin, Clarissa tried to stifle the involuntary flinch that followed, but she wasn't very successful.

Simon turned his dark eyes on her once again and she felt the strange passion beginning, the same way it had arisen the night of their first carriage ride. Her body temperature rose to an uncomfortable level as he kept staring at her, his gaze so intense that she had to close her eyes to keep its probing quality at bay.

They opened in wide alarm when she felt the apple being pressed to her mouth.

"Take a bite," Simon said, turning the red fruit so she would be forced to sample it from the same side where he'd already eaten. The apathy of the last few weeks was gone, replaced by his steamy gaze and husky voice.

A velvet silence overtook the carriage as Clarissa opened her mouth and took a small bite of the cool, sweet fruit. Simon's smile was pure devilry as she chewed the apple.

"Now kiss me," he said, placing the apple aside and reaching for her. He lifted her onto his lap, holding her in place when she tried to return to her original seat. "Kiss me," he commanded in a rough whisper that spoke to the sexual frustration he'd suffered for the last six weeks. "You're my wife now. Kiss me."

Clarissa wasn't sure who kissed whom. Simon's mouth covered hers, and suddenly she was tasting him along with the apple. Once again, her senses were overwhelmed by the exotic pleasure of a kiss. His mouth was warm and moist, and his tongue dipped between her lips, sending tiny shivers up and down her spine. She could feel the hard strength of his thighs as she remained perched on his lap like a puppy. The hand holding her head in place moved down her arms and back up again as they both realized her resistance was nonexistent. The sudden realization that the earl could now do with her as he pleased was enough to make Clarissa pull back, her eyes sparkling with indignation as she assumed the kiss had been meant as a lesson in obeying her husband's every word.

Once again, Simon seemed to read her thoughts. "I've missed kissing you," he said, tightening his hold on her. His hands moved to her waist, and he smiled. "I'm glad you left your corset at Hartford

Hall. I like feeling you much better than a whalebone cage."

Clarissa was trembling inside as his hands continued to flex and relax, his long fingers inching up her torso until his thumbs were resting under her breasts. "You've missed me, too. Admit it."

"I'll admit no such thing," she told him, wiggling to be free of his tempting embrace.

Her movements only served to bring a soft groan from her husband's throat and a tightening of his grasp as he told her to be still and stop being stubborn.

"I'm not stubborn," she scolded him, keeping her voice low so the driver of the coach wouldn't hear them arguing.

"Yes, you are," he replied, clearly amused by the personality trait. "But I'm much more stubborn than you, my lovely wife, and it's time you learned that fact. You can pretend that what passes between us is embarrassing and beyond the realm of what a well-bred lady, such as yourself, could admit to enjoy. But enjoy it, you do."

"I don't enjoy your insults," she snapped, thinking the man reveled in embarrassing her. It was so unlike the gentleman he appeared to be to everyone else.

"Ahhh, but not I'm insulting you," he countered. His dark eyes glittered with mischief as he took another bite of the apple. "I admire your beauty, and I find your natural passion quite beguiling. Don't you find my words complimentary?"

His tone was teasing as his hands moved closer to the gold buttons that kept her jacket closed over a pale silk blouse. Under that she wore only a chemise.

"Let me go," she said, trying to forget how wonderful it had been to truly kiss him again. "Or are you planning on forcing me to submit to your outrageous marriage terms here and now. I'm sure the driver might find the results entertaining."

"You'd be surprised how quietly and slowly passion can unfold," Simon replied, tossing her bluff right back at her. "I could toss up your skirts and undo my trousers and the driver would be no more the wiser for my actions. My mouth would mask your moans of satisfaction, and when we arrived at Sheridan Manor, you would be my wife in more than name. Would you like that, bold lady?"

"You are the one who's bold," Clarissa chided him. How dare the man treat their wedding day so shamefully. She could feel her face turning red at the mere suggestion of coupling in a carriage.

Simon's soft chuckle was followed by a trail of kisses that started at Clarissa's throat and ended up sealing off more protests. This time the kiss went on and on until she was clinging to his shoulders, the coach and its driver completely forgotten. One kiss turned into another and another until Simon's body was shouting for release and Clarissa was straining against him, trying to get closer instead of pulling away.

His bride's acquiescence sent desire stabbing through Simon's body until he, too, almost forgot where they were. Wanting to kiss her for the rest of his life but knowing if he didn't stop Clarissa's skirts would indeed be tossed up to her waist, Simon forced himself to change the tempo of his seduction. He slowly began to soothe her stimulated senses with light kisses; his hands stopped caressing her through the blue fabric of her clothing and began a less aggressive path up and down her back, slowly quieting her female ardor until she was resting in his arms, her cheek pressed against his chest.

Clarissa was still too dazed by the sweet seduction of Simon's mouth to think beyond the moment. The short drapes that covered the coach windows allowed in enough light for her to see that the sun was setting beyond the thick trees that lined the country road. The setting sun played hide-and-seek through the green boughs as the coach rocked and swayed over the rough lane. The air was cooling as well, but she couldn't feel its effects because Simon's arms were warm and strong about her. Her eyes slowly lifted to his face, and she found him smiling down at her. That damnable smug smile that she hated one moment and loved the next. *Like the man,* she thought.

When she tried once again to leave his lap, Simon held her in place. "Rest," he said. "There's plenty of time for you to take a nap. I'll wake you when we reach Coventry."

"I can't sleep sitting in your lap," she complained, albeit less fervently than she should have. It did feel good to be held in Simon's arms, and she was tired from all the activities of the last few days. Getting married was an exhausting experience.

"You'll be sleeping in my arms tonight," he reminded her. "Now close those beautiful eyes and rest before I grow impatient again and forget that a bride should have the comfort of a feather mattress before she becomes a wife."

With the beat of Simon's male heart echoing against her feminine ear, Clarissa closed her eyes. She didn't see the smile of satisfaction that crossed her husband's face as he lifted his booted feet and placed them on the opposing seat, nor was she privy to the desire that was rushing through his veins along with the life-giving blood. Holding her contently against his chest, Simon thought of the night ahead.

Once he had Clarissa settled in at Sheridan Manor, he intended to keep her very busy. He'd spent years eluding the altar, but having been there, he was suddenly impatient to become a husband in every sense of the word. More certain than ever that Clarissa would settle into the role of wife and mother without too much difficulty, Simon found himself thinking of a name for their firstborn son. His father's name had been Alexander, and he supposed it would be right to pass the name along to the next earl, but then Clarissa had been very fond of her grandfather. He rolled the name Richard around in his head. Since both the late earl of Hartford and Simon's uncle shared the same name, it would be wise to consider it as well. Then again, Simon couldn't be sure that Clarissa would give him a son the first time she delivered a child. It could very well be a girl. The thought wasn't totally displeasing, since he fully intended to get her pregnant more than once or twice. In fact, the more he thought about children, the more he favored a large family. A very large family.

Keeping Clarissa with child would ensure him some peace and quiet. After all, how much chaos could a pregnant woman create? Ladies kept to the country when their bodies began to round with child, and once the babe was delivered, their maternal instincts usually kept them content until the next child was conceived. The more Simon thought about it, the more the thought of giving Clarissa a child that very night pleased him.

As the coach turned off the main road that connected Norwich and Coventry, Simon placed a kiss on the top of his wife's auburn head and smiled. Clarissa moaned softly as she cuddled closer to him. The movement seemed to break some feeling loose inside the earl's chest, and he stared down at the woman sleeping so peacefully in his lap. He brushed a tendril of cinnamon hair away from her face, letting his fingers linger for a moment against the ivory perfection of her skin. He stared at her, once again unable to identify the vague emotion that seemed to be growing with each kiss they shared. Trying to cool his ardor by not thinking about the wedding night ahead of them, Simon concentrated on the things about Clarissa that he did know. She was beautiful and pleasant in her disposition when she wasn't arguing with him. Her education by private tutors and her manners suited a lady of her rank, and she had a sharp mind. He smiled at the thought of the dinner conversations they would share. It would be a pleasant change from the silent meals he was used to taking.

Simon quickly realized that everything about his life had suddenly changed. He'd given Clarissa his name, but he'd promised her much more than the eloquent words they'd exchanged in the chapel. Never again would he think in singular thoughts. He'd share more than his bed. From this day forth, every moment of his life would include the lovely lady sleeping in his arms. He had a wife and the promise of children. The ramifications were complicated but not displeasing. The certainty of his desire was tempered by the undeniable knowledge that he felt more than he should, having only been engaged to the lady for a few short weeks. The feeling didn't go away as the traveling coach rolled through the gates of Sheridan Manor to deposit the earl and his new wife at the doorstep of their honeymoon home.

Nine

Although Clarissa had been to Sheridan Manor before, she'd never entered it as the mistress of the house. Simon led her up the front steps, past the stiff-lipped Higgins, and into the foyer. As expected, the housekeeper was waiting with the full staff of house servants lined up like chess pieces by her side.

"My lady," Mrs. Talley said after Simon had introduced Clarissa as "his wife, the countess of Sheridan."

Mrs. Talley was a slender-built woman with gray hair pulled back into a prim knot at the nape of her neck. She was dressed in a black broadcloth dress with a white starched apron. Clarissa looked into her pale blue eyes and smiled. Although the housekeeper didn't smile back, the new countess of Sheridan got the impression she wanted to, which meant Mrs. Talley ran the house with as much respect as she did fear.

The butler, who had taken his position next to the housekeeper, was formally introduced. He gave Clarissa an appraising glance, as if his inspection and approval were required before she could take her rightful place in the earl's home. She wasn't entirely sure she liked the grim-faced Mr. Higgins, but then Huxley would be arriving tomorrow. The manor didn't need two butlers, but she'd explained to Simon that her butler also served as a secretary of sorts and there would be no competition between the two servants. Higgins would continue to rule the roost at Sheridan Manor, and Huxley would assist her in other matters.

Clarissa smiled politely as the housekeeper began to introduce the individual servants. Higgins took over the task when it came time to present the footmen, who served under his direct supervision. Once Clarissa had been bowed and curtsied to almost three dozen times, Mrs. Talley dismissed the staff and turned to her employer, the earl.

"Mrs. Talley, after you've shown Lady Sheridan to her room, please arrange for a light supper to be served in the master sitting room."

"If your ladyship will follow me," Mrs. Talley said in a soft voice that Clarissa silently predicted could turn into a lion's roar if things weren't done properly.

Clarissa watched as Simon turned and walked into his library, shutting the door behind him. Feeling a little out of place, even though she was perfectly comfortable with the way an aristocratic manor house was run, Clarissa followed the housekeeper up the wide mahogany staircase to the second floor of her new home.

Clarissa's eyes absorbed the luxurious details of the large house as they climbed the stairs and began to walk down the open gallery decorated with Sinclair family portraits. Mrs. Talley turned off the gallery and down a wide, thickly-carpeted corridor, not stopping until she reached a set of ornately carved double doors.

"This is the master suite, your ladyship," Mrs. Talley said, pushing open the doors, then stepping aside so that Clarissa could enter.

Feeling a new flock of butterflies take over her stomach, Clarissa stepped into an elegantly decorated sitting room with two sets of adjoining double doors. The room was wallpapered in royal blue and gold. A long settee sat against one wall, with a pedestal table and two chairs occupying the place of honor beneath a brass chandelier. The room was larger than the front parlor at Hartford Hall. Clarissa barely had time to notice the walnut desk and matching chair next to the fireplace before Mrs. Talley opened the door to the left of the impressive sitting room.

"Your room, my lady. I hope you find it comfortable."

Clarissa stepped through the second door and came to an abrupt stop. Comfortable was an understatement. The lady's suite was furnished in red and gold and was three times the size of the one she occupied at Hartford Hall. A white marble fireplace took up the entire north wall. A massive bed, sitting atop a mahogany dais, was draped by deep red curtains, tied back with gold braids, and covered with a gold-and-white brocade coverlet that looked heavy enough to suffocate anyone sleeping under it. Small gold-fringed pillows of white and red were tossed gracefully against the thick feather pillows. The bed's tall canopy had matching gold fringe. The furniture, consisting of a small cherry-wood writing desk and chair, a chaise longue covered in rich red velvet and a settee in gold brocade cloth, was artfully displayed in the large chamber. The carpet was red and gold, with the Sheridan family crest displayed in the center of the room, just below a chandelier that was twice as large as the one in the sitting room.

Mrs. Talley closed the drapes, shutting off the French doors that led to the balcony, before walking across the room and opening the door to the dressing room and bath area.

Clarissa peeked inside and smiled. Beyond the closet area was a white silk dressing screen decorated with red roses and flamboyant blue birds perched on gold tree branches. The bathing area was done in gold, with a white marble tub and gold faucets. There was a tall chifforobe opposite the claw-footed tub as well as a large vanity table and matching brass stool with a red velvet cushion.

"I've assigned Prissy to be your maid until your personal staff arrives. The trunk that was sent ahead has already been unpacked." Mrs. Talley said as Clarissa removed her gloves and laid them on a dainty table situated between two Queen Anne chairs. "I'll send Prissy up to draw your bath."

"Thank you," Clarissa said, realizing that Simon's room was just across the common sitting area where he'd instructed a light dinner to be served later. He'd meant a *private* dinner, of course. Now that she'd been shown to her room, Clarissa knew he expected her to be changed out of her traveling suit and into something more appropriate for her wedding night. "I'm sure Prissy will do just fine. Unlike most ladies, I don't require a lot of attention."

Mrs. Talley's expression didn't change until she reached the doors leading to the sitting room. She hesitated for a moment, then smiled. "Everyone at Sheridan Manor is pleased that the earl has taken a wife. I hope you will be happy here."

Clarissa smiled in return. "Thank you, Mrs. Talley. Other than my butler, who will be acting as a temporary secretary, the only servant who will be arriving tomorrow is my personal maid, Lillian. In all other matters, I will defer to your expertise."

"I will do my best, your ladyship," the housekeeper replied, her smile still intact.

The door shut behind the housekeeper, and Clarissa heard the jingle of the house keys, attached to Mrs. Talley's belt, dissolve into the distance. It never hurt to have an ally on your side, and she knew that most housekeepers dreaded a new mistress. It meant changes that all too frequently led to servants being dismissed for no other reason than personal whim.

A few moments later, there was a discreet knock on the door. Clarissa responded, knowing that it was Prissy, the maid. The young girl came into the room, looking as nervous as Clarissa felt. A mass of freckles stood out against her pale face, and she stumbled when she dipped into the expected curtsy.

"My name's Prissy, milady. Mrs. Talley sent me up to draw your bath."

The girl's ashen face and quivering bottom lip brought about an uncontrollable need to put the young maid at ease before she fainted dead away. "Thank you, Prissy."

The girl scampered into the dressing room before Clarissa could say anything. The sound of water flowing into the large brass tub filled the outer room as Clarissa unbuttoned her jacket and laid it on the bed. While the water was running, Prissy came back into the bedchamber and asked which gown her ladyship would like to wear to dinner.

Not sure what Lillian had packed in the single trunk that had arrived two days ago, Clarissa walked to the closet and opened the door. Wondering how long she'd be wearing anything she chose, Clarissa decided against the white dressing gown and sheer undergarment that was too scanty to be considered clothing at all. Hanging beside the customary virginal white bridal nightwear was another dressing gown of frosty peach with ivory lace. Clarissa dismissed it as well, thinking it would be best to dress as formally as possible, since she'd be meeting Simon in the sitting room, not her bedchamber. That left a royal blue dress that was more suited to the morning than the evening and an emerald green gown that she had favored before going into mourning for her grandfather.

"This will do," she said, withdrawing the green gown and handing it to Prissy.

A short time later, Clarissa was sitting in front of the vanity table in her chemise while Prissy brushed her hair. Some of the maid's nervousness had left her, and she smiled as she complimented her new mistress on the color of her thick mane of hair.

"It's like cinnamon and brown sugar with a touch of mahogany," Prissy remarked, pulling the ivory-handled brush through Clarissa's waist-length hair.

"My mother was Scottish. My hair is more red than brown, especially in the sunlight, but hers was the color of a new copper coin. She was very beautiful."

"So are you," the maid said, giving Clarissa a sheepish smile. "I heard the earl telling Viscount Thornton that very thing."

Clarissa arched her brow at the girl's reflection in the mirror.

"I wasn't eavesdropping, milady," the maid said in quick defense. "I was cleanin' the foyer, and the library door wasn't closed all the way."

"That's perfectly all right," Clarissa assured her. "A lady always likes to hear that her husband thinks she's pretty."

A short time later, Prissy had been dismissed, and Clarissa was pacing the red-and-gold bedchamber. The emerald gown flowed around her feet, and small diamond earrings gleamed against the rich color of her hair as she wondered how she was going to handle her wedding night. Although she knew some of the things that were going to happen, she didn't have enough information to feel comfortable about the upcoming "deflowering." She loved Simon, and she wanted to be his wife, but she didn't like the idea of having her nuptials turned into a contest of wills, and she feared that that was exactly what her husband had in mind. His *conditions* had been clearly stated, and she knew Simon well enough now to suspect that he was going to put her cooperation to the test.

Being in love was such a complicated thing, Clarissa decided as she swirled around to retrace her path across the plush carpet. She did love Simon, and she wanted to be his wife. But she also wanted to be his friend. She wanted to share his confidence and his respect. She wanted to laugh with him and cry with him and do all the things that only a husband and wife could do together. She wanted the fact that she was his wife to mean something to him. Something real and substantial. But most of all, she wanted him to love her.

The sound of a footman wheeling a serving cart into the sitting room interrupted Clarissa's marathon. She stopped dead in her tracks as Simon's voice came through the doors of her bedchamber. The sound of china and crystal being set in place was followed by the closing of the sitting-room door and a light knock on the door of her bedchamber.

Knowing that Simon was standing just beyond the engraved oak doorway, Clarissa took a deep breath and prayed that she wouldn't embarrass herself more than the average bride. She reached out and, using the brass handles, pushed the doors open wide. Just as she suspected, Simon was waiting for her. The sight of him was enough to make her mouth go dry and her feet forget how to function. He was dressed in a blue silk smoking jacket with black velvet lapels. His trousers were black, as were his slippers. His hair was damp, and he appeared to be freshly shaven.

"Madam," he said, motioning toward the table with a graceful sweep of his hand.

Clarissa stepped into the sitting room, taking note of the elegantly set table and the bottle of wine. The gaslight chandelier had been turned down, and a candelabra decorated the center of the table. The candlelight flickered and danced on the walls and ceiling, and Clarissa tried her best to smile.

Her mouth felt as if it were made of stone, and she knew that she'd failed miserably when Simon chuckled softly and took her hand, leading her toward the intimately set table like a lamb to slaughter.

He seated her, then leaned down and brushed the lightest of kisses across her earlobe. "I know you must be hungry. Relax and enjoy the meal."

Clarissa didn't get much relief from her husband's words. He was standing entirely too close, and she could feel the heat of his body as he leaned over her shoulder and filled a crystal goblet with red wine. How was she supposed to eat when she'd left her stomach in the bedchamber, along with her courage?

She watched as his long, slender fingers held the wine bottle. He had strong hands, and she could remember the way they'd held her in the coach, capturing her in a gentle vise that had held her in place as surely as the ardent gaze of his eyes and the low, seductive tones of his voice. She'd told herself time and time again over the last six weeks that when her wedding night finally arrived, she'd meet it with all the dignity and grace of a proper lady. But with the ominous event staring her in the face, all Clarissa could think about was the crisp dark hair on the back of Simon's hands and how those hands would feel on her body.

After pouring the wine, Simon walked around

the table and sat down. She stared into his eyes, mesmerized by some unknown power, unable to avert her gaze as he stared back. A frisson of sensation went through her, tickling her nerve endings; apprehension, excitement, desire, or a combination of all three. She wasn't sure.

"Eat," he said simply, finally breaking the intangible contact between them as he lowered his eyes and reached for a piece of silver flatware bearing the Sinclair family crest.

The impulse to get up from the table and flee teased Clarissa's mind for a brief moment, but there was no place to run. She nibbled at the food, her senses overwhelmed by Simon's masculine presence and what he expected of her later in the evening. Never had she felt so out of control. It was disconcerting to think that she'd managed to secure a quarter of her grandfather's fortune, a remarkable feat considering the times in which she lived, and yet at this moment she felt completely helpless.

Simon sensed Clarissa's trepidation. It pleased him to some degree. As much as he admired her spirit, he didn't want her too comfortable with her new situation. She needed to learn to trust him, to depend upon his ability to take care of her and his right to determine their future as man and wife. She'd accused him of being archaic in his attitudes, and admittedly he was, at least about the roles of husbands and wives. He disliked men who allowed their wives to become complacent in the bedchamber, giving the gentlemen an excuse to seek their sexual satisfaction elsewhere. Regardless of the prudish notions young ladies inherited from their mothers and maiden aunts, it was a husband's duty to see that his bride not only accepted her role but enjoyed it. The innocence of a woman's wedding night should be rewarded with pleasure, not degraded later because the man had been too busy rutting to take the time to find the passion that Simon believed God had disbursed equally to both genders.

He was known as a considerate and giving lover among the women who had shared his bed over the years, but Simon's determination to break through the ladylike veneer Clarissa wore like a shield went beyond the pleasure he would gain by teaching her to be a participant instead of a victim of their marriage bed. The need to reach her on a physical level was fueled by more than his own sexual satisfaction. There was more to his charming wife than she wanted to admit, and he was determined to find out everything about her. He wanted her to respond to him for the sheer pleasure of his touch, for her life to become so linked with his own that she stopped building walls to keep him out. He wanted all she had to offer—all her thoughts, all her dreams, and all her *secrets.*

The metallic clatter of silverware was the only sound in the room as Clarissa put down her fork and reached for the glass of wine. She sipped it slowly, savoring the sweet, rich taste, hoping that it would calm her nerves. She hated silent meals. They were bad for the digestion. But she couldn't think of a single word to breach the heavy stillness of the room. What did a bride say on her wedding night? There were no words of undying love that she could speak, not without admitting that she cared for Simon more than he cared for her. A lady didn't talk about passion and the marriage bed, so she didn't dare ask him which of the two bedchambers they would occupy later.

She looked over the rim of her glass to find Simon's eyes resting upon her once again, but this time they seemed to be smiling rather than brooding. He took a sip of his own wine, then finally spoke.

"Whatever you said to Mrs. Talley left her smiling. A rare sight indeed. She also remarked that she was sure the staff would find you to be a benevolent mistress."

"How long has she been here?" Clarissa asked, thinking to direct the conversation toward something more benign than the husbandly rights Simon would claim once they'd finished eating.

"For as long as I can remember," he replied. "When I was a little boy, she used to scare me. Higgins, too."

"I can't imagine anyone scaring you," she said, trying to envision Simon as a little boy. It was difficult, considering how manly he looked at the moment.

His smile brightened the room, competing with the candles adorning the center of the table. "I was a boy, like most boys," he said, as if he had followed her thoughts. "I climbed the trees in the orchard, hunted ghosts in the attic, scaled the garden walls. The usual mischief. Once I tried to ride my father's prize thoroughbred. I don't know what made my bottom more sore, the dirt I landed in after the stallion threw me or the palm of my father's hand when he instructed me to keep away from the stables."

Clarissa laughed, releasing some of the tension that had been imprisoned inside her since arriving at Sheridan Manor. Having Simon share an incident from his childhood, especially one that attested to having his backside bruised, made him seem a little less threatening.

"Grandfather spanked me once."

His dark eyes took on an inquisitive gleam.

Clarissa replied to the silent question with a candid answer. "I was a bit on the precocious side as a child."

"Do tell."

She ignored the gleam in his eye as she recited the story of her one and only spanking. "It was just before my eighth birthday. I slid down the banister."

"The earl spanked you for sliding down a banister?" The infraction seemed small compared to the consequences, but then young ladies of good breeding weren't supposed to act like street urchins.

"He didn't spank me for sliding down the banister, although he insisted that I never do it again," Clarissa told him. "He spanked me for landing on the vicar. I knocked the poor man right out of his wits."

The image of a little girl with cinnamon curls hanging in a tangle down her back and the ruffles of her pantaloons showing as she came sliding down the wooden railing was amusing. The image of her landing on an astonished member of the clergy made Simon laugh.

"I see that I'll have to keep an eye on our daughters as well as our sons," he said, reaching across the table to refill her wineglass. "If they inherit their mother's adventurous spirit as well as her beauty, I'll have my hands full."

The compliment brought a flush of color to Clarissa's face. She wasn't vain, but it was nice to know that Simon found her attractive. Once again, the room went mute. The clock on the white marble mantel in her bedchamber chimed the hour. Simon folded his napkin and stood up. He looked at her for a long moment before coming around the table and offering her his hand. The silent gesture sent a rush of emotions through Clarissa, and for a moment she was afraid that if she stood, her legs wouldn't support her. When she took his hand, the candlelight made the sapphires on her wedding ring gleam like tiny blue stars, reminding her of the woman she'd become earlier that day. She was the countess of Sheridan, Simon's legal wife.

For a moment, all he did was hold her hand gently in his, watching her from beneath the thick dark lashes that framed his walnut colored eyes. A female heat swept through Clarissa's body, and once again the impulse to flee seemed overwhelming. But she didn't move. Her feet seemed to be glued to the carpet, her body no longer hers to command.

Slowly, Clarissa met his gaze, her eyes searching his face for something that said he felt more than passion. A soft tremor ran through her as his mouth curved into a smile. Reaching out with his other hand, he caressed the curve of her cheek, letting his fingertips slowly descend to the skin of her throat, burning her whenever they touched. The invisible fire made the warmth in her blood ignite like a match to fresh kindling. Her eyes closed.

"Look at me," Simon told her, his voice as irresistible as the need overtaking her senses.

Clarissa knew that opening her eyes would mean some sort of surrender, and for a scant second she hesitated.

Simon watched her face as he slid his hand around her throat until it was resting at the nape of her neck. When her eyes finally opened, he scanned their violet depths, seeing both indecision and the female fear of the unknown. It was as if she were standing at a crossroads, unsure of which way to turn. He could see the doubt; left or right, yes or no.

She was so beautiful, and he had spent the last six weeks imagining this moment, anticipating her surrender, planning it, wanting it so much at times that he'd been forced from his bed, doomed to pace the floor with a brandy glass in his hand until his ardor cooled and he could once again find sleep.

Now there was nothing left to say. Nothing left to do but begin the process that wouldn't end until she was his wife in every way.

He kissed her.

For a moment, she stiffened, and he knew she was struggling with that private part of her mind that didn't want to admit she was finally his. He held her head in place, offering her no escape as his mouth moved over hers, gently at first, then more demandingly. His left arm circled her waist and brought her body in close enough contact with his to feel the evidence of his need but not so closely that she felt trapped. He was determined to go slowly, to evoke her response the way sunshine enticed the petals of a rose to open.

Clarissa felt her willpower dissolving like sugar in a hot cup of tea. Simon's mouth moved teasingly over hers, intensifying the effects of the kiss like a musician building on each note of a shattering crescendo. Never had his kiss meant more than it did at this very moment, never had she felt its beckoning quality as surely as she felt it now. She hovered on the brink of the unknown, yet at the same time she felt a certainty that swept away any ambivalent feelings she might still have about the man she'd married.

Besides, who was to say that love couldn't beget love?

Simon was narrow-minded, but he wasn't cold-hearted. All she needed was time and patience. The problem being that she had a lot of the first and very little of the second.

As Simon's mouth became more demanding, Clarissa's mind went blank. Devoid of thought, all she could do was feel, and all she could feel was Simon.

Reluctantly, Simon raised his head. Clarissa's eyes had closed again, but he could see the flush of desire that was warming her skin. He allowed his gaze to linger on her parted lips, then slide slowly down to her breasts, pressing suggestively against the emerald satin of her dress. Her chest was rising and falling with a gentle rhythm, and her head was leaning back against the cradle of his open hand. He wanted to scoop her up in his arms, kick open the door of the bedchamber, and dump her in the middle of the feather mattress, coming down on top of her. He wanted a lot of things, but none of them was going to happen in the sitting room. And they weren't going to be rushed. Never in his life had he wanted to stop time, but he wanted to do so now, to make the next few hours an eternity, because it was going to take him that long to satisfy the need his beautiful wife aroused in him.

"You need to change your gown," he said, releasing her. "Come, I'll help you with the buttons."

Clarissa regained her wits with the slowness of a contented cat sleeping lazily on a warm hearth. Simon's embrace always seemed to have that effect on her. She hated leaving the circle of his arms the way anyone deplored stepping onto a cold floor after being tucked into a warm, cozy bed on a winter's night. When he walked to the double doors that led to her bedchamber, opening one side of them and then waiting for her to enter the inner sanctum, Clarissa tried her best to stroll toward the room as normally as she'd enter a library or parlor.

Once inside the bedchamber, Clarissa realized she had no idea what to do next. Thankful that her back was to Simon as he closed the door and locked it with a soft click, she stared at the large bed. If he had conducted the evening the way most gentlemen would have arranged it, she would be given some privacy to prepare herself. Then, upon his arrival, she'd be wearing a white gown, with her hair freshly brushed, or perhaps she'd be in the bed, reclining against the feather pillows with a book of poetry on her lap. But Simon wasn't most men, and apparently he intended to play the role of lady's maid by helping her out of the gown she'd worn to dinner. Clarissa might be able to think of the gesture as thoughtful after they'd been married for a year to two. But not now. Now it was only another reminder of the conditions he'd demanded before accepting her marriage proposal.

Whenever, wherever, however, he wanted her.

Ten

Clarissa felt her knees grow weak as Simon walked toward her, his footsteps muffled by the soft carpet on the floor of the elegantly decorated bedchamber. She tried to think of Haven House and the ladies who were depending upon her to make a success of her marriage, thereby guaranteeing the continuance of the charity she'd begun, but her mind refused to focus on the pragmatic side of her relationship with Simon. His presence and the significance of the night they were about to share stripped away the practicality of the situation. There was only the night, the man, and the hot-blooded, restless feeling that was flowing through her veins like warm honey.

Simon kissed the nape of her neck, and Clarissa reacted instinctively, turning to meet the warmth of his embrace. His gaze wandered over her once again, and he murmured. "I want you to trust me."

The request seemed a bit absurd to Clarissa, and she said so, her voice betraying some of the nervousness she felt as Simon caressed the curve of her cheek. "I promised to submit to my wifely duties. I won't fight you."

His mouth thinned into a disapproving line. "I

don't want your submission. I want your trust. They aren't the same thing."

Clarissa didn't want to argue the point, although she could have. She wanted to be able to trust Simon, but she couldn't. She couldn't trust a man with his antiquated viewpoints to understand her commitment to Haven House and the unwed mothers she protected there. She longed to be able to tell him why she'd accepted his *conditions,* why she would continue to accept them, but she didn't dare. Not yet.

Her silence pricked at Simon's temper, but he didn't let it show. Instead, he kissed her lightly on the tip of her upturned nose and smiled. "Granted, I expect you to honor the promise you gave me, but that isn't the reason I want you to trust me."

"I don't understand," Clarissa replied, wishing that Simon would stop playing with her earlobe so she could concentrate.

"Becoming my wife involves more than becoming my bed partner," he told her patiently. "I want you to trust me enough to know what's best for us both. What will give us both pleasure and satisfaction. I want you to trust me the way a wife should trust her husband."

She was beginning to understand, and she didn't like it. She pulled back, preventing Simon from placing another kiss on the curve of her throat. "You want me to trust you enough to let you run my life. Is that it?"

"I see my freethinking lady is back," he replied, smiling.

"She never left," Clarissa retorted. She disengaged herself from his embrace and stepped back. "I accepted your conditions, I married you, and I'm willing to share your bed. But that doesn't mean I'm going to become a different person. I'm not going to stop thinking the way I think or reacting the way I normally react, and I most certainly am not going to let you take control of my life."

"I already have," Simon reminded her. "When you married me this morning, you accepted my name. In return, I accepted the responsibility of taking care of you and whatever children you give me. That means I have both the moral and legal right to control whatever aspects of your life I think need controlling. Excluding the right to manage your personal accounts, of course."

Arrogant man, Clarissa thought as she began to move about the room, taking off her diamond earrings and placing them in the velvet-lined jewel box on the vanity table. She gave Simon a quick glance over her shoulder as she walked toward the doors that led to the balcony. A gentle tug of the drapery cord and the glass-paned doors were revealed. Outside, the sky was filled with stars, and the moon hung like a silver platter against the dark mantel of the night. Clarissa opened the doors, deciding the room was entirely too warm for her liking, and stepped outside.

She walked to the stone railing and rested her palms against it to cool the fever in her blood. Clarissa tried to put her feelings for the man in the room behind her into some kind of perspective. It would be much easier if she could contain those feelings in a distant place, but they refused to be shepherded into a safe corner, where they offered no threat to her heart. Like the man she loved, her feelings were bold and strong, demanding so much at times that she feared she would not be able to hide them for long. If Simon only knew, she thought, as he stepped up beside her. If he knew how she felt, would he use it against her? Would he try to manipulate her, justifying his actions in the name of love?

Unfortunately, Clarissa feared that he would.

Most men would under the circumstances and although Simon was unique in many ways, he was still a man.

"You don't like being under anyone's thumb, do you?" Simon asked, his voice as soft as the breeze cooling Clarissa's hot skin.

"Would you?" she replied, looking up at him. Simon studied her as though he were trying to figure out where the absurd question had come from.

"It's hardly the same thing," he remarked. "You were under your grandfather's supervision until a year ago. If your parents hadn't been killed, you would have been under your father's supervision. A husband's authority isn't all that different."

Clarissa almost laughed. She was tempted to remind Simon that neither her grandfather nor her father would have demanded the things he had demanded from her, but she thought better of it. Instead, she spoke from a more generalized point of view. "Why should a husband have *any* authority over his wife? A marriage should be a partnership, not a dictatorship."

It was Simon's turn to laugh. "The institution would cease to exist under those circumstances. There would be social chaos."

"History is full of social chaos," Clarissa retorted. "It's also full of wars. Fought by men, not women. Perhaps if more governments were actually run by women rather than female figureheads who bend to the advice of their male counselors, we would have less social chaos and more social progress."

Simon's smile was deceptively lazy. His eyes gleamed in the moonlight like a predatory animal as he reached out and lifted Clarissa's hand away from the cold banister. He pulled her close, tipping up her chin until their eyes met. "If you're trying to delay our wedding night, madam, I advise you to try another tactic. I am not in the mood for a political or social debate."

"Just as I thought," she said with false sweetness. "Our marriage is to be a dictatorship."

"I am not a dictator. I'm your husband. And as such it's my responsibility to see that you enjoy our wedding night."

The word *responsibility*, used for the second time that night, hit Clarissa's ears like the high-pitched whistle of a train. She didn't want to be a responsibility. She wanted to be loved. "I see," she said blandly, hiding her disappointment. "I suppose I shouldn't be surprised. Most men look at their wives as a responsibility, a necessary evil, so to speak."

Simon knew if he let Clarissa take control of their conversation, he'd spend his wedding night arguing about the archaic role of husbands and the progressive destiny of the female gender. He led her back inside, refusing to let her go until the balcony doors were once again closed and she was standing at the foot of the large double bed.

"I'm not most men," he told her calmly. "I'm the man you married. The one you promised to love, honor, and obey. Now, turn around and let me help you out of that dress."

There was a finality in Simon's tone that said he wasn't in the mood for conversation.

With a strange sense of anticipation and a forced indifference that she came no way close to feeling, Clarissa offered Simon her back and easy access to the row of tiny jet buttons. She forced herself to stand perfectly still while he reached out and began to unfasten her dress. Less than a minute later, the dress was hanging loosely from her shoulders, and he was caressing the bare skin of her neck and shoulders. Each gentle stroke of Simon's hand sent the dress and the straps of her chemise farther down her arms until Clarissa was clutching them to the front of her to keep the garments from dropping to her waist.

"Turn around," Simon instructed her.

Holding her bodice up, the sleeves of her dress gathered between her wrists and elbows, the straps of her chemise dangling off her shoulders, Clarissa turned to face her husband.

"Let go," Simon told her.

Clarissa hesitated for a moment before dropping her hands to her side. The front of her dress sagged to her waist. The silk chemise stayed in place, the sheer fabric covering the swell of her breasts and the pink tips that were beginning to harden under Simon's feverish gaze.

He bent over and kissed her, his mouth warm against her lips as his hands found the chemise and tugged it gently out of the way. His arm slid around her waist, pulling her closer until her naked breasts felt the cool silk of his smoking jacket. Clarissa's female instincts took over, and her arms curled around him, her palms moving over his back, letting him know she was helpless to fight the effects of the kiss. His hands became more insistent, and the dress drifted down her legs, the emerald satin pooling around her feet.

He continued to kiss her. Soft, warm, gentle kisses that shattered her resolve like a hammer striking fragile glass. The anger and doubts drained away from Clarissa as he slowly, carefully, seduced her senses. There was the ticking of the mantel clock and the coolness of the air against her naked back and the heat of Simon's hands as they moved slowly up and down her bare arms. There was the delicious texture of his mouth as it pressed against her, his tongue teasing and darting in and out, his breath flavored by the French wine he'd had with dinner.

Clarissa felt his hands pushing the chemise past her hips and the almost-tickling sensation of the silk as it slid down her legs and joined the emerald dress on the floor. Then there was the heat of his hands as they moved around behind her and cupped her bottom, lifting her up at the same time they pressed her closer to his body. She could feel his body more intimately than ever before and the arousal pushing against his black trousers. She moaned softly as his hands kneaded the soft flesh of her backside.

"Trust me," Simon whispered as his hands moved from the lush curves of her bottom, up her back, and down again, leaving a trail of goose bumps behind them.

He felt as if he were on fire as Clarissa began to return his kisses, her tongue shyly meeting his in a sensual duel. His hands quickly moved from her naked back to her hair, pulling out pins and tossing them to the carpet. The thick mane of auburn hair toppled to her waist, spilling over her shoulders in a simmering sea of cinnamon that felt like cool silk to Simon's touch.

Clarissa's head fell back, and he buried his mouth against the soft curve of her neck and shoulders, savoring the female scent of her and the warmth of her skin. When he lifted his head, his eyes were burning with the desire he had forced himself to control for the last six weeks.

"I want to look at you," he said, holding her at arm's length.

Clarissa blushed under the sensual surveillance of his dark gaze as she let him look his fill. This was no insubstantial fantasy, like the dreams she had had for so many years. This was real. Simon's hands were warm and strong as they held her, his eyes on fire with passion, his breathing becoming more labored as he sought to control the desire they ignited so easily in one another.

Simon was more than pleased at what he'd only been able to imagine up to now. Clarissa was perfectly proportioned. Her breasts were full and high, with dark pink nipples that reminded him of fresh raspberries. Her waist narrowed above lushly curved feminine hips that flared to long, graceful legs. The nest of cinnamon curls at the junction of her thighs almost tempted him beyond his limits, but he gathered his resolve to go slowly and savor each wonderful inch of her.

His need for her growing by the minute, Simon swept her up in his arms and carried her to the bed, cradling her against his chest with one arm while he reached down and jerked the rose coverlet back, disrupting the hodgepodge of velvet and satin bed pillows.

Clarissa sank into the coolness of the sheets as Simon stood by the bed, staring down at her. She found herself watching, spellbound, as he shed the smoking jacket and white silk shirt. He had a broad, well-muscled chest covered with a crisp carpet of dark hair that narrowed as it approached his flat stomach, then swirled around his navel. Her fingers itched to reach out and touch him, to feel that soft covering of hair, to comb her fingers through it and touch the warm flesh under it.

She'd lost her shoes along with her dress and silk chemise, but she was still wearing her stockings. Clarissa sucked in her breath as Simon reached down and began removing them, his long fingers caressing her calves as he slowly rolled the sheer silk down her legs and off her feet. Her clothes were scattered about on the floor, forgotten in the sexual tempest her husband was creating. When she was lying completely naked, Simon smiled and reached for the waistband of his trousers.

She'd never seen a naked man before, and the sight of her husband, fully aroused, was enough to give Clarissa more than a moment's pause. Her face must have revealed her apprehension, because Simon quickly tossed his trousers aside and leaned down to kiss her again.

"Trust me," he said again. "I won't hurt you."

Clarissa didn't believe him, but she was helpless to do anything about it. He'd already joined her on the bed, his body stretched out alongside hers, his hands caressing her hips and thighs as he kissed away her fears. She could feel the hard male planes and angles, the heat of his arousal pressed against her leg, and the sweet warmth of his breath as he rained kisses over her face, neck, and collarbone. When he covered one aroused nipple with his mouth, laving the small kernel with his tongue, Clarissa almost jumped out of her skin.

"Easy, sweetheart," he mumbled softly. "Relax and trust me."

Clarissa closed her eyes, wishing he'd stop telling her to trust the complete unknown. And this was the unknown. There were no vague, feverish dreams now. There was only the hot reality of Simon's touch, burning her skin and making her insides tremble in a restless attempt to understand what he was doing to her. The tantalizing pleasure she was feeling was a little frightening. She felt helpless and vulnerable, and she didn't like it.

"Relax, sweetheart," Simon instructed her one more time. "I'm not going to hurt you. I want to please you all the way to your pretty toes."

Clarissa couldn't feel her toes for all the sensations taking place in the upper half of her body. Simon's hands seemed to be everywhere, touching, caressing, exploring every inch of her breasts, stomach, and hips. She shivered as his hand moved between her thighs, gently forcing them to part so he could caress her even more intimately. Arrows of nerve-shattering heat shot through her as his hand moved over the nest of curls at the center of her body and probed carefully, seeking out the soft folds of female flesh. She arched against his hand unable to control her response to the shocking invasion.

"You feel so warm. So wet," Simon breathed against her ear. "Don't be afraid or embarrassed It's natural for me to touch you like this. But only me," he added as Clarissa turned her head and closed her eyes to avoid meeting his eyes. Simon wouldn't let her hide from the intimacy of his gaze any more than he was going to let her deny the pleasure she felt from his touch. He could feel it too. She was getting warmer and wetter with each stroke of his fingers.

"Look at me," he said in a more demanding voice.

Clarissa turned her head.

"Open your eyes," Simon said, almost laughing The bold young vixen who had marched into the downstairs library and proposed marriage was now a shy bride.

Slowly, her eyes opened, and Simon looked down into their violet depths as his fingers moved slowly in and out of her snug female channel. "Move against my hand," he whispered as he bent his head to kiss her. "Don't be afraid of the pleasure Let it happen. Stop thinking about what I'm doing to you and just enjoy it."

That was the problem. She was enjoying it too much. Her body no longer belonged to her. It belonged to Simon, and he was controlling it with a sweet expertise that had Clarissa afraid of losing her soul along with her virginity. His hands were delicious instruments of torture, and his mouth, suck ling greedily at her breast, was enough to make her moan.

"That's it, sweetheart. Relax and enjoy it," he prompted her as he moved from one breast to another.

His velvet tongue flicked at her nipples as his mouth sucked harder and harder, making her stomach muscles clench and unclench as the sensation moved from her breasts to the very center of her being. Clarissa moaned again, her hands coming up to hold Simon's head in place, while she let sensation overtake her. She stopped thinking, she stopped hearing, she stopped doing anything but feeling. And it was wonderful.

Simon continued kissing her, suckling her breasts, teasing her with his fingers, determined to bring her to a climax at least once before he entered her. He murmured reassuring words when Clarissa tried to make him stop the sweet, sensual torture that was quickly taking her beyond her self-control. He refused to let her dislodge his hand, telling her not to be afraid of what she was feeling, that it was what he wanted her to feel.

The sweet torment went on and on as Clarissa tried to hold on to her sanity. She couldn't. Simon kept moving his fingers, whispering for her to let go, to feel the pleasure. She responded to his provocative beckoning like a wave to the shore, unable to do anything but follow the natural inclination of her body, unable to stop the crashing climax that came in a rush of hot, sweet convulsions.

Simon muffled her cry of release with a kiss that left her trembling gently against his body as he moved over her. She buried her face in the hollow of his throat and whimpered with the almost painful pleasure she was still feeling. He withdrew his hand and caressed her stomach and breasts, slowly bringing her back to the reality of the moment, soothing her with gentle words that she could barely hear through the humming haze that seemed to surround her.

"That's what passion is all about," he said as he wedged his knee between her legs, forcing them to open wider so he could rest in the natural cradle of her body. "There's nothing shameful or sinful about it. It's what a wife should give her husband."

"I thought you wanted me to trust you," Clarissa managed to say, flinching slightly when she felt his hardness rub against her moist center.

"Real passion takes trust," he whispered, kissing her between the words. "You have to trust me before you can surrender to the passion. Spread your legs a little wider, sweetheart. I can't wait much longer."

Clarissa was still trying to relate passion to trust and trust to surrender as she did as Simon asked, spreading her legs until she could feel every hard inch of him pressing intimately against her. He reached between their bodies, opening her, until his aroused flesh was touching the entryway to her body.

Her arms were around his neck, her lips searching out his for more of the delicious kisses he had taught her to enjoy. His mouth covered hers again, and his hands moved to her hips, then under her, until he was cradling her bottom. Clarissa couldn't hold on to one exotic sensation before another one took its place. Simon kissing her, his manhood rubbing against her, his hands lifting her, forcing her to feel every inch of him as he moved against her, teasing her already sensitive female core. She could feel his heart beating and the perspiration beading on his skin. The muscles in his arms were stiff as he supported his weight, giving her just enough to make her want more. Kissing her just enough to make her want more. Touching her just enough to make her want more.

She strained toward him, letting her hands explore the taut ridge of his shoulders and upper back before they moved to the wide plane of his chest. She combed her fingers through the thick male hair, loving its texture. She found a small, hard male nipple and teased it with the edge of her fingernail.

Simon groaned like a man in pain. He pulled back for a moment, and she smiled up at him, unable to hide the female pride she felt at making him feel a small portion of the sensual torment he was inflicting upon her.

"You little witch," he said as her hands continued their exploration, moving down until they found the small indentation of his navel. "Go ahead," he coaxed her. "Touch me. I'm not immune to passion, either."

Allowing her normally bold nature to take control, Clarissa followed the masculine lines of his body, downward over the hard muscles of his lower abdomen to the thick thatch of hair around his aroused male flesh. Her fingers skimmed lightly over him, and he groaned again.

"Trust me," she said, tossing his words back at him as he reached down to remove her caressing hand before it was the end of his self-control.

Simon gritted his teeth and endured the shy exploration of her hand as she moved it up and down his throbbing length. His breathing increased as her hands roamed over him and around him, touching the sensitive sacs between his legs. When Clarissa's exploration took her hand to the flexed muscles of his buttocks, he pushed back against her, liking the feel of her touch more than he'd ever liked a woman's touch before. He had to have her. Now.

He mumbled something she couldn't understand, then began to lower his body until his manhood was pushing against the warm, wet flesh of her channel. He filled her inch by slow, sweet inch, not stopping until he encountered the natural barrier of her virginity.

Her hands dropped to her side on the feather mattress, and she closed her eyes against the extraordinary sensations he created as he carefully probed her body. She felt incredibly full, but it wasn't painful. Instead, it felt as though Simon were giving her something that she'd always been lacking, completing her in some strange way that didn't make sense at the same time that it felt so wonderfully perfect.

Clarissa's eyes popped open as he increased the pressure, pushing farther inside her.

"Relax," he whispered, brushing kisses over her face. "Take a deep breath and let it out slowly. I don't want to hurt you, but I can't be satisfied until I have all of you."

She burned inside, but she did as he asked, taking in a deep breath, then holding it for a moment before she released it like a soft breeze that caressed his neck. He pushed a little harder, and Clarissa felt something inside give way. It wasn't truly painful, but it took her by surprise as he suddenly surged deep inside her, filling her so completely that she was amazed she'd been able to take all of him.

"God, you're so hot inside," Simon said, awed by the sensation more than he should be. Clarissa was the virgin, not him, but it felt as though he'd never been inside a woman's body before. He could feel her tight channel squeezing him as she wiggled around trying to get comfortable. It was enough to make his control come close to shattering. "Don't move," he said before his mouth moved to her ear and he nibbled for a moment, then told her that he could stay inside her forever.

Clarissa wanted to tell him that was impossible, but she had to admit the idea had merit. He shifted his weight, pulling gently out of her but stopping before he left her completely.

"Look at me," he said, seeing her smile as his body continued its gentle conquering, moving in and out in slow strokes that began to rekindle the passion she'd felt a few minutes earlier.

Clarissa met his gaze, enthralled by the experience of actually being joined with Simon in such a way. No wonder the poor women at Haven House didn't regret the children they'd conceived. If their lovers had made them feel half as good as Simon was making her feel, it was easy to understand why they hadn't pushed the men away. It was mysterious, this intimate act of a man joining his body to a woman's. Intimate and intriguing. And too wonderful to waste time trying to understand. Clarissa arched against her husband's invading body and moaned softly.

"That's it," Simon encouraged her. "Give the passion back to me, sweetheart. Let me feel how much you want me."

Clarissa shivered with delight as his lower body pressed against her again and again. His palms cupped her breasts while he kissed their rosy peaks, then moved downward until he was holding her hips, gently lifting her to meet him as he continued stroking in and out of her. The slow, sensual rhythm began to build as he talked to her, using seductively persuasive words and phrases that made their joining seem even more intimate. Clarissa clung to his shoulders as he increased the pace of his sexual assault, bringing her closer and closer to the unknown promise she longed to claim.

His kisses became more demanding as their bodies strained toward the inevitable conclusion. Clarissa bit her lip to keep from crying out when he lifted her legs higher around his waist, increasing the angle of his penetration. His body pressed more deeply into her, his hips pushing her down into the lush feather mattress as he forced her past the point of sanity and into the realm of shivering, simmering sensations that danced like flames on a hearth.

"Simon . . ." She whispered his name feverishly, sensing that whatever was happening to her would soon be beyond her control.

"Hold on to me, sweetheart." He brushed the words across her ear as he kissed her. His hands moved over her body with the skill of an artist putting a paintbrush to canvas, stroking and touching with just the right amount of pressure to increase her pleasure. "Don't fight it. Let it happen. Let me have you."

Clarissa couldn't have stopped the sensual glory that exploded in her body any more than she could have stopped the moon from glowing in the midnight sky. The ecstasy poured through her, making her shudder softly in Simon's arms, forcing her eyes to close and her lips to part with a gasp of pure, sweet, indescribable pleasure.

Simon felt the first tremors of his wife's release and speared his hands into her mane of auburn hair draped over the pillows. He plunged into her, deep and hard, savoring the wonderful feel of her female body convulsing around him. His own control was held by a thin unraveling thread, and as Clarissa arched up to meet him, Simon surrendered to his own climax.

SHANNON DRAKE
THE KING'S PLEASURE
ROSANNE BITTNER
TEXAS PASSIONS
ANNE STUART
PRINCE OF MAGIC
NEW YORK TIMES BESTSELLING AUTHOR
JANELLE TAYLOR
WILD WINDS

Eleven

Clarissa awoke to the sound of her husband stoking the fire. The drapes were closed, but a thin sliver of grayish light, seeping through the folds, said dawn was approaching. She stretched like a contented cat, feeling the slight discomfort of her wedding night as she moved under the heavy coverlet that Simon had retrieved from the floor sometime during the night.

His back was to her, and he was gloriously naked. The muscles in his broad shoulders and back rippled as he added wood to the orange-and-blue flames. Unable to avert her gaze, Clarissa watched him with a sense of wonder. Never in her wildest dreams could she have imagined the things Simon had taught her during the night. His lovemaking had been both gentle and insistent as he'd tutored her in the limitless aspects of physical passion. Just thinking about some of the things he had done, the ways he had touched her, kissed her, was enough to bring a flush of embarrassment and exhilaration as he turned to look at her.

"Good morning," he said, strolling to the bed without a bit of shame as Clarissa's sleepy eyes devoured the sight of him.

"Good morning," she replied as the fire leaped

and crackled and the corners of the dim room absorbed the amber light like a sponge soaking up water. Her eyes swept over him as he pulled back the coverlet and joined her again. He was strong and masculine, and for the first time in her life, Clarissa realized that she didn't need to resist a man taking care of her. Simon might be arrogant and prudish in his politics, but he was her man. Her husband. After last night, the word held a new meaning for her. One she would have to reconcile with other aspects of her charitable life once she was fully clothed and thinking rationally again.

"You're even beautiful in the morning," Simon said as he lay on his side, his elbow bent and resting on one of the four original bed pillows. He had used one of them to lift her hips during one of their more demanding couplings.

She tried to read the unspoken emotion in his eyes as he pulled her close but at the touch of his hand, her eyes drifted closed, and she moaned a soft, contented purr of a sound. He stroked her back and legs as his mouth rained kisses over her face and neck. It was all Clarissa could do not to swoon at the incredibly delicious feelings his touch created. The hours that had passed since they'd walked into the bedchamber had been luxurious ones that had taught her body to respond to his every touch.

"Would you like a bath?" Simon asked as his mouth came in contact with an aroused nipple. "I'll draw the water."

The thought of soaking in a hot, steamy tub was almost as tempting as the violent surge of pleasure that assaulted her senses when Simon began suckling on her right breast. Before she could respond to the unexpected question, he was lying on his back, with Clarissa covering him like a blanket. He reached down and arranged her body so she was sitting astride him.

He told her what to do while his hands played havoc with her ability to refuse him anything. He urged her on in a husky whisper. "That's it. Do what comes naturally, sweetheart. Ride me. Hard and fast. Slow and deep. However you want."

It was sometime later when Clarissa remembered the promise of a bath. Simon was resting beside her with a sated smile on his face. Slowly, she got up from the bed and walked into the dressing area, where a robe was hanging from a brass hook. Clarissa slipped it over her naked body, tying the sash loosely about her waist. She went into the marble tiled bathroom and turned on the brass spigots, adjusting the water. While steam overtook the room, fogging the mirror, Clarissa brushed her hair and secured it in a thick knot atop her head. Thoughtfully, she considered the consequences of her wedding night.

Although she had responded to Simon, and he to her, with an uninhibited passion that had frequently caused the posters of the double bed to shake, there was no reason to assume that his feelings toward her had changed. Sharing an exciting desire for each other's bodies wasn't the same as sharing their hearts. Clarissa couldn't let herself forget that her new husband saw their marriage in the same traditional light that her grandfather had viewed his marriage to her grandmother. Simon had said as much last night, reiterating his role as the head of the family and hers as the submissive, subservient wife.

Clarissa also reminded herself that she had married him out of necessity—to keep a portion of her inheritance—but Haven House didn't seem as relevant this morning as it had that day six weeks ago when she'd walked into the library downstairs and laid her grandfather's will on Simon's desk.

She didn't resent the marriage the way former ladies of society might have abhorred being forced to take a husband because of rank and obligation. In fact, Clarissa realized she didn't resent her wedding night. Simon had promised to make it a pleasure, and he had done just that, so much so that she was finding it difficult to separate the necessity of her current circumstances from the love in her heart.

Clarissa turned off the spigot, then untied her robe and let it slide to the floor. She had one foot in the tub when her husband interrupted her with another sleepily spoken "good morning."

She looked at him over her bare shoulder and smiled. Whatever embarrassment she'd felt the first time he'd seen her completely naked was long gone. "I'll be glad to draw you a fresh bath after I'm finished," she offered, sinking into the steamy folds of water.

"That would be a waste of water and time," Simon replied, sauntering over to the tub and grinning down at her. "Besides, I can wash your back much easier if I'm in the tub with you."

Before Clarissa could protest, Simon was pushing her forward and stepping in behind her, his long legs encasing her as he made himself comfortable and drew her back so that she was resting against his hairy chest. "Now, isn't this much more practical? One tub, one husband, and one wife."

"How very efficient of you to think so," Clarissa said as she reached for a bar of scented soap. "However, a lady does expect some privacy."

Simon kissed the back of her neck. "Not when the lady is my wife. There will never be locked doors or secrets between us, my love. I won't allow it."

My love! Clarissa longed to hang on to the words like the ray of hope they seemed to be, but she knew better. Simon had whispered endearments to her all night, but none of them had come from his heart. He had been a man bent on seduction, not love. As for secrets, there were more than he realized. Secrets that had to remain undisclosed.

Clarissa soaped up a soft square of cloth and began washing her arms. When Simon's agile fingers took the soapy rag from her hand, she didn't protest. It was rather nice to be pampered, especially by a man. While her husband's hands and the warm water soothed away the discomforts of her wedding night, Clarissa wondered what the day would bring. She assumed that most newly married couples spent a great deal of time together, but that assumption was grouped with a second assumption that those couples loved each other and therefore wanted to partake of each other's company.

Clarissa knew enough about running a manor house to realize that she would be expected to voice her preferences to the cook as to the evening meals and assign any other duties that she pleased. Except for her slight role in the overall management of the house, which would be handled by Mrs. Talley and Higgins, her time was her own. At Hartford Hall she had occupied the morning hours with rides in the country and the afternoon hours with correspondences between Haven House and Mrs. Quigley in London, but she had to be very discreet now that she was living under Simon's roof. Even with Huxley to help her, she was sure Simon would scan the post, and too many letters, especially ones arriving from Yorkshire, might draw his attention. If she arranged to receive her letters elsewhere, the news would reach her husband in a short time. A proper wife didn't intentionally detour her postal deliveries.

While Clarissa was thinking of the deceptive way she'd have to maintain her business ventures, Simon was thinking about spending the balance of their honeymoon locked in the suite of rooms on the second floor of Sheridan Manor. Clarissa's response had been more than he'd originally wished for, and he couldn't be more satisfied with her at the moment. In fact, the intensity of his happiness surprised him. Simon hadn't expected that much to change once he'd married Clarissa and dispensed with the physical act of making her his wife. But then he hadn't expected making love to her to be akin to finding a small chunk of heaven. Rather than taking her virginity with gentlemanly finesse, then returning to his own room to sleep a sated sleep, he'd remained in her bed, unable to satisfy the need she aroused more desperately after having her than before. Even now, only a few minutes after having her ride him to a shattering climax that had left him gasping for breath, he could feel his body responding to her. He'd never let his sexual appetites rule his common sense, but he found it increasingly difficult to ignore the naked woman resting so casually against his bare chest. She was magnificent, all warm pale skin and dark russet hair. And her eyes. The more responsive she became, the more brilliantly they glowed. Seeing her in the first light of day, drowsy and obviously satisfied, her eyes had reminded him of an amethyst bracelet he had once considered purchasing for one of his previous mistresses. They had also reminded him of the sapphire necklace still tucked in the pocket of his smoking jacket.

He would give her the necklace this morning. There was an old hunting lodge on the northern edge of the manor property. It would be the perfect place for a late-morning tryst. Isolated and secluded, he could hold Clarissa in his arms until she ried out loud with pleasure. The thought brought smile to Simon's face as his wife instructed him to ub her back a little harder because it felt so good.

Simon did as she requested, but a nagging hought in the back of his mind warned him that heir blissful relationship would be short-lived. larissa had become much too independent over he last few years, and although he admired her pirit, Simon had no intention of letting her coninue on an unconstrained path. She had to learn hat his role as her husband went beyond the conines of the bedchamber. He didn't want to totally lominate her, but he did want her to rely on him. s he rubbed the soapy cloth over her shoulders nd down her back to the lush curves of her hips nd buttocks, he told himself that it was only natual to want to keep her tucked under his wing. His ossessive attitude had nothing to do with the feelngs she stirred in him. Feelings that had become nore intense and even more indefinable since sharng a bed with her.

"Would you like to go riding this morning?" he sked, then amended his inquiry by asking if she as too uncomfortable to enjoy an outing in the hick forest and open meadows that made up the ulk of his Coventry estate.

"I'd very much like to get outside in the sunhine," Clarissa told him. "I always rode at Hartford Iall. It was a morning tradition, of sorts."

"I hope you rode with an escort," Simon stated, lready knowing the answer wouldn't be in the afrmative.

"Rarely," Clarissa replied honestly. "I preferred ne privacy of my own company."

Simon dropped the cloth into the water, then eached around to turn Clarissa's head so that she as looking at him over her shoulder. "I'm afraid ou will have to seek your privacy within the confines of this house from now on, madam. If you are not riding with me, then at least two grooms or Mr. Pearsall, the stable master, will accompany you. You are not to ride alone. Is that clear?"

"I should have known." Clarissa sighed wearily, rolling her eyes toward the frescoed ceiling and the band of naked cherubs resting their plump elbows on puffy white clouds. "The tyrant assumes his throne with the rising sun."

"The restrictions I place on you will be few, but they will obeyed," Simon said in his most authoritative voice. "To do otherwise will place your beautiful bottom in a very vulnerable position. Is that clear?"

Clarissa left the tub with an indignant splash that left Simon wiping the water out of his eyes. She snatched up the silk robe and stomped out of the room, unaware that the soft fabric was clinging suggestively to the very posterior her husband had just threatened to abuse.

The new Lady Sheridan couldn't remember the last time she'd been so furious. Pacing the floor and leaving a trail of wet footprints behind her, Clarissa fumed under her breath. On her fourth turn across the red-and-gold carpet, she found her husband leaning smugly against the door to the dressing area, clad in a white linen towel.

"I see my lady's temper came up with the sun as well," Simon mocked her in an arrogant tone that came close to shredding the last of his wife's control.

"Your lady's temper is hot enough to boil tea," she shot back at him. With her hands on her hips, she glared at the man she was silly enough to love. "I will not be threatened or treated like a child. It's preposterous! And degrading, not to mention insulting. I won't stand for it. Have I made myself clear?"

Simon strolled across the room, discarding his

towel along the way before stooping down to retrieve the black trousers he'd shed in the heat of passion. "The only thing you've made clear is your tendency to demand things that aren't in your realm to demand," Simon replied patiently.

"I will not allow you to—"

"Spank you." Simon supplied the humiliating word. "I don't doubt it," he added with a smile, envisioning the fight he would have on his hands if he ever did put Clarissa across his lap. "But that doesn't mean it won't happen. The possibility is entirely up to you, madam. As for being preposterous, I assure you, gentleman have been spanking disobedient ladies since the beginning of time. It may be insulting, but it's perfectly acceptable and as legal as any husband's decision to restrict his wife's freedom if he decides her actions are a threat to her safety and well-being."

"Of all the ridiculous logic," Clarissa stammered, so mad she could spit. "If this is your opinion of a husband assuming his responsibility, then I fear we will have a very short marriage, my lord. I will not be threatened or intimidated."

Simon finished buttoning his pants. He was wise enough to keep his amusement to himself as he looked at his new wife. "As I said, madam, the choice is yours. Disobey the few rules I impose and pay the consequences or do the logical, obedient thing and keep your very spankable bottom safe and sound."

Simon watched her eyes turn a deep violet as she jerked the sash of her robe more tightly around her waist. She was undoubtedly the most gorgeous creature he'd ever seen, especially when she was seething with anger. He was sorely tempted to carry her back to bed and prove to her that his male strength could easily overpower her female temper. It was only one of the many interesting ideas running through his mind as Clarissa respectfully asked him to get the bloody hell out of her room so she could dress.

"I don't approve of ladies using crude language," he noted in a matter-of-fact tone. "I suggest you rid yourself of the habit as well as your preference to ride without an escort."

"Crude!" Clarissa hissed the word at him. "How dare you call me crude after what you've said to me this morning."

She couldn't believe this was happening. She'd always suspected that Simon was much too rigid for a man of his age, but actually threatening to take her over his knee was beyond belief. Some men might still think the abusive action respectable and acceptable, but she couldn't fathom her husband being one of them. Yet Simon sounded sincere in his threat to force her to accept the *few* restrictions he seemed determined to impose on her.

He was heading for the door to the sitting room when Clarissa stopped him with a question. "Just how many restrictions make a few?"

Simon turned around to face her. "Three or four."

"I see." She was surprised that her voice sounded normal. She felt like screaming the roof down. "And what would they be?"

He gave her a pensive look before replying. "As I have said, you will not ride without the appropriate escort either here or in London. You will not take up the fashionable art of flirting with other gentlemen."

"I have never flirted in my life!" she raved at him. "Of all the insulting—"

Simon cut her short as he continued reciting what he considered a very reasonable list of demands. "You will behave in the manner and fashion expected of a woman of your rank and social status. I will not tolerate a fractious wife."

The item covered a lot of territory, especially when it was applied to a young, freethinking woman who believed in speaking her mind without hesitation. Clarissa was about to point out to her arrogant husband that the last restriction was akin to a prison sentence when he surprised her with one more.

"And you will never lie to me. Any falsehood, no matter how slight, will gain you the very thing you wish to avoid. I detest dishonesty, especially between a man and his wife."

Although she hadn't actually lied to him so far, Clarissa doubted if she'd be able to conceal her unorthodox charitable endeavors and the business ventures Mrs. Quigley had hired Lionel Nebs to investigate without coming very close to the disastrous boundaries Simon was setting.

"They aren't unreasonable conditions," Simon said, seeing the disapproving expression on Clarissa's lovely face. "Now, if you'll excuse me, I need to dress as well. I will have Mrs. Talley serve breakfast in an hour. After that, I will introduce you to Mr. Pearsall, the stable master, and you can select a mare for our morning ride. There are several that should suit you."

Clarissa was unsure if she should be happy that Simon's restrictions were so few or furious that they literally built a wall around her. The one that confused and infuriated her the most was the second. How could Simon possibly think her capable of *flirting?* She'd never been overly fond of any gentleman's company, and after the verbal exchange she'd just had with her husband, Clarissa doubted if she could muster up enough fondness for Simon to last through the morning meal.

Dressed in a fawn-colored riding habit and shiny black boots that hugged her calves, Clarissa descended the staircase. Prissy had told her that the earl frequently took his morning meal in the small dining room that opened onto the east garden. Still angry over the casual way Simon had threatened her backside if she strayed from the straight and narrow, Clarissa greeted the flock of servants in the foyer, polishing and scrubbing. She offered them a cordial smile and a pleasant "good morning" before joining her husband for breakfast.

The small, informal dining room where Higgins was serving breakfast smelled of delicate flowers, with an underlying fragrance of beeswax and fresh spring air. The butler pulled out her chair, seating her a good ten feet away from her husband, who had yet to acknowledge her presence. Simon had his head buried in a London newspaper. Clarissa didn't mind. She needed a cup of tea to fortify her spirits before confronting her husband again.

Once a plate of fluffy scrambled eggs and thinly sliced sausages had been placed in front of her, she dismissed the butler with a thank you and went about eating her breakfast. The dining room door closed in conjunction with the lowering of the newspaper, and Clarissa found herself looking into Simon's dark eyes.

"Do you prefer privacy for your meals as well, or would you like some conversation?"

"What I would like is for you to stop treating me as if I'm a sulking child," she replied a bit too tartly for Simon to think that she'd gotten over her upset. "I'm quite capable of eating a meal without any more of your patronizing dialogue."

"Drink your tea," Simon told her, undaunted by her response. "Perhaps it would soothe your frazzled disposition."

It was on the tip of Clarissa's tongue to tell her handsome, dictatorial husband a thing or two, but she decided a second argument on an empty stomach was one too many. She ate her breakfast, doing her best to resist asking Simon for the paper when he finally put it aside.

At the opposite end of the cherry-wood table, Simon sipped a second cup of tea and decided that he'd never wake up bored again. When he was in residence at the manor house, he usually rose early, spending a good part of the morning riding about the estate. He returned for lunch and then secluded himself in the library to attend to correspondence and ledgers. It was refreshing to have that routine interrupted, especially by a fiery wife who was quickly discovering that she hadn't gained everything with her bold marriage proposal that she had assumed she would. All in all, Simon was very pleased with how things were going. He'd shown Clarissa a blissful wedding night, teaching her in the course of events that passion wasn't something to be ashamed of, and he'd also let her know that becoming a husband hadn't changed his status. He was still master of his own home.

He reached inside the jacket of his hacking coat to touch the small velvet pouch holding the sapphire necklace. Looking at his wife now, sitting quietly at the opposite end of the table, doing her best to ignore him, Simon couldn't wait to get her away from the house and all to himself. He'd give her the necklace at the hunting lodge, after he disposed of her riding habit and before he made love to her again.

"If you're finished eating, we can go for our morning ride," he said, coming to his feet.

"That would be nice," Clarissa replied. She knew enough about human nature and arrogant men, having lived with her grandfather for over fifteen years, to know that it was too soon to resurrect the difference of opinion she and Simon had had upstairs. It was a beautiful day, and she was anxious to be outside, enjoying it. For the time being, she was willing to let Simon think he'd had the last word.

The stable master was waiting for them. Mr. Pearsall was a tall, thin man with friendly blue eyes and a jovial smile. He was wearing stained breeches and scuffed boots, with an unlit pipe dangling from the corner of his mouth. He was leading a wide-chested bay stallion. The animal pranced and danced, its hooves clicking loudly on the cobblestone drive that circled from the main house to the stables. An indignant snort and a restless toss of the stallion's head proclaimed his impatience at having to wait for his owner.

"He's beautiful," Clarissa said, admiring the thoroughbred. The animal stood a good sixteen hands high, with a glossy black mane and a long, flowing tail.

"His name is Prancer," Simon told her with a undeniable tone of pride.

"It suits him," Clarissa said laughingly as the stallion took a sidestep that caused Mr. Pearsall to take a firmer grip on the reins.

"And what mount should I be saddlin' for her ladyship?" the stable master asked, transferring the stallion's reins to the earl.

"I think Venus," Simon replied, "but I promised the lady she could choose for herself."

"Right this way, yer ladyship," Pearsall said, taking off his plaid cap with a flourish and motioning her toward the large double doors of the stable. "We've got a fine bevy of mares here at Sheridan. I'm not a bit partial in sayin' you won't find a better horse in all of England."

While Simon gave his stallion a few words of praise, Clarissa followed Pearsall into the large, well-kept barn. Black wrought-iron gates separated the mounting and grooming area from the private stalls. The pungent scent of fresh hay, leather, and horses assaulted her nostrils as she looked around, impressed by the stable's size and its selection of riding mounts. Her eyes were immediately drawn to a strawberry mare with a pale mane and tail.

"That be Venus," Pearsall told her. "She's a good mare, she is. And a good runner. A bit too feisty for some ladies, but I think she suits you."

Clarissa smiled at what she interpreted as a compliment. "She's beautiful. And yes, I'd like to ride her."

"I'll have her saddled right away," she was told.

Clarissa wandered about the stables while two grooms rushed to do Pearsall's bidding. She stopped to admire a superbly built hunter with a white blaze interrupting his otherwise majestic black coat as well as another mare. The second mare wasn't as striking as the strawberry mare, but her conformation attested that she was just as expertly bred.

By the time she mounted, Clarissa was in fine spirits. The morning fog had been burned away by a rich vanilla sun, and the lush greenery of the Coventry countryside soon had her thinking more pleasant thoughts. True to her reputation, Venus was a good runner, and she had no trouble keeping up with Simon's stallion. After a few minutes of observing the way Clarissa handled the mare, Simon relaxed, seeing that his wife was an excellent rider and he needn't fear that she'd end up being tossed over the mare's head or dumped onto the dew-dampened ground. After a lively jaunt across a meadow dotted with wildflowers, they crossed a narrow stream. Simon turned down a bridle path, leading the way toward an unknown destination. Nothing had been said between them since leaving the stables, both apparently content to enjoy the fresh air and the freedom of being out of doors.

Riding slightly behind him because the thick

branches of stout oaks and graceful elms prohibited the width of the path, Clarissa observed her husband in silence. He was as magnificent as the stallion he rode. Both man and animal were lean and powerfully built, exhibiting the best of their gender.

Her husband chose that exact moment to look over his shoulder at her, and Clarissa hoped that her thoughts wouldn't betray her. No matter how familiar she'd become with Simon's good looks, she couldn't see him now without remembering how it had been between them last night. If she closed her eyes, she could still feel the heat of his powerful body, moving over her, teaching her things that could bring a blush to her face if she dallied on the thought too long. It had been astonishing, their joining, and Clarissa couldn't help but feel enthralled by the idea of having Simon make love to her again.

Her husband stopped abruptly, his stallion pawing the soft ground at the edge of a clearing. She nudged her mare forward and looked at an abandoned building. Wild ivy had taken over the oblong stone structure, covering it in a tangle of green leaves and twisted brown vines. Winter storms and the rain that fell as predictably as a maid serving up tea in the afternoon had eliminated most of the shingled roof. Unpainted wooden shutters sagged over the narrow windows, and the door, once thick and sturdy, now hung haphazardly from rusty hinges.

The style of the building, or what was left of it, told Clarissa that she was looking at an old hunting lodge. One that had probably seen the presence of England's first virtual prime minister, Robert Walpole, who had been a close friend and confidant of the second earl of Sheridan.

"It's a bit run-down," Clarissa remarked.

"A bit," Simon said noncommittally, then nudged

his stallion forward. He had played in the old lodge as a child, and it brought back fond memories of a time when he hadn't been concerned with Parliament or the obligations of his rank. "Let's have a look, shall we?"

They rode closer, then dismounted and walked through the tall grass. Clarissa could feel the tension mounting between them as Simon tied the horses to a sprawling hawthorne bush and pushed open the door of the deserted lodge. Once inside, Clarissa wiggled her nose at the musty smell of neglect that had overtaken the building. Gone were the lavish draperies and tapestries that had once decorated the walls. The only furnishings that were left behind were a long, battered table and a set of benches, pushed against the far wall. The massive fireplace, constructed from creek rock and mortar, lay cold and empty, but her lively imagination could envision what the lodge was like once upon a time, filled with boisterous hunters with their tankards of ale raised high in salute to the man who had brought down the day's best stag.

"Why did you bring me here?" she asked, looking around her but avoiding Simon's dark eyes.

"I wanted to be alone with you," he replied honestly. He took off his gloves and fanned at the dust that had accumulated on the tabletop.

"We've been alone since we left the stables," she pointed out, feeling a wave of anticipation overtake her.

They stared at each other, the moment filled with what had been left unsaid between them for so many hours. The silent admission that they both had enjoyed their lovemaking seemed to ring through the air like chapel bells on a cold, crisp morning.

"I have something for you," Simon said, reaching into the pocket of his coat.

When her voice came, it was barely more than a whisper. "What?"

Simon reached out and grasped her hand, pulling her toward him. "A token of my appreciation as a husband," he said, withdrawing the velvet pouch and dangling it in front of her.

Loving surprises, Clarissa reached for the pouch, only to have Simon pull it back.

"First a kiss," he said, giving her no time to protest before he covered her mouth with his own.

Clarissa let her arms find their way around his neck as Simon overpowered her senses with his masculine taste and power. Their tongues matched in a wild prelude to what they both knew would happen next. When Simon lifted her onto the table, Clarissa pulled back, but she didn't let go of his shoulders. His hands moved to the front of her riding habit, undoing buttons and pushing the garment aside until he could reach the softer fabric of her under blouse. Her soft moan encouraged him, and more buttons were undone until he was cupping one bared breast in the palm of his hand.

Clarissa gasped in pleasure when he pinched at a hardened nipple. "What about my present?" she said as she arched into the demanding caress.

"Not yet," he said. He closed his mouth over her distended breast, his tongue flicking at the rosy crown until she wiggled on the dusty tabletop, trying to get closer.

The next few moments brought more feverish kisses and Simon's hands pulling and tugging at her riding habit until Clarissa found herself naked and quivering in her husband's arms. Spreading her knees wide with his thigh, Simon reached for the buttons of his trousers while Clarissa's fingers found their way inside the linen shirt covering his chest. It was Simon's turn to moan as her fingernails raked up and down his torso.

"I want you," he said, barely finishing the demand before he joined their bodies with a deep thrust that would have sent Clarissa off the table if he hadn't been clutching her hips.

Outside the deserted lodge, the horses grazed peacefully, and the late morning sun danced through the thick oak foliage. Inside, Clarissa discovered that her husband was as sexually talented in the light of day as he was in the shadows of the night. She cried out his name as her body turned to molten fire, then splintered into a thousand tiny needles of sensation.

When Simon could breathe normally again, he opened the velvet pouch and withdrew the sapphire necklace. "Your eyes look like sapphires after I've made love to you."

Clarissa bit her tongue to keep from pointing out that a man could hardly make love to a woman when he didn't love her, but she didn't think she could win an argument without her clothes on, for they were scattered about the lodge like leaves in a gale. Instead, she thanked Simon for the present and promised herself that one way or the other she'd find the key to her husband's elusive heart.

Twelve

Clarissa touched the sapphire necklace lying against her bare skin. It had been almost two weeks since Simon had taken her to the abandoned hunting lodge and in that short amount of time she'd discovered that her husband wasn't only insatiable, he was very, very creative. At least when it came to the *conditions* of their marriage.

Now, with the house quiet around them and the last embers of the fire dying on the hearth, it was hard to believe that the man sleeping peacefully beside her could be so bold as to lock the library door and make love to his wife on the chaise longue. Not as bold as seducing her in the butler's pantry, of course. That adventure had almost ended with Higgins walking in on them before Simon could get his trousers properly buttoned and Clarissa's bodice back in place. Then there was the morning that he'd decided to forgo breakfast and make love to her until she was so exhausted that she'd practically slept right through to dinner.

But the afternoon they'd spent on the roof would be one Clarissa wasn't likely to forget. The memory of the sensual escapade could still bring a blush to her face. Simon had enticed her to the top of the house, telling her that the view was spectacular and she simply had to see it. Once the door, used by the chimney sweeps, had been locked, he had pulled her to the center of the rambling rooftop and kissed her resistance away. It wasn't until she'd been lying on her back, with her skirts bunched up around her waist and her husband's handsome face looming over her, that Clarissa realized just how innovative the earl of Sheridan could be. Their lovemaking had been frantic, and toward the end, Simon had covered her mouth to keep her cries of ecstasy from being heard by everyone on the estate.

Clarissa shifted in the large bed, easing up on her elbow and looking down at her husband's face. He was such a handsome man, and in slumber, with his dark hair tousled over his forehead and his features relaxed, he reminded her of a naughty little boy, exhausted by too much mischief. She reached out to stroke his right shoulder, and he mumbled her name as he found her nude body under the coverlet and instinctively pulled her closer. The gesture brought a smile to Clarissa's face, and she couldn't help but wonder if some of the ardor she'd experienced at her husband's greedy hands during the last two weeks couldn't be attributed to his *feeling* something for her besides lust.

Was a man interested only in lust so demanding of his wife's constant attendance that she didn't have time to write a letter or finish the first chapter of the book she'd been reading the day he'd locked the library door and insisted that she kiss him? Would a man interested only in his own physical pleasure make every kiss he shared, every caress he gave, so intensely rewarding that his wife couldn't deny him no matter the time or place? Surely not.

Simon might not love her, but he felt something for her. Clarissa was sure of it. It was trying to figure out what that "something" was that had her staring at the fringed canopy of the bed and wondering what would happen once the honeymoon was over and they returned to London so that Simon could finish up some business before beginning a tour of the properties he had accumulated by taking a wife. Would the fire of their passion be squelched by the presence of English politics being discussed in the gentlemanly clubs that kept a husband out until all hours of the night? Would the feelings that seemed to explode with each touch they shared fade to memories as London once again consumed her husband's time and energy?

"It's almost dawn," Simon mumbled. "You should be asleep."

"I was thinking," Clarissa said as she snuggled closer within the warmth of his embrace.

"About what?"

"About things?"

Simon opened one skeptical brown eye and stared at her. "What things?"

Clarissa shrugged. "Just things."

He pinned her to the bed with a powerful sweep of his right leg and looked down at her. "What things, and why do they have you brooding when you should be sleeping?"

Clarissa purposely avoided his gaze as she wiggled, trying to get more comfortable. She should be ashamed of herself for forgetting the real reason she'd married Simon. She needed to think about Haven House and its ladies. She needed to concentrate on her work there and accept the fact that the man hovering over her like a hungry hawk didn't have to love her to make love to her.

"Clarissa . . ." Her name was an impatient question.

"I was thinking about London," she ground out. "About the last party before the city loses its noble inhabitants and why you accepted the invitation. I thought you didn't like parties."

"I don't," he said. "But this party is different. Or at least the guest list is different."

"Who's on the list?" she asked, her curiosity piqued, as it always was when she realized that Simon had been keeping things to himself. The dreadful man couldn't seem to grasp the concept of partnership.

"A friend of mine, recently arrived from America," he mumbled while he trailed a path of moist kisses over her collarbone and down toward a plump, ripe breast.

"An American!" Clarissa sat up in spite of her husband's affectionate attention. "You actually know someone in America? How wonderful."

Simon let out a frustrated sigh as his head fell back onto the pillow. "Only you, my rash wife, would consider America wonderful. It's an unpredictable country, if you ask me."

"It's wild and full of adventure," she scolded him lightly. "Why, one of the books I read said that women actually own and control thousands of acres in the western part of the continent. Imagine being able to ride for days and days without ever leaving the security of your own land. It must be thrilling."

"The country isn't that wild anymore," Simon pointed out. "They have trains and constables to enforce the law."

"Marshals," Clarissa corrected him. "In the west constables are called marshals, and they carry guns. I've always wanted to travel to America. Do you think . . ."

"No," Simon stopped her. "I have no interest in traveling abroad, and if I did, it wouldn't be to America."

"Why not?" she challenged him. "Don't tell me that the American lack of respect for titles and English nobility frightens you. I would think that a man of your confidence would find the country as inviting as the colonists who eventually rebelled against old Georgie."

"You're the only rebel in the Sinclair household," Simon told her. He didn't speak again until Clarissa was lying under him, her eyes bright with fresh-kissed passion and her hands clinging to his naked shoulders. "Now, back to my original conversation. A man, who just happens to be an American, will be attending Lord Criswell's dinner party. I've known Garrett Monroe for a good many years. We share a few common investments, one of which is a textile mill in Wakefield. He's in London to attract some investors in a business endeavor he is currently organizing in San Francisco, and I am taking advantage of the situation to refresh our friendship and discuss the possibility of investing in the American enterprise myself. Since marrying a very beautiful but somewhat audacious young lady, I find myself with money to spare."

Clarissa pounded his shoulder with her fist, but Simon only laughed. He kissed her again, and it was much later in the morning before she remembered that her husband had said a "textile mill in Wakefield." Wakefield wasn't all that far from Haven House, and as she stepped into the hot bath Lillian had prepared, Clarissa hoped that she and Simon would never cross paths while traveling in the Yorkshire countryside. Explaining her presence in the northern province could be very awkward.

After a leisurely bath, Clarissa went into the music room. She favored the elegantly decorated room, with its gold draperies and cream-colored furniture, in the early hours of the day. As she expected, shortly after entering the room she was joined by Huxley. The butler had formed an amicable truce with Higgins, and the two men tolerated each other's presence while they served their individual masters. Thankful that Simon had decided to spend the morning in Coventry, attending to some local business, Clarissa greeted Huxley with a bright smile and a summons to close the door behind him so they could have some privacy.

"Have you heard from Mrs. Flannigan?" Clarissa asked, anxious to find out if the newest arrival at Haven House was settling in properly.

"A letter came by yesterday's post," the butler informed her as he poured tea into a fragile China cup decorated with blue flowers and tiny hummingbirds. "All is well, or so the housekeeper informs us. Miss Eldridge has recovered from her journey and is getting along quite nicely."

"Thank goodness," Clarissa remarked. "Although I didn't see her during the interview, I sensed a certain frailness to her voice. I suspect she is more remorseful of her condition than most. I wonder if the man who fathered her child is as guilt-ridden as Miss Eldridge."

Huxley retrieved Mrs. Flannigan's letter from the inside pocket of his jacket and handed it to Clarissa. "I'm not sure the frailness you attribute to Miss Eldridge has anything to do with guilt," the butler commented. "During our trip to Yorkshire, I found the young lady very determined in her plan to deliver a healthy child and to keep that child at her side, no matter the cost."

Clarissa gave his remarks a thoughtful going-over in her mind before responding. "Then perhaps the weakness I detected was due to the initial embarrassment of having to seek help for her situation. I hope so. It takes a strong woman to raise a child alone. I can give the ladies a roof over their heads and a safe haven in which to bear their children, but I cannot hold their hands forever. Sooner or later, they have to face the world again. It is then that I fear the most for them."

"You give them more than anyone else thinks to

give," Huxley reassured her. "Much more. You give them back their self-respect. It is a difficult thing to recover once it has been taken away."

"What of the renovations?" Clarissa asked, deciding there was very little she could do about the future happiness of her *ladies*. Especially since she had so little control over her own happiness. All she could do was hope that one day Simon would whisper the words "I love you" as fervently as he currently announced his physical desire for her.

"The painting is almost complete," the butler replied, unaware of Clarissa's private train of thought. "Mrs. Flannigan is satisfied with the work and feels confident that the nursery will be ready by summer's end."

"Excellent. And have we word from Mrs. Quigley? What of Lionel Nebs and his investigation? Has he found a suitable site for a seaside investment?"

"Of that I am uncertain, my lady," Huxley informed her. "I will send an inquiry if no news arrives by post this week."

"Dispatch a letter either way," Clarissa instructed him. "I want to meet with Mrs. Quigley as soon as possible after my arrival in London. If Mr. Nebs is unsuccessful in finding a suitable piece of property in the south, then we shall look elsewhere. I'm convinced that a resort will be a profitable venture, and I want to make sure we acquire the property within the year."

The remainder of the morning was spent discussing plans for expanding the gardens at Haven House to include a small fruit orchard and the possibility of diversifying her charities to include a home for retired servants. It was customary for the aristocracy to give an elderly servant with a loyal record a generous retirement bonus, but there were a sizable number of the servants who had no home to return to when the time came for them to step down from their duties. Knowing Huxley was such a servant, Clarissa had always harbored a secret desire to provide him with comfortable surroundings, where he could live out his life. Noting that the butler received the concept with an approving nod of his head, Clarissa instructed him to mention the idea in his next letter to Mrs. Quigley. Now that she was confident of the funding for such an endeavor, Clarissa was anxious to see her dream become a reality.

It was late afternoon when Simon returned home to find his wife in the east garden. The setting reminded him of the first day that she'd come to Sheridan Manor, armed with her grandfather's will and a marriage proposal that had both outraged and intrigued him.

Seeing her now, dressed in a light gray skirt and white silk blouse, her auburn hair reflecting the sunlight and her long, elegant fingers touching the petals of a yellow rose, Simon was stunned by the fierce emotion that gripped him. For one heart-throbbing moment he wasn't sure what he was feeling except that it was the same intense emotion that overtook him whenever Clarissa surrendered in his arms. He knew the feeling contained more than a small portion of pride. What man wouldn't be proud to call such a beautiful woman his wife?

Content to remain in the shadows of the portico a while longer, Simon studied his wife's features. He'd seen that expression before. The one that said her thoughts were elsewhere. But where? The question had plagued him more and more in the last few days. He had no intention of breaking his promise and actually inquiring into her personal accounts, but he couldn't help but wish that she trusted him enough to disclose the nature of her private business. What could be so private about her charitable endeavors? Even if she was determined to keep them anonymous, there was no reason not to divulge her activities to her husband.

Simon knew that the real reason for his curiosity lay in his inability to gain Clarissa's unquestionable trust. It bruised his ego to think that he could make her melt in his arms but he'd failed at gaining more than her physical submission. Knowing that he wouldn't be satisfied with anything less than her complete being, Simon stepped out of the shadows and into the late-afternoon sunlight. Clarissa greeted him with a bright smile that vanished the moment he told her they'd be having a guest for dinner.

It wasn't having a guest that upset her as much as the guest they were having.

Lady Martha Wenshaw was the most ruthless gossip in all of England. She was also the most unforgiving person Clarissa had ever had the misfortune of meeting. Married to a man almost three times her age, Lady Wenshaw had inherited a sizable fortune upon the death of her spineless husband. A fortune that she used to her personal advantage. If the lady's reputation as a coldhearted gossip didn't dispel Clarissa's appetite for the evening meal, then Lady Wenshaw's known rudeness toward servants and anyone else she thought beneath her certainly did. She couldn't believe Simon had actually invited the insufferable woman to dinner, and she said as much.

"Her carriage suffered a broken axle as she was traveling through Coventry," he explained, as aware of and as disapproving of the woman's reputation as Clarissa. "Unfortunately, it happened as I was departing a nearby shop. The woman practically fell out of the carriage window trying to hail me. There was little I could do but offer her the comforts of Sheridan Manor until her conveyance is repaired and she is once again on her way to Oxford to visit her nephew."

"You mean she's here now?"

"I had Higgins show her to one of the guest rooms." He laughed at the disgruntled expression that overtook Clarissa's face. "Don't worry. After offering Lady Wenshaw the temporary comfort of my own carriage, I made sure the livery owner was promised a generous bonus if the lady's carriage was ready first thing tomorrow."

The thought of actually having to entertain the wrinkled-faced Lady Wenshaw for more than one day was enough to make Clarissa insist that she needed a nap before dinner. It was going to take all the stamina she could muster to endure the evening ahead.

"I must say, Lady Sheridan," Martha Wenshaw remarked after inspecting the parlor like a general surveying raw recruits, "I have to admire your choice in husbands. The earl is certainly a handsome man."

"I think so," Clarissa replied, forcing a smile. Her handsome husband had retired to his study after dinner, leaving her alone with the plump, overdressed woman who never had a kind word for anyone.

"And to think that he kept your engagement to himself for so long. It's an admirable trait, that. A man's ability to keep a confidence."

"Yes, isn't it," Clarissa responded, knowing Lady Wenshaw was fishing for the details of the unexpected marriage that had taken place only a few weeks ago. Although Simon had been considered an eligible bachelor for some time, society hadn't been prepared for him to wed the earl of Hartford's granddaughter.

"I've always been fond of Simon," the voracious gossip went on. "I was a very close friend of his mother's, you know."

Clarissa didn't know any such thing, and her mouth watered to say those very words to the two-hundred-pound woman whose corset was straining at the seams. Instead, she offered Lady Wenshaw another sip of sherry, hoping the elixir would make the woman sleepy and thus bring a quick end to what was becoming a long, boring evening.

"Have you heard that Viscount Thornton is about to announce for Lady Avondale's hand?" Martha Wenshaw said, smiling around her crooked front teeth. "Of course you haven't. The assumption has only been circulating for a few days, and you've been secluded here in the country."

"If it's an assumption, how can you say that Viscount Thornton is about to do anything?" Clarissa replied in her most courteous voice. "Surely one should wait until an engagement is properly posted before speculating upon its existence."

Lady Wenshaw wasn't deterred by the polite set-down. She walked over to the mantel, taking the time to run her finger along its marble rim to check for dust before looking at her hostess once again. "Everyone knows that Lady Albright is anxious for her son to wed, and Lady Avondale is a most respectable young lady."

"There are many respectable young ladies in London," Clarissa reminded her. "As I recall, the viscount has been seen with several of them on his arm."

"Well, yes, of course." There wasn't a moment's hesitation in her words. "But then everyone also knows that Lord Avondale, Melissa's father, hasn't been well of late, and there's the rumor that his estate is lacking the funds for a proper funeral. One only needs a few facts to turn an assumption into gospel, my dear."

"A few facts is what you seem to be lacking," Clarissa said, knowing she shouldn't allow herself to react so strongly to venomous gossip, but she liked Melissa Avondale. She also knew that Viscount Thornton thought the girl boring and totally ill suited as a candidate to satisfy his mother's quest for a daughter-in-law. He'd said as much to Simon after escorting Lady Avondale to the opera. "Lord Avondale's estate is as healthy as ever, and his daughter has no interest in marrying Viscount Thornton. She's taken with another gentleman, or so she told me herself only a few weeks ago. I sincerely doubt that the announcement you have described is forthcoming."

"Well," Lady Wenshaw stammered indignantly, insulted that anyone, even the new Lady Sheridan, would turn away a bit of juicy gossip. "Time will tell, of course. But I'm better prepared to predict the social future than you, my dear. After all, you've hardly been out and about, have you? What with your grandfather's death and the earl's inclination to place his privacy ahead of his social obligations."

The verbal jab at her husband's decision to keep the parties they'd attended to a minimum during her recent visit to London wasn't missed. Simon had been very discreet in accepting invitations, and blessedly they'd been able to avoid Lady Wenshaw until today. Coming to her feet in a rustle of royal blue satin and black lace, Clarissa was about to excuse herself from the room when Simon came strolling into the parlor.

"Madam," he said, wrapping his arm around Clarissa's waist and giving her a kiss on the cheek. "Excuse me for leaving you alone, but I had some business that demanded by attention before the morning post."

Clarissa gave him a disbelieving scowl that turned into an amicable smile when Lady Wenshaw asked the earl's opinion on the state of Viscount Albright's bachelorhood.

"Whatever Albright decides, I wish him all the happiness my own union has given me," Simon replied with diplomatic skill. "I for one find marriage very rewarding."

"That is very apparent," Lady Wenshaw remarked in a censoring tone. "I don't believe I've ever seen a more happily married couple. But then the union is still in its infancy."

Simon met her challenging words with a cold stare as he suggested that the ladies retire for the evening. After all, Lady Wenshaw had to be on her way to Oxford early the next day. Knowing she was being dismissed, their plump guest gathered up the folds of her lime green dress and left the parlor in a flourish of starched petticoats that said she didn't like being sent upstairs like a wayward child. Clarissa was silent until the lady disappeared into the depths of the house. Then she sank into a chair and sighed a breath of relief.

"Someone needs to sew that woman's mouth shut," she remarked.

Simon laughed, then helped himself to a brandy. "For once we are in complete agreement," he replied.

"She insists that Clarence Albright is going to offer for Miss Avondale," Clarissa told him.

Simon laughed. "Clarence likes his women with a little more life than that," he said, clearly amused by the gossip.

Clarissa frowned. "Why is it that men like *their women* to have spirit, yet as soon as those women become their wives, they're quickly told to be obedient? It's sheer hypocrisy, if you ask me."

It was Simon's turn to frown. "I'm not in the

mood for a verbal jousting match," he told her. "Nor am I interested in whomever Albright eventually selects as a wife."

"What does interest you?" Clarissa challenged, knowing that Simon enjoyed their debates as much as she did. He was a born politician. "Surely you want your friend to be content in his marriage. You said as much to Lady Wenshaw."

"Of course I want Albright to be content. And I'm sure he will be."

Clarissa almost asked if Simon was as content as he'd professed to their house guest, but she already knew the answer. Of course he was. And why shouldn't he be. He had a wife who melted in his arms every time he touched her, along with a sizable fortune that was likely to grow larger under his keen supervision. The man had to be deliriously happy. While she, on the other hand, was growing more miserable with each passing day.

As always, when they were alone, the room assumed an air of tension. Simon leaned against the mantel, sipping his brandy and staring at Clarissa. Her heart began to beat erratically as his gaze took on a warm glow that promised another night of lovemaking.

"The evening is warm," he announced unexpectedly. "Shall we walk in the garden?"

Clarissa fiddled with the fringe on one of the settee's pillows. She knew Simon was up to no good when he set down the brandy glass and held out his hand. Like so many of the invitations he'd extended in the last two weeks, they had a double meaning.

She accepted his hand, and a few moments later they were in the garden. Clarissa looked toward the heavens. Here and there a star twinkled brightly, its light finding a way through the heavy clouds that covered the moon and promised rain before morning. In spite of a brisk breeze, the air was unusually warm for this time of year, or perhaps it was the heat of her husband's hand that was keeping her warm. Either way, Clarissa allowed the natural mystery of the night to banish her worries as Simon led her toward the small fountain in the center of the garden.

Once there, he turned to face her. His hands untied the light woolen shawl that covered her shoulders, revealing the sapphire necklace. After little more than one passionate kiss, Clarissa was clinging to him, as greedy as Simon for the pleasure they always found together.

His mouth closed over hers again as his hands found the buttons at the back of her dress and began undoing them with an agility that said he was impatient to see her skin bathed in moonlight. When his mouth moved to her ear and he whispered that he wanted to make love to her while the breeze cooled their skin and the moon paid witness to their passion, Clarissa couldn't find the words to protest, although she did remind him that Lady Wenshaw's room overlooked the garden.

"Excellent." He chuckled. "It will give the old hag something to talk about for a good, long time to come."

"What of your reputation as a gentleman?" Clarissa goaded him as he sweep her up in his arms and started toward one of the marble benches placed at convenient intervals along the garden's meandering walkways.

"I stopped being a gentleman the day I married you," he told her. "I find I like being a husband much better."

When he sat down and pulled her onto his lap, Clarissa looked over her shoulder. The lights in Lady Wenshaw's room were burning brightly, but the overhanging branches of the garden's trees and the night shadows blocked their presence from anyone's invading eyes.

"Stop worrying about propriety and kiss me," Simon demanded in a gruff whisper. "I haven't been able to think of anything but kissing you for several hours now."

Clarissa smiled at the backhanded compliment and did as her husband requested. Her hands grasped his shoulders as he lifted her again, bringing her down so that she was straddling his lap. The full skirt of her dress was pushed out and up, and she could feel the cool texture of his trousers pressing against the center of her body and, beneath the coolness, the hard length of his arousal. Soon everything was warm. Their hands explored, pushing against clothing to find each other and the lightninglike passion that ignited so easily between them.

Clarissa's arms were linked around his neck as Simon struggled to release himself from the confines of his trousers. He cursed. She laughed with the delight of knowing that in this, their most private moments, she at least had the ability to rid him of the stuffy, gentlemanly veneer he painted on for the rest of the world.

When he entered her in a deep thrust that ended the sensual foreplay they always enjoyed beforehand, Clarissa closed her eyes and gritted her teeth to keep the overwhelming pleasure from escaping her with a flamboyant cry of delight.

"God, you feel good," Simon mumbled against her throat. "So good. So damn good."

His hands gripped her derriere, controlling her movements, drawing out the pleasure until Clarissa feared she might faint. She could feel his heartbeat keeping time with her own as he raised and lowered her in an exquisite dance that had them both panting for breath. Somewhere a night bird sang, and Clarissa felt the love within her answer in its own sad tones. The scent of roses mingled with the scent of the man she loved, and the bittersweet fragrance brought a tear to her eye. If only Simon could feel her love, she thought to herself. *How can he hold me like this and not feel it?*

Simon was asking himself another question. Why couldn't he get enough of this woman? What was it about her that called to his body like water to a thirsty man? Why couldn't he keep his hands to himself for more than a few hours? Hours that seemed to last an eternity when she wasn't in the same room with him, her smile lighting up his life like fireworks at a country carnival.

He moved again, filling her and feeling the tight, warm fit of her stealing his control. He didn't want to come now. He wanted this feeling to last forever.

"Please, you're killing me," she said against his mouth.

Simon moaned a response, then lifted her again. "Slowly and quietly," he told her. "I could stay inside you all night."

"I'll die from the pleasure," she confessed weakly.

"Then die for me, sweetheart," he prompted her, his strong hands lifting her again. He brought her down on his hard length and held her there for a moment, letting her feel his heat and the need that had them both hovering on the brink of ecstasy. "Love me, darling. And I'll die with you."

The night exploded in a kaleidoscope of shimmering colors. Silvers and golds and bright reds. The clouds swirled around the moon, and the stars turned into white, hot blossoms of light that floated on the midnight blackness like lily pads on a summer pond. Simon surged deep inside her, giving to her and taking from her all the wonderful things a man and woman could exchange. Their mingled

Thirteen

The magic disappeared with the morning. Rain was drenching the Coventry countryside as Simon and Clarissa bid farewell to Lady Wenshaw. Thankful to see what she hoped was the last of the round-bellied gossip, Clarissa smiled as Huxley served her tea in the music room. But her relief was short-lived when Simon announced that it was time to return to London.

Hiding her disappointment, Clarissa went about preparing for their journey while Simon closed himself in the library. As Lillian readied her trunks, Clarissa walked to the balcony doors of her bedchamber and looked out at the rain. The sky was a deep gray, the clouds so thick and full of moisture that one couldn't tell where the horizon ended and the sky began. The blissful days of her honeymoon were over, and the reality of her marriage loomed ahead of her like an unwanted dose of foul-tasting tonic.

For the last two weeks she had shared Simon's bed and his passion, but she was no closer to knowing the man she had married than she was to understanding why she loved him. After making love to her in the garden, he had carried her upstairs, tucked her under the covers, and told her to have sweet dreams. Then he'd disappeared downstairs, presumably into his library, where he remained far into the night. Although Clarissa had awakened to find him at her side, she admittedly missed falling asleep in his arms.

She sighed, drawing an inquisitive glance from Lillian as the maid carefully folded dress after dress and placed them gingerly into the heavy traveling trunk. While the rain splattered on the balcony, Clarissa began to pace the room. She'd gotten very good at pacing over the years, finding it a physical release for all the secrets she was forced to keep to herself, secrets she longed to share with her husband but didn't dare.

There was still so much to be done. At times it seemed as though the more she tried to help people, the more people there were to help. Still, she couldn't let the scale of the problem keep her from doing what she could. Nor could she allow her husband's restrictive reasoning to keep her from the tasks at hand. Focusing on the resort she hoped to open and staff with socially acceptable widows, Clarissa stopped pacing the room and went in search of her husband.

For some inexplicable reason, she had to see him, needed the reassurance of his dark gaze and the crooked smile he frequently gave her whenever she came upon him unexpectedly. She was just outside the library door when she heard Simon's voice, not raised in anger but plainly angry.

"Have her dismissed at once," he said. "I'll not tolerate that kind of behavior."

Clarissa paused, her ear to the door, her breathing soft and hopefully silent as she tried to discern if one of the staff had been caught stealing.

"What of the man?"

Clarissa recognized the questioning voice as belonging to Mr. Dobbins, the estate steward.

"What of him?" Simon asked dryly. "Since he already has a wife, it's impossible for him to take another. Besides, the girl should have known better. She admitted that she wasn't forced. Her fate is her just reward. Give her a month's wages and show her to the gate."

Clarissa felt her heart sink to the vicinity of her knees. She didn't need to hear anything else to realize that one of the young ladies in Simon's employment had overstepped the boundaries of good sense and gotten herself into the worse kind of trouble.

Taking a quick breath to compose herself, Clarissa turned the brass doorknob and made a regal entrance, feigning surprise that she'd interrupted her husband's conversation with his steward. "Excuse me, gentlemen," she apologized immediately.

"That is all." Simon dismissed Mr. Dobbins with a wave of his hand.

The steward walked by Clarissa, giving her a respectful nod of his head as he took his leave. Once the door was closed again, Clarissa approached her husband's desk. She stood in front of the mahogany fortress, smiling demurely, while her husband locked the desk drawer he had opened to withdraw the unwanted servant's final wages.

"I didn't mean to interrupt," Clarissa said.

"Our business was finished," Simon said rather abruptly. Realizing that his anger was still showing, he immediately pushed the unsavory business from his mind and pocketed the key to his desk. "To what do I owe your lovely but unexpected appearance?"

Clarissa kept her frown from showing as she walked to the window. She didn't need to be reminded that a man's library was his personal domain, especially a man like her husband. Of course, he hadn't minded her company the day he'd made love to her on the chaise longue. Turning away from the window and any reminders that might weaken her resolve to do something for the unfortunate young lady who was about to be cast out into the inhospitable weather, Clarissa gave her husband another smile. "I didn't mean to eavesdrop," she began, "but it was impossible not to comprehend some of the unpleasantness you and Mr. Dobbins were sharing. Have you been forced to dismiss one of the servants?"

"It's nothing to be concerned about," Simon answered her. "An unpleasant affair, to be sure, but not one that you need to become involved in."

Clarissa bit back a blunt retort, changing her tactics to meet the situation. "I am mistress of Sheridan Manor now, my lord. If a servant has earned a dismissal, I think it only right that I should know about it. After all, when you are absent from the house, it will fall upon me to make similar decisions in the future."

"I certainly hope not," Simon remarked. "My reaction should set an example that won't need to be repeated in the future."

"What happened? Did Mr. Dobbins catch one of the servants stealing the silver?"

"It's unimportant now," her husband replied in a brisk tone that said the subject was closed.

"I must insist," Clarissa challenged him.

"Insist, madam?"

"Really, Simon, don't be such a prude," she chided him lightheartedly. "I managed my grandfather's home for years. If one of the servants has done something to warrant their being tossed out on their ear, then so be it. I am merely asking to have the circumstances explained to me."

"Very well." He sighed heavily. "But it's an unsavory thing to discuss with one's wife."

"Ahhh . . ." Clarissa gave him a wicked smile. "One of the maids had a lover's quarrel with one of the footmen, and she bashed the poor man over the head with a family heirloom. Tell me, which silver platter was dented? Not the one your mother received from the queen. The one Higgins covets like the Holy Grail."

"It's a little more consequential than a dented platter."

"What?" Clarissa wasn't about to give up. She knew if she asked Lillian, the answers to her questions would be served up with afternoon tea, but she didn't want to hear gossip from a maid. She wanted her husband to share something besides passion with her. She wanted him to share the day-to-day events of their lives. Nothing miraculous, mind you. Just the normal, average things that husbands and wives all over the world shared.

"A maid has gotten herself pregnant," he said bluntly.

Clarissa gave a soft laugh. "The deed requires a partner, my lord. A male partner."

"It is no laughing matter," Simon said harshly. "I dislike having to dismiss anyone."

"But you dismissed the maid," she pointed out. "Not her partner in crime, so to speak. A bit unfair, don't you think?"

"Are you questioning my solution? Of course I dismissed her. I can't let—"

"What?" she interrupted him. How long had she been fighting the very indifference that her husband was justifying? "You can't let a woman get away with being indiscreet while, on the other hand, the man keeps his job and the security of knowing that no matter how many times he unbuttons his trousers, the earl will understand and see that his wages are dispensed on a regular basis."

"Henry has been in my employ for several years.

He has a wife and two sons. The girl knew the possible consequences of her actions and chose to ignore them."

"And Henry didn't?" she snapped back at him, unable to hide her disgust over the situation a moment longer. "But then it's always that way, isn't it? The woman bears the consequences and the bastard child, while the man goes about his business like a saint on Judgment Day."

Simon took a menacing step toward her. "That is enough."

"I'm afraid it isn't nearly enough, my lord," Clarissa replied calmly. "The topic may be unsavory, but it's necessary. I do know what goes on between a man and a woman when passion rules the moment. Or have you forgotten that you made love to me in this very room?"

"You are my wife."

"Yes. And Henry should have shared his passion with *his* wife instead of seducing an unmarried girl."

Simon blinked at her as if she'd grown an enormous wart on the end of her nose. His disbelieving stare was followed by a tightening of his jaw. "This discussion is at an end, madam. I suggest you take yourself upstairs. Now."

"I won't be sent upstairs like a wayward child."

Simon admired his wife's spirit, but he wasn't about to let her get away with being disrespectful. "The girl is on her way out of this house. And you are on your way to—"

"I am not questioning your authority," she told him. "I am merely trying to point out that it is unfair to dismiss one lover without dismissing the other. Surely you can see the logic of my reasoning."

"I see no logic at all to this conversation," Simon replied. "A conversation that wouldn't be taking place at all if you deferred to my judgment, as a wife should."

Clarissa knew she was venturing into dangerous territory, but she desperately wanted Simon to reconsider his decision. One that would stand unless she could convince him otherwise. She walked to his side, hoping that he wasn't as coldhearted as he appeared to be at that moment. "Simon, please try to understand. I hate to think of a young girl cast out like a criminal. And what of the babe? Does she have a family who will take her and the child in? Where will she go? What will she do?"

"She should have thought of that before she hiked her skirts in the stable."

Clarissa realized then that she should have handled the situation differently. She should have gleaned the girl's name from one of the other maids and sent Huxley out to find her. Instead, she'd offered her husband a chance to prove himself, hoping against hope that he would try to help the girl instead of throwing her out.

Of course, Simon had no idea that he was being tested. All he knew was that his wife was acting like a raving maniac because he'd done the customary and acceptable thing. She tried one more time to salvage the situation.

"Simon, I'm sure if you give the situation some thought—"

He couldn't believe that his wife was actually arguing with him about a pregnant maid of all things. He spoke over her words. "I've given the situation all the thought it deserves. The girl has been dismissed. The matter is settled."

Simon sat down and opened one of many ledgers scattered across the top of his desk. He paused for a moment and looked up at her as if to ask why she was still standing there. He couldn't recall the last time he'd been this furious. But then he couldn't recall the last time anyone had blatantly argued with him over a household decision. Clarissa hadn't only argued, she'd very eloquently called him a hypocrite. He was tempted to put her over his knee and smack her lovely bottom until she started thinking like a rational human being again. If she had to spend two days in a carriage, sitting on a sore backside, she might be more hesitant to challenge him in the future.

Knowing her husband considered the matter settled, Clarissa raised her chin a stubborn inch and walked out of the room as proudly as she'd walked into it. The library door closed behind her with a soft click that sounded as loud as the ominous chimes of the foyer clock when it struck midnight.

The matter is far from settled, Clarissa said to herself as she went in search of Huxley. She found the butler in the kitchen, discussing a favorite Hartford Hall recipe with the cook. Knowing her far better than Clarissa feared her husband ever would, Huxley had only to catch a glimpse of her expression to know trouble was brewing. He excused himself from the busy kitchen with an apologetic smile and followed Clarissa into the music room. Once they were sealed away from prying ears, she told him what she'd just discovered.

"Do you know which maid it is?" Clarissa asked.

Huxley nodded. "Prissy, my lady. The young maid who attended you until Lillian arrived. I overheard Mrs. Talley and the steward discussing the girl's dismissal this morning. I thought to pick up some information in the kitchen, but you arrived before the cook could tell me the latest gossip."

Clarissa frowned as she sat down on the sumptuous ivory settee. "I tried to talk Simon out of dismissing her, but he wasn't inclined to be forgiving. We argued over it, I'm afraid. I'm also afraid that

I've married a narrow-minded, hardheaded lord of Parliament who—"

"I assume you wish me to intervene in our customary fashion," Huxley inquired, preventing Clarissa from expounding on her husband's faults.

"I don't think our customary methods are going to work in this situation," she replied. "The proximity to my husband's loyal servants and Prissy's family, if she has any, will make whisking her off to Yorkshire too risky."

"What, then?" Huxley asked, knowing Clarissa intended to do something to ease the girl's plight.

"I'm not sure," Clarissa said thoughtfully. "But I intend to so something. The right or wrongness of what Prissy did has nothing to do with the child. If her family's reaction can be gauged by those we've seen in the past, the girl will be sleeping in the woods tonight, rain or no rain." She met Huxley's patient gaze. "Make some discreet inquiries. Find out what you can about the father—Simon called him Henry—and about Prissy's family. If possible, talk to her directly. Make a fatherly inquiry into her welfare and see if she is agreeable to taking another post, one where she can perform minimal duties in exchange for a place to live until the child is born. If she has been thrown out of her home, then offer her enough money to take a room at one of the local inns for the night. There isn't much time. Simon intends to leave for London in the morning."

"Do you think to offer her sanctuary at one of the Hartford estates?"

"All the Hartford estates are Sheridan estates now," she replied sadly, then added, "I'm not sure what I'm going to do with her. But I do know I don't want her seeking out the sort of assistance that could kill both her and the child."

* * *

Clarissa dressed for dinner, but she lacked an appetite for the stuffed goose and glazed carrots the cook had prepared. By the time she descended the staircase, she was thoroughly angry again. Not only at her husband but at the world in general. Huxley had returned a short while ago with the news that Prissy had indeed been cast out by her own family. He'd found the maid in the stables, hiding in an empty stall and planning to sleep there for lack of a better bed.

With his usual finesse, he'd expressed his regret over the situation and gained her trust by offering to pay for a room at one of the local inns. During their brief encounter, he'd also gleaned enough information to reach the assumption that Prissy was too upset over discovering that she was pregnant to think about what she was going to do next. Unsure of what Clarissa's final solution would be, Huxley had left Prissy at the inn, informing her that he would return first thing in the morning and telling her to rest and try to think of the future instead of past mistakes that couldn't be undone.

With only a few hours between now and their departure for London, Clarissa had decided the only solution she had at her fingertips was to send Prissy to the city under Huxley's watchful eye. She'd penned a note to Mrs. Quigley and asked her friend to give the maid a temporary job in the millinery shop until she could find a more long-term solution. Once Prissy had had time to recover from the shock of finding herself with child, being dismissed from her post at Sheridan Manor, and being tossed out into the cold by her very own family, she might be able to think clearly about the babe she was carrying. Then, and only then, could the maid be given the option that Haven House offered.

Life could be so complicated at times. Why were people so unforgiving, and why did they find it easier to harden their hearts than to open their minds? The question had no definitive answer, which made it all the more difficult for Clarissa to put a smile on her face when Simon stepped into the foyer to escort her into dinner.

As usual, Simon looked irresistibly handsome in a dark jacket and white silk shirt, and as usual, the slightest touch of his hand sent a wave of anticipation through Clarissa's body. He had remained in his library most of the day, and this was the first time she'd laid eyes upon him since their verbal confrontation.

"You look lovely," he told her as he sent an approving glance up and down her body. "Although I'm surprised you chose a black gown. After a year of mourning, I would think you would prefer more lively colors."

"Black suits my mood this evening," she replied politely.

He searched her face but found nothing but an innocent composure that would have fooled anyone but him. She was sulking. It was the first normal, predictable thing he'd seen her do since the day she had proposed marriage. It was also extremely irritating. He disliked brooding women who pretended to be fine when they were raging inside. Surprisingly, Simon realized he preferred Clarissa's temper to the charade of indifference she was displaying toward him now. The disagreement they'd had that morning was far from forgotten on both their parts, but he'd decided to approach the evening meal as though it were a new day. Deciding to continue with his plan until Clarissa forced him to resurrect the issue, Simon led her into the dining room, where Higgins and four footmen were waiting to serve them.

"Would you care to join me for a stroll in the

garden after dinner?" he asked as he pulled out the chair and seated her himself.

"I'd rather not," she told him in the same polite tone she'd used in the foyer. "If you still plan on leaving for London in the morning, I should get a good night's rest."

"Ahhh," he whispered as if he'd just found the answer to a perplexing problem. "Has our wedded bliss ended so soon?"

"I find nothing blissful about your attitude toward women," Clarissa told him, keeping her voice low so that the servants wouldn't hear. "In fact I find it just the opposite."

Simon moved to the head of the table without replying. When Higgins stepped forward to serve the first of several courses, he waved the butler aside. "We won't be needing your assistance tonight, Higgins. You may dismiss the others as well. I'll make sure my wife is attended to properly."

Clarissa maintained her cordial composure as two footmen carried dishes from the sideboard to the table and Higgins put the bottle of white wine within easy reach of his employer's hand. Once the door had been closed behind the butler and footmen, Clarissa looked at her husband. Although his instructions had been spoken in a normal tone, she knew that Simon wasn't going to lavish the kind of attention on her that his words had implied. This wasn't going to be an intimate dinner, it was going to be a lesson in accepting her place as his wife. Her submissive, subservient place. A prim, proper wife who accepted her husband's word as law and received any decision he reached as irreversible.

"Would you care for some soup?" Simon asked, ladling some into a small gold-rimmed china bowl.

"No, thank you," she answered, wishing he'd get the anticipated lecture over with so she could retire.

She wouldn't have to feign a headache to avoid his attention. The day's events had her head pounding.

"As you wish," he replied, unfolding his napkin.

"What I wish is for you to stop acting like this is a normal meal. I have no intention of sitting here while you offer me a dish of stewed tomatoes."

"What are your intentions, then? To sit and sulk until the goose is cold and the sorbet has melted?"

The tension between them shimmered like a mirage. She ended the illusion by averting her gaze and reaching for her water glass. Once she'd taken a sip, Clarissa scrounged up her best smile.

"I came down to dinner in hopes that we might have a normal conversation about what happened this morning. I am still upset over it, as you well know, my lord."

"What happened this morning happened. I suggest we put it behind us and move on to a more amenable topic."

"What?" she asked somewhat angrily. "Perhaps you would prefer to discuss Gladstone's campaign for reform or Lord Jonworth's rebuttal to the charges that he's becoming overly concerned with the advancement of the trade unions."

His calm response belied the anger blazing in his eyes. "If a discussion of politics stimulates your appetite, then by all means, let's discuss Gladstone's tendency to forget that as prime minister he is to represent the interests of the entire country, not just a zealous few."

"Gladstone's first loyalty is to the people who restored him to the position of prime minister," Clarissa countered with enthusiasm. If she couldn't argue over the way Simon had handled the dismissal of a maid, then she'd argue for arguing's sake. At least she'd be able to release some of the tension making her neck hurt and her shoulders stiff. "Unlike your esteemed Disraeli, who is so focused on upholding the British Empire in Africa and Asia that he's forgotten the homeland that colonized those territories, Gladstone is at least keeping his attention closer to the shores of our modest isle."

Simon laughed. "Disraeli may be self-indulging, but no one's ever accused him of being narrow-minded. Of course he's concerned with our colonies. And rightfully so. With the increase in tariffs by the United States and Germany, our colonies are more important than ever. They are the backbone of our economic success. A success, I might add, that caused the Hartford coffers to overflow."

"Thus allowing me the indulgence of a personal allowance." Clarissa bridged the gap in the conversation with sarcastic ease. "Are you saying that I should be thankful for Disraeli's preoccupation with everything but the social decay of our society?"

"Social decay!"

"What else would you call it?" she challenged. "The population of our cities is increasing with little regard to the strain it puts on the already overcrowded conditions. The aristocracy is flourishing in its prosperous complacency, while the working class is shut off from the political process and dependent upon the trade unions for what little representation they are allowed. The most needy of our citizens are completely ignored. People are begging on the streets of London, my lord, within sight of Parliament's sacred halls. Women are seeking out illegal abortions instead of bearing children they cannot hope to feed."

Simon put down his fork with a soft click of silver against fine china. "You, madam, have a distinct talent for getting your way. I said any discussion regarding this morning's events was not to be brought to the dinner table."

"I was not referring to Prissy, my lord, but to the general malice of women in poverty. Women who frequently find themselves caught between the desperation to feed the children they already have and the despair of discovering that they are carrying another babe." Never shy when it came to what was important to her, Clarissa didn't allow Simon to interrupt her before she finished what she had to say. "We are too far from London for a country maid to seek out the illegal assistance that prospers in the dark alleys of the East End."

Realizing that Clarissa wouldn't be satisfied until the unsavory issue had been thoroughly aired, Simon gave her an intense frown. "Is that why you were so upset this morning? Do you think the girl will endanger herself by trying to get rid of the child?"

Wishing she could tell Simon that Prissy had been shunned by her own family but knowing she didn't dare without revealing that she'd involved herself in the girl's plight, Clarissa evaded a direct answer. "I'm not sure what a young woman in her situation might or might not do, my lord. Since the father is unable to offer restitution for his actions by marriage, Prissy's options are somewhat limited."

"As they should be," Simon told her. "Consequences are excellent boundaries, madam. Without them civilized society cannot exist."

"Was it civilized to dismiss the woman and indirectly reward the man by ignoring his participation?"

The question pricked more than Simon's temper; it came dangerously close to making him second-guess his decision, something he'd never done before. He'd always dealt with his servants in what he considered a fair and equitable manner. "What would you have me do, madam? Seek out the maid and reinstate her? Or perhaps you think I should take it upon myself to find her a husband. One who would ignore the fact that she is pregnant with another man's child."

It was on the tip of Clarissa's tongue to say the idea had merit. After all, Myles Garfield had married one of her *ladies* under similar circumstances. Seeing the fury building in Simon's expression, she wisely decided to temper her response with something less dramatic. "What I would have you do, my lord, is to consider that people often make mistakes. Mistakes that can be understood and forgiven."

"You think I should condone a young woman's unwed pregnancy?"

"Certainly not," she replied. "Prissy will face the consequences of her actions, as you suggested. But that doesn't mean she has to be shunned for the rest of her life. And what of the child?"

The conversation was getting out of hand, and Simon wasn't quite sure what he could do about it. It was becoming increasingly apparent that his wife didn't harbor the characteristic indifference of her peers. She seemed genuinely concerned about the maid's welfare. A part of him admired her concern, while the other warned him that he was engaged in a no-win situation. As an employer, he had to maintain both the official and unofficial rules of his household. As a man, he could understand the temporary-insanity passion so frequently kindled and excuse the behavior of both servants. As Clarissa's husband, he couldn't afford to back down from the decision he'd had every right to make. As a future father, he didn't like knowing that he may have endangered an unborn child. Whatever course he took now was secondary to the one he'd already taken.

Clarissa waited for Simon's reply, praying that he would say something, anything, to redeem himself. So far, there was nothing about his actions or remarks to offer her any hope of ever broadening his horizons. He'd dismissed Prissy because her actions had been unacceptable, and that was that.

Simon was about to offer a philosophical response to her question when Clarissa excused herself from the table. "I will apologize to Cook in the morning. Please excuse me, but my appetite seems to have vanished along with my enthusiasm for stimulating conversation."

Fourteen

Simon sat alone in the library at his Belgrave Square town house, scowling at the fire and sipping on a glass of claret. His mood was one of deep contemplation as he tried to sort out what had gone wrong in the space of a few short days. Since their last night at Sheridan Manor, Clarissa had been distant but polite. She'd withdrawn, and although Simon knew the reason why, he couldn't quite grasp why the events surrounding a permissive young maid should affect his wife so dramatically. It wasn't as though the servant had established a bond of friendship with the new mistress of Sheridan. Indeed, the two women had barely spent more than a few minutes together. He supposed that it was possible for Clarissa to be sincerely concerned about the girl's welfare, but her response seemed a bit overreactionary for there not to be more to it.

Simon drank the last of the claret while he speculated on whether or not his lovely wife might be more involved with the folly of women's rights than she was willing to admit. She was certainly well versed in the current political situation, and her ability to converse on almost any topic standing before Parliament spoke to her intelligence. Still, she didn't keep company with the zealous females who had a reputation for wanting to spread grief among the males of the land. Her friends, or at least the few whom he had met so far, seemed perfectly normal and fairly sensible in their attitudes.

And although Clarissa still came willingly into his arms, he could sense a reluctance that hadn't been there since their wedding night. Once he fired her passion, she was as unable to control it as he was to control his need for her. The wild and urgent hunger that had plagued him for the last few weeks still remained unsatisfied, and although he tried to tell himself that it was no more than a healthy case of lust, Simon knew better. No matter how many times he physically possessed Clarissa's body, he wanted it again. And yet after each exhausting and extremely satisfying joining, he still felt as if he'd missed obtaining that one essential element that would make them both completely content.

Even more puzzling was the simple fact that he missed having her at his side during the day. In Coventry, he'd used the excuse of their honeymoon to insist that she read in the library, filling the room with the soft fragrance of her perfume and the light of her smile, while he worked at his desk. They had dallied away the days riding in the countryside or sitting in the garden, debating politics. But here in London, he couldn't indulge in the simple pleasure of her company. He had business that took him away from the house, and when he returned, as he had this evening to find his wife attending some social function, he couldn't deny his disappointment.

Clarissa was at the opera with Lady Albright. She'd told him that she'd accepted the invitation, and he'd encouraged her to enjoy herself, but . . .

Simon looked around the room. He had always felt comfortable here, surrounded by his personal selection of books. He had always felt satisfied with his life until a certain lady with auburn hair and violet eyes had invaded his domain, filling his body with an insatiable need and his mind with questions that kept him from concentrating while his solicitors rambled on and on about railroad shares and whether or not he should buy a small estate that neighbored one of the larger ones he'd gained by marriage to the late earl of Hartford's granddaughter.

He should be content now. He had a beautiful wife, one who might disagree with his political and social views but certainly kept his sexual appetite fed. Soon Clarissa would give him the son he required, and after that there would be more children. He was now, thanks to the terms of her grandfather's will, one of the wealthiest men in all of England. He had the respect of his peers and the admiration of his friends. He was the man other men envied, yet at this moment he couldn't find enough contentment in his life to retire and get a good night's sleep.

The sound of the front door being opened by one of the two butlers brought Simon out of his chair. He listened through the open library door as his wife greeted Huxley with a cheery salutation, then asked if her husband had retired for the evening.

"I believe his lordship is in the library," the servant responded.

Simon waited, expecting to see Clarissa waltz through the doorway in a wave of satin and lace, her eyes sparkling. When she did appear, he felt the same vague sense of need that she always kindled in him. Her dress was a shimmering shade of pearl gray that seemed almost alive as the fabric swirled around her. Her hair was arranged in thick curls on the top of her head and held in place by an ivory comb. The color of her gown made her eyes seem even more violet than normal, and he found himself wanting to march across the room and take her into his arms.

Instead, he greeted her with a smile and an inquiry about the opera.

"It was nice but rather exhausting." She sighed as she tossed her white fur wrap onto a chair and walked toward the hearth to warm herself. It had been raining most of the day, and the night air, though dry, was still damp with fog. "Lady Albright told me that the viscount is still unable to find himself a wife. It seems that each of the young ladies he has courted has too many faults to list."

Simon wasn't interested in his friend's quest for a wife, not when he had one of his own so close at hand. He moved toward her and saw the same emotional shield she'd been wearing since arriving in London come over her features. The diamonds adorning her throat sparkled like raindrops, and he wanted to kiss the soft skin of her neck before exploring the rest of her body.

Clarissa saw the all too familiar gleam in her husband's dark eyes and turned her back to him, extending her ungloved hands toward the warming flames of the fires. She heard him exhale in a frustrated sigh that said he was growing impatient with her attitude of late, and she wondered how much longer she would be able to pretend that things were right between them.

"You didn't have to wait up for me," she said, watching as he removed the top of a crystal decanter and refilled his glass of claret. "Did your meeting with Mr. Knightley go well?"

"It went well," Simon told her before raising the glass to his mouth. He studied her over the rim of the glass, wondering if a rousing argument would clear the air between them. He was more than willing to raise his voice to the rafters if it would restore the candor they had shared at Sheridan Manor. Damn, he wanted Clarissa moaning in his arms again, not looking at him like a wounded animal.

"I didn't wait up for you to discuss business," he said, sitting his drink aside. "We received an invitation this morning. One I thought you might like to know about."

Clarissa waited as he opened his desk drawer and withdrew a pristine envelope. When he walked across the room and handed it to her, the royal crest embossed into the fine parchment was unmistakable. "From the queen!"

Simon watched in pensive silence as Clarissa opened the invitation and began to read.

He told her the gist of the eloquently penned words. "We've been invited to a royal hunt this fall. At Balmoral."

"Scotland! I've never been to Scotland," she replied softly, sinking onto the soft leather of a nearby chair. The silver fabric of her gown billowed out around her like fiery moonlight as she held on to the royal invitation with trembling fingers. "The queen . . ." She mumbled the words as though they belonged to a foreign language.

Simon smiled at her befuddled reaction. "I've been expecting an invitation of sorts for some time," he told her. "I'm sure you'll enjoy Balmoral. It's a wild, wind-blown estate, but it's the queen's favorite, and she rarely invites anyone there that she isn't sincerely interested in meeting. The grouse hunting is excellent. I'm looking forward to it."

"You've been there before," Clarissa said, suddenly realizing just how much power her husband did wield in Parliament. A personal invitation from Queen Victoria wasn't an ordinary occurrence for most lords.

"A time or two," he said matter-of-factly.

She looked at him, wondering what thoughts were going through his mind. A mind she was trying very hard to understand. The last two weeks had been filled with confusion, spurred by the disagreement they'd had before arriving in London. Simon had refused to discuss it with her again, and although Clarissa knew he considered the matter laid to rest, she did not. Huxley had delivered Prissy into Mrs. Quigley's capable hands, and the young maid was now a shop clerk, dusting and keeping the millinery window spotless and living in a small but comfortable room in the rear of the store.

Clarissa had intentionally avoided the shop, not wanting to stumble upon Prissy too soon and create questions that were best left unanswered for the time being. The girl thought Mrs. Quigley an old friend of Huxley's, which explained things well enough for now. But the question that was keeping Clarissa from feeling content had little to do with the former maid and everything to do with her husband's willingness to discharge the girl in the first place.

She still loved Simon, but Clarissa had growing doubts that she'd ever be able to make him understand her need to champion the cause of her gender, especially unwed mothers who were considered little less than whores by society and their own families. It was disheartening to think that she might never be able to share her innermost thoughts with the man she had married.

Simon watched a flood of emotions wash over his wife's face, and misunderstanding them as nervousness over meeting the reigning queen, he felt a need to reassure her that there was nothing to be frightened of. The queen was strict in her thinking and conservative in her attitudes, but she was a gracious hostess.

Somewhere in the house a door closed, and the unexpected noise brought Clarissa's violet eyes up to meet Simon's darker ones. A tense moment of silence followed as he tried to think of what to say. He'd seen Clarissa function in the swirl of society enough to know that her social skills were better than most women's, and her intellect was certainly enough to make dinner conversation anything but boring. So why did she looked bewildered?

"Are you anxious about meeting the queen?" he asked.

"A bit," she replied honestly.

"Then there's more on your mind than a trip to Balmoral? Would you care to share it with me?"

Oh, how she wanted to share everything with him. To spend the night sitting beside him or lying in his arms while she told him all the troublesome thoughts that clouded her mind like fog over the slate roofs of London. It would be wonderful to share her plans with him, the resort she'd instructed Mr. Nebs to purchase, set just a few miles east of Plymouth, and her plans for the nursery at Haven House. She'd decided on yellow and white. The drapes were being sewn and would be ready to hang within the week. How she longed to tell him about her *ladies* and the hope she held for the children they would soon bring into the world. As much as she loved Huxley and Mrs. Quigley and all the others who shared her secret endeavors, she loved Simon much more. She loved him so much that withholding a part of herself from him was akin to nursing a constant bellyache. It made her feel sick not to be herself. She wasn't sleeping properly, and she was feeling restless. Too restless for her husband not to eventually discern that something was wrong.

Now there was an invitation from the queen, and although the hunt wasn't to take place for several months, he would expect her to behave in an exemplary fashion until the day they traveled to Scotland for her first presentation to the royal monarch. What would Simon think if he discovered between now and then that she was harboring a pregnant maid and eight other ladies in Yorkshire? How would he react if he found out that she'd transferred funds from her private account to buy a hundred-acre estate in Plymouth, complete with a twenty-bedroom manor house and stables, so that two of those ladies could oversee the venture and eventually make a place for themselves and their illegitimate children.

Mrs. Quigley had suggested that once the transaction was complete, Prissy might make herself useful in the conversion of the property. The maid, with the companionship of a hired housekeeper, could take up residence until the ladies from Yorkshire were up to making the trip and claiming their new home. Clarissa had spent most of the evening going over the possibilities in her mind while she'd pretended to listen to Lady Albright's endless stream of London gossip.

"Talk to me," Simon said, sinking onto one knee beside her, his hand gently taking the queen's invitation from hers and putting it on the table beside the chair.

His hand felt warm and strong as she looked into his eyes. Clarissa wondered if she'd ever be able to tell the man she loved what she did with her money and why she was willing to risk almost anything to keep doing it. She idled with the thought of confessing everything right then and there, but she couldn't muster the courage that could very well end with Simon's proclaiming her a madwoman and locking her in the attic. His smoking jacket was a dark emerald green, and she reached out and dusted a speck of lint off the velvet lapel.

"What should we talk about?" she asked in a whispery voice.

He touched her cheek. All thought of speech left them both. Moments later, they were entwined in each other's arms, their passion burning more brightly than the fire on the nearby hearth. Helpless to do anything but surrender to the need that grew with each passing day, Clarissa used her body to express the love she was afraid to speak aloud. Simon moaned under the tender caress of her hands as he rolled onto his back and allowed her to take control of their lovemaking. Clarissa pushed her worries aside and concentrated on pleasing both her husband and herself. The joining was both tender and primitive, and Clarissa let the power of it control her entire being. She loved Simon, and she needed him to love her. If all she could have of him was his body, then she'd take it willingly, praying that one day she might have his heart.

Simon dismissed his valet and wished for the hundredth time that he could avoid the social obligation of attending Lord Criswell's party. He was looking forward to seeing his friend Garrett Monroe, but that could be done at his club. Monroe was a handsome man with a reputation that put Thornton's to shame when it came to women. As Simon opened the door that separated his suite of rooms from the one his wife occupied in the Belgrave town house, he realized that he was feeling a spasm of jealousy. He'd seen Garrett woo women with little more than a glance, and he wasn't looking forward to introducing Clarissa to the charming American wolf.

Simon found his wife standing in front of the mirror while Lillian chided her for not wearing a corset often enough to make the tying of one an everyday event. "It's like wearing a suit of armor," his wife said, grimacing as the maid's beefy hands pulled the strings taut and tied the whalebone cage. "A man must have invented it. It's a torture device."

Simon's laughter brought Clarissa around, the starched layers of her petticoats fanning out around her as she swirled to find him standing in the doorway. A random breeze, drifting through the half-opened window, caught a wisp of her auburn hair and made it dance around her face. She brushed it aside. "I'm not dressed yet," she said, stating the obvious as Lillian walked to the bed and gathered up a dark blue taffeta gown. "I didn't realize you'd be so anxious to attend the party."

"I'm not," Simon announced, noting the maid's unease at having him in the room while she helped his wife dress. "But I am enjoying the preparations."

Clarissa blushed, something she was surprised she could still do since marrying Simon. Lillian cleared her throat as she smoothed some nonexistent wrinkles from the expensive gown.

"I'll wait for you downstairs," Simon said, turning to leave but not before he let his eyes roam from the swell of Clarissa's lush breasts to the tips of her stocking-clad feet.

Trying to ignore the rush of heat that always accompanied one of her husband's lusty stares, Clarissa turned her attention to Lillian and the gown the maid would have to help her into. The dress was a thick brocaded satin with a black lace underskirt and full, billowing sleeves that narrowed to a tight fit just below her elbows. As always, she wore the sapphire pendant Simon had given her on their honeymoon. A matching pair of earrings, a gift discovered on her pillow this morning, finished off her ensemble. Once her waist-length hair was brushed and artfully arranged in a cluster of curls at the nape of her neck, Clarissa descended the staircase.

A short time later, Lord Criswell's butler announced them in an imperious voice that echoed through the vast ballroom like a sailor's call of "land ahoy." The room was ablaze with bejeweled ladies and well-dressed gentlemen, while red liveried servants scurried here and there serving chilled champagne. Clarissa walked across the polished marble floor on the arm of her husband. The whispered hum of voices went unheard, and the bright reflection of the gaslight chandelier off the gold and crystal of the room went unseen, pushed aside by the warmth of Simon's arm lying beneath her gloved hand.

"Sinclair," Lord Criswell said in a deep, crisp voice after Simon had introduced his new wife to their host. "Monroe's in the library. I'm to send a footman to fetch him. He's anxious to meet your wife. Said he thought you'd never marry."

Simon laughed softly. "The beautiful evidence is here on my arm for all to see."

Clarissa's heart swelled with pride at her husband's public compliment. There was a lot of undiscovered territory between them, but she was confident that Simon didn't regret marrying her. In that, they were equal. She had no idea what she was going to do if she couldn't make Simon love her, but Clarissa didn't regret marrying him. Loving him so much it hurt, she couldn't imagine life without him now.

Garrett Monroe was one of the most handsome men Clarissa had ever seen. His hair gleamed like India ink, blacker than a raven's wing. He was tall, with bronzed features that boasted of a life in the American sunshine and strong hands that gripped his champagne glass with elegant ease while at the same time appearing capable of causing great harm if his temper was aroused. But it was his eyes that caught and held Clarissa's attention a moment longer than was polite. They shone like polished pewter. The combination of his ebony hair and silver eyes were a striking contrast, accented by a devilish smile.

"She's beautiful, Simon. Much too beautiful for a man of your limited tastes," Garrett Monroe said, bowing low over Clarissa's hand and brushing the acceptable kiss over her gloved knuckles.

"Clarissa, this is Garrett Monroe. A friend, as long as he remembers his manners."

She noticed the tightening of Simon's jaw and the cold glare of his gaze as he looked at the handsome American. Not having seen the expression before, it took her a moment to realize that he was warning Mr. Monroe not to think of entertaining himself with another man's wife. The brief show of jealousy boosted Clarissa's spirits like a warm cup of tea on a cold winter day. If Simon was jealous, then he had to feel more than desire for her.

"Manners can restrict a man's pleasure, but if you insist," Garrett said, still smiling. He stepped back and offered Simon his hand. "So tell me, old friend, are you still wielding words like a double-edged sword? I hear Parliament is getting ready to pack its bags and head to the English countryside for the summer."

"The last session was three days ago," Simon told him, motioning for a servant. He lifted two tall-stemmed glasses from the silver tray and offered one to Clarissa. "I'm looking forward to a few months of touring my estates and enjoying my wife's company."

"I can't blame you," Garrett replied with a mischievous wink that said he knew just how Simon intended to enjoy his new wife. "As for me, I'm still footloose and fancy free. Although Grams is forever lecturing me that it's time to get on with growing up and all the responsibilities that go with it."

"Grams?" Clarissa asked, thinking that Garrett Monroe had the look of a gentleman but sensing he was far more dangerous than the American outlaws she'd read about. His voice was soft and slow, with a hint of several accents blended into a subtle melody that reached a woman's ear like music. Tall, dark, and handsome, he wore his confidence like a king wearing a crown. This was a man who could win a woman's heart with little effort and just as easily cast it aside.

"My grandmother," he explained. "I love the old woman, but she's a proverbial pain in the . . . backside. My thirty-fifth birthday is looming on the horizon, and she's determined to see me married and rocking babies on my knee before I reach the ripe old age of thirty-six."

Simon laughed. "I'll introduce you to Clarence Albright. Viscount Thornton to his peers. You two have a lot in common."

"Speaking of having things in common," Garrett remarked. "When you can drag yourself away from your lovely new wife, join me in the library. I've got an idea that might interest you."

"Your ideas usually do," Simon replied.

They were interrupted by the viscount, leading a petite brunette on his arm and looking totally bored. He introduced the young woman as Miss Belworth, a niece of one of the many lords attending the ball. Clarissa saw Garrett eye the girl casually, then smile. Miss Belworth's face lit up like a holiday hearth.

The conversation was polite but limited until Simon whisked her off to the dance floor, leaving his friends behind them. As they danced, Clarissa's mind was filled with fanciful thoughts, and she forgot the doubts that were never far away when she thought of the future. She held on to Simon's strong hand, unaware again of the speculative gazes that followed them as they moved to the music. The magic was back, and Clarissa surrendered to it willingly as Simon swirled her around the floor.

Several of the ladies commented that the earl must be truly in love, for they'd never seen his eyes appear so soft, and why not? His wife, indeed a beautiful woman, seemed just as smitten. They made a perfect couple. All one had to do was to look at them waltzing; they swept across the room in perfect unison to the music, their eyes locked on each other, their bodies moving as if they were floating on air.

Of course, there were the rumors that Lady Sheridan was a bit on the ascetic side, preferring her privacy, but she seemed like such a nice lady that one could understand, especially when she'd only recently exchanged her mourning garb for a wedding dress. Next year she would surely be more inclined to accept the dozens of invitations that had arrived at the Belgrave town house since her reappearance in the city.

The remainder of the evening was spent dancing and dining. The music played on, soft and sweet, as Simon escorted her into a large dining room. Clarissa found herself seated next to Garrett Monroe and across the table from the viscount.

"I hope you don't find England boring, Mr. Monroe. I've heard that your country offers one so many exciting things," Clarissa remarked, making conversation. She looked up the table, where her husband was seated. He was busy discussing politics with their host, and for a moment Clarissa regretted the custom of intentionally separating a man and wife. "Were you born in San Francisco?"

"Actually I was born somewhere in the Rocky Mountains; I'm not sure if the place had a name."

Clarissa gave him an inquisitive look.

The American's responding smile would have shattered the heart of a woman who wasn't already in love. "My parents were on their way west. My father wanted to open a bank in San Francisco, and my mother didn't want to be left behind in St. Louis. I was born along the way."

"I can't imagine just packing up one's belonging and marching off to a new life," she replied. "It must have been thrilling."

Garrett chuckled. "I'm afraid I don't remember the trip west."

"I've read a great deal about your country," Clarissa told him. "I would love to see it for myself, but Simon doesn't seem inclined to travel." Clarissa leaned a little closer and lowered her voice. "Some Englishmen aren't as adventurous as they would like people to believe."

Garrett's eyes danced with amusement. "I think one Englishman is, or should I say Englishwoman. I always know a kindred spirit when I meet one, Lady Sheridan. And my instincts tell me that my friend has acquired a rare treasure."

"And what would that be, Mr. Monroe?"

"A true lady," Garrett replied, raising his glass in a salute. "To your happiness. May it last a lifetime."

Surprised by the sincerity of his words, Clarissa smiled shyly, then turned her attention toward her husband. Simon's dark eyes quickly found hers, and in that brief moment all she could think about was how much she loved him. The emotion was strong and uncomplicated, and it filled her so completely that for a moment Clarissa forgot that she was sitting at a table with twenty other guests. She quickly averted her gaze, staring down at her plate, but not before Simon smiled at her, that smug male smile that said he knew she was thinking about how it had felt to make love on the floor of the library.

His wife's warm gaze had a rejuvenating effect on Simon's bored body, and he cursed silently, hoping that he wouldn't embarrass himself when their host called an end to the meal and the gentlemen adjourned to the library for brandy and cigars.

He managed to control his desire until they were in the carriage, the windows closed and draped against the cold drizzle that made the cobblestone streets gleam in the moonlight. Sitting down beside his wife, Simon waited until the footman shut the door before he lifted Clarissa onto his lap and kissed her until she melted against him. Surprisingly content to do nothing more than hold her until they reached the town house and the comforts of the large double bed they shared, Simon wrapped his arms around Clarissa and held her tightly against his chest. No words were spoken as the carriage rolled gently to and fro, the sounds of the London night softened by the thick drapes that covered the windows.

Clarissa wasn't sure why Simon was holding her on his lap like a child, but she didn't protest. Instead, she savored the warmth of his arms and the tangy scent of his cologne. She enjoyed her husband's physical attention, and it slowly dawned on Clarissa that it was something she hadn't received in normal proportions as a child. Her parents had loved her, but she'd been very young when they had died, and her memories of them were vague. Sometimes she could close her eyes and recall her mother's voice, but no matter how hard she tried, she couldn't evoke the memory of being hugged or held on either of her parent's lap. Her grandfather had loved her, she was certain, but Richard Pomeroy hadn't been a tactile person. There had been no hugs from her grandfather, either.

Clarissa smiled, perfectly content to let Simon give her what she'd lacked up to now. She could hear the faint echo of his heartbeat as her cheek pressed against the damp wool of his cloak. It was raining again, and the sharp splattering of raindrops on the roof of the carriage sounded like the tick-tock of a mantel clock. Once again the absolute certainty of her love for Simon flooded Clarissa's senses. A small tremor raked her body as she realized that the very thing she had feared would happen had happened. Simon had laid claim to her heart and soul as surely as their wedding vows had given him legal claim to her body.

"Are you cold?" Simon asked, feeling Clarissa tremble in his arms.

"No," she whispered, but snuggled a bit closer, anyway.

With a gentleness that brought tears to Clarissa's eyes, Simon lowered his head and brushed a tender kiss across her forehead. There were no words, only the kiss, and Clarissa felt a glimmer of hope light up her heart.

The contentment she felt in Simon's arms vanished the moment Clarissa walked into the foyer of the Belgrave town house. Higgins opened the door, taking Simon's cloak and her fur wrap, then inquiring if they had enjoyed the evening.

Simon grunted an answer, anxious to take Clarissa upstairs, but the butler stopped him by announcing that there was a messenger waiting in the kitchen.

"In the kitchen?" Simon turned on his heels and looked at Higgins.

"He was soaked to the bone, my lord," the butler replied. "Cook's warming him up with a bowl of hot soup. He walked from the rail station."

"The rail station? Where's he from?"

"Yorkshire, my lord."

Clarissa's heart stopped for a frantic second, and her insides went numb. She looked anxiously around the foyer and gave a sigh of relief when Huxley made an appearance. The butler had apparently been in the kitchen with the rain-soaked messenger. His expression said she should prepare herself for the worst.

"Fetch the man," Simon told Higgins, then mumbled something under his breath that Clarissa couldn't hear. He turned to her, softening his expression, and said, "Why don't you go on upstairs. I'll join you shortly."

Clarissa was trying to think of a way to remain downstairs without seeming too obvious when Higgins appeared once again. She recognized the man following behind the butler as one of the workmen Mrs. Flannigan had hired.

"Milord," the man said as he reached the center of the tiled entryway. His clothing was still damp from the rain, and his face was shadowed with several days of unshaven beard.

"You have a message for me," Simon said, giving the man's ragged appearance a curious going-over. It was apparent that the messenger wasn't a footman dispatched by one of the earl's business associates.

"The message is for your lady," the man said, glancing passed Simon to where Clarissa was standing. Reaching inside his ill-fitting jacket, the man withdrew a soiled envelope. "I was paid a good dose of coin to put this piece of paper in her hand."

Simon gave him a disgruntled look that quickly shifted to his wife. "I don't recall any business in Yorkshire being listed on your grandfather's inventory of affairs. Who would be sending you a message, and from Yorkshire of all places?"

Clarissa hovered on the brink of a lie, then pulled back, knowing she needed to act quickly before Simon snatched the letter from the man's hands and all hell broke loose. Marshaling as much grace as she could, Clarissa walked to where the messenger was standing and held out her hand, accepting the envelope. "Thank you," she told him, then looked to where Huxley was standing at the foot of the stairs. "Please see that—"

"Keevers," the man replied.

"Please see that Mr. Keevers is given a room for the night and as much of Cook's soup as he likes. I'll send a reply in the morning," Clarissa said, looking once again at the man who was apparently the bearer of bad news. "Will you carry the letter for me?"

Mr. Keevers smiled, revealing two rows of crooked teeth. "I'll be honored, your ladyship. I'm a man to be trusted, no fear about that."

"I'm sure your services can be relied upon," she said, holding on to the letter. "Thank you."

When everyone had left the foyer but her perplexed husband, Clarissa took off her gloves and dropped them on the teakwood table next to the library door. Without a word of explanation to Simon, she ventured into his library. He followed her, as she knew he would, closing the door behind them and watching her as she took a chair and opened the letter.

The news hit her like a cold blast of arctic wind, making her stomach knot. There had been a fire at Haven House. The east wing of the house had been damaged, and the roof, which had just been repaired, was now sagging, or so Mrs. Flannigan had written. No one had been injured in the blaze, but her *ladies* were rightfully nervous. The fire had started in the kitchen and spread, but not overly far, and the workmen insisted that the once-grand manor house could be restored to its former luster. Mrs. Flannigan wrote that she regretted having to send such news, but she didn't feel right in commissioning repairs without Clarissa's guidance and advice.

"It is bad news?" Simon asked, assuming that the note came from someone who didn't trust the telegraph services, which were gaining on the post in delivering sordid news and death notices.

"I'm afraid so," Clarissa said. She walked to the hearth and tossed the letter into the fire, then watched as the flames curved around the paper and sent the evidence of her charitable endeavors up the chimney. She didn't want to lie to Simon, but there didn't seem to be any choice in the matter. "A friend has found herself recently widowed, and she seeks my comfort."

"What friend?" Simon asked. He didn't recall Clarissa mentioning a friend in Yorkshire.

Clarissa's mind raced to put together a plausible story. One that Simon would believe. She turned to look at him, hating the fact that she had to deceive him in order to make her dreams come true. "Her name is Martha Calberry," Clarissa said, using the first name that came to mind. "We attended school together and have kept in touch through the post. She has only been married a short time. She begs my forgiveness for asking, but she wants me to come visit her in Yorkshire as soon as possible. She finds herself unable to recover from the shock of her husband's death, and she needs my company."

"I see," Simon replied, searching her face. She did appear to be upset, but his instincts told him there was no recently widowed friend. Clarissa was hiding something. But what?

He knew she hadn't had a lover before their marriage, so there was no reason to believe that she was sneaking off to Yorkshire to meet a man. Unless, of course, she'd recently found a man that interested her. Is that why she'd burned the letter? Given the attention she received whenever they were in public, Simon couldn't dispel the notion. London was full of married men who thrived on seducing beautiful women, especially married ones.

The thought gave him more than a moment's pause, but he finally dismissed it. Clarissa might be wild in her thinking, but she wasn't promiscuous in her actions.

Simon was sure that the messenger had something to do with her private account. There was more to Clarissa's demand for control of her allowance than she was willing to admit, and it was time that Simon put aside his infatuation with her and discovered what that something was. He anticipated her next remark and managed not to frown when she recited it perfectly. His wife might be able to keep a secret better than any woman he'd ever met, but she couldn't lie worth a damn.

"With your permission, my lord, I would like to go to her. Martha was always frail, and I fear that in her grief she might not see to her own welfare."

"Please send Mrs. Calberry my sympathies," he said, pouring himself a drink. "But I cannot allow you travel to Yorkshire. It is a long journey, either by carriage or train, and my business requires that we travel south, not north. Surely there is someone else who can comfort her during her grief. We can stop in Yorkshire for a visit before we travel to Balmoral at the end of the summer."

Clarissa took a deep breath and hoped she wouldn't kindle another argument. "Please, Simon. I know it isn't the best of timing, but I could take Huxley and a full entourage of servants with me. I can join you in a few weeks. You should be done with your tour of the mills in Birmingham by then, and we can meet in Lincoln at Viscount Thornton's estate. I heard you accept his invitation this evening."

Remembering his promise not to inquire or interfere, Simon decided the only way to discover what Clarissa was hiding was to let her go to Yorkshire. He'd follow at a discreet distance and find out once and for all what his lovely wife had up her sleeve. It wasn't a direct breach of his word, and he justified it by telling himself that he couldn't be content as long as he suspected that his wife was engaged in something that might be dangerous.

Pretending to ponder her request for a thoughtful moment, Simon sipped his brandy. When he looked at Clarissa again, his dark eyes held none of the suspicions racing through his mind. "Very well," he relented, "but I want Huxley and at least six footmen with you. And you have only three weeks. I expect you in Lincoln on schedule."

Thinking she'd accomplished the impossible, Clarissa donned a bright smile and walked to where Simon was standing. She placed a chaste kiss on his cheek. "Thank you."

"You can thank me better than that," Simon said, setting aside his brandy and pulling her into his arms. "If I'm to sleep alone for the next few weeks, I don't intend for either one of us to get much rest tonight."

Clarissa laughed, then kissed him again.

Fifteen

Simon sat in a rented carriage and watched the rain dripping off the black locomotive and onto the wooden platform of the Carlisle train station, forming oily puddles as it washed the coal soot from the mechanical giant. It had been raining for the last two days, and the roads were little more than muddy bogs, trapping carriages and their occupants while rain-soaked footmen and drivers heaved and cursed to get them moving again. His brown eyes scanned the mud-encrusted platform for his wife. The porter, who had received a hefty coin in exchange for the information he'd given the earl, had told Simon that a lady would be getting off the train before it assumed its journey to Newcastle.

Simon was becoming more suspicious of his wife's actions with each passing day. Clarissa had dispatched Mr. Keevers the morning after his arrival with a note supposedly informing Mrs. Calberry that her friend was on the way and would be arriving within a week's time. Deciding there was little to do but behave normally, Simon had told Higgins to pack for a trip to Birmingham. The household had been in a tether, what with half the servants sending their master off in one direction and the other half preparing for their mistress to go to Yorkshire.

That had been four days ago, and Simon was quickly tiring of the cat-and-mouse game. As she'd promised, Clarissa had left London with a butler, six footmen, and a maid. But instead of traveling by coach, as six footmen indicated she would, she'd boarded a train at Paddington Station and rolled out of London. If it hadn't been for the discreet runner Simon had hired to keep track of his wife's whereabouts, he would have thought her bogged down on the road somewhere between London and her final destination. Instead, she'd eliminated the damaging effects of the weather by taking the train and was now preparing to enter a hired coach to begin what he assumed was the final leg of her journey.

Simon knew that if he hadn't been right on her heels, she would have slipped through his fingers, and he'd have no idea where to look for her. Fortunately, he'd been prepared for a quick chase, and he'd managed to catch up with her in Carlisle. Unlike most men, he rarely underestimated women.

His eyes took on an ominous shade when he saw Clarissa get off the train. She was wearing a dark brown cloak with the hood pulled up, but Simon would have known her anywhere. In the course of the last few weeks, he had learned every inch of his wife's scheming body, and no amount of clothing could conceal her charms. Huxley was at her side, and Simon waited patiently for the other servants to appear. When they didn't, he realized that Clarissa had apparently found some excuse to rid herself of them, and he made a mental note to give her an extra hard thrashing for disobeying him in that regard as well.

She didn't look left or right as Huxley escorted her toward the hired carriage. Like the one Simon had procured, it was old but sturdy. The driver tipped his hat and spoke, and although Simon couldn't make out his words, he got the distinct impression that this wasn't Clarissa's first trip to Carlisle. After the baggage was loaded, the carriage pulled away from the station.

Simon rapped on the roof, instructing his driver to follow. The next two hours were spent watching the barren Yorkshire countryside as rain continued to drizzle on the moors and thick clouds hovered on the horizon, promising more of the same weather well into the night.

"This blasted weather," Clarissa mumbled as the carriage jerked back and forth so violently that her head bumped against the seat and her hood fell back, revealing a mass of auburn hair. "I pray that we reach Haven House before nightfall. I don't wish to spend one more night on the road."

Huxley nodded in full agreement as the driver issued a string of curses meant to encourage the horses through a muddy section of road. "We'll be stopping to rest the animals at the next inn. A hot cup of tea will soothe your nerves."

Clarissa frowned. "I don't know what's got me worried the most," she admitted wearily. "The damage to Haven House or lying to the earl. God help me if he ever finds out."

Although she wanted to tell herself that Simon wouldn't make good on his threat to physically chastise her, Clarissa couldn't be absolutely sure. There was still so much she didn't know about him, and his temper was something she'd only touched upon a time or two. It was hard to say how he would react if he discovered that she'd blatantly lied to him. She doubted that her good intentions would go very far in protecting her posterior.

"The circumstances were rather rushed," Huxley said, offering what consolation he could. "Had we been at Hartford Hall, I could have intercepted the messenger. As it was, there was no way for his lordship not to be told."

"Don't blame yourself," Clarissa said. "I knew the risk when I married Simon. But I hadn't planned on a fire."

While Clarissa sat in one carriage, debating the ramifications of her actions, Simon traveled a few miles behind her, wondering what in the world his wife was doing in the middle of Yorkshire with no one but a butler for company. The lack of a maid told him that Clarissa was intentionally reducing the number of people who knew her destination. Apparently, Huxley knew, which meant that the servant had probably been here with her before. The realization was another thorn in Simon's side as the driver called down that there was an inn ahead, and did his lordship want to stop for a bit of something to ward off the chill of a rainy day.

"Stop here," Simon called out as the slate roof of a roadway inn peeked over the horizon. Smoke curled from the stone chimney, and the air was heavy with the scent of burning peat.

The carriage slid in the gray mud as the driver pulled back on the reins and the horses came to a stop. Simon opened the door and stepped out, sinking ankle deep in the mud as he looked around him. There was nothing for miles around but the isolated inn. The rain was still a thin drizzle that kept the ground from drying out. There was a chill to the air that came from the North Sea, and the thick layer of pasty clouds shielding the sun didn't appear to be in any hurry to vanish. All in all, it was a dismal day.

"We'll wait here awhile," Simon told the driver. "If you've got a flask in your coat pocket, feel free to open it."

"You've a kind soul, milord," the driver replied,

reaching inside the worn woolen greatcoat that was keeping his spindly body warm. He'd been around enough years to know that his fare didn't want whoever was in the carriage ahead of them to discover they were being followed. The driver got the impression that the woman he'd seen get into the other rig belonged to the man who had hired him, and if so, there was going to be bloody hell to pay somewhere up the road. He gave Simon a crooked smile as he raised the flank high. "I'm willin' to share."

"No, thank you," Simon replied, getting back inside the coach. He had his own spirits, thanks to Higgins's careful packing. But he didn't intend to open the bottle of French brandy until he'd confronted his wayward wife. His temper was raging high enough without the added effects of liquor.

Having stopped at the inn before, Clarissa knew it served a reasonable cup of tea, along with soup and bread. She'd never had the courage to sample the establishment's other fare, nor did she have the appetite today. While she made herself comfortable at a corner table, keeping her hood up and her face averted, Huxley made sure the horses were properly fed and the driver made content with a wedge of cheese, hard bread, and a tankard of ale.

Two more hours, she told herself. Two more hours and she could soak in a hot tub. After that, she'd inspect the damage the fire had done, arrange for repairs, and hopefully eliminate the anxiety of her *ladies*. Then she could see to her own anxiety. It had been increasing with every mile she put between herself and London until she was sick with worry and unable to think of any way out of the hole she'd dug by lying to Simon. What if he insisted on meeting Martha Calberry one day? What if he decided that they should stop on their way to Balmoral just to make sure her friend had regained her strength and accepted her widowhood?

The possibilities of being caught in the falsehood she'd blurted out seemed more and more likely as Clarissa sipped her tea. At the moment, they were overshadowing the hope that she might ever make Simon fall in love with her. That particular possibility would become less and less likely if he discovered that she'd lied to him. Her husband's staunch nature and unbending personality weren't going to soften once he'd deemed her untrustworthy.

Huxley escorted her back to the carriage, which was covered with mud, slung up by the carriage wheels and the heavy hooves of the horses. Making herself comfortable for the last segment of the trip, Clarissa wondered what she would find when she reached Haven House.

Simon reined in the mount he had rented at the inn. The gelding was several years past his prime, but he was strong-legged and had made his way across the moors with little difficulty. Both Simon and the horse were covered with mud and soaked to the skin from the cold drizzle that hadn't let up since early that morning. Simon had taken the time to have a tankard of ale at the inn. He'd also made a few inquires. The innkeeper had seen the lady before, but he didn't have any idea who she was. Her manservant did the talking and made sure no one disturbed his mistress while she enjoyed her tea. Deciding he could follow Clarissa more efficiently on horseback, Simon had rented the innkeeper's horse.

Now, sitting atop the exhausted animal, Simon watched the carriage deposit his wife at the front door of a country manor.

The house, dating back to the sixteenth century, had been constructed of limestone and appeared to be in salvageable condition. The roof, however, was almost completely gone. The second-floor windows were rimmed with soot and filled with jagged teeth of glass, broken out by the flames that had overtaken the house. Questions piled up in Simon's mind as he rode around the house, keeping to the trees because there was still enough daylight to be seen.

Upon further inspection, he could see that the fire had originated in the back of the house, probably in the kitchen, and spread to the second floor. Most of the damage was to the eastern wing and servant quarters, and he wondered if perhaps he hadn't overreacted to his wife's news that a friend had found herself unexpectedly widowed. Of course, that didn't explain why Clarissa hadn't mentioned the fire or why she'd excused her maid and the six footmen.

Taking a deep breath, Simon decided it was time to confront his lovely wife. He wasn't surprised when Huxley greeted him at the front door.

"My lord," the butler said, stepping back so Simon could enter.

"Where is my wife?" he asked, giving the servant a scowl that would have sent most men running for cover.

"In the parlor, my lord," Huxley replied calmly, indicating a closed door to the right of the foyer.

Simon stomped across the parquet floor, leaving a trail of rain and mud behind him. He didn't hesitate but threw the door open and marched into the parlor like a conquering general.

"What is the meaning of this?" He roared the words. Simon wasn't sure what he'd expected to find, but it certainly wasn't a flock of gestating females.

His wife was sitting on a blue-and-white striped settee, surrounded by a bevy of pregnant women. Simon counted eight in all. Some were very, very pregnant, while others looked to be in various stages of the delicate condition. Clarissa came to her feet so quickly that she almost spilled the tea she was holding. One of the woman took the cup from her hand, while another looked at Simon and proceeded to faint dead away. Two of the woman rushed to where the young girl had slumped into a chair. The others continued to stare at him.

"Ladies, this is my husband." Clarissa said, along with a silent prayer for her life. "Please excuse his grand entrance."

"Ladies," he said evenly.

Clarissa looked from her husband's menacing smile to the shocked faces of the women in the room and realized that she only had a few moments to get control of the situation. "I wasn't expecting you, my lord. If you'll wait for me in the library, I'll be with you as soon as I've seen to Miss Eldridge. You seem to have startled her."

Simon whirled on the heels of his muddy boots and went back into the foyer. As expected, Huxley was waiting. "Where's the library?" Simon snapped. He'd deal with the butler later.

"This way, my lord."

"Does my wife own this house?" Simon asked with a sweep of his gloved hand.

"Yes."

"Then have someone fetch my belongings from the inn where you stopped for tea. I need a bath and a hot meal. But first I want a drink."

The butler nodded, then opened the door to the library. "There aren't any spirits in the liquor cabinet, my lord, but Mrs. Flannigan usually keeps a bottle of Irish whiskey in the kitchen."

"Whiskey will do," Simon replied curtly. Who in the hell was Mrs. Flannigan, and why were there eight pregnant women in the parlor? He'd only had a brief glimpse of the one who had fainted. Something about the female stuck in his mind. He'd seen her before. But where? A maid, or a tavern wench perhaps? God knew he'd encountered hundreds of them in his life. Yes, perhaps that was it. She'd been employed at one of his friends' homes, or perhaps she'd served him a tankard of ale in some unremembered tavern.

Across the foyer, Clarissa was trying to calm eight hysterical women and one very worried housekeeper. "Mrs. Flannigan, I'm sure his lordship would like something to eat once he's overcome his shock. Would you see to it, please. As for Miss Eldridge, I suggest we put her to bed and keep the rest of the ladies out of sight until I've had time to deal with my husband. It might be a good idea to send Huxley to fetch Dr. Hayward. I daresay some of us may need a tonic before this is over."

The housekeeper hadn't gotten a look at the earl yet, but several of the women had likened his unexpected appearance to that of a devil in muddy boots. She gave Clarissa a skeptical look as she told the ladies to go into the dining room. Until the rain stopped and the workmen repaired the damaged roof, the second floor was off limits. The formal dining hall was now the women's dormitory.

Clarissa took a moment to assure each of the women that Simon wasn't going to toss them out into the night. As she smoothed the skirt of her wrinkled traveling suit, she prayed that she wasn't telling another lie. The look on Simon's face had promised retribution, and Clarissa wasn't looking forward to confronting him.

Simon's strides ate up the library as he paced back and forth. He couldn't recall ever being as furious as he was at this specific moment in time. He'd spent the last four days on trains, in hired carriages, and riding a swaybacked horse, only to track his wife to a deserted estate in the middle of nowhere. And what had he found? Not the lover most husbands would expect. No. He'd found his lovely wife cloistered in the parlor with a collection of pregnant women!

Simon turned, his hands behind his back, his expression set in lines as cold as the rain pelting the sagging roof over the east wing, when Huxley appeared with a bottle of Irish whiskey and a glass perched on a serving tray. The butler poured a generous helping into the glass before handing it to Simon.

"I assume you knew where my wife was going when she left London?" Simon inquired in a brutal tone.

"Yes, my lord," Huxley responded, his amber eyes meeting his employer's furious gaze. "I always travel with her."

"I see," Simon mumbled, although he didn't know enough facts to see anything clearly. The only thing he did see was that Clarissa's butler possessed the dedication of a good hunting hound. The man had only one master, and Simon wasn't it. "When did she purchase this house?"

"I'll answer whatever questions you have, my lord," Clarissa interrupted from the doorway. "That will be all, Huxley. Please check in with Mrs. Flannigan. I believe she may need your assistance."

Leaving the cork out of the whiskey bottle, Huxley gave a curt nod of his head before exiting the room and leaving Simon alone with his wife.

"You have exactly one minute to explain yourself, madam." Simon's voice was low but firm.

"It will take considerably longer than that, my lord. Why don't you sit down and make yourself comfortable."

Just before turning the doorknob and letting herself into the library, Clarissa had decided the only way to explain anything to Simon was to tell him the whole truth. She eyed the whiskey bottle, and for the first time in her life she wondered if a good stiff drink really did make things better. If so, she was going to have Huxley fetch her a bottle as soon as she left the library. *If* she left the library. At the moment, her husband looked as if he could cheerfully strangle her.

There was a fire blazing in the hearth, and Simon stepped closer, shedding his greatcoat on the way. He sat his whiskey glass on the oak mantel and extended his hands toward the warming blaze as he tried to contain his temper. It was several long moments later before he retrieved the whiskey from the mantel and turned to face his wife.

"I've instructed Mrs. Flannigan to prepare you a hot meal. The kitchen suffered considerable damage during the fire, but the cook is a very resourceful woman. Although it won't be what you are used to, the food will be hot and well prepared."

"The cook isn't the only resourceful lady in this house," Simon remarked. "What are you doing here, and why did you lie to me?"

Clarissa grimaced inwardly with guilt, but she kept her chin up and her voice calm. If she let Simon back her into a corner with his first question, it would be all downhill from there. "This house, or what is left of it, belongs to me."

"For how long?"

"I purchased it with the money I inherited from my mother on my eighteenth birthday."

Simon took a deep breath and a short sip of whiskey. "Did your grandfather approve the purchase?"

"No," Clarissa told him.

"I assume this is one of your charities."

"One of them," Clarissa said candidly.

The thought of other estates scattered around the English countryside was enough to make Simon stifle a groan. "The messenger who arrived in London brought you news of the fire."

Clarissa nodded. She was standing in the center

of the room, her hands folded in front of her, and for all intents and purposes she felt like a little girl being chastised for climbing a tree in the orchard when she should have been practicing her embroidery. She had never heard Simon speak in the House of Lords, but if his tone was anything like it was now, she didn't doubt his ability to hold the attention of an audience.

"Who do those women belong to?" he asked.

Clarissa almost smiled. "To themselves, my lord."

"You know what I mean," he snapped. "My patience is dangling by a thin thread, madam. I don't recommend that you test it further."

"If you mean, do their husbands know they are here, then the answer is no. Only one of them has a husband, and he's away buying supplies to repair the roof."

Simon downed the rest of the whiskey in one long gulp, then reached for the bottle. He filled the glass to the rim, walked back to the mantel, and prayed that he would wake up in London and the last few days would all be a bad dream.

Clarissa watched as the only plausible explanation soaked into her husband's brain. She knew the second he had sorted it all out. His eyes went wide.

"What in the name of God do you think you're doing?" he roared.

Clarissa almost staggered back from the fury of his question. Whatever doubts she had about her husband possessing a formidable temper had vanished. Praying she wouldn't melt under the heat of his angry gaze, she did her best to explain. "I'm trying to keep a roof over their heads and food in their bellies until they can birth their children. They have noplace to go and no one who wants them. Haven House is the only thing standing between them and the gutters of London."

All of Simon's questions got answered at once. It

was all beginning to make sense. No. Not sense. Everything about it was incredulous! Insane was a better word. Clarissa's demand for control of her private allowance, the way she'd reacted to his discharging Prissy, the lie she'd told him to cover up why she needed to leave London and where she was going.

Thinking there wasn't enough Irish whiskey in the world to ease the cold, hard fact that his wife was skating on the thin ice of scandal, Simon set down his drink and walked to the window. Night was fast approaching, and the moon was barely more than a sliver of light in the darkening sky. Rain splattered the window in soft droplets and ran randomly down the glass pane as Simon tried to find some logic in the chaos he'd discovered.

"Where do you find the women?" he finally asked, praying that his wife wasn't advertising for them in the London newspaper and that her identity couldn't be traced.

"I don't," she said. "They find me."

He turned, his silent but lethal stare daring her to draw out the explanation.

"They are not trollops," Clarissa insisted. "Some are shop girls, others were employed as servants, while others are simply young women who trusted the wrong man."

"How do they find you?"

"There is a shopkeeper in London," Clarissa replied. "We're friends."

"Friends?" Simon was almost afraid to ask how a shopkeeper fit into the scheme of things.

"Her name is Mrs. Quigley. She owns a millinery shop off Bond Street."

"And . . ."

Clarissa decided to sit down. Her knees were rattling so badly, she was afraid Simon could hear them. "Her occupation makes her privy to certain types of gossip. When she hears of a woman who needs the type of refuge I offer, she arranges for them to be interviewed. If they meet our requirements, they're invited to come to Haven House."

"And what are your requirements, madam? Or need I ask? A house filled with unmarried pregnant women speaks for itself."

"My ladies are not whores!" Clarissa came to her feet. Her fists were balled at her side, and her fear of Simon's reaction was pushed aside by her need to vindicate the women she sheltered. "They might have given their bodies foolishly, but they're not whores. They are women. Women who thought themselves in love with the men who fathered their children. Men who deserted them when the consequences were known. What would you have me do, my lord? Turn them out the way you turned out Prissy? Or perhaps I should give them the money to pay an East End abortionist and rid themselves of the babes instead of wasting my funds trying to give them back their dignity."

"Is Prissy one of them?" Simon asked. After his argument with Clarissa at Sheridan Manor, he'd had Higgins seek out the young maid, but she'd already left the village.

"No," Clarissa told him. "Prissy is in London with Mrs. Quigley."

Under normal circumstances, Simon was more than willing to engage in a shouting match, but there was nothing normal about this situation, and he needed to get to the bottom of it as quickly as possible. "Sit down, Clarissa. No one is accusing anyone of being a whore. Nor am I suggesting that these women be turned out. I am merely trying to discern what I've stumbled onto."

"What made you stumble onto anything, my lord?" she asked, still standing. "What of our agreement? No inquires. No interference. Yet here you stand, in my library, demanding answers to questions that you have no right to be asking."

"I'm your husband! That gives me all the right I need." It was Simon's turn to lose his temper. "My wife receives a message, which she promptly burns, then asks me to believe an outrageous story about some poor widow when it's apparent that she's lying through her lovely teeth. Then she dashes out of London, loosing her footmen and maid somewhere along the way. And where do I find her? In a scorched estate in the middle of Upper Yorkshire with eight unwed mothers-to-be clinging to her skirts. Believe me, madam, I have every right to expect my questions answered."

"Seven," Clarissa corrected him. "Miss Calberry was married last month."

Simon's jaw clinched as he tried to regain control of his temper. It was a formidable task, since he'd like nothing better than to drag his wife back to Coventry and lock her in the coal cellar until she came to her senses. "Very well," he finally replied. "Seven unwed mothers-to-be."

"Actually, there are ten. In all the confusion, I almost forgot about them. Three ladies live here with their children. They earn their keep by helping Mrs. Flannigan. One of them is the cook."

A knock at the door interrupted Clarissa's interrogation. Simon marched across the room and almost jerked the door off the hinges as he opened it.

"Who are you?"

"Mrs. Flannigan," the housekeeper replied. "I run this house for Lady Sheridan, and I've brought your dinner."

Simon stepped aside as the stout housekeeper, dressed in widow's black with a white starched apron tied around her thick middle, walked into the room. He watched as she carried a tray to the desk, then pulled away the linen towel covering it to reveal a plate of food. The aroma of fresh-baked bread filled the library and his stomach rumbled. "Thank you," he said, regaining his manners. "There's only one plate. What about my wife?"

"Her ladyship usually takes her meal with the other women when she's in residence," Mrs. Flannigan told him in no uncertain terms. "That won't be for another hour."

"I'm not very hungry," Clarissa chimed in, trying to sound lighthearted.

The meal wasn't elegant, but it smelled delicious. Deciding to give himself some time to assimilate what Clarissa had told him so far, Simon picked up the knife and fork and sliced into the thick meat pie.

If he was getting the facts straight, his wife was operating a refuge for unwed mothers who were apparently from the middle and lower classes. With the assistance of a shopkeeper named Mrs. Quigley and a devoted butler, Clarissa was shepherding the pregnant women away from London and sheltering them until their children were born.

But what did she do with them after that?

Simon forced himself to finish his meal before addressing the additional questions. Once he'd cleaned his plate of the meat pie and stewed vegetables, he reached for the whiskey glass. No matter how he looked at his wife's bizarre charity, all he could see was disaster looming on the horizon. What if the queen found out that Clarissa was hosting a house for immoral women? And that was how society would view the *ladies* hiding under his wife's scorched roof. No matter how wrong it might be to judge them, his peers would do just that, and they'd waste no time rendering a similar decision about his wife.

Sixteen

Clarissa watched as Simon folded his napkin and stood up. His jaw had relaxed, and his gaze didn't seem nearly as angry, but she knew she had a long battle to fight before the war was won. Bracing herself for the next offensive, she smiled, thinking it was the only thing she could do under the circumstances.

Simon smiled back, but there was no humor in the expression. "Before we leave this room, I want to know everyone involved in your charitable activities. Everyone and everything."

Clarissa sighed. "It isn't all that bad, Simon. Really, it isn't. All I'm trying to do is help people."

"Unmarried pregnant people."

"What's so terrible about that?" she countered sharply. "They need help. And understanding. And a little sympathy."

"I'm not blind to the situation," he said, hearing the conviction in her voice. Beneath the anger, he had to admire Clarissa's courage. He couldn't think of another woman who would risk what she was risking just to help someone. "And neither are you or you wouldn't have lied to me from the very beginning."

"I don't want to lie about anything," she told

him. "How can I do what needs to be done any other way? I can't solicit help from my peers. It's perfectly all right to toss a coin in the poor box as long as we don't get our pristine hands dirty. Well, I for one don't give a damn about getting my hands dirty. I won't abandon these women or others like them. The only difference between them and me is that I have a title and money and they don't."

Ten years in Parliament had taught Simon when to press forward and when to retreat, and he knew he was engaging in an argument he couldn't win. His wife was right, of course. Their Christian upbringing demanded that they be charitable, and he couldn't fault her reasons. He could, however, fault her methods.

"Who else contributes to your charity?" Simon continued, determined to find out everything Clarissa had kept hidden from him.

"Huxley and Mrs. Quigley have been with me since the beginning," she told him. "I hired Mrs. Flannigan after I bought the house. The other only person is Dr. Hayward."

"Dr. Hayward?"

"He retired from his practice in Manchester a few years ago. And he's very discreet."

"Most physicians are," Simon replied. "Anyone else?"

"Not directly."

"Who?" he demanded, thinking his wife had a virtual underground railroad at her disposal.

"Mr. Nebs. He's a friend of Mrs. Quigley's." Clarissa prepared herself for another rafter-shaking roar when Simon learned of her plans for a seaside retreat.

"And what does Mr. Nebs do?"

"He finds things for me," Clarissa said with a smile.

"What sort of things?" This was getting more

complicated by the moment, Simon decided. As it was, there were at least fifteen people who knew his wife was involved in a scandalous situation. Which meant that fifteen people knew the woman he was sleeping with better than he did.

"Houses and things."

"Don't tell me you have other havens like this one."

"No," she told him. "The house Mr. Nebs just purchased for me isn't like this one. It's on the southern coast just outside Plymouth."

Simon wanted to pull his hair out. Instead, he continued watching his wife and praying that she was almost at the bottom of her pocketful of surprises. "What do you plan on doing with a house in Plymouth?"

Clarissa's smile brightened. "I'm going to open a resort. You know, a seashore retreat. They're quite popular of late, and Mrs. Quigley agrees that it's a wonderful idea. Two of the ladies have already agreed to run it for me."

"Posing as widows, of course." He was beginning to get the picture. Clarissa didn't want her charity work to stop with giving room and shelter. She had latched onto the idea of reinstating the women into society as well.

"Of course," she told him. "Actually, I'm convinced that it will be a very profitable venture. Mr. Nebs acquired the house for a very good price, and he assures me that it will only need a few renovations."

Simon held up his hand. "That's enough for now," he told her. "It's getting late, and I need a bath and a few minutes to digest what you've told me. In the meantime, I suggest that you have your dinner. We'll talk again later."

Clarissa wasn't sure if she should be relieved or not. Simon had stopped yelling, but the look on his face said he had a long way to go before he was ready to accept what he'd discovered when he'd walked into the parlor. She was heading for the door when he stopped her.

"From this moment on, madam, there will be no secrets between us. And no lies. Do you understand?"

Clarissa nodded. "I never wanted to lie to you, Simon."

Simon believed her, but his temper hadn't cooled enough for him to give her the reassurance she needed. He was torn between a need to keep her safe and the overwhelming urge to hike up her skirts and thrash her within an inch of her life. For a moment, he decided it would have been easier to have discovered Clarissa with another man. He could shoot the bloody bastard and be done with it.

"One more thing, madam. From this day forth there will be no privacy for your allowance. I will distribute your funds in the future. Charitable or otherwise."

Clarissa's temper went over the edge. "You're going back on your word!"

Simon's expression didn't soften. "I'm going to make sure that my wife doesn't end up in the middle of a scandal."

"There is nothing scandalous about what I'm doing here," she argued. The small glimmer of hope that she'd held on to vanished. Simon was going to use the lies she'd told him to justify the withdrawal of his promise.

"You know better than that," Simon told her. His eyes snapped with fury. "Don't doubt me in this, madam. If you so much as breathe without my permission, you will find yourself dancing with the Devil, and I will be your partner."

Clarissa quit the room, slamming the door on her way out.

She was too angry to eat, but she couldn't let the other ladies at the table sense her irritation without causing them distress. Forcing herself to act as if her husband's appearance was an asset rather than a liability, Clarissa let the women talk among themselves while she listened. When she noticed that Miss Eldridge was absent from the table, Mrs. Flannigan told her the young lady was resting in the parlor.

Clarissa decided to let the newest arrival at Haven House enjoy her privacy. There was so little of it now that the women were confined to the first floor.

After dinner, Clarissa went in search of some privacy for herself. It was still raining, so the weather kept her from seeking out the solace of the garden. She needed to do some thinking before she saw Simon again. If the man thought he was going to use the day's events as an excuse to tighten her purse strings, he had another thing coming. The more she thought about his following her like a thief in the night, the harder it was to forgive him. Wasn't it enough that she had to tolerate his lovemaking when she knew it was nothing more than lust? Now he expected her to tolerate his constant interference. It wasn't possible. She couldn't function with Simon breathing over her shoulder like a medieval dragon.

Being very careful where she stepped, Clarissa climbed the stairs to the second floor. Although the staircase and walls had been washed free of soot, it was easy to see where flames had licked at the wood. Once she reached the second floor, she could see where the oak panels had been blistered from the heat of the fire. The hallway carpet had been removed, the doors leading to the rooms taken off their scorched hinges and discarded. Looking inside the room that had once been reserved for her, Clarissa fought back tears. The windows were bare of drapes, and the bed had been stripped down to a naked frame of wood. The Oriental rug was stained, and the oval mirror over the vanity was cracked down the middle. Gone were the comfort and security she had tried to incorporate into every room of the house. No wonder the ladies were worried. The fire-ravished rooms looked like cold, dark skeletons.

Clarissa turned toward the west wing, hoping to find a room that didn't smell like the inside of a chimney. Carrying a candle because Mrs. Flannigan had had the gaslights on the second floor disconnected, Clarissa prayed that she could make Simon see reason. Now, after the fire, she needed funds more than ever before. She couldn't abandon Haven House. It would be too much like deserting the women she had brought here. And she refused to do that.

"What are you doing up here?"

Clarissa flinched as Simon stepped out of the shadows just in front of her. "I could ask you the same thing, my lord."

He was wearing clean clothes, and his hair was still damp from his bath. "Huxley assigned me to the room at the end of the hall," he said, motioning toward the dark corridor ahead of them. "At least it has a bed. That's more than I can say about the rest of them."

"This wing is still being renovated," Clarissa replied, refusing to let him intimidate her the way he'd done downstairs. "Would you like to see the nursery?"

Not waiting for an answer, Clarissa stepped around him and headed toward a set of richly carved double doors. She pushed them open and stepped inside.

Simon followed her. He was about to chastise her

for not thinking of the danger and coming upstairs when he saw the cradle. It wasn't the first cradle he'd ever seen, but it seemed small and lonely in the empty room. The way he felt whenever Clarissa wasn't nearby. He watched as she walked over to the tiny bed and gave it a nudge with the tip of her toe. It rocked to and fro, and he found himself thinking of the nursery at Sheridan Manor and the cradle that was waiting to hold his firstborn child.

"I suppose it's a good thing that the draperies hadn't been delivered yet," Clarissa said, looking around the room, then at Simon. "It's hard to imagine with things in their present state, but this room is going to be bright and cheery when it's finished. The drapes are white and gold, and I've commissioned a local artist to paint murals on the walls. What do you think about butterflies?"

"I think you're trying to avoid the subject," Simon replied.

Knowing that the longer she allowed Simon to think he had taken command, the more control he would absorb, Clarissa faced him head-on. "And what is the subject, my lord? Is it Haven House and the ladies sewing in the parlor or the fact that a proper lady of the peerage isn't doing what a proper lady should be doing?"

"Both," he answered candidly, then drew a hand through his damp hair as if he could rake the answer out of his head. "What you have here is hardly an acceptable charity."

"Then to hell with acceptability," Clarissa almost shouted. "I'll find a way to keep this house open with or without your approval."

Simon didn't want to argue. What he wanted was to hold his wife in his arms. He took a step toward her, wondering if he'd lost his mind. He should be furious that she would risk a scandal by doing what she'd done. He should be, but he wasn't. For some bizarre reason Clarissa's unorthodox approach to things made him proud. But he couldn't let her know that, at least not yet. Nor could he let her run around the country without some restraint. She had to understand that there were limits to what she could get away with.

"Is my approval important to you?" he asked in a soft whisper.

Clarissa hesitated before answering. She shouldn't give her arrogant husband the satisfaction of knowing that she longed for a small glimmer of anything that came from his heart, but she didn't want to put another lie between them. "Is it so unthinkable for me to want you to understand how important Haven House is to me? After all, you are my husband."

"Aye, madam, that I am," he said almost teasingly.

She looked at his face, revealed in the moonlight streaming through the undraped windows. There was something in his gaze that charged the air between them like heat lightning on a sultry summer night. Clarissa wet her lips. There was so much she wanted to say to this man, so much she wanted to share, yet she held back, unsure how her private thoughts would be received.

He was staring at her mouth, and Clarissa knew that the gleam in his eyes was caused by passion not anger. She shouldn't let Simon kiss her, not when things were so unsettled between them, but she couldn't deny that she wanted his kiss. The passion was there between them, as viable as an electric current, strong and powerful and waiting to be felt.

Slowly, Simon reached out for her, his hands spanning her waist. Clarissa took a step forward her face raised, her lips parted. When the kiss finally happened, her knees almost buckled from the sheer delight of it. His arms claimed her with a vengeance, holding her so tightly that she couldn't catch her breath. His mouth covered hers, hot and demanding, and oh, so wonderful. Her body felt as hot as Simon's lips. Her blood raced through her veins, and her heart pounded. She curled her arms around his neck and felt his body, his need. She could smell the scent of soap on his skin and taste the whiskey he'd drank earlier.

Simon's hands roamed up and down her back, then moved to her breasts, molding them to fill his hands. He breathed a deep male groan into her mouth, and Clarissa answered with her own sound of female need.

He kissed her again as he fitted his hands to the curve of her bottom and lifted her against him. He walked her back against the wall. "I want you. Right here. Right now."

Clarissa mumbled what could have been words of protest or surrender, but there was no denying the passion. There was only the empty room and the moonlight stretching out across the wooden floor like long silver fingers reaching for a cherished treasure. There was the echo of her heartbeat filling her head like the roar of a cavalry charge and the heat of Simon's hands as he pushed her skirt up and stroked the back of her thighs. He pinned her against the wall with his hips, and his hands found the buttons on the front of her blouse. He flicked them open one by one, kissing the skin he revealed. When his mouth covered the tip of her right breast, Clarissa moaned out loud.

"Hush, my love," he said in a throaty whisper.

Clarissa's eyes drifted closed as his hands found more and more of her. His touch set her on fire. The world blurred around her until it was only a tiny space surrounded by shadows and moonlight and the exquisite caress of her husband's hands as he raised her legs and locked them around his hips.

"Hold on to me," he instructed, his voice hoarse, his breathing as labored as hers. "Don't let go."

As if she could, Clarissa thought silently. She rained kisses over his face as he circled his hips and rocked slowly back and forth, making her body tighten in tiny waves of pleasure. Wanting to touch him, her hands found the buttons on his shirt and undid them hastily. When she slid her fingers inside to comb the thick mat of hair that covered his chest, then pulled it, Simon groaned against her throat.

His hand gripped her bottom as he drove into her harder and harder, unable to stop the flow of passion one kiss had ignited. Simon pulled back and thrust even harder, wanting to possess as much of Clarissa as he could, needing to remind himself that she did, in fact, belong to him, that he had a right to her, to all that she was. He couldn't account for the unnatural hunger that had been triggered by discovering what she was up to in Yorkshire. He didn't think it could be explained. All he knew was that he wasn't going to let her keep a part of herself separate from him.

From the corner of his eyes, Simon could see the empty cradle. The thought of giving Clarissa a child added fuel to the exotic fire burning in his body. Maybe a child would calm her outrageous behavior? Once she was too big to do more than waddle about the house, perhaps she wouldn't go about plotting and scheming social scandals? Maybe giving Clarissa a child would give him some peace?

Maybe? But Simon doubted it. He looked at her through the heat of passion and saw more than he'd ever seen before. God, she was lovely. With her eyes closed and her lips moist and swollen from his kisses, he couldn't deny that she made him feel more alive than he'd felt in his entire life. With the heat of her body hugging him so exquisitely, he couldn't stop wanting her. And he did want her. All of her. Especially her heart. A heart that was big enough, generous enough, to reach out to those other people turned away.

Such a loving heart.

And he wanted that heart to love him, too.

Suddenly, the hunger had a name. Desire was no longer desire. It was that deep, unexplained need that he'd felt the first time he'd kissed her. As Simon moved inside her, he knew that he wanted Clarissa to love him. That's why he'd demanded what he had of her, thinking their physical union would eventually leave her heart open and vulnerable. Instead, it was his heart that was lying open and exposed.

The passion rose higher and higher with each stroke of Simon's body. Clarissa couldn't open her eyes. It was as if they'd been welded shut. All she could do was feel that wonderful, shimmering sensation that he evoked with each thrust. It grew and grew until her nails were making crescent marks on his bare shoulders and her body felt as if it were going to explode. But still Simon didn't stop. He continued moving, plunging deeper inside her with each thrust, stealing a part of her soul, until her body did explode and she moaned against the damp skin of his neck.

Clarissa was still floating somewhere between a dream and reality when Simon's muscles grew taut and he drove inside her one last time. An instant later, she felt him surrender to the same passion that had stolen her senses.

Seconds turned into minutes as they clung to each other. Clarissa was still holding on to his shoulders, but not as tightly now. Simon was still breathing heavily, but his body had finally relaxed. His hands made their way from her bottom to the curve of her knees, and he lowered her feet back to the floor. She slumped against the wall, unable to stand.

When Simon finally raised his head, he kissed her gently on the mouth. "You are a very distracting female, madam."

Because his voice was as soft as the moonlight and his eyes were glowing with satisfaction, Clarissa smiled up at him. He stared at her for a long moment, then kissed her again. His tongue parted her lips, and he tasted her as deeply as he'd claimed her body. When he pulled back this time, he was frowning.

"What have I done now?" she asked, thinking she'd never understand the man.

Simon shook his head, not answering her. He righted his clothing, then reached out and began buttoning her blouse as quickly as he'd unbuttoned it earlier. "I want to meet the women."

Clarissa shook her head, sending a mass of disheveled auburn hair falling around her shoulders. "You've already scared them to death."

Simon's frown grew fiercer. "The one who fainted . . ." His voice trailed off as the memory came rushing back, no longer blocked by a physical desire he'd had to satisfy or go mad. "Bloody everlasting hell!"

"What?"

"What's her name?" he demanded, forgetting the buttons.

"Who's name? And what has you cursing now?"

"The girl!" Simon threw his hands up in a frustrated gesture. "The one who fainted. What's her bloody name?"

"Eldridge," Clarissa replied. "Miss Sara Eldridge."

"No, it isn't," he roared like a hungry lion. "Damnation. Of all the rotten luck . . ."

His curses trailed off as he turned on the heels

of his boots and marched out of the room. Clarissa rushed after him, trying to button her blouse and tidy her hair at the same time.

"Simon, for the love of God, stop and tell me what you're mumbling about."

Her husband didn't acknowledge her words. Instead, Simon stormed down the stairs. When he reached the parlor door, he gave Clarissa a scathing look before pushing the doors open and invading the room. By the time she reached the doorway, her ladies were scattering like kittens in a thunderstorm. All but Miss Eldridge. Simon had the young lady pinned to her chair with a disapproving glare that was sure to send her into another faint.

"Simon?"

Clarissa's husband silenced her with another one of his scolding looks. His feet were braced apart like an ancient warrior ready to do battle. Then, with a sweep of his hand, he introduced her to the young lady Clarissa thought was Sara Eldridge.

"Madam wife, may I introduce Lady Beatrice Dalton."

Miss Eldridge or Lady Dalton, whoever she was, cringed in the chair. The young woman looked at her hands, folded demurely in her lap. Rain pelted the parlor windows as Clarissa shut the door behind her, thinking her husband had surely lost his wits. Lord Dalton was one of the most powerful men in England.

"How did you manage to evade your uncle and end up here?" Simon demanded.

Her uncle! Clarissa's stomach began to churn. If Lord Dalton found out about Haven House, it would be ten times worse than having Simon discover it. Unsure what to do or think, Clarissa waited as her husband continued his interrogation.

He rephrased the question. "Where are you supposed to be?"

"Scotland," the young woman replied, confirming her true identity. "I have some relatives there. On my mother's side. Uncle Alec thinks that I'm visiting them."

Clarissa slumped onto the settee. "But how . . ."

Lady Dalton looked at her. She was barely eighteen years old, and her youth showed her confused features. Medium-brown hair framed a pale face. Her eyes were brimming with tears, and her bottom lip was quivering. "My uncle is my guardian, but he couldn't care less where I spend my time as long as it isn't under his feet. He's too preoccupied with politics and his own personal agenda to care if I'm whiling away the summer in Scotland or sitting alone at one of our family estates."

Simon could see Clarissa softening under the tearful explanation. He interrupted, intent on getting some answers and getting them quickly. "That doesn't explain how you managed to carry off this little charade. Nor does it supply the name of the man who fathered your child."

Lady Dalton began wringing her hands. "My maid helped me. She's been with me since my parents died. When I discovered that I was going to have a child, she—"

"Found the generous Mrs. Quigley," Simon supplied.

"I want to keep my baby," Lady Dalton said with surprising conviction for a woman who looked ready to swoon.

"And how do you think to manage that?" Simon's voice grew harsh. "A lady of your position can't return from a trip to Scotland with a babe under her arm and not be noticed. What about your uncle? Indifferent or not, he's bound to realize his household has increased."

"Really, Simon, must you be rude?" Clarissa said, recovering from the shock of finding Lord Dalton's niece among her flock. "Stop badgering the poor girl."

"The poor girl has a pedigree that links her to the royal family," Simon said, gritting his teeth. "My God, am I the only one who realizes the ramifications of her being here?"

"No, you are not," Clarissa replied calmly. "And if you'd stop ranting long enough for Lady Dalton to regain her composure, we might be able to make some sense of this mess."

"Trust me, madam, there is nothing sensible about any of this. It's mayhem at its finest."

Beatrice began crying in earnest. Clarissa frowned, and Simon began to pace the room. Every time he thought he'd never been more angry in his life, he found something that made him more furious than the last time. And all within the last twenty-four hours. It was enough to make a man take to drink.

"Now, now," Clarissa said, trying her best to soothe Lady Dalton. Of course, she couldn't blame the poor girl for crying. In fact, Clarissa could do with a little crying herself. The last few days had been anything but normal. "Calm yourself and tell me how you think to keep the child with you. My husband is right. It won't be easily done."

Lady Dalton sniffled into the lace hankie Clarissa produced. "I plan on hiring a maid to raise the child. My uncle has hundreds of servants; one more won't be noticed. If she arrives with the baby, everyone will assume that it belongs to her."

"The idea sounds a bit flimsy," Clarissa told her.

"It's preposterous!" Simon announced. "And totally unnecessary. All Lady Dalton has to do is give me the name of the man and she will be legally wed before week's end. Unless, of course, the man is already married. Is he?" Simon turned on the still-sniffling young lady.

It took another ten minutes for Lady Dalton to

answer him. Her brown eyes were red and swollen when she looked up at him. "He is not married."

"Excellent," Simon said, thinking he'd finally found something he could handle. A discreet call upon the gentleman and a special license would take care of things.

"I won't marry him," Beatrice announced firmly. "He doesn't love me."

"Of all the silly, romantic notions!" Had every female in England gone suddenly mad? "That didn't stop you from—"

"That's enough," Clarissa said, coming to Lady Dalton's rescue. She wasn't about to relive the argument she'd had with Simon the day he'd dismissed Prissy. "I think you should retire to the library, my lord, and let me handle this."

"I have no intentions of retiring anywhere unless it's to Bedlam," Simon replied bluntly. Taking a deep breath, he tried again. "Now, Lady Dalton. Who is the man?"

The young woman blew daintily into the hankie and shook her head. "I won't tell you. And I won't be forced into marriage. If I have to be miserable, I'd rather do it on my own."

Simon was on the verge of demanding an answer when a knock on the door stopped him. He jerked it open and demanded. "Who the hell are you?"

The jovial-looking man on the other side smiled. "Dr. Hayward, my lord. I was told that Miss Eldridge wasn't feeling up to snuff."

"Miss Eldridge is fine, sir. Nevertheless, do come in. I have been outnumbered since my arrival this afternoon. The addition of another man is most welcome."

Understanding completely, Dr. Hayward sauntered into the room. The physician was a heavy man with silver hair and a ruddy complexion. His face was pouched, and his nose was wide and flat.

His bright blue eyes sparkled as he set his medical bag on the table and reached for Lady Dalton's hand. "Now, my dear. Crying isn't good for the babe. Take a good deep breath and let it out slowly. That's the trick. Now another one."

While Dr. Hayward attended the frazzled Lady Dalton, Simon took Clarissa by the arm and escorted her to the corner of the room. Keeping his back to the subject at hand, Simon kept his voice down and his wife within his grasp. "You had no idea who she was?"

"Of course not," Clarissa chided him. "Even I don't have enough brass to take on Lord Dalton."

Simon disagreed but wisely kept his opinion to himself. "Has she made mention of the man?"

Clarissa shook her head. "It isn't something I insist upon," she told him. "My experience here has taught me that the man has very little to offer once the damage is done."

Simon thought it best not to comment on the insult to his gender. "If he's unmarried, then he has more than enough," he retorted. "We have to get her married. Her uncle won't be as easily fooled as she wants to believe, and he isn't above casting her out if he discovers the truth. Marriage with or without love is preferable to what she'll face if Dalton gets wind of this."

Clarissa was tempted to tell Simon that marriage without love had little to offer any woman, but she decided to postpone that debate until another time. Right now, they had more important things to discuss.

"Do you recall hearing any gossip about Lady Dalton or her preference in gentlemen?"

"I don't listen to gossip," Clarissa said adamantly.

"Now isn't the time to get huffy," Simon reminded her. "Damn, the man could be one of a hundred gentleman. She may be a mouse of a woman, but her uncle's fortune would attract a pack of wolves. One must have seduced her."

"I don't think it was seduction," Clarissa said. "She wouldn't be so determined to keep the child if she thought she'd been used, then cast aside."

Simon considered the possibility, thinking it didn't make much difference now. Blind love or seduction, the girl was pregnant, and he had to find out the man's name. Her uncle's rank and wealth could attract a husband easily enough, but he couldn't think of a single man in the peerage who would take a woman to wife knowing she was carrying another man's child. Heirs were too important, not to mention a man's pride.

"I need time to think," he said, glancing over his shoulder. Lady Dalton was stretched out on the settee, with Dr. Hayward hovering over her like a mother hen. He doubted he was going to get any useful information out of the young woman tonight. "I think it's time for Lady Dalton to retire for the evening. And you've had a long day as well. I'll join you upstairs after I've spoken with the good doctor."

Clarissa didn't like the idea of leaving Simon alone with Dr. Hayward. On the other hand, Lady Dalton wasn't up to another bout of questions. Deciding between the two evils, she helped Beatrice to her feet and led her from the room, insisting that the young lady shouldn't make herself sick worrying over things. A solution would be found.

Simon wasn't sure there was a solution—short of murdering his wife.

"Shall we retire to the library, Dr. Hayward?" Simon suggested as his wife and her pregnant fledging disappeared down the hall. "I could use a drink."

"I'm right behind you," Dr. Hayward said, grabbing up his bag. "From what Huxley told me, it's been an eventful day."

"You could say that," Simon said over his shoulder.

He walked across the foyer and into the library. A few seconds later, he and the country physician were both sipping the last of Mrs. Flannigan's Irish whiskey. "I'm almost afraid to ask how my wife got you to join her band of renegades," Simon remarked, relaxing in the leather chair behind the desk. "I'd like to think she stopped short of blackmail."

"I'm afraid there's nothing that spectacular in my past," the physician replied with a light chuckle. "I've always led a rather boring life."

"Until now," Simon countered.

Dr. Hayward grinned. "Taking care of the ladies does keep me busy. I've got two ready to deliver any day now. I'm surprised your arrival didn't put them into labor."

"Perish the thought," Simon mumbled. "Now, tell me. What exactly do you think of my wife's little charity."

"Frankly speaking?"

"By all means," Simon assured him. "I've had enough deception to last me a lifetime."

The physician gave him a pensive look. "I think your wife is afraid to trust anyone with her little secret."

"I'm not anyone," Simon reminded him. "I'm her husband. And she's certainly trusted enough people with her little secret up to now. From what I gather, she's got a regular band of volunteers just waiting to do good deeds."

"What she's doing here is more than a good deed, my lord. It's a blessing," Dr. Hayward replied firmly. "I've had the misfortune of seeing the other side of things. There's nothing pretty about watching a young woman die in childbed because she's malnourished or half-dead with pneumonia. The children don't do much better than their mothers. The ones who do survive end up being carted off to an orphanage, where they're not likely to last a year."

Simon heard the loyalty in the physician's voice and knew that everyone else associated with his wife felt the same way. Nor could he contradict the man's description of what happened to young ladies who found themselves with a child but no husband. "I'm not faulting your dedication to my wife, Dr. Hayward. But I'm forced to take a more pragmatic view of things. Angel of mercy that she is, she is still my wife."

"Will you close the house?"

Simon took a swallow of whiskey and walked to the window. Somewhere in the house a clock chimed ten. As he stared out the window, Simon suddenly realized just how important Haven House was to his wife. It was important enough for her to propose marriage and to humble herself by accepting the outrageous conditions he'd attached to his acceptance. She cared enough about the women and children under her care to risk her reputation to protect them. The magnitude of her compassion went beyond anything Simon had ever encountered before. It was humbling to think how little he'd done for others in his life compared to what his wife was attempting to do here in Yorkshire. Eight unborn children. It was a heavy weight to carry, yet Clarissa's shoulders didn't seem burdened by it.

"I will not close the house," Simon finally responded, turning to face the doctor. "As to what I will do, I'm not entirely sure. But rest assured, I will do something. Things cannot continue as they are. The situation is far too volatile."

* * *

While Simon drank whiskey and contemplated the scandalous situation waiting to explode in his face, Clarissa paced the upstairs bedroom, wondering what she was going to do with a pregnant aristocrat. Lady Dalton might appear to be a mousy woman, but she'd managed to get herself to Yorkshire without raising anyone's suspicions. Clarissa felt a certain empathy with the young lady. What would she have done under the same circumstances? It was hard to say. The only thing she did know was that if their roles were reversed, Clarissa would feel just as adamantly about wanting to keep Simon's child.

Clarissa stopped pacing and dropped languidly into the chair by the fire, regarding the orange flames with disinterest. What was Simon going to do? She was certain that he was going to do something. Her husband wasn't the kind of man to stand idly by while things unraveled around him.

"I thought you'd be asleep by now," Simon said as he entered the room. "It's after midnight."

"I'm exhausted, but I'm not the least bit sleepy," Clarissa replied as she watched her husband shed his jacket. Her fingers twisted in the soft fleece of her robe as she tried to contain her impatience. "Is Dr. Hayward still about?"

"I had Huxley show him to one of the habitable rooms," Simon told her. "But don't fret. He looked in on your ladies before he retired. He assured me that they were all resting peacefully."

"Even Lady Dalton?"

Simon shrugged his shoulders as he untied his cravat and began unbuttoning his shirt. "I doubt that Lady Dalton will sleep as well as the others. She no doubt realizes that I will not give up my pursuit of the name of the man who sired her child."

"What if she simply refuses to tell you?"

Simon's gaze became dangerously cold as he sat

down on the bed and took off his boots. "She *will* tell me, one way or the other. Until then, the only thing we can do is get some sleep. Come to bed, Madam."

Clarissa eyed him uneasily. "You can't force the man's name from her, Simon. And what if you do, only to discover that he refuses to acknowledge that he fathered her child? Just because you assume him to be a gentleman doesn't make him one. He could be a rake who thought to seduce her into marriage because his own estates are lacking."

"You thought differently in the parlor," Simon reminded her. "You seemed convinced that Lady Dalton harbored strong feelings for the man."

"I believe she does," Clarissa replied. "But that doesn't mean the man harbors any feelings for her. If he did, she would have told him about the babe."

Simon released a frustrated sigh as he shed his trousers. "At the moment, I'm not capable of gauging a pregnant woman's emotions or those of an unknown gentleman. In fact, I'm finding myself incapable of gauging anyone's emotions. Especially those of my adventurous wife."

"I'm not adventurous," Clarissa said, defending herself.

Her eyes were drawn to the sleek muscles of Simon's body as he pulled back the coverlet and got into bed. He folded his arms behind his head on the pillow and gave her one of his arrogant smiles. "Perhaps rash, impetuous, and unorthodox would be better adjectives."

"I am none of those things," she flared. "I'm only trying to help people."

"I know, sweetheart," Simon's voice turned soft. "Now come to bed. I'm cold."

Clarissa frowned, then stalked to the bed. She shed her robe, draping it over the footboard, then joined her husband. Once she was settled in his arms, Clarissa peered up at him. "Do you really intend on taking over my personal account?"

Simon placed a kiss on top of her upturned nose. "Yes," he told her. "As of this moment, I manage all of our affairs, including your notorious charities."

"There is nothing notorious—"

"Hush," he said, brushing a kiss across her mouth. "It's too late to argue. You trusted me enough to propose, now you must trust me enough to take care of things."

Clarissa didn't like the sound of that. "If by taking care of things you mean to turn me into a pliable, submissive wife who's afraid to purchase a bonnet without your advance approval, then I fear we will spend the remainder of our lives at cross-purposes, my lord."

When Clarissa received nothing but silence as a response to her admonition, she looked at her husband again. Simon's eyes were closed, and he appeared to be sleeping. "I will not be ignored in this, Simon," she whispered fervently.

Still no response.

Thinking her husband was either a very good actor or totally exhausted from the day's activities, Clarissa snuggled against him and quickly fell asleep.

Seventeen

Over the course of the next several days, Clarissa wrestled with feelings of relief and frustration. Her husband had, in his usual efficient manner, taken over the running of the estate. A part of her was relieved, because she didn't relish dealing with the carpenters, painters, and masons that had been hired to right the damage the fire had done to the house. On the other hand, she didn't like having the responsibility of Haven House snatched out of her hands as if she had no business being involved in the repairs that were taking place. Whenever she made an inquiry of Mrs. Flannigan or Huxley, she was told that his lordship had already seen to the matter. Haven House belonged to her, and she didn't care for the way Simon was currently ruling the roost.

The library clock struck eleven as she strolled into the room to find her husband sitting behind the desk, his head bent over a pile of papers that consisted mostly of bills submitted by the workmen he had hired to replace the fire-scarred roof. "Excuse me, my lord," she said, shutting the door behind her. "Huxley said you requested my company."

Simon raised his head and studied Clarissa for a

short moment. Looking at his wife wasn't an unpleasant task. Dressed in a blue-and-white striped gown that called attention to her female form she looked extremely lovely this morning. Her gleaming auburn curls were pulled away from her face and secured with a velvet ribbon. The casual style accented her features and the brilliant shade of her eyes. A bleached straw bonnet, adorned with silk daisies and a blue scarf, was dangling from her right hand.

"Huxley said you requested the carriage," Simon said to her. "May I ask why?"

Clarissa's violet eyes took on a deeper hue as she looked at him sharply. "I wasn't aware that you wanted to know my whereabouts every moment of every day, my lord. Should I prepare a list of activities for you to review and approve before breakfast?"

"There is no need to raise your voice or lose your temper," he replied calmly. "I am merely inquiring into your plans for the day."

"Oh, of course," she retorted sharply. "You now have the right to make such inquiries. Forgive my lack of memory."

"Sit down," Simon countered gruffly.

Ignoring his order, Clarissa strolled to the windows that overlooked the garden. The hedges needed trimming, and the fish pond was empty, but if one overlooked those inadequacies, the garden seemed light and cheerful. Several rosebushes, heavy with new buds, were straining toward the sunlight that had replaced the on again, off again rain of the last several days. The sounds of male voices, mingled in conversation and curses, could be heard drifting on the light wind that brought with it the scent of the moors. The pounding of hammers and the brittle sound of timber being cut joined the voices of the workmen. Feeling confined by the secrets she'd kept and the restricted living quarters of the house, Clarissa longed to be outside, where she could feel the sunshine on her skin and see the magic of the summer day.

"Madam . . ."

"I'm not in the mood to idle away the day," she said over her shoulder. She hated having to explain her actions, but she feared that Simon would countermand her order if she didn't offer him some explanation. "I asked Huxley to have the carriage brought round so I could go into the village. With Miss Lullumber's baby due, I thought to do some shopping. Besides, it's a lovely day. I want to enjoy it."

Simon leaned back in his chair. He was feeling as restless as his wife, but it had little to do with the weather and everything to do with the guilt that was weighing more heavily on his shoulders with each passing day. Like the jealousy he hadn't felt until he'd seen Clarissa dancing with another man, guilt was a new emotion for him. Until arriving in Yorkshire, he'd no reason to duel with the sentiment. His life had been simple and straightforward. But there was nothing simple about what his wife was doing, and he feared that like it or not, he was now a partner in her clandestine charity.

The last few days had revealed a lot of things. Some of them Simon was finally beginning to understand. Others were still giving him pause. For one, he was no closer to discovering the father of Lady Dalton's child than he'd been the night he'd confronted her in the parlor. The young lady avoided him at all cost, and if it wasn't for Huxley's constant reassurance that she hadn't fled to parts unknown, Simon wouldn't know she was living under the same roof. He could almost say the same thing about his wife. Clarissa seemed to prefer the company of her *ladies* to that of her husband, and

Simon knew that one of the reasons he was feeling restless was because he wanted his wife to himself. He didn't like sharing her with other people, even if there was no reason to be jealous of the women residents, who demanded her attention on an hourly basis.

His expression hardened to an intense frown as Clarissa continued to stare out the window, keeping her back to him. The reason for his guilt was because he'd hurt his wife's feelings and he wasn't sure how to go about mending the situation. There was no way he could make her understand that his concern was more than an arrogant male need to oversee her every move. They'd spent the last few days exchanging polite pleasantries and the last two nights sleeping stiffly by each other's side. Being unsure of so many things, Simon had spent the morning brooding over his sudden inability to sweep Clarissa off her feet and into his arms.

Perhaps a change of scenery would put a smile back on his wife's lovely face.

"I have some business to attend to in the village," he said, coming to his feet. "I'll accompany you."

Clarissa misunderstood his desire for her company. To her way of thinking, Simon had decided she wasn't to be trusted out of his sight. "Am I to have a chaperone at all times, my lord? Surely I can be trusted to buy some muslin and strands of ribbon."

"You can buy all the muslin and ribbon you want," Simon replied. He refused to be baited by the sarcasm in Clarissa's voice. She'd been pushing him in the direction of a fresh argument for the last two days, but he had no intention of surrendering to the temptation. Clarissa needed to understand that he would deal with things in his own way.

Experience had taught him that losing his temper rarely accomplished anything.

Clarissa didn't hear Simon rise from his chair. He was suddenly behind her, his strong arms coming around her waist. He hugged her close, then bent down and began nibbling on the lobe of her right ear. "If all you required was a chaperone, my dear, I'd send Huxley along. God knows the man has become an expert at the job."

Clarissa stiffened in his arms, but she didn't pull away. She could feel the warmth of Simon's body slowly seeping through her clothing, and she realized that she missed being held in his arms. The physical closeness they shared was different from the passion that was so easily kindled between them. She simply liked being close to him. It brought a certain contentment with it, as if she'd finally found her true place in the world.

If only Simon could feel the same contentment. If only he whispered words of love rather than teasing chastisements meant to remind her that she'd broken the rules and now had to suffer the consequences.

Simon's mouth wandered from the tip of his wife's ear to the soft skin above the collar of her dress. The palm of his hands flattened against her lower stomach, and he found himself thinking of what it would be like to place his hand over her rounded belly and feel his child kicking. He'd been surprised the previous morning when he'd come down to breakfast to find a chubby toddler racing about the foyer. Simon had stared at the little boy, with his topping of brown curls and wide blue eyes, and found himself lost in the thought of having a son of his own. One of the women, who he'd incorrectly assumed wasn't far enough along to show her condition, had scooped up the little boy and disappeared into the kitchen.

Simon had eaten his breakfast alone after being informed by Huxley that the mother of the little boy was one of the women who was waiting to take over the house Clarissa had just purchased in Plymouth. The other was Miss Lullumber, who looked like an overripe pumpkin and whom Dr. Hayward had restricted to short walks in the garden until her child was delivered.

When Simon turned Clarissa in his arms and lowered his head to kiss her in earnest, she pulled away. She hated to break the spell he was casting over her senses, but Clarissa wasn't ready to be seduced again. "The carriage is waiting, my lord."

"So it is," he said, releasing her.

A short time later, Simon helped her into the carriage. Clarissa placed her bonnet on the seat beside her, forcing her husband to sit across from her to keep from ruining one of Mrs. Quigley's creations. Clarissa didn't care for the atmosphere within the carriage once Simon had tapped on the roof to send them on their way. Her husband looked far too handsome in a rust-colored, snug-fitting jacket and black trousers that emphasized the strong muscularity of his legs. He crossed his feet at the ankles and relaxed against the leather cushions. As the hem of her dress brushed against his gleaming black boots, Clarissa realized she'd have little luck in purging her mind of its current thoughts. Having Simon within kissing distance made staying angry at him almost impossible.

"What business awaits you in town?" she asked, preferring polite conversation to the steely silence that was beginning to make her nervous.

"Myles told me the village had a telegraph office," Simon told her. "Supervising the repairs is going to keep us here for several more weeks. I need to cancel some previously scheduled appointments to accommodate the new schedule."

"I'm perfectly capable of overseeing Haven House," she replied. "If you wish to continue the summer schedule you had arranged, you are free to do so."

"Am I?" Simon said in icy amusement. "Are you suggesting that I forgo my responsibilities to my wife in favor of my business investments? That doesn't sound like a new bride. Are you tiring of me so quickly, love?"

Clarissa didn't care for the endearment Simon tacked on to his question, because it reminded her that he didn't love her at all. In fact, she was less certain about what he felt for her now than she had been prior to his arrival in Yorkshire. "What I'm growing tired of, my lord, is your increasing interest in my personal affairs. Although you think our agreement voided, I do not. I would prefer for things to return to the way they were."

"Ahhh, yes," he said slowly. "They way they were. Which means that you found yourself free to do whatever you wished with your money while I presumed that you were acting with some intelligence."

"I am not lacking in intelligence," she snapped, clearly insulted.

"You think what you are doing is intelligent," Simon scoffed, knowing the argument he had hoped to avoid was now inevitable. "Your good intentions could be discovered at any moment, madam. And with that discovery comes the ruination of your reputation. What will the queen think if she hears of your charitable endeavors? Do you think she will applaud your generosity? I think not. Victoria isn't as forgiving as her subjects would like to think. When it comes to matters of morality, she is inflexible in her attitudes. I will not be called to court to defend an outrageous wife."

"Then why haven't you closed Haven House?

Why risk hiring workmen who may boast of their occupation after a cup or two of ale? Why, all of Yorkshire could learn about your outrageous wife before another week passes," Clarissa countered almost savagely. "Wouldn't it be easier to let the walls crumble from fire and neglect than to risk the Queen's displeasure?"

"Would barring the door of Haven House end your enthusiasm for the work you have begun?" Simon asked. "I think not. Which means I have little recourse except that which I have taken."

"And that is?"

"To become enthralled in your unorthodox plot to right the wrongs of society," Simon admitted somewhat reluctantly. He held up his hand as a smile began to lighten his wife's face. "Don't mistake my intentions, madam. I am still opposed to your surreptitious activities. Unfortunately, your endeavors can't be dispatched as easily as they were begun. Nevertheless, I will not lower myself to the standards you expect from me and bar the door. I will see the house restored and the residence comfortable. After that—"

Clarissa interrupted him. "What I began shouldn't be undone. It's too important. Surely you can see that much, Simon. When I look at my ladies, I don't see their immorality. I see their need. A need that no one in our civilized world cares to recognize. We are too busy judging them to offer them the compassion we would eagerly give a stray dog."

"I am not concerned with society's lack of compassion," Simon told her bluntly. "My first responsibility is to your reputation. I will not have your name spoken with disdain."

"You mean the Sheridan name, don't you?"

"I mean that you will not engage in any more secret charities without my knowledge," Simon replied, keeping his temper in check. It wasn't easy.

His wife was hitting her target much too expertly for him to feel comfortable about the course of their conversation.

Clarissa was about to send another volley of disagreeable words toward her husband when the carriage came to a stop in front of the village telegraph office. The building's low-pitched roof displayed a wooden sign that informed the hamlet's residents that they could send a wire or pick up their mail, while another smaller sign informed them of the name of the local magistrate. A chimney at the back of the scrubby building was blackened with soot but lacking smoke, attesting to the day's warmth.

Simon opened the carriage door and stepped out. After extending a helping hand to his wife, he waited until she had tied the bonnet's blue scarf into a perky bow under her chin before informing her that he would join her as soon as he'd sent a wire. Clarissa managed a smile, more for the benefit of the villagers lingering outside the telegraph office than for her husband, before she gathered up her skirts and started off down the narrow lane that formed the hamlet's main street. Finding the shop she desired, Clarissa opened the door and stepped inside.

She was greeted with the pungent aroma of dried spices and fresh-cut wildflowers. The apothecary wasn't as large as the ones she'd visited in London, but it was well stocked. Dingy curtains had been pulled back to allow the day's light into the rectangular room. Several wooden cases with dull plate doors displayed jars and bottles, all filled with herbal remedies and elixirs that promised the restoration of one's good health.

"Can I be of service, milady?" A man stepped out from behind the curtain that shielded the back of the shop from customer scrutiny. The proprietor was a scruffy, pitiful looking man with shaggy gray hair and more space in his mouth than teeth, but his eyes sparkled with kindness, and Clarissa smiled back. She withdrew the list Dr. Hayward had given her from the pocket of her dress and requested the appropriate herbs for the tea the physician frequently prescribed for his patients.

"This smells lovely," Clarissa remarked as she lifted a ceramic jar to her nose.

"It's dried mulberry," the shopkeeper informed her. "It's good for keeping your bed linens fresh and moths out of your wardrobe. I have several ladies who use it to perfume their baths."

"I'll take a pouch," she said before ambling over to another table littered with small amber bottles. She pulled the cork from one of the bottles and took a sniff. Her eyes began to tear, and she gasped for breath.

"I doubt that your ladyship would be interested in that remedy," the proprietor said, chuckling.

"It smells like horse liniment," she muttered, wiggling her nose in disgust as she replaced the cork and set the bottle away from her.

While the shopkeeper filled her order for herbs, Clarissa turned her attention to the small bundles of dried flowers lying on a narrow table in front of the window. The flowers looked so delicate that she was reluctant to do more than gaze at them.

While his wife was comparing her tenuous relationship with her new husband to the fragile petals of a wildflower, Simon was listening to the sharp click-clack of the telegraph key. The man behind the counter had gray hair. Underneath his bushy brows, his eyes were small and pouched. His chin ran into the bulge of his thick neck, and his mouth was twisted into a determined line as he turned Simon's request into short metallic dots and dashes that would be interpreted in London. Shortly after his message was received, a runner would be dispatched to the town house near Hyde Park's north entrance, and help would be on its way.

Simon had thought long and hard about seeking his friend's assistance and had finally reached the conclusion that he had little choice. He knew he could trust Albright to keep the unsavory nature of his wife's Yorkshire business to himself after he'd gotten over the shock of it. Besides, the viscount, still a bachelor and with a bachelor's appetites, was Simon's best source of information regarding Lady Dalton. If anyone could ferret out the news of the young lady's recent romance, it was Viscount Thornton.

After paying the clerk, Simon stepped outside and began the search for his wife. Clarissa wouldn't be hard to locate considering the limited number of shops the village of Shipley offered. He found her in the narrow confines of the dressmaker's shop, sorting through a table of fabric. Clarissa was studying the bright paisley pattern of a shawl. The colorful, swirled design, with its heavy gold fringe, reminded Simon of a Persian rug. Taking the garment from her hands, he draped it over her shoulders.

"The bold colors suit you," he said.

Clarissa once again misunderstood his words, thinking he was referring to her personality instead of her physical features. A retort was ready to pass her lips when Simon's mouth brushed lightly across her forehead. He looked over her head at the gaunt shopkeeper and smiled. "My lady seems to like the shawl. I shall buy it for her."

"Aye, milord, it's a pretty thing, to be sure," the woman replied, smiling. Her face looked like a withered apple, but her bright green eyes danced with amusement as she watched the fancy lord try to please his lady.

Clarissa was tempted to put the shawl back on the table, but she didn't want to offend her husband under the watchful eye of the shopkeeper. Instead, she allowed Simon to tie the shawl loosely around her shoulders, his hands brushing ever so lightly over the bodice of her dress. She looked up at him and realized her clothing hadn't completely concealed the effect the gentle caress had had on her. Simon's voice, when he spoke, was soft and seductive.

"Is there anything else my lady desires?"

"Not at the moment," Clarissa replied stiffly, knowing her body had betrayed her. Simon was smiling as she turned away from him and began sorting through a pile of unbleached muslin.

Damn the man! She'd planned on having some time to herself today, thinking the village offered the distance she would need to sort out the jumble of thoughts that had collected in her head over the last few days. But how was she to think at all with Simon hovering over her shoulder like a bee flitting around a flower? Forcing herself to think of the quality of the cloth she was buying, Clarissa asked the shopkeeper to cut several yards of the buttercream muslin to go along with the other goods she had selected before her husband had strolled into the shop. Once her purchases had been wrapped in brown paper and tied securely with twine, Clarissa thanked the shop owner and walked outside, leaving Simon to settle the bill.

Once they were in the carriage and on their way back to Haven House, Clarissa gave Simon a skeptical glance. "You didn't send a wire to Lord Dalton, did you?"

Simon laughed. "Lord Dalton is the last man I want to communicate with at the moment," he told her. "Besides, what would I say to the stately old gentleman? 'Pardon me, my lord, but your niece is growing fatter by the day, and I haven't the slightest idea who caused the problem.' "

"Then who did you wire?" she asked.

"Clarence Albright," Simon replied, wishing every word they exchanged wasn't linked to Haven House and its questionable future. How he longed to return to the political debates and verbal jousts he and Clarissa had engaged in while at Sheridan Hall. Of course, now he could understand why she opposed his more conservative approach to things. His wife was as liberal in her thinking as she was fiery in her passion.

"The viscount!" Clarissa exclaimed. "Whatever for?"

"Because he's the only man I can trust at the moment," her husband replied stiffly. "And I have no intention of leaving you in Yorkshire while I return to London and investigate Lady Dalton's recent past."

Clarissa wanted to argue with Simon's reasoning, but she didn't. He was right about the viscount being able to shed some light on Beatrice's unnamed lover. Since Albright was currently looking for a wife, he had been invited to every soiree and ball of any consequence to be held in London for the last six months. If there were rumors of Lady Dalton's indiscretion, he would be privy to them. Still, she had to voice her doubts. "I'm not so sure that discovering the name of Lady Dalton's lover will accomplish your ultimate goal, my lord. If the man's intentions held any honor, he would have pursued her hand in marriage."

"Not necessarily," Simon replied. "Her uncle isn't an easy man to please, and I fear that Dalton has someone already in mind for his niece."

"Who?"

"Anyone that can strengthen his already massive influence, for one," Simon said dryly. "Which limits the number of suitable gentlemen he would welcome should they come calling."

Simon was right again. Clarissa didn't know a lot about Lord Dalton, but she had heard from her own grandfather that the man's arrogance surpassed his political greed, which was said to be formidable.

They arrived back at Haven House to find Miss Lullumber in labor. While Mrs. Flannigan was helping Dr. Hayward, the other ladies waited in the parlor. Finding himself in unknown territory, Simon secluded himself in the library, while his wife joined Dr. Hayward.

The afternoon stretched into the evening, and Simon wondered how long it took a woman to actually have a child. Pouring himself a drink, Simon settled into a chair and waited.

It was just past midnight when Clarissa cautiously opened the door of the library and stepped inside. She smiled when she saw Simon sleeping, his legs stretched out in front of him, his head resting against one side of the wing-backed chair near the fire. He'd removed his jacket, and his shirt was unbuttoned at the top, revealing a sprinkling of dark chest hair. An unfinished glass of brandy rested on the table beside him.

He awoke at the sound of the door being closed. Rubbing the sleep from his eyes, Simon glanced at the clock. "My God," he grumbled sleepily. "Does it always take this long?"

"Sometimes," Clarissa replied. "But Miss Lullumber is resting, and the babe is healthy." She smiled. "It's a little girl."

Simon returned her smile, then held out his hand.

Clarissa walked to where he was sitting. When he tugged her down onto his lap, she went willingly. He twisted his fingers into her loose hair and covered her mouth. The kiss was soft, yet demanding, and she returned it. Afterward, she laid her head against Simon's shoulders and sighed.

"You're tired," he said, wrapping his arms around her.

"Not as tired as Miss Lullumber," she replied with a soft laugh.

Her smile brought sunshine into the dark room, and Simon felt something inside him grow warm with the knowledge that he loved someone as special as his wife. It was more than desire, and he knew it now. When had passion turned into love? He wasn't sure. And it didn't seem to matter all of a sudden. What did matter was that he loved Clarissa more than he'd ever thought it possible to love anyone. Realizing that he loved his wife only strengthened Simon's resolve to shelter her from the malicious gossip of their peers. He also realized that protecting her meant protecting the women and children she had gathered under her wing.

He almost laughed at the irony of his present situation. Who would have thought such a thing possible? Still, here he was, sitting in a house in Yorkshire doing just that. He was paying the workmen twice their normal wage, under the strict requirement that they were to keep their mouths shut about anything they saw or heard around the estate. He'd instructed Huxley and Miles to make sure that the men were kept as far away from the *ladies* as possible, and he had made it abundantly clear that any man who broke the rule of silence would have a very difficult time finding work again.

Simon glanced down at his wife. Clarissa's eyes were closed, and she was smiling gently. Simon's breath brushed over her hair as he thought of how boring his life had been before she'd waltzed into his home and boldly asked him to marry her. Until that day, he'd been content with politics and the duties of his rank, never knowing how sterile his surroundings really were, how cold and abstract his life had become. But there was nothing abstract in how he felt about the woman sitting on his lap.

Clarissa had brought something uniquely precious into his life. Her laughter, her wit, the way she cared so deeply for those around her—everything about her had called to his heart from the beginning, but he'd been too proud and too stubborn to admit it.

Dare he admit it now?

Simon wondered if he had the courage to confess his love, knowing that it might be rejected. He suspected that Clarissa harbored some affection for him, but he couldn't be sure. He wanted to believe that the willingness of her arms, the passionate responses he drew from her, were proof of her feelings, but he didn't want to deceive himself. Discovering Haven House, watching Clarissa with her ladies, seeing her concern, and knowing how much she had risked to establish the charity, Simon could now understand the boldness that had brought her to his doorstep and the determination that had sent her down the aisle on their wedding day.

Like so many of the peerage, past and present, Clarissa had married for duty.

Duty.

The word sounded dry and unrewarding as it rolled around inside Simon's head. He'd felt the burden of his title most of his life, but along with it had come his identity. He was Lord Sheridan. The name said more about him than anything else. He'd been raised from the cradle to accept his title and everything it endowed. Knowing that, he could relate to Clarissa's sense of obligation when it came to the women she sheltered. But, she hadn't inherited the responsibility; she'd willingly petitioned it.

Unlike Lady Dalton, who would have to eventually accept the consequences of her own actions and reveal the name of the man who had fathered her child. With every day that passed the possibility of her being discovered loomed closer, and Simon couldn't think of any way to avoid a disaster if Lord Dalton learned of his niece's current whereabouts. He hoped Albright would be able to shed some light on the subject. Just thinking about Lord Dalton's reaction to Haven House was enough to make him reach for his brandy glass.

Clarissa sensed the change in Simon's mood. She raised her head and looked at him.

"Has Lady Dalton retired for the evening?"

"Hours ago," she told him. "Mrs. Flannigan runs a strict house."

"I want to talk to her in the morning," he said stiffly.

Clarissa assumed that the birth of Miss Lullumber's baby had rekindled Simon's curiosity about the father of Lady Dalton's child. "I hope you don't intend to badger the poor girl again."

"I am not going to badger her," Simon said. "I only want to ask her a few questions."

"Questions she isn't going to answer," Clarissa pointed out. "I've discovered that Lady Dalton isn't as meek as she looks. She's determined to keep the man's identity a secret. I'm not sure that I fault her for her resolve," Clarissa added. "No woman wants to be tied to a loveless future."

Simon grimaced inwardly, wondering if Clarissa felt tied to him. He decided that she probably did. After all, her reasons for marrying him were clear now. And the conditions he'd attached to their engagement had forced her to walk into his arms whenever he opened them. He sipped his brandy and tried to convince himself that Clarissa's passion wasn't totally due to duty. Granted, she was a fiery woman by nature, and he had done his best to convince her that following her sensual instincts wasn't shameful, but Simon couldn't persuade himself that what they shared was totally physical.

Simon was tempted to test his theory, but the dark circles under Clarissa's eyes told him that his wife needed sleep more than she needed him at the moment.

"You should go to bed yourself," he said, putting down the brandy.

Wrapping an arm around her waist, he led her from the room. The house was quiet. Everyone had taken to their beds after an exhausting day. Even Huxley. Simon had to smile as he realized that the butler was more parent than servant, and he felt another pang of jealousy. The butler knew Clarissa better than anyone, but nothing about the man's demeanor had indicated to Simon that he was displeased over her choice in husbands. If anything, Huxley had begun to soften in his attitude, and the two men had even shared some stimulating conversation once the servant had realized that Simon didn't intend to close Haven House and restrict Clarissa to Sheridan Manor.

It was Huxley who had told Simon about Mrs. Quigley's niece and the incident that had spurred Clarissa into her first act of charity. It was also Huxley who had assured Simon that no one connected to Haven House would ever say or do anything to dishonor Clarissa's generosity. Mrs. Flannigan had assured him of the same thing, clearly stating that she'd personally strangle anyone who dared to breath Clarissa's name publicly.

"I want to check in on Miss Lullumber and the baby before I go upstairs," Clarissa said.

She stepped away from Simon and tiptoed to the closed door of what had once been the music room. Simon followed her, suddenly curious about the little girl who had been born a few short hours ago. The room was dark except for a candle burning on the table. Its light revealed the housekeeper sitting quietly in a corner chair while the baby and its mother slept peacefully.

Simon stood in the shadows just outside the door as his wife walked to the small cradle at the foot of the bed. Most of the room's previous furnishings had been removed to make room for the bed and cradle. The drapes were drawn, but the candle offered enough light for Simon to see Miss Lullumber. The young mother looked pale, but none the worse for wear, and Simon found himself admiring a woman's ability to withstand the pain that accompanied the wonder of bearing a child.

"She's so beautiful," he heard Clarissa whisper.

She motioned him inside, and although Simon was slightly embarrassed at the thought of invading Miss Lullumber's sleeping chamber, he found himself drawn toward the cradle. Peering inside, he smiled at the cherubic face of the newborn infant. A dusting of dark hair covered the baby's small crown, and a tiny fist showed above the blanket's edge.

Simon was awed by the translucent quality of the baby's skin and the peaceful expression on its tiny face. He'd never seen a newborn infant before, and he was humbled by the miracle of life as he gazed down at her. He'd fallen asleep in the library with the thought of how he'd one day pace his own library while Clarissa delivered their firstborn child. The thought had turned into a dream when he'd fallen asleep in the chair and slept with the image of a little boy dancing around in his mind.

The abstract idea of producing an heir took on a new dimension as Simon looked at the sleeping infant. His son wouldn't be just an heir; he'd be an extension of the two people who had created him.

A combination of himself and Clarissa, a unity of flesh and blood, a new life.

"Has she decided upon a name?" Clarissa asked, looking toward Mrs. Flannigan.

"She wants to name the child after you," the housekeeper replied.

Clarissa blushed. "That isn't necessary."

"I doubt that necessity had anything to do with it," Simon told her, keeping his voice low. "It's Miss Lullumber's way of thanking you."

Clarissa looked at her husband. She'd been surprised by the gentle tone of his voice, and she was even more surprised by the soft gleam of his eyes as he looked from her to the sleeping child. A smile came to her face. "Do you like the baby?"

Realizing that he was wearing his heart on his sleeve, Simon stepped back from the cradle. "What's not to like about a sleeping child?" He glanced at his pocket watch. "It's time we were all abed."

"Very well," Clarissa said.

She followed Simon from the room and up the stairs, wondering if she'd mistaken his reaction twice in one evening. He'd seemed glad to see her when she'd walked into the library. Granted his eyes had been dazed by sleep and he had yawned, but there had been a softness in his gaze when he'd held out his hand, and his kiss had been just as gentle. She'd seen the softness again when he'd looked at Miss Lullumber's baby, as if for a brief moment he had been gazing upon his own child.

Looking at him now, his shoulders stiff, his eyes once again dark and unreadable, Clarissa couldn't help but wonder if she'd ever be able to melt the aristocratic ice around his heart. Most men had defenses of some sort—it was their nature—but Simon seemed determined to keep her in her place. Every time she felt herself getting close, he pushed her away with a hard glare or a curt word. The only time he didn't hold up an invisible shield was when they were making love. When their bodies were joined, their heartbeats intermingled with the sounds of sensual moans and the whisper of skin against skin. Clarissa could almost feel their souls touching. It was a fanciful thought, but she'd felt it more and more of late. Simon could call it passion if he liked, but she knew it was more.

In spite of their differences over Haven House and her determination not to let Simon take over every aspect of her life, Clarissa still loved him. During their short marriage, she had learned a lot. Simon was proud and stubborn, but he wasn't coldhearted, and the fact that he hadn't stuffed her into a carriage and taken her back to London was proof enough that he had a heart. All she had to do was reach it.

Eighteen

Simon met Viscount Thornton as he stepped off the train in Carlisle. It was a warm day, with a fault-less blue sky and a crisp breeze that carried the shrill sound of the locomotive's whistle over the slate roofs of the village. After exchanging the cus-tomary pleasantries, the two men shared a pint of ale at the local tavern before climbing into the car-riage.

Not knowing their ultimate destination, Clarence Albright quickly asked: "I didn't realize Lord Pomeroy had an estate in Yorkshire." He stretched out his legs, making himself comfortable along with the assumption that Simon had inherited the York-shire residence when he'd married Clarissa. "Tell me, how's the beautiful Lady Sheridan doing?"

Simon smiled. "My wife is fine. She's also the reason you're here."

The viscount groaned. "Don't tell me she's found some proper young lady in need of a husband. I thought I'd met them all. God, but it's been a long six months. And I've six more to go before I'm forced to sacrifice myself for the sake of an heir."

Wanting to tell his friend as much as he could before they reached the boundaries of the estate where Clarissa sheltered her unlikely crew, Simon decided there was no need to choose his words carefully. "The estate didn't belong to Lord Pomeroy; in fact, the old gentleman would probably turn over in his grave if he knew about it."

He'd gotten the viscount's attention. Albright eyed Simon carefully for a long moment, then smiled. "I though I detected a hint of mystery in your telegram."

Simon's chuckle was sardonic. "Mysteries are things we don't know. I'm afraid my wife's activities here in Yorkshire don't fall into that category. At least not anymore."

The viscount glanced out the carriage window for a moment before looking at Simon once again. The gaiety in his gaze had vanished. "Bloody hell, that's a disappointment," he confessed. "I would have bet a tidy sum at White's that you owned the lady's heart."

Simon laughed. "I haven't been cuckolded. Though God knows it would be easier to handle than what I found waiting for me when I followed Clarissa from London."

Albright's interest grew, and he straightened himself until he was sitting up. "What did you find?"

Simon let out a frustrated breath before he began the lengthy explanation. He was interrupted several times along the way as the viscount either cursed in agreement with his friend's dilemma or laughed at its outrageous nature. When Simon got to the part about discovering Lady Dalton among Clarissa's band of wayward women, the viscount went pale.

"Lady Beatrice Dalton!"

Simon nodded. "I've got a bloody damn mess on my hands, Albright. If Dalton finds out that my wife has his niece tucked up in the country with a babe growing in her belly, he'll— What's wrong?"

Simon no sooner got the words out before he

uttered a groan that matched the one his friend was making. A flickering memory turned into a blaze of recognition as Simon recalled the conversation he'd had with his uncle in London.

"Rumor has it that Dalton is ushering his niece off to Scotland to visit a maiden aunt just to keep Thornton from getting too close to her."

"My God . . ." Simon slumped against the carriage cushions. "I should have known. You never could keep your britches buttoned."

The viscount recovered from his shock, adding a string of curses to relieve his spleen. "Why didn't she tell me? Bloody hell, her uncle will have my head."

"That's not all he'll have if you don't marry her," Simon said gruffly. He stared at his friend for a good long while. The wildest stretch of Simon's imagination couldn't conjure up the image of Clarence ridding Dalton's bashful niece of her virginity. He didn't have to verbalize the question; the viscount saw it when he met Simon's questioning gaze.

"She's a sweet little thing when her uncle isn't about."

Another spell of silence filled the carriage as the two men absorbed the ramifications of their individual actions; Simon had inherited a houseful of unwed mothers along with the Hartford fortune, and the viscount had just found himself the wife he'd promised to wed before Boxer Day. Both of them had Clarissa's boldness to thank for their bounty.

The silence turned into astonished merriment as the two friends looked at each other and burst into laughter.

"Damn it, Sinclair, this wasn't what I expected when I boarded the train in London," Albright said, shaking his head.

"Now you know how I felt when I walked into the

parlor and found my wife surrounded by a pack of pregnant women," Simon retorted. "I've aged ten years in the last ten days."

"Better you than me," the viscount said, realizing that Simon's problem outweighed his. "All I've got is *one* woman to worry about; you've got a bloody houseful."

"Don't forget about the uncle," Simon reminded him. "Dalton isn't above retribution if he decides you seduced the girl to get to her fortune."

Albright began to look worried. "Damnation. I'll have to take her across the border to Scotland. Either way, Lord Dalton isn't going to offer his congratulations."

"One problem at a time," Simon said. "For now, I'd concentrate on the lady. Until a few days ago, I would have thought the solution easy. A special license and the deed is done."

"What more do I need?"

Simon frowned, something he'd been doing a lot of lately. The frequency of the expression was his wife's fault, of course. That and the fact that he still hadn't decided if loving Clarissa was a blessing or a curse. "The lady's consent for one."

The viscount went back to looking confident. "She'll marry me. What else can she do?"

Simon didn't have an answer, but he was sure about one thing. His friend was in for a dose of Clarissa's temper when they arrived at Haven House.

"You don't seem overly upset about marrying the girl," Simon remarked.

The viscount gave him a shrug. "I suppose I've reconciled myself to the thought of marriage in the last few months. Beatrice is an amicable enough young lady, and I'm not above admitting that she'll please my mother."

"Trust me," Simon replied. "There's more to

marriage than you realize until after the vows are spoken; then it's too late to take them back."

"I know you're unhappy about your wife's little hobby. Can't blame you there, old chap, but am I detecting a hint of discontentment where the charming lady herself is concerned?"

Simon hadn't come to terms with his recent feelings for Clarissa to share them with anyone, even his best friend. He peered out the carriage window, noting that the small violet flowers growing alongside the road were the exact same color as Clarissa's eyes when she got angry. Everywhere Simon looked there was something to remind him of his lovely wife; the bright sunshine made him think of her smile, and the soft breeze carrying the scent of the spring day brought to mind the fragrance of her skin after she'd bathed.

The birth of Miss Lullumber's baby had brought Simon face-to-face with his deepest feelings, and he wasn't sure what to do with them now that they had finally been identified. He'd sought marriage thinking that his desire for Clarissa and his obligation to produce an heir would be enough to keep their relationship active for a good long time. Now that he'd admitted that desire was merely one of the many things he felt for his wife, Simon wasn't sure how to go about discovering her true feelings for him. He'd spent his childhood learning how to be the earl of Sheridan and most of his adult life maintaining the dignity of his rank. As a young man, he'd learned how to control his emotions, how to use them to his best advantage, and how to keep his personal life separate from the duties his title required of him.

Now, knowing that he loved Clarissa and doubting how she felt about him, Simon found himself unable to explain the discontentment the viscount had heard in his voice. He had awakened that morning and every morning for the last three days with the intention of pulling Clarissa into his arms and telling her out loud how he felt. But each time he'd reached for his wife, his tongue had refused to say the words, and he'd ended up kissing her until his intentions had been consumed by desire. Even after they'd made love, while she lay content in his arms, her body pressed intimately against him, her hand lightly caressing his chest, he'd been unable to make himself confess what shouldn't be a confession at all but an exclamation of joy.

He recalled Clarissa's words about women being forced to marry men they didn't love. Although the words haunted him, Simon tried to convince himself that they didn't apply to his wife. Clarissa hadn't been forced to wed him because of a child. Simon had told himself that several times over the course of the last three days, but he was nowhere near believing it.

Clarissa had married him because she'd felt compelled to protect the women at Haven House. Knowing that she'd traded her body for that security didn't sit well with Simon. He wanted his wife to love him as passionately and as wholeheartedly as he loved her.

"Speak up," Thornton said, interrupting Simon's private thoughts. "Have you grown tired of the lovely lady so quickly?"

"No," Simon replied bluntly. "I've been too busy rescuing her reputation to grow bored."

There was no more time for conversation, as the carriage rolled up in front of the scorched country estate. The carriage came to a halt, and Simon opened the door, motioning for his friend to step out. Huxley greeted them on the front steps. Simon inquired about the whereabouts of his wife and Lady Dalton, aware that Clarissa had informed the butler of the young woman's identity after they'd jointly decided that it wasn't necessary for anyone else in the household to know. Simon had quickly learned that there were no secrets between Clarissa and the stout servant, and he tried not to let the fact intimidate him. For a moment, Simon dallied with the idea of asking Huxley if he was privy to Clarissa's feelings, but his pride wouldn't let him go that far.

"Please ask my wife to join us in the library," Simon instructed the butler.

"As you wish, milord," Huxley replied, taking the viscount's hat and gloves. "Should I inform Mrs. Flannigan that Viscount Thornton will be joining us for dinner?"

"No," Simon told him. "It won't be necessary to inform anyone of the viscount's presence." He headed for the library, then stopped and looked over his shoulder. "Send for Dr. Hayward. I have a favor to ask of him."

While the butler went in search of Clarissa, Simon poured himself and his friend a brandy. "You look like you could use this."

Thornton accepted the medicinal elixir with a nervous smile, then started pacing the room. "Damn it, Sinclair. Just knowing the house is full of pregnant women is making me witless."

Simon laughed. "I suggest you concentrate on the pregnant woman you'll be marrying before day's end and leave the rest to my wife and Mrs. Flannigan."

"Before day's end? It's a good three day's journey to Scotland."

"I don't think it will be necessary to flee across the border," Simon said, settling into a chair. "Although I haven't met the man personally, I understand the local magistrate isn't above looking the other way if the reward is tempting enough. I'm sure a few coins will see the right date on the necessary documents. Besides, the sooner you wed the charming Lady Dalton and whisk her away for a blissful honeymoon, the sooner I'll have one less female to worry about. It's a pity I can't get rid of the rest as easily. I shudder to think what will happen if anyone else finds out about my wife's little charity."

"From what you've told me, it's lucky she hasn't been discovered before now. And I thought you had brass."

Simon took a moment to compare himself to his wife. He came up short. How did a man compare words to actions. He'd stood in front of Parliament countless times, talking about the principles of government, reciting the reasons why it should maintain an open ear and an open heart to those it governed. He believed in those things and had spoken out for them. Yet his wife had gone beyond words. She'd acted upon her conviction, disregarding the risk, believing so strongly in her cause that she'd even married because of it.

"I'm afraid my political fortitude is paled by my wife's sense of compassion," he admitted. "Nevertheless, I can't fault her reasoning. Where but here would these women be welcome?"

Thornton didn't bother with the obvious answer—*nowhere.*

Clarissa prepared herself mentally for the meeting with Viscount Thornton. She had no fear of the man, but it would be the first time she'd face another member of the peerage who was aware of her private endeavors. Excluding her husband, of course. She'd been too surprised when Simon had popped into the salon to think about being embarrassed. She wasn't ill at ease now, either, only anxious about how her husband's best friend would greet her.

Simon didn't live his life to please other people, but Clarissa knew he valued the viscount's friendship and therefore his opinion.

She smoothed the gathered folds of her blue dress before tapping lightly on the library door. Simon's deep voice bid her to enter. Hoping that the viscount would be able to shed some light on Lady Dalton's current condition, Clarissa turned the knob and entered the room.

Both her husband and the viscount greeted her with cordial smiles.

"I hope your trip from London was a satisfactory one," Clarissa said, addressing the viscount as she walked across the room to sit next to her husband. "Yorkshire is lovely in the spring."

The viscount neither agreed or disagreed. He poured himself another drink, then sat down. Clarissa sensed his discomfort and hoped that it wasn't because he thought his best friend had made a mistake by marrying her.

"Where is Lady Dalton?" Simon asked, acutely aware of his wife's presence in the room.

But then, he was always acutely aware of Clarissa. She had filled all the empty crevices in his life, especially his heart. He looked up at her. Their eyes met and locked, and a current of emotion pulsed just below Simon's skin, like a ripple on a pond. He'd felt the sensation a hundred times during his short marriage to Clarissa, but it wasn't until the last few days that he'd known it was caused by his heart rather than his groin.

Clarissa watched as her husband's eyes darkened the way they always did when he wanted to kiss her. His gaze probed deeply, and she felt as if he'd reached inside her and touched her heart. It was a fleeting sensation, but she felt it with an acute certainty, and for a moment she thought he might forget that they weren't alone in the room.

"Sit down," Simon said softly before giving her a wolfish smile. "I don't want you to faint when you discover who fathered Lady Dalton's child."

More than curious and slightly relieved because she'd begun to worry over the young lady's health, both physically and emotionally, Clarissa sat down on the settee next to her husband. When Simon reached out and took her hand, she wasn't sure if it was an act of reassurance or affection. Feigning a dignified serenity, Clarissa let the touch of her husband's hand warm her until the anxious knot in the pit of her stomach melted and she could relax.

The viscount put down his brandy glass. "Blast it, Sinclair. You don't have to be so bloody melodramatic about the affair."

Clarissa looked from the viscount's unhappy features to her husband. Simon was smiling. It took her less than a second to match Thornton's disgruntled tone with her husband's amused expression and come up with the answer. "Oh, my goodness!"

Simon laughed out loud, drawing an even fiercer frown from the viscount. "It seems that my handsome friend is the father of Lady Dalton's child. Although the timing is a bit awkward, the problem has been solved."

"What about Lord Dalton?"

"He'll come around," Thornton said matter-of-factly. "What else can he do?"

Clarissa wasn't sure how to react. She'd imagined a number of London gentleman responsible for Beatrice's condition, but Clarence Albright had never entered her mind. He was a dashing rogue of a man, but envisioning him with Lady Dalton hadn't occurred to her. Looking at him now, she tried to imagine his casting a charming spell over the shy young woman. Of course, she didn't know either one of them very well, which meant she was a poor judge of their feelings for one another. However, she sensed that Beatrice loved the father of her child. But how did the handsome viscount feel about the lady? The thought of a forced marriage didn't sit well with Clarissa, and she knew it wouldn't sit well with Lady Dalton, either. They both wanted the same thing, to be loved by the men they loved.

"Is Lady Dalton still resting?" Simon asked, watching as his wife absorbed the news.

"I believe she is up and about," Clarissa said, wondering how Beatrice would react when she found out that Thornton had arrived at Haven House.

"Excellent," Simon said. "Fetch her."

Clarissa turned her attention back to the viscount. "I assume you're prepared to marry the lady."

"Of course," Thornton replied, sounding neither enthusiastic nor reluctant. "The child is mine, after all."

Clarissa had a dozen other questions on the tip of her tongue, but she dared not ask them. It was apparent that the gentlemen had discussed the matter and reached the obvious conclusion. Duty demanded a wedding.

She came to her feet. "I will see if Lady Dalton is up to receiving visitors."

"Is she ill?" There was enough concern in the viscount's voice to give Clarissa some hope.

"She has been overly tired of late," she told him. She wanted to say that Lady Dalton was a bundle of nerves and had been since Simon's arrival, but Clarissa didn't want to lay all the fault at Simon's feet. "It's not unusual, considering her condition."

The viscount seemed to be having some trouble

with his own nerves, and Clarissa wondered if he worried about how Beatrice would receive him. *A little worry will be good for him,* she decided as she left the library and went in search of Lady Dalton.

She found Beatrice in the small parlor that opened onto the back garden. The doors were open, letting in the day's warmth and a bright stream of sunshine. A book was laying unnoticed on Beatrice's lap as the young lady stared out the window. It wasn't the first time Clarissa had found her alone and gazing off into the distance, as if she were trying to find her future.

Clarissa knew how the young woman was feeling. How many times in the last few weeks had she herself stared out the window or stood on the balcony and gazed at nothing in particular, her mind racing with thoughts that had no final destination. Since marrying Simon, her future lacked the clarity it had once had. Her plans for Haven House and the other retreats she envisioned for women who needed a second chance at life stilled burned in her mind, but something was missing. Clarissa realized that the something was her own happiness, her own chance at life. She'd become so consumed with helping others that she'd allowed her own dreams to be pushed aside. She knew now that she'd married Simon hoping against hope that one of those dreams would come true. That one day he'd love her with the same consuming obsession that had stolen her heart and labeled it his for the taking.

As Clarissa stood in the doorway of the parlor, looking at Lady Dalton, she felt as if her heart were being torn in two. She was being ripped apart by her convictions. One part of her knew that what she was doing, what she was risking, was right. The other told her to put aside anything that might jeopardize her future happiness. It was as if she were standing on the deck of a sinking ship, knowing she could save one of two people but loving them both. How would she chose? What was more important? Her life or the lives of her *ladies,* women who would be exiled and endangered unless homes like Haven House were allowed to exist.

Perhaps she was asking herself the question prematurely. Simon wasn't pleased with her activities, but he hadn't demanded that she retire to Sheridan Manor while he dispatched the women. That was the fuel for the hope still burning in her heart. But the uncertainty of what Simon would do was also burning, the question still unanswered. She hadn't asked him outright, fearing the answer, but Clarissa knew she couldn't postpone the inevitable. Sooner or later, she had to know Simon's intentions.

"Excuse me for interrupting you," she said as Beatrice turned away from the placid scene of the garden. "My husband is requesting your presence in the library."

Lady Dalton frowned, changing her appearance from one of demure innocence to one of worry. "I mean Lord Sheridan no disrespect, Clarissa, but I fear if he asks me one more question, I shall scream."

Clarissa smiled. "He can be persistent at times. But I think this interview will be different, so please indulge me and come along."

"Very well."

By the time they reached the closed library doors, Clarissa was wondering if she shouldn't have prepared Beatrice for her upcoming surprise. Praying that the young lady didn't faint again, Clarissa tapped on the door, then pushed it open. Fortunately, Simon was standing nearby, because Lady Dalton had taken no more than two steps into the room when her eyes went wide and her face pale. Simon caught her as she crumpled to the floor.

"Damnation, not again," he cursed as he lifted

Lady Dalton in his arms and carried her to the settee.

"Get out of my way, Sinclair," Thornton said, pulling Simon away from the settee so he could sit down on the edge of the small sofa and take Lady Dalton's hand. "Fetch me a glass of water," he ordered, sounding upset. "You should have warned her," he added, glancing over his shoulder at Clarissa. "She has a delicate disposition."

Simon laughed. "Ladies with delicate dispositions don't run away to Yorkshire." Nevertheless, he poured the water and handed it to his friend.

Clarissa watched as Thornton dipped his fingertip into the glass and moistened Lady Dalton's lips. The caress was both careful and tender, and Clarissa knew in that moment that the viscount had more feelings than he was willing to admit. His voice was low but soothing as he said the young woman's name, then softly scolded her for scaring the blithering wits out of him.

Dark lashes fluttered for a moment before Beatrice opened her eyes. She groaned out loud. "Clarence, what are you doing here?"

Thornton sat up, assuming his aristocratic veneer. "I should be the one asking that question." He gave his future wife a deep scowl. "Why didn't you tell me?"

Beatrice turned her head away. "I sent you a note asking you to call upon me, but there was no reply."

Thornton cursed long and hard. "It was that meddling uncle of yours. I did call. And I was promptly shown the door before I could hand my hat off to the butler."

"You tried to see me?" The surprise in Beatrice's voice was followed by a satisfied smile that was quickly kissed away by the man leaning over her. It was apparent to anyone watching that it wasn't the first kiss the two people had shared.

Clarissa looked at Simon. Her husband smiled, then reached for her. Wrapping his arm around her waist, he drew her near. "I think we should leave them alone. Thornton seems to have everything under control."

Clarissa wanted to drag her feet, but Simon wouldn't let her. He propelled her out of the room. "No eavesdropping," he teased as he shut the library door.

"What if she still refuses to marry him?" Clarissa asked.

"She won't," Simon announced. "Thornton persuaded her to be his lover. I'm sure he can persuade her to be his wife."

Clarissa shook her head. "I'm still in shock. Thornton and Lady Dalton."

Simon laughed. "I know what you mean. But then, it's always difficult to imagine another person's feelings." He looked down into Clarissa's eyes. In the dim light of the foyer, her eyes looked more sapphire than violet. "Sometimes it's impossible to see inside another person's heart."

Held in place by her husband's penetrating gaze, Clarissa felt her breathing slow down and her pulse start to quicken. Was Simon making an observation or asking a question? Silently, she studied his face, unsure how to reply. The need to tell him how she felt shivered through Clarissa, but her mouth refused to form the words. Dare she strip her soul bare? Dare she tell Simon that she loved him, that she had for a very long time and would go on loving him? Dare she take the step that could send her into his arms or reeling over the edge of a cliff, exposing her heart to the disastrous consequences of being told that he didn't love her in return? Was knowing worse than not knowing?

Before Clarissa could decide, Simon pulled a gold watch from his vest pocket. "You look tired. Why don't you take a nap. If things go as I suspect they will, we're in for a busy evening."

"I'm not sleepy," she told him, still unsure about what she'd heard, or thought she'd heard, in his previous remark. She was in the process of asking him why this evening should be busier than any other when Simon leaned down and kissed her.

It was a good thing that the ladies were either taking their own naps or busy in the kitchen, because what Simon had meant to be a chaste, do-as-you're-told kiss turned into something much more lasting when his mouth brushed over Clarissa's parted lips. He eased his fingers into the russet curls at the nape of her neck, holding her in place while his tongue dipped and teased.

A shudder ripped through Clarissa. It was different from the wild, sensual storms that Simon always created when he touched her. This kiss was softer, more caring, and the sensations were warmer. Instead of hot flames, the feelings overtaking her body were slow and gentle, like the first rays of sunshine seeping over the horizon. Her hands slid up his arms and around his neck as she returned the kiss and clung to the hope that Simon's outward affection concealed an inner emotion.

The satin heat of Simon's mouth made her tremble. She was arched against his body, her head titled back, her breasts pressed ever so lightly against the front of his body. Being close, but not close enough, made her nipples harden and her body ache with a sweet anticipation. His teeth gently raked against her bottom lip, and Clarissa couldn't stifle the soft sound of female satisfaction that escaped her.

With a savage intensity that would have shocked his peers, Simon pulled Clarissa more tightly into his arms. The husky whimper he drew from her throat magnified Simon's pleasure, and he deepened the kiss. He felt the fine tremor that raked Clarissa's body and smiled inwardly. No matter how devoted Clarissa was to her unique charity, he refused to believe that her response was triggered by duty alone. She was too responsive in his arms, too willing, too hot.

His heart swelled with the possibility that his wife might harbor real feelings for him. Along with that hope came a rush of desire so strong that he felt his knees weakening and his blood running hotter than the flames that had consumed a good portion of Haven House. Clarissa was more than beauty and passion, she was everything he'd ever wanted. The bittersweet longing mixed with the fire in Simon's blood as he broke the kiss.

The sound of Huxley, discreetly clearing his throat, kept Simon from sweeping Clarissa into his arms and carrying her upstairs to finish what he'd started.

"I sent one of the workmen to summon Dr. Hayward, milord. Is there anything else before I have a room prepared for the viscount?"

"Nothing at the moment," Simon replied as he looked at his wife. Clarissa's face was flushed with color, and he smiled at her embarrassment. "Just make sure no one ventures into the library; I wouldn't want them blushing like my lovely wife."

Clarissa wanted the floor to open up and swallow her whole. As active as her relationship had been with Simon up to now, they'd managed to keep the more intimate side of their relationship private. It was embarrassing to be found kissing in the foyer, by Huxley of all people.

"I think I'll check in on Miss Lullumber."

She exited the foyer with a graceful haste, scowling at the amused laughter of her husband as she quickly opened, then shut, the door to the music room, where the young mother and her new baby were still residing.

"When Dr. Hayward arrives, I'll be in the . . ." Simon hesitated. The library was the only male domain in the otherwise female-dominated household, and most of the rooms on the second floor were still empty of furnishings. "I'll be in the garden," he said, for lack of a better place.

"Very well, milord," Huxley replied before returning to his duties.

Simon strolled outside, feeling content with things for the moment. When Dr. Hayward arrived, he intended to solicit the physician's help with the magistrate. Having resided in the area for some time now, Simon was confident that Dr. Hayward would know the best way to approach the local official. Once Thornton and Lady Dalton were legally wed, he would still have a household of unmarried, pregnant women to contend with. After that, he'd deal with his lovely wife.

Nineteen

The bride wore a soft blue dress with silk embroidery around the collar and sleeves. The corsage front formed a pointed bolero at the waist, but the cream-colored shawl, tied in an elegant knot just below her bodice, hid her expanding waistline. The viscount stood beside her, tall and handsome, and Clarissa couldn't help but think of her own wedding day. She glanced at her husband, standing regally by Thornton's side. Simon returned her gaze, and Clarissa knew that he was remembering, too.

The magistrate was a short man with a raspy voice and a rounded belly that pushed against the buttons on his vest. His hair was steel gray, and his blue eyes sat in deep sockets atop a wide nose. A thin mouth and a rather stern disposition made the man almost froglike in appearance. Since arriving at the country house, he had remained quiet, sitting in the library and sipping a brandy while Clarissa hurried the bride through her toiletries. The only other occupants in the room were Huxley and Dr. Hayward, who would sign as witnesses.

The ceremony lacked the eloquence of a church service, but it was just as binding, and neither the bride nor the groom seemed to mind the lack of finery that usually accompanied a wedding between two socially acceptable people. One of the women had cut some flowers from the garden, and the bride was holding the small bouquet as she looked at the man beside her.

Once the magistrate pronounced Viscount Thornton legally wed to his bride, Lady Beatrice Dalton, Simon breathed a sign of relief. Beatrice's uncle could rant and rave until the Second Coming, but there was little else he could do now without casting a shadow on his own family name. As for the viscount, Simon had come to the conclusion that Thornton could do worse than marrying a soft-spoken young lady with a quiet demeanor and shy brown eyes.

He couldn't help but compare the two wives. Clarissa's bold coloring was only a hint of the fire that lay beneath her polished surface. Simon felt fortunate that he was the man to discover that fire. Nothing about Clarissa was mediocre or mundane, and Simon smiled, knowing that his life would continue to be as adventurous and challenging as it had become since agreeing to marry her.

As Huxley and Dr. Hayward stepped forward to sign the necessary documents, Simon moved to his wife's side. As always, his first close impression of her was the soft floral scent that floated up from her body and hair. "Thornton wants to leave for London first thing in the morning."

"I assumed as much," Clarissa replied. "Beatrice is anxious about seeing her uncle again. She's not sure how he will react."

"That's Thornton's worry now," Simon told her.

Clarissa frowned. "Why is it that men always presume that the moment a woman marries she forfeits her identity? Lord Dalton is still her uncle, and although she may not openly declare a fondness for him, I'm sure it exists."

"I thought women wanted their husbands to be knights in shining armor. Don't tell me that Beatrice would rather face her uncle alone than have Thornton slay the dragon for her?"

Clarissa shook her head. "You're deliberately misunderstanding me."

"I know," Simon teased her.

Before Clarissa could respond, Dr. Hayward walked across the room, smiling proudly at his part in the day's events. "The magistrate accepted his *fee* with the assurance that no one will know the time schedule in which certain events took place."

"Excellent," Simon replied. "That's one less woman I have to worry about."

The physician laughed when Clarissa reached out and cuffed her husband on the arm. "You should be ashamed of yourself, my lord."

"Perhaps," Simon relented as the viscount joined them. Beatrice was clinging to her husband's arm, and Clarissa was forced to admit that they did make a handsome couple. "But I'm also relieved."

Thornton laughed. "Not as relieved as my mother will be."

The new bride blushed, but her eyes were shining with a happiness Clarissa shared. Whatever the viscount had said to her in the short time they'd been alone had worked. Beatrice looked like a woman in love.

"Where's the champagne?" the viscount asked. "I promised my new bride a taste. With the good doctor's permission, of course."

"I think a small sip or two would be good for her," Dr. Hayward replied.

"I'm in your debt, sir," Thornton said in a more serious tone. "Beatrice tells me that you have been a comfort to her these last weeks. And she insists that you attend her when our child is born."

Dr. Hayward's smile filled the room. "I would be honored."

The conversation stayed light and amusing as the

day's tension drained away. When Mrs. Flannigan announced that dinner was being served, Simon took his wife's arm and pulled her close. "After dinner, we will retire early. The bride and groom are due a wedding night, and we have a lot to talk about."

Clarissa wasn't so sure she liked the look on Simon's face. She'd told herself time and time again that the temporary truce they'd reached since his arrival at Haven House was sure to come to an end soon. It seemed that the time was at hand.

"I won't do it!" Clarissa said, crossing her arms over her chest. "I won't leave. There's too much to be done."

Simon's jaw tightened as he discarded his dinner jacket. Before the sun rose again he was determined to have things set straight between him and his unpredictable wife. He corrected his thoughts as he removed his cuff links. Clarissa wasn't unpredictable at all. She was reacting exactly as he'd expected.

The balcony doors were open, and a soft breeze filled the room. He unbuttoned his shirt and tossed it over a chair. "There's nothing to be done here that can't be done by someone else. The workmen are making excellent progress, and the house should be back to its former state by summer's end."

"That's not what I meant, and you know it," Clarissa said, glaring at her husband as he continued disrobing. He was down to his black trousers before he looked at her again.

"I know exactly what you meant," Simon retorted. "But it's time you realized what I mean."

"And what is that?" she dared to ask, holding her

head high. She crossed her fingers as she folded her hands in the folds of her skirt.

Simon crossed the room in three long strides and looked down at her. "I mean to have some degree of normalcy in our lives. We are returning to Sheridan Manor at week's end."

A little voice inside Clarissa warned her not to push Simon too far. What little she'd seen of his temper so far had been formidable, and she knew she couldn't win in the end. That Simon wasn't ordering Huxley to dispatch the women and bar the doors should be enough of a victory for her. But it wasn't. She wanted more. Perhaps more than her husband had to give.

"I don't belong at Sheridan Manor," Clarissa said, deciding it was time to get more than a few things out in the open. "I belong here at Haven House."

Her declaration got Simon's undivided attention. He scooped her up in his arms and marched to the bed, then tossed her in the middle of the feather mattress and watched her bounce twice before coming to a stop. Clarissa was in the process of returning to her feet when Simon came down on top of her, his dark eyes blazing.

"You belong wherever I want you to belong," he said firmly. "You belong to me. Or have you forgotten your marriage vows?"

"I haven't forgotten them," Clarissa replied shakily. She was seeing a side of Simon that she'd never seen before, and for the first time since he'd stormed into the parlor, she feared that he might make good on his threat to thrash her.

Simon looked down at her as he struggled to keep his control. He wanted to make love to his lovely wife until she relented and told him that she loved him. But he wanted to beat her black and blue at the same time. God, she was the most infuriating female he'd ever met.

Deciding he'd do the former, Simon lowered his body until his arms supported his weight and his lovely wife was pinned between his bare chest and the soft down of the feather mattress. One hand inched behind her lower back, arching her up and onto the obvious proof of his aroused flesh. "You are my wife," he said just before he kissed her.

Clarissa fought the response that welled up inside her the moment Simon's mouth covered her own. She pulled back as best she could and turned her head to the side. "I thought you wanted to talk to me."

"I do," Simon said as he placed a kiss on the exposed skin of her throat. "But later, when you're more willing to listen to what I have to say."

Clarissa's skin was hot, and she could feel the feathery touch of Simon's breath on her neck as he nibbled at the sensitive spots he'd discovered over the last few weeks. "I'm willing now," she whispered, then realized she was speaking two truths at once. She wanted to talk to Simon, but she wanted to make love with him as well. Deciding that words had to come first, she pushed him away. "You're right, we need to talk. And regardless of your arrogant assumption, I doubt that I'll be more willing to listen after you've ravished me than before."

Simon laughed. He couldn't help it. "Very well," he said, lifting himself away from his wife's tempting body and sitting down on the bed beside her. "We will talk first."

Clarissa sat up. Her hands were shaking, and she wasn't sure if she'd made the right decision. Simon was back to looking determined. "Why must we return to Sheridan Manor so soon?"

"Because the longer we stay here, the greater the

chance of someone discovering your identity, my dear wife."

"What about—"

Simon shook his head, stopping her. "As I said, there is nothing left to be done here that can't be done by someone else. Mrs. Flannigan runs the house like a military encampment. The ladies are all well, and if they so much as sneeze, Dr. Hayward is summoned immediately, and a cup of herbal tea is administered. The roof will be completely repaired within a few days, and the workmen will begin on the inside of the house. What remains to be done?"

Clarissa bit her tongue to keep from saying what was really on her mind. For some strange reason she'd equated leaving Haven House with Simon's inability to love her. She didn't want to budge from Yorkshire until she knew the nature of her husband's true feelings.

Simon saw the apprehension on Clarissa's face. He was sure he was doing the right thing. "I have spoken with Huxley, and he's agreed to stay behind. Surely you can't fault his management."

Clarissa suddenly felt as if the bed had magically transformed itself into the pitching desk of a sailing ship. "I can't return to Coventry without Huxley."

"Why not?"

"I've never been without him," she said. "I've never . . ."

"Trusted anyone else," Simon finished for her. He'd predicted Clarissa's reaction on this issue as well. Taking her hands, he covered them with his own. "I know Huxley is more than an efficient butler to you. But it's time you trusted me. I'm your husband."

The words sank into Clarissa. She didn't like them. Huxley was more than a servant. He was family. The only family she had left since her grandfather's death.

Tears brimmed against her gold-tipped lashes, and Clarissa fought to pull them back. She rarely cried, and she was afraid if she started now, she'd never stop.

Grimly, Simon fought the urge to give in to Clarissa. It had only taken him a short time to realize the role Huxley played in Clarissa's life, one that had become crystal clear once Simon had discovered Haven House. The butler was both parent and friend to Clarissa. It was for that very reason that Simon was forcing the breach in their relationship. Without the trusty butler at her beck and call, Clarissa would have to accept Simon's authority in her life, but more than that, she'd have to trust her husband. Simon hoped that gaining his wife's trust would eventually gain him her love.

Clarissa looked at him with a question in her eyes.

Simon smiled.

"I'm not exiling him. I know how much Huxley means to you."

"Do you?" Clarissa whispered. "Funny, but I've only just realized it myself."

Simon pulled her onto his lap and held her close. His hands moved up and down her back until she relaxed against him. "Trust me," he whispered against her hair. "I trust Huxley to make the right decisions for Haven House. You need to trust me to make the right decisions for us."

With tears still burning behind Clarissa's eyes, she looked at her husband. "I've never told Huxley how much I love him," she admitted. "Do you think he knows?"

Simon smiled. "I'm sure he does."

Inside, Clarissa was aching to tell Simon how much she loved him, but she was afraid that he'd gloat over the victory of winning her heart along with her body. She looked at the hearth. Fresh wood was neatly arranged on the red brick, but the warm night didn't need the added heat of a fire. She glanced toward the balcony doors, then around the room, anywhere but at her husband.

Simon wasn't to be denied. Taking hold of Clarissa's chin, he turned her head until she was looking at him. "I won't force you to close Haven House," he said, "but I will insist that you allow Huxley and Mrs. Flannigan to run it. You've gotten very close to the edge of propriety, my love, and I'm going to pull you back before you fall."

Clarissa stiffened in his arms. Simon hadn't changed his mind about the role of a lady and her image as a proper wife. She felt as if a plug had been pulled out of her heart and all her hopes and dream were draining way.

"You're taking everything I care about away from me," she said bitterly.

Simon didn't let Clarissa see the impact her words had on him. "I had hoped that you'd be content to be my wife once you realized that your work at Haven House would go on."

"Content!" She hissed the word. She tried to free herself from his grasp, but Simon refused to let her up. "How am I supposed to be content when everything I believe in is kept just beyond my reach? Do you really think I'm going to sit in the parlor and knit while someone else lives my dream?"

Simon was reaching the end of his patience. He flipped Clarissa back onto the bed, looming over her. "You are the most exasperating female I have ever encountered. What more do you want of me, madam? Any other man would have closed this house and returned you to London without a second thought."

"I want . . ." Clarissa couldn't say the words.

God, how she wanted to. How she longed to tell Simon that all she wanted was for him to love her. Instead, she closed her eyes against the harsh reality that he was only going to keep her away from the very thing that had given her life purpose for the last four years.

Simon took a deep breath and tried to hang on to his control. He was back to being torn between the need to strangle his beautiful wife or making love to her until neither one of them had the energy to crawl out of bed. As always, Clarissa had him second-guessing himself. Well, he was tired of playing second place in her life. She was his wife, damn it, and it was time she gave him her total attention.

"I've written Mrs. Quigley," he said as he lowered his head and nibbled on the lobe of her right ear. "It was a lengthy letter. I sent your regards and informed her that you would be indisposed for any further interviews. She will have to use her own judgment in selecting future candidates for Haven House."

"You're interfering," Clarissa said, wishing that Simon would stop kissing her. She couldn't stay angry at him when he was making her feel such delicious sensations. And the arrogant man knew it. "I won't have my movements restricted. Mrs. Quigley is my friend, and she will remain so."

"I have no objection to your friendship," Simon replied as his hands found the buttons on Clarissa's dress and began unfastening them. "On the contrary, from what I've been told, Mrs. Quigley is an admirable woman."

Simon paused to place a kiss on the tip of Clarissa's nose. When she wiggled it at him, he laughed out loud, then ran his fingertip over the seam of her mouth. When her lips parted, he kissed her, deep and hard, ending their conversation for several long, shimmering moments. When he raised his head, Clarissa's eyes had softened to a warm shade of violet, and her breathing was unsteady, telling him she had enjoyed the kiss as much as he had.

His body was hot and damp from the passion firing his blood, but Simon took his time undressing his wife. He stopped to kiss the pale softness of her shoulders as he pulled the silk blouse down her arms. Pleased that Clarissa didn't wear a corset, Simon continued on his slow unveiling of her body. The warm pressure of her hands on his bare back and arms was more pleasure than he could stand, and Simon pulled them away, anchoring them over her head while he feasted on her naked breasts.

Clarissa moaned softly as Simon's tongue teased and taunted her, making her body flush with heat and a sweet ache swell deep inside her. The velvety heat of his mouth played havoc on her senses until she was moving under him, wanting what he wanted, needing it so desperately that she wanted to jerk her hands free and rip away the rest of their clothing so that they could touch bare skin to bare skin.

The sweet, erotic movements of Clarissa's body under him tore at Simon's control, but he refused to be hurried. He lingered over the soft skin of her belly, circling her navel with his tongue, then teasing her with soft, nibbling bites that made her moan again.

Her skirt disappeared with a quick jerk of her husband's deft hands. Clarissa closed her eyes as Simon's hand slid underneath her petticoat and began drifting up her leg, inch by sweet tormenting inch, until he reached the inside of her thigh.

"Tell me about your dreams," he said in a husky whisper as his hand moved over her skin in slow, random circles that threatened to have her screaming if he didn't get on with things.

"I can't think," she replied, her voice part moan, part whisper, as he withdrew his hand to find the strings that held her petticoats in place.

Once untied, they disappeared, landing on the floor atop her discarded skirt. Her stockings followed, pulled down her legs with a slow, caressing motion that made Clarissa wish he'd never stop touching her. It felt so good. His hands were warm and strong, and she loved the feel of them as they drifted over her body, touching, caressing, undressing her so slowly that she feared she'd faint before he was done.

"Tell me," he demanded as his mouth found her breast once again. The pressure of his mouth drew stronger and stronger, and Clarissa felt something inside her burst. All reason vanished with the tiny explosion. There was only Simon and the simultaneous pleasure she felt everywhere he was touching her.

"I dream of . . ." She couldn't think for the heat boiling up inside her, nor could she talk. All she could do was feel the texture of Simon's tongue as he flicked at her nipples and the rougher texture of his palm gliding up her leg until he was inches away from the place where she ached the most.

His wife's inability to form a coherent word sent a victorious tremor though Simon. His body tightened with its own need, and he wanted to be buried deep inside her warmth, held prisoner by her silk and satin muscles. His fingers skimmed the ginger curls at the apex of her thighs and found the warm, moist center of her womanhood. Clarissa moaned again and pushed against his hand.

"Tell me what you dream about," he insisted in a rough whisper as he pushed inside her body, caressing her with his fingers until she was arching against him with each retreat of his hand.

But there was no way Clarissa could tell him anything. Simon's mouth had replaced his hand, and she was floating somewhere between dreams and reality. The sensual advance and retreat of Simon's tongue sent Clarissa into a different world, one where colors blurred, then exploded, into a thousand tiny stars, gleaming against her closed eyelids. She was astonished by the new intimacy and unable to resist it at the same time. Her nails dug into the muscles of his shoulders and upper arms as she said his name.

Shock turned into pleasure as Simon found the center of her being and did his magic. With a tenderness that consumed Clarissa until tears broke through her closed lashes, Simon continued stripping away her senses, one by one. The sounds drifting in through the open balcony doors faded into a mute silence. Her eyelids felt like iron weights, and all she could see was a glorious, hazy world that stopped and started with her husband.

When a searing spiral of sensation seemed to take Clarissa outside herself, she cried out Simon's name.

With a powerful movement, Simon moved between her legs, stopping just short of entering the inviting folds of her body. Poised over her, he brushed a feverish kiss over her lips. "I've been dreaming about a child," he said in a husky whisper. "Do you want a child?"

"Yes," Clarissa whispered, reaching for Simon, running her hands up and down his sweat-dampened body. "I want a child."

"My child?" Simon inched inside her, sucking in his breath as the feminine wonder of her body engulfed him.

Clarissa's eyes searched his face, seeing the need that had his body taut with passion, the deep glow of his eyes as he looked down at her, feeling the masculine strength of his body as it slowly joined with her. "Yes." She managed the word as Simon flexed his hips, burying himself even farther inside her aching body. "Yes, I want your child."

Groaning, Simon drove into her, ending the torment and beginning the hot, savage mating that they both wanted. He moved deep and strong, uniting them in a primal union of male and female, sensing that this was the night when Clarissa's womb would accept his seed. Wanting that acceptance as much as he wanted her love. Needing it at some unnamed level of his being, the place where man and gentleman became one, where lover and husband became one.

Clarissa felt the same unnamed longing. Her body arched, meeting the almost violent thrusts of Simon's hips as he drove into her, sensing that this time was different, knowing somehow that something had changed between them.

When Simon's body could take the torment no longer, when he was beyond controlling the need that raced through him like an ancient wind, he pushed deeply into Clarissa's warm womb and stayed there, relinquishing his control and letting the fiery tongues of satisfaction consume him.

After bidding Lord and Lady Thornton much happiness and a pleasant trip back to London, Clarissa looked around her. The house was abuzz with activity. Workmen were stripping away the scarred woodwork and ceiling tiles in the upstairs chambers. Mrs. Flannigan was busy supervising the women who were cleaning and polishing the furniture in preparation for once again having their old rooms back. Miss Lullumber was sitting in the garden, holding her new daughter, while Huxley and Simon were closeted in the library, talking about whatever business still needed to be discussed before their departure.

Feeling confused and restless, Clarissa sought the sanctuary of the bedchamber she and her husband shared. It was another beautiful day, and she sat on the balcony overlooking the estate gardens. The wind blew softly, sweeping through the moors and bringing with it the scent of wildflowers. The apple orchard, neglected because the house had demanded so much attention, was a patch of green against the flawless blue of the sky. Clarissa looked at the sprawling branches of the trees. Some were dotted with blossoms, while others hung naked over the thick carpet of spring grass that covered the western edge of the estate. She made a mental note to have Huxley see to the neglected orchard, knowing it could still bear fruit. All it needed was a little attention.

The thought of bearing fruit brought a belated blush to Clarissa's face as she remembered the fury of last night's lovemaking. Simon had always been an attentive lover, but last night had been different. Unconsciously, her hand slipped to her abdomen, and Clarissa wondered if she had indeed conceived the child her husband had confessed to wanting.

As much as she longed to have Simon's child, Clarissa wanted his heart more. One without the other was compromising her dreams, and she'd never been one to compromise.

She sat on the balcony for a long time, letting her thoughts drift like the wind until she decided that daydreaming wouldn't gain her what she knew she needed. She'd always found a way to achieve what she wanted, and she'd find a way to make Simon love her. Remembering the words he'd whispered to her last night, while they were lying in each other's arms, gave her hope.

The hope was still there when she stood on the steps of Haven House and bid Huxley good-bye.

The butler had assured her that he would see that everything was done to her strict standards and for her not to worry. He'd join her and Lord Sheridan at summer's end. It was unthinkable that Clarissa could venture to Scotland to see the queen without the faithful butler at her side.

"It's time to go," Simon said, standing by the carriage door.

Clarissa looked over her shoulder at the man she had married, then back to the stout butler who had raised her like a daughter. It would take days to list the differences between the two men, yet she loved them both. Huxley was the past. Simon was the future. Torn between the two, Clarissa didn't move.

"His lordship is waiting," Huxley said

"I know." Clarissa's mouth began to tremble. "It's just that . . . Oh, damn, I don't know how to say good-bye."

"It isn't good-bye," the butler told her, taking a step forward. He took her arm and began leading her toward the carriage, where her husband was waiting. "It will only be a few short months, milady. When I see you next, I expect to see a smile on your lovely face."

Clarissa made a sound that was somewhere between a laugh and a sob. "I'm going to miss you."

"And I you," Huxley replied. "But in this I agree with his lordship. It's time you returned to Sheridan Manor. Your first responsibility is to your husband. Mrs. Flannigan and I will keep things running smoothly while you're gone."

Once they reached the waiting carriage, Huxley released Clarissa's arm. Simon stepped forward and took it. The symbolic transfer didn't go unnoticed by her misty eyes, and Clarissa knew that Huxley was pointing her toward the future. She allowed Simon to help her inside the small coach. He joined her after exchanging a few words with the butler.

Clarissa leaned out the window and waved good-bye as the driver snapped his whip in the air, urging the horses to be on their way.

Simon sat across from her, saying nothing as Clarissa pulled a linen hankie from her reticule and wiped her teary eyes. "I suppose you think it foolish for a lady to cry because she's leaving her butler behind."

"I think nothing of the sort," Simon said, stretching out his legs. His booted feet brushed against the hem of Clarissa's hunter green traveling suit. "Cry, if you feel the need."

"What I need to understand is your arrogant decision to whisk me away from Haven House. I would prefer to spend the summer here while you tour the estates and factories you inherited the day you married me."

Simon didn't let her frustrated words bait his temper. In fact, he doubted that anything Clarissa might say could provoke his temper. Not after what she'd said last night. Although the lady seemed to have forgotten her remarks with the light of day, Simon hadn't. They'd been echoing in his ears since Clarissa had wrapped her arms around him and declared her love just before she surrendered to the passionate climax that had left her trembling in his arms.

She probably didn't realize that she'd uttered the confession, Simon thought to himself. He'd never taken their lovemaking to the sensual heights they'd climbed to together last night, although he'd been tempted to on several occasions. He'd never made love to any woman the way he'd made love to Clarissa last night, with every fiber of his being, giving and taking everything two people could share. And he'd certainly never told a woman that he wanted to give her a child.

Simon's eyes drifted to the narrow expanse of his

wife's waist. After almost three weeks in a house filled with pregnant women, he couldn't help but think of Clarissa's body changing as his child grew inside her. In fact, he was looking forward to the experience.

They traveled in relative silence as Clarissa looked out the window and Simon relaxed with the newspaper he'd been too busy to read that morning. It was late afternoon before they stopped at an inn on the road to Manchester. Simon had some business interests in the milling town, and he'd decided to stop and look into the state of affairs before catching the train for London. After a few days spent tidying up the business he'd left behind him, they'd travel on to Sheridan Manor.

The inn was a steep-roofed building with large front windows. Once inside, the aroma of fresh-baked bread mixed with the smell of ale and the tobacco the innkeeper used in his long-stemmed pipe. Simon ordered them a light meal of stewed beef and vegetables. Clarissa wasn't very hungry, but she forced herself to eat. She couldn't go on sulking about things forever.

Although Simon hadn't said it, she knew he wouldn't divest her of the funds needed to maintain Haven House. As she sipped the spring water that had been brought to her along with her meal, Clarissa wondered if she dared to ask Simon what he planned on doing with the house she'd purchased in Plymouth. She looked up, posed to ask the question, but before she could form the words, Simon spoke.

"Would you like to take a walk before we get back in the coach?"

It was a lovely day, and Clarissa wasn't looking forward to spending the remainder of it sitting on the cushioned but less than comfortable seats inside the carriage. "Yes, I'd like that."

Simon paid for their meal and escorted her outside. The inn sat back from the road, and there was a long stretch of meadow to their left. "Walk a while," he said. "We won't reach Manchester before nightfall. While you stretch your legs, I'll see about the driver and the horses."

Clarissa nodded, grateful for a few moments of privacy.

Simon found the driver sitting on an upturned keg just outside the livery door. He'd fed and watered the horses, and now he was doing the same for himself. After giving the man instructions, Simon turned to join his wife for a short stroll before they resumed their journey. The muffled sound of someone crying caught his ear.

"Is someone inside the stable?" he asked, glancing at the shadowy interior of the small barn where horses were kept for hire.

"Not that I know of, milord," the driver replied before popping a piece of bread and cheese into his mouth. "I've not heard or seen anyone about."

The sound came again, and this time Simon was certain that it was someone crying. He walked into the narrow barn, grimacing as the odor of the stalls assaulted his nose. The innkeeper kept a clean establishment, but the same couldn't be said of his stables. There were only three horses, and Simon gave them a quick glance, assessing their healthiness and ability to carry a rider or draw a carriage. The animals seemed fit enough.

He was approaching the last of the stalls when a young girl darted out in front of him and ran for the door at the back of the stables. Startled by her sudden appearance but not immobilized by it, Simon reached out and grabbed her arm.

"I say, where do you think you're going?" The girl struggled against his grasp, but Simon didn't release her. "Stand still and answer me."

The girl went limp, but she didn't turn around. From what Simon could see of her, she was full grown but skinny. Her clothing was soiled, and her hair was hanging in a limp mass of tangles down her back.

"Who are you?" he asked, afraid that the girl might be a runaway or worse. It wasn't uncommon for an inn of this sort to keep a female about for male customers who weren't particular about what kind of women they bedded. "Do you work here?"

The girl shook her head. "No."

The word was filled with fear, and Simon realized she was trembling with the same emotion. He released her arm, but not until he'd made it clear that his driver was just outside the door and if she thought to bolt again, she'd surely be caught.

The girl took a step back when he dropped his hand, and the light seeping through the rough planks of the stable fell over her face. It was bruised and swollen. There was dried blood clinging to the corner of her mouth.

"Who did this to you?" he asked, furious that anyone would abuse a woman so brutally.

"My brother," the girl answered, her words slurred by the swelling of her mouth and left jaw.

"Why?"

She looked at the dirt floor with its scattering of hay. "He found out I'm going to have a babe. Said I'd shamed the family and that I'd get worse from my dad once he found out."

"So you ran away," Simon stated, wondering if the innkeeper was her father.

"Aye," the girl mumbled, then started to cry. "I'm not a bad girl," she insisted. "Tommy said he'd marry me, but then he went off. His cousin told me he'd gone to the city to find work, but I don't think he's coming back It's been too long. I asked the innkeeper for a job, but he said he'd not have the likes of me about the place."

Simon listened to the girl's words, muffled by tears and sobs, and frowned. A quick glance took in her rounding belly and her obvious lack of good health.

"Stay here." he ordered her. "Right here. Do you understand?"

She nodded wearily.

He walked outside and told the driver to find Clarissa, then returned to where the girl was leaning against the wall, still crying.

"Stop that," Simon said, more out of frustration than anger. At least he wasn't angry at the girl. However, he'd like nothing better than to meet her brother. Any man who used his fist on a woman deserved a good thrashing himself.

"Simon, what's wrong?" Clarissa's voice came from the wide doorway behind him. "The driver said you seemed anxious about something."

"Come here," Simon told her. "And be careful of your skirts. This is a stable."

Clarissa stepped inside, wondering what in the world could be wrong. The last time she'd heard Simon use that particular tone of voice, he'd been lecturing about the ills of Haven House.

It didn't take Clarissa long to figure out what had her husband so angry that he was clenching his fists as if he wanted to hit something. Mindless of the damage the dirt floor could do to her clothing, she rushed to the girl's side. Simon watched as his wife soothed the girl with soft, caring words that eventually stopped the crying.

"She needs a good meal and a bath," Clarissa said, looking up. "Please ask the innkeeper to prepare a room. I doubt that she's had a good night's sleep since she ran away."

"I can't go in there," the girl said, pulling back.

"You most certainly can," Clarissa corrected her. "Don't worry, my husband will see that the proprietor keeps his opinion to himself."

"But why . . ." The girl stammered, then wiped her bruised face with a dirty sleeve. "Why would the likes of you be helpin' the likes of me?"

"Because you need help," Clarissa stated, then began tugging the girl toward the door. "Come along. You'll feel better after you've had something to eat."

Simon walked ahead of them, preparing himself for a confrontation with the innkeeper. The man proved to be difficult but not impossible. Once Simon had paid more for the rooms than they were worth, he instructed the driver to unharness the horses and prepare for an overnight stay. Simon knew Clarissa wasn't going anywhere until her newest fledgling was properly cared for.

"I can't believe her own brother would beat her like that," Simon said as he paced the narrow compartment he'd rented for himself and Clarissa. The room had one chair, a small dresser, and a bed. There was barely enough space left over for him in which to turn around.

"I can," Clarissa said. "I've seen women treated much worse by their families."

Simon didn't ask his wife to expound on what she'd seen. He was only too aware that women were frequently mistreated by the very men who professed to love them, but this was the first time he'd actually seen the evidence of such abuse. It sickened him.

"How is she?" he asked.

"Sleeping," Clarissa replied. "Her name is Nora. She wouldn't tell me anything else except that she's certain that if she returns to her family it will be only to receive more of the same thing. It isn't the first time she's been mistreated."

Simon reassured her that Nora wouldn't be mistreated again.

"It's late. Get some rest."

"What about Nora?" Clarissa asked.

"Haven House is only a few hours away. Come morning, I'll arrange for the girl to be taken there."

Clarissa's eyes grew blurry with tears as she looked up at Simon. "Thank you."

The two words didn't take the place of the three simple ones Simon wanted to hear. He pulled Clarissa into his arms and kissed her. "Do you think me so coldhearted that I could turn my back on a girl like Nora?"

"No, my lord" she told him. "I've never thought you coldhearted, only hardheaded."

Simon laughed. "I am that, madam, but I'm not too stubborn to change. Whatever you do from this day forth, you do with me, not without me."

The words made the hope in Clarissa's heart blaze anew. She smiled as tears dimmed her vision. Simon was looking at her the same way he'd looked at her the previous night. His eyes were glowing with emotion. Taking the step she'd feared since the day they had married, Clarissa reached up and traced the angles of his face.

"I have never thought your heart cold, my lord."

The feel of Clarissa's hand against his skin was like a soft fire, burning Simon at the same time as it pleased him. He sucked in his breath as her fingertips moved to his mouth, outlining it with a gentleness that forced him to smile. "I never gave my heart much thought until I met you."

Clarissa looked into his eyes for a long moment, remembering the way he'd kissed her in the library the day he'd accepted her proposal, and the times they'd made love. Each time he'd touched her it had been with loving hands. She thought of the way he'd fumed about her charity, then how he'd treated her *ladies*. Every word he had spoken, every gesture he had made toward them, had been colored with respect and concern. The way he'd taken over the house, hiring workmen, making sure they had everything they needed to restore the fire-ridden estate, had been done to please her and to help the women she sheltered.

Why hadn't she seen it before? Why hadn't she been able to put her fear of rejection and her pride aside and realize that Simon did care for her? She'd been too busy worrying about her own heart to see the one Simon was laying at her feet.

Still, she needed the words. She needed to hear them, and she sensed that Simon had the same need. *"Tell me about your dreams."*

"I have given your heart a great deal of thought," Clarissa said, reaching up to brush her mouth lightly over his. "In fact, I have spent an enormous amount of time trying to devise a way to capture it."

Unable to contain the joy he felt at hearing Clarissa's confession, Simon sank onto the bed, taking her with him. He pinned her beneath him. "Then you can cease trying, madam, because you have my heart. You captured it the day you came to Sheridan Manor and asked me to marry you. It's been in your possession ever since." He kissed her quick and hard. "Did I forget to tell you?"

Clarissa slapped at his hands as they began undressing her. "You are impossible," she chided him, laughing and crying at the same time. "And you call yourself a gentleman."

"Ahhh, but I am a gentleman," Simon told her as he tore at the buttons on her suit, scattering them about the room like peas being popped out of a shell. "If I weren't a gentleman, I'll simply hike up your skirts and take you this very minute. But

I'd much rather take my time and enjoy every inch of you."

Clarissa's reply was cut off as Simon covered her mouth. She returned the kiss with all the love she felt. More buttons disappeared as Clarissa's hand found the front of Simon's shirt and tore it open. Soon they were struggling to keep their mouths pressed together while their hands fumbled with more buttons and hooks and petticoat strings.

"God, you're beautiful." Simon breathed out the words in an exclamation of delight once Clarissa was finally naked and lying beneath him. "More beautiful and more courageous than any woman I've ever known."

Another kiss and he was gliding into her, their bodies joining with the same sweet passion that both surprised and thrilled Clarissa all the way to her soul.

"You're also unduly stubborn, unnaturally independent, and totally captivating. I don't regret losing my heart at all." He retreated just far enough to gaze down at her. "What about you? Any regrets?"

"No," she said as he began moving again. "I love you."

The words trapped Simon for a long moment. Then he smiled, his heart totally satisfied. "I love you," he said before kissing her again. "Much more than any man should love a disobedient, outrageous wife. I shall have to be on my guard or you will have me standing in Parliament, spouting liberal prose and encouraging my peers to support progressive politics."

Clarissa was about to laugh, but the sound turned into a female moan as Simon turned his attention to her breasts. Their lovemaking was slow and tender, and when she was finally lying sated in his arms, she couldn't think of anything more pleasing than being Simon's wife. When she told him as much, he smiled.

"How about the mother of my children?"

"That, too." She sighed as her husband shifted position and looked down at her. "In fact, I'd like that very much."

"Good," he said, brushing the hair away from her neck so he could nibble on it. "I want to spend the rest of my life holding you in my arms at night and watching our children grow during the day."

"Only at night, my lord?" Clarissa pouted. "What about our agreement? Whenever, wherever, and however you want me."

"Ahhh, yes, our agreement," Simon replied as he continued his assault on her senses. "I think it should remain in force, don't you? Unless you'd consider giving up your allowance and living on my charity."

"I have no intention of giving up anything," Clarissa replied between kisses. "Especially the man I love."